Praise for the novels of Rona Jaffe

"A minor genius."
—*New York Times Book Review*

"Rona Jaffe's deft storytelling is irresistible."
—*Los Angeles Times*

"Jaffe comprehends the ambivalence of women in love like few other contemporary novelists."
—*New Woman*

"Diverse characterizations...entertaining."
—*Booklist*

The Cousins "is the book Rona Jaffe's fans have been waiting for."
—Gail Parent, author of
Sheila Levine is Dead and Living in New York

"Rona Jaffe has her finger squarely on the pulse of the times."
—*Washington Times*

"Reading Rona Jaffe is like being presented with a Cartier watch; you know exactly what you're getting and it's exactly what you want."
—*Cosmopolitan*

"Vivid and trenchant...wry and very readable."
—*New York Times Book Review*

Dear Reader,

FIVE WOMEN is a novel about survivors. It is also about women's relationships with their mothers, their fathers, their children, their men and their own bodies. At a certain point in our lives, maybe at thirty or forty, we start to wonder how much longer we can carry the destructive baggage of the past without moving on. The devastating events of childhood led to the mistakes and pain of adult life, to the personality that keeps making the same errors or is afraid to live at all.

The young couples after World War II had their dreams, and this is what happened to their daughters—us—after those dreams fell apart. Our parents all had such high hopes for a better life. But through the years, and even half a century later, their daughters grappled with the necessity to create that life for themselves, in a way that their mothers would never have imagined.

I hope you enjoy this story of five women trying not just to survive, but trying to make their dreams come true.

Sincerely,

Rona Jaffe

RONA JAFFE

Five WOMEN

MIRA

ISBN 1-55166-424-0

FIVE WOMEN

Copyright © 1997 by Rona Jaffe

First published in the United States under the title FIVE WOMEN by Rona Jaffe.

Published by arrangement with Donald I. Fine Books, an imprint of Penguin Books USA Inc.

"Chain of Fools" by Don Covay. Copyright © 1967 (Renewed) Pronto Music, Inc. and 14th Hour Music, Inc. All rights reserved. Used by permission. Warner Bros. Publications U.S. Inc., Miami, FL 33014. "Down On Me." Copyright © 1967 Strong Arm Music. All rights reserved. Used by permission. "Piece of My Heart." Copyright © 1967 Web IV Music, Inc. and Ragmar Music Inc. Renewal rights secured by Web IV Music, Inc./Unichappell Music and Sloopy II Music Inc. All rights reserved. Used by permission.

"Me and Bobby McGee." Words and Music by Kris Kristofferson and Fred Foster. Copyright © 1969 Temi Combine Inc. All rights controlled by Combine Music Corp. and administered by EMI Blackwood Music Inc. All rights reserved. International copyright secured. Used by permission.

Printed in U.S.A.

An unhappy childhood is the wound that never heals.

———◆———

Recently I saw a medical ad in a magazine that read:
"Do you have a wound that will not heal?
Come to The Wound Center."
And I thought:
"What about my heart?"

AUTHOR NOTE

This novel and all the characters in it are a work of fiction in which I have let my imagination fly. Nonetheless, because a novelist wants her readers to identify with the story and characters, it is not unlikely that the fictional universe that I have created is populated with bits and pieces from the real world—bits and pieces acquired through research, partly by accident, and partly because our collective experiences and consciousness link us all in some strange way so that what happens to a fictional character in the novel may have actually happened to someone in the real world. Also, although we sometimes don't like to admit it, the monsters from the id may arrive unbidden to our keyboards, so that characters and situations are constructed in part from some of our own secret feelings, from situations that we might never act out, but which give us great satisfaction to create. Why is a novelist drawn to tell a certain story and not another? This is why.

ONE

New York is a city always in flux, where people are constantly remaking their lives. It is like the filing system in a computer: folder within folder within folder, neatly hidden away but accessible. You can navigate skillfully from place to place, from old friend to new friend, or hide and see no one. Sometimes people wonder what has happened to you; more often they just think you're busy. Often you are. Sometimes they think you don't like them anymore. Sometimes you don't. As you remake your life you also remake yourself.

On a Wednesday evening in January 1995, Gara Whiteman had these thoughts as she dressed to go out for what had become a weekly ritual of drinks and dinner with three other women with whom she had recently become friendly. She had always liked Wednesday: she thought of it as the day that broke the back of the week. She was a successful psychologist, with her own busy practice, and she loved it, but by the weekend she'd had enough of worrying about other people's misery and confusion. Of course, you never really stopped.

Gara was a very attractive, trim, youthful woman of fifty-five, with dark hair and light eyes and a look of receptivity. She smiled easily and warmly. She had always been a caretaker all of her life, in one way or another, and after the years of therapy she had been in she realized quite well that she had never felt entitled to anything and therefore had deprived herself of many of the pleasures she could have enjoyed. She was slowly trying to rectify that.

She looked around her apartment—a lot of white, a lot of silk, very feminine, part of the reinvention of herself as a successful single woman after the divorce she had never wanted. Her ex-husband, Carl, had been as careless as a large, golden furred animal, and she had made their apartment together into a brown cave filled with the memories and possessions he had had before she entered his life. She had lived with him in that cave in love and trust, in safety, and there had been nothing she would not do for him, freely. It had obviously not been enough.

Her weekly evenings with her new friends at Yellowbird, a lively East Side bar and restaurant where they felt comfortable, was another step toward ending her isolation. People always asked how the four of them had met. She supposed they asked because the little group seemed so different from each other but laughed so much together, or perhaps because those people who asked were lonely and isolated, too, and wanted to know how to meet people.

She had met them at New York parties, they had gotten to talking; it was simple. She enjoyed that they were not in her field. She had never really liked to socialize with other psychologists when she wasn't working, preferring a more eclectic group of friends. It was one of the things she had liked about her ex-husband, that his life was so different from hers; that she had been able to learn about art, about business, that they traveled in such an interesting way.

He was an art dealer, and because of their separate, time-consuming careers he had often traveled without her. Never let them take trips alone, she thought now. But then she would also have to say, Never let them go to the office, never let them meet anyone they don't tell you about. But what good would that do? Even if they told you things, it wouldn't necessarily be the truth. What was the saying: The shoemaker's children have no shoes? Physician, heal thyself? Do what I say, not what I do?

One of her patients had asked her once if a therapist shouldn't have a perfect life, as an example of what mental health and happiness could be. As a role model. Gara had laughed. "We're only human," she said. "I'm here to help you, I'm not a goddess."

For years it had been only in her therapy sessions that Gara felt that kind of power. Now she sometimes felt it with her friends. Because she was trained and comparatively wise, they often used her as a sounding board, advice dispenser, and good mother figure. Sometimes she got fed up with this, because just like many of her patients, they nodded agreement while on another level they weren't listening at all. But sometimes she liked doing it anyway. This support was what friendship was supposed to be about.

She changed from her sedate professional clothes to black leggings, cowboy boots, and a long, thick ruby red chenille sweater. Whenever she dressed like this, admiring her hard-earned muscles, she remembered the uncomfortable girdles her mother had sent her off to college with. She had worn them on dates, with nylons and high heels, in the snow. When pantyhose came out she considered them one of the greatest inventions of the twentieth century. Her mother, however, was too fat, out of shape, and modest to try them, too. For years she had been an old woman, and she had been younger than Gara was now.

Gara brushed her teeth, put on ruby red lipstick that matched her sweater, and tied her hair up in a ponytail under a peaked wool cap. From a distance she looked forty years old. Maybe there would be some interesting men in Yellowbird tonight, maybe even one for her. Of course, she thought, I wouldn't know what to do with him, but that's a different story. I'll settle for a smile.

In her penthouse apartment overlooking the twinkling lights of the city and the empty, moonwashed paths of Central Park seen through the black sticks of leafless winter trees, Kathryn O'Mara Henry hummed along to Bobby Short and poured herself a glass of wine as she got dressed to go out and meet her new friends at Yellowbird. Life was wonderful; she'd just had another great day. An hour at the gym with her trainer at seven a.m., followed by an aerobics class, two hours of tennis with some new girlfriends at the health club, lunch at Cipriani's with some other ladies who were spending their fuck-you alimony, a quick turn through the Metropolitan Museum to see what was new, a pass through Barney's to buy a Chanel belt, a bubble bath by candlelight overlooking her view, and now a night out.

She wasn't that crazy about Yellowbird—she would have

preferred to try a different restaurant every week, but her little group felt safe there. They were creatures of habit. Kathryn knew there was no such thing as safety; it was a total illusion. She also knew you could never trust anything to be what you thought. This was not a bad or dangerous thing; it was just a fact. She was still here. She was a survivor. She spent very little time even thinking about it. She was like a cork on the ocean: whenever a wave smashes it down it bobs up again.

Kathryn was a chic, pretty, happy, bubbly redhead, a woman who drew others to her not only because she was attractive but because when she wanted to be she was so friendly. She'd had a good face lift and was a young fifty-seven. She didn't mind telling her age, although she usually took a few years off. This was not too easy when your oldest child was nearly forty. She'd had three marriages and had four grown children whom she adored, and she thought that in a few years she might even marry again, not because she particularly liked marriage after all her mistakes, but because the men she became involved with wanted to marry her and she always thought: Why not?

She couldn't understand why Gara thought her own life was over in that way, thought she'd never find love or romance or companionship. You didn't have to have all three anyway. One was enough, for as long as it lasted. She'd seen a lot worse. You had to make your own life great. And *she's* the therapist, Kathryn thought, smiling to herself. Sometimes it was better to let the past lie, put it out of your mind. You healed and went on. Gara worried too much.

Late as always, Felicity Johnson was hurriedly refreshing her makeup in her cream-colored marble and mirrored bathroom in the East Side townhouse she shared with her husband, Russell Naylor. She had so much work at the office she could have stayed there until midnight, but she had brought it home as usual even though tonight she was going out with her friends.

Her house was a double-width four-story building that had once been the mansion of a large, rich white family around the turn of the century. She and Russell, a very successful builder, were the only black people on the block, but she was used to that. Her father was a doctor, and she had been brought up in an affluent white suburb because her parents wanted her to have "all the advantages." There had also been the disadvantages: bigotry, loneliness, not fitting in. But now she was a literary lawyer, with a good career and a husband people considered a catch, she was sexy and smart, everybody told her she was beautiful—although she was the only one who didn't think so—and she seemed to move easily between the two worlds of black and white.

Actually, she knew she didn't really fit into either. In case she didn't know it, her husband told her all the time. "You're deluding yourself," he would say. "Our black friends don't really like you. You don't try to be a part of their lives."

"I do so," she would say. "I know they like me. Who said they don't like me?" Silence. That bull's glare of his with lowered head and folded arms. Russell was a short, compact, muscular man, and a bully. If she had known then what she knew now, she would never have married a man who was only her height, and nearly old enough to be her father. He treated her like a trophy wife and a silly, disobedient child.

"And my white friends accept me," she would say. Sometimes she really hated him.

"That's what you think," he would say.

Once a week, for dinner, she got away from him and was able to see her women friends at Yellowbird. It was a night she looked forward to. She could pretend she was single again and out on the town with the world full of limitless possibilities. Not that she would do anything. She had a jealous husband she was afraid of, and an unpredictable, irresistible lover she was obsessed with, and that was almost more than she could handle as it was. The guilt over cheating on her husband, of being such a bad person, tormented her all the time. But it had seemed a natural progression, a desperate restoration of her desirability, after what Russell had done to her during the first five years of their marriage, when she had been even more vulnerable than she was now.

Felicity let her hair loose from the bun she wore it in at work. It fell free, long, dark, and wavy. She had high cheekbones and slightly slanting greenish eyes. Her skin was light brown. Maybe she wasn't so bad-looking. She wished she had more confidence. The only thing she knew was that she didn't have a line on her face: her mother's great genes. She was forty and looked twenty-five. Almost too late to have a baby, though. She wanted that more than anything.

But Russell didn't want her to have a baby. She was *his* baby, and he didn't want to share her with anyone. How could she have been so stupid to have chased him all those years, to be so thrilled when she finally got him, never realizing that she didn't know him at all? She was probably lucky she had never become pregnant. He would have been as domineering a father as he was a husband. She would have been stuck in her unhappy marriage forever.

Who was she kidding? She was stuck in this marriage anyway. Jason, her lover, was never going to get a divorce, and she wouldn't marry him if she could. She couldn't trust him not to cheat on her, too. She was a fool for love, but not that big a fool. And Russell might have been a wonderful father. Babies and little kids were infinitely malleable. She, of all people, should know that. Russell could have had a child who worshipped and adored him, no matter how he behaved toward it. She certainly knew about that, too.

She went out into the den. Russell was watching college basketball on TV. He would watch anything as long as it was a sporting event. It was a kind of meditation for him, an altered state. In the early years of their marriage she had tried to watch with him, but she got sick of it, and she had too much work from the office anyway. The pressure to churn out the firm's mandatory individual billable hours was incredible. Russell was lucky. During the day he could deal with the hard hat guys and at night he could turn into a vegetable.

The remains of the chicken dinner their housekeeper had prepared for him, which Felicity had heated up, was on the coffee table in front of him. "Was that good?" she asked solicitously.

"Great. Who did you say you were meeting?"

"I told you. Gara and Kathryn and maybe Eve." She hoped not Eve. Maybe she could get out of the house before Eve called.

"Call me from the restaurant," Russell said.

"You know I will."

She hated the way she had to check in all the time like a parolee. She had to carry around her cellular phone, which meant she could never have a decent evening bag unless she was out with her husband; the rest of the time she had to lug a big one.

"You like Yellowbird so much," Russell said, "maybe I should go with you some time."

"I told you that you were invited," she said, hoping she was disguising her lack of enthusiasm. But she knew he would never join them. He wasn't interested in being with her girlfriends, of whatever color. He didn't even like having them around, which was why she never had guests unless they were his friends. He was jealous of her friendships, of the easy laughter women had together. He felt shut out.

"Good night, Slugger," Felicity said, kissing him lightly.

"Good night, Baby."

She was almost to the front door when the phone rang. She knew it was Eve. Damn.

"Will you get that, Baby?" Russell said. "Maybe it's for me."

Yeah, sure. "Hello?" she said cautiously into the receiver.

"I want to go to Yellowbird tonight," Eve Bader said, in her abrupt, demanding voice. She never said hello, considering pleasantries a waste of time. Silence. "Are you going?"

Felicity sighed. "Yes," she said.

"What time?"

"Now."

Eve Bader was only a peripheral member of their little group because she kept trying to be with them and they kept trying to get away from her. An actress somewhere in her forties (she would never tell just where), Eve was a volcano of anger and pushiness, with manic energy, a dangerous quality, hot hands and hot eyes and flying hair.

"I just had an audition for an off-Broadway play," Eve said brightly. "I was wonderful. The director liked me. He said he'd let me know in a few days if I have a callback. I have a feeling this is going to be my year. I was really marvelous—I felt the energy. Remember I keep telling you, when I feel the energy I'm unstoppable! I could see he felt my energy, too."

"That's good," Felicity said.

Eve was only moderately successful, but she never gave up the feeling that she was destined to become a star when she met the right people. Twenty years ago she had landed a role in a daytime soap opera that she kept for five years. During that period she was able to put away enough money to have the luxury of pursuing her career full time. On the show, Eve got the reputation of being difficult, and she never worked in a soap again, but she thought soaps were beneath her anyway and wanted to be on Broadway or in a movie, perferably a Woody Allen movie.

"Even if I get this play, I'd still rather do Broadway," Eve said. "I need to expand. Maybe there will be contacts for me at Yellowbird tonight. You never know."

"Well, then, I'll see you there, I guess."

"Are Gara and Kathryn coming?"

"Yes."

"Maybe I should call some men to join us. What do you think?"

"I just want to be with my friends. I'm tired."

"Why are you tired?" Eve snapped. "It's a state of mind." Oh, Eve...

Kathryn didn't mind her, because she liked everybody, but Felicity and Gara often asked each other why they put up with Eve. They admitted that sometimes she was fun to be with, and her unremitting narcissism and ego made them view her as a creature from another planet, which they found amusing. Gara, who as a therapist knew about these things, said that it was an interesting phenomenon of female bonding that some women tended to put up with and befriend another woman whom they really didn't much like. Felicity wondered if it was the scapegoat factor. There was something childish and nastily satisfying to have someone to complain about.

Or maybe she herself, dissatisfied with her life, was just passive and lonely. Eve got on her nerves, but she wished she had some of Eve's eternal optimism and confidence. "So I'll see you there," Felicity said.

"Get the table I like. You know the one."

"Gara made the reservation."

"She doesn't care where we sit. I need to see and be seen."

"Okay."

"If I don't like the table they give us, I'll make them change it," Eve said.

"I'm sure you will," Felicity sighed. She hated it when Eve had their table changed. Eve always wanted to sit near the smoking section because she thought her important contacts would be sitting there, and then she complained when people smoked. She also hated how Eve insisted on dividing the bill up to the penny, and always managed to come out ahead. This time she was going to get there before Eve did and tell the waiter from now on Eve had to be given her own check.

She hung up. "Was that Eve?" Russell said.

"Yeah."

"I could tell from the tone of your voice. I thought you couldn't stand her."

"She's all right," Felicity said. Russell even knew whom she was talking to. A closeness she would have happily welcomed from someone else made her feel frightened and trapped when it came from her husband. There were many reasons for that. But she wasn't going to think about them now. Right now she just wanted to get out of the house.

She hit the street running, hailed a cab, settled into it, gave the address of Yellowbird, and smiled.

TWO

Among the noisy singles hangouts, the bars, the bagel shops, the nice little neighborhood Italian and French restaurants, the Korean all-night grocery stores, the Chinese takeout places, the pizza parlors, the coffee bars, the big supermarkets, the high rise apartment buildings, and the beat-up tenements that had been reconverted into too expensive little apartments was Yellowbird: a place like none of the others in the area. You could miss it if you walked past it too quickly. The sign was hard to read, and the windows were purposely kept inscrutable. Inside was a carefully created other world, a throwback to the past.

Yellowbird was a monument to Janis Joplin. Dark and warm, the brick walls were completely unadorned except for a huge framed black and white photograph of Janis Joplin singing—passionate, drugged-out, drunk, wild-looking, unexpectedly young, and with that great blues voice that was stilled much too early. The albums of the legendary women blues singers played, sometimes scratchily, on the sound system. From time to time, at the whim of the owner, there was someone contemporary, or even new. Interesting people came in here; you could make a friend, find love of sorts, or just not be alone. The one thing you would never have to be at Yellowbird was alone, unless you chose to be.

Billie Redmond owned this place. Forty-eight, tall, rangy, and dramatic-looking, she prowled her domain. For a few years, in the early seventies, she was a singer in the Janis Joplin style, and had a couple of hits. So for a few incandescent years she had been a rock star. You found this out quite quickly when you came here. Sometimes she had a look about her as if she were still on stage, or was remembering it—a way she moved, or tossed her head, a glance. When Billie was around you always knew who was in control, and she was always there.

Gara had asked Billie once why the place was called Yellowbird—was it a song she had written, was it the town in Texas she came from?

"No," Billie said, sounding bored. People had asked her that same question a lot over the years. "I just like it. It sounds hopeful, you know?"

She had a strange, low, hoarse voice and a scar on her neck. Sometimes she covered the scar with a turtleneck or a scarf, and sometimes not. It seemed to Gara to be a kind of stigmata, a literal representation of the scars all of the others carried inside, but no one ever dared ask her about it. They were sure that in her brief glory days as a singer she hadn't had the voice they heard now, it would have been impossible, but of course no one would ever ask her about that either. Gara found her fascinating.

"I'm from Plano, Texas," Billie said. "Ever heard of it? Probably not. You're a New Yorker." She still had her Texas twang. "You didn't miss anything," she said with a little smile. "I left real young."

Gara knew that Billie didn't have a husband or any kind of permanent partner, but it was clear, if you watched carefully, that Billie was a lusty, independent woman who had an occasional lover when she wanted one. She would sit at the bar, watching over the reservation book, talking to men who were there alone, sometimes buying them a drink. Gara could see the electricity growing in their eyes, the subtle change in body language.

She thought of Billie's bar stool as the catbird seat. They were all her guests, albeit paying guests, and there was a certain currying of favor. When Billie was bored with the bar she would wander around the room, sometimes alighting at a table or a booth, particularly later at night when she'd had a few drinks and was feeling mellow and in a mood to reminisce about interesting people she had known in the late sixties and early seventies.

Billie had a nine-year-old son, Little Billie. You could tell he was hers—they had the same eyes—but anything more about his origin was another of her mysteries. He was a very well-behaved child, with golden curls, the face of an angel, and the matter-of-fact sophistication of a child who has always lived among adults. Billie had told Gara once that she had been taking Little Billie to Yellowbird since he was born. Everybody adored him.

He was there tonight, as always, doing his homework at a back booth, with his little computer and his Walkman and his plastic violence doll. There was a cot in his mother's office in case he got sleepy. Since Billie's formal education had been minimal due to lack of interest, Little Billie was being helped with his homework by the two transvestites Gara called the Larchmont Ladies. They dressed like middle-aged suburban matrons, wearing cheap copies of Chanel suits, sensible pumps, and wigs set in the long-outdated petal look. They had become a kind of fixture here, preferring Yellowbird to the downtown clubs.

After the initial shock of their appearance, or the discovery that they were not what they pretended to be, the Larchmont Ladies turned out to be quiet and pleasant. One of them was an accountant, and he helped Little Billie with his math. The other one was reputed to be a cop. They were not lovers, only friends, or sisters if you will, although they both claimed to be straight. No one had ever seen either of them with a woman. They didn't mind being baby-sitters. They called themselves Gladys and Lucy, but Little Billie called them Ralph and Tom.

Gara had been the first to arrive tonight, so she nabbed the seat with the best view of the rest of the room and ordered a bottle of white wine. Janis was singing on the sound system and she hummed along. *"Take another little piece of my heart now, bay-bay…"* She liked the old songs more than the new ones; the lyrics made more sense in relation to her life. Or maybe they really had been better.

"Hey," Billie said by way of greeting.

"Hi."

"Who's coming tonight? Kathryn? Felicity?"

"Yes," Gara said.

"Eve?"

"I don't know."

"She'd better not ask to have her table changed," Billie said ominously, and walked away. Gara laughed.

The waiter arrived with the wine, menus, ice water, and biscuits. The food here was sort of Southern and not very good, and Billie hardly ever changed the menu, so there was something about it that Gara found reassuring. It was like the food of her childhood. Growing up in New York they'd had a black, Southern housekeeper who didn't cook well, but Gara's mother hadn't cooked at all. Gara had never been able to decide if this was her mother's one gesture toward being emancipated from the role of housewife, or if it was her way of being privileged. Gara had grown up to be an indifferent cook, but her ex-husband hadn't minded; he liked the two of them to eat out nearly all the time anyway, as if they were on a permanent date.

When she thought how romantic Carl had been when he wanted to be, she felt sad. She had finally gotten to the point where there were whole days when she forgot he existed, but she knew it was an act of will. She had been married to him for twenty-two years, most of her adult life. She had known him when they each had both parents. She had helped bring up his two sons from his previous marriage, on the weekends and vacation weeks that he had custody, a time that seemed so long ago. She could finish his sentences, and often he looked at her hopefully to do so. How close their bond had been—two minds with the same thought, the same references, the same memories. Perhaps that had been part of the problem. She had become too familiar. Strangers were more enticing. And at the end he had turned into a stranger, so that she was the one left yearning and enticed.

"There you are," Kathryn said cheerfully, emerging from the dimness with a glass in her hand. "I was at the bar. I didn't see you come in." Her skin was luminous, her hair glowed a soft, shiny copper, and she was smiling a white-toothed, perfect smile. Her outfit had probably cost four thousand dollars.

"Don't you look glamorous," Gara said. "That suit! That handbag!"

"Well, thank you," Kathryn said. She sat down. "God bless Mr. Henry."

"Who?" Gara asked. She and Kathryn had a running joke about Kathryn's husbands: Gara pretended never to be able to remember their names or keep them straight. Not that three were so many these days.

"My last husband, the multi-millionaire. I finally learned how to do it right."

"Practice makes perfect."

"I only slept with three men in my life," Kathryn said matter-of-factly. "And I married them all. I was a nice Catholic girl."

And a strong one, Gara thought. Of them all, she thought Kathryn had probably had the worst trauma to deal with. Or perhaps it had only been the most dramatic. Whenever she saw Kathryn, Gara saw the scene again; an event she had not been part of, which she could only imagine. So this was Kathryn's story:

A cold, dark winter night in Boston. The woman is hiding in the backseat of the car, lying on the floor under the heavy raincoat, the man and the other woman in the front, the man driving. The woman in the back is trying not to tremble, hardly breathing. The man turns around. The woman in the back holds up the gun and blows his head off.

She had never understood how Kathryn had managed to survive this event of her past and seem so well-adjusted. It was something she wondered about often. Gara asked her sometimes, but Kathryn just shrugged with her devil-may-care attitude and said she didn't know.

The waiter poured them glasses of wine. "Well, cheers," Kathryn said.

"Cheers. To health."

"Oh, look who's here."

Gara saw Felicity heading for their table, beaming with delight at the prospect of an evening out with her friends.

"How pretty she is," Kathryn said. "All the guys are looking at her." She chuckled in a motherly way, and Gara remembered that Kathryn's oldest son was only a year or two younger than Felicity.

"I know. She's gorgeous."

"What are you saying?" Felicity asked.

"That you're fat and ugly," Kathryn said. "Sit down and have a drink, we've started already."

"I'm fat and ugly?" Felicity said in horror.

"I'm just joking, you twit. You know you're beautiful. I don't want to listen to any false modesty."

Felicity kissed them both hello and sat next to Gara. "A drink, yes! I do need a glass of wine." She smiled at the waiter when he poured it. "Eve Bader gets her own check," she said. He nodded.

"I was going to pay for everybody," Kathryn said.

"No, you can't," Gara said.

"Okay."

"It's so great to be away from my husband," Felicity said.

"Well, you're taken care of, but by spring Gara and I are both going to have boyfriends," Kathryn said. "I'm going to find them for us. You'll see."

"For you, maybe," Gara said.

"No, for both of us. There were some nice guys at the bar. I was talking to two of them. They're going to come over to the table later. I need a next husband."

"You wouldn't marry *again*...?"

"I'd settle for an escort at the moment," Kathryn said. "A man to go to things with."

Gara winced. "That makes me feel so old. An escort."

"You're confusing it with a walker. I mean a nice, heterosexual guy who wants to have fun."

"That's a date."

"Nothing wrong with a date."

"I've given up," Gara said. "It's too late. I've forgotten how to have sex."

"Nobody forgets."

"I'm afraid to tell you." She felt like a freak. Why not admit the truth? She trusted her friends. "I haven't had sex in five years," Gara said. When the words came out and she had to listen to them, she wanted to cry.

"Five years?" Felicity gasped. "You're kidding! Five years?"

Kathryn did not gasp. She had not had sex in longer than that; but, of course, *she* didn't care.

Gara shrugged. The time had gone by fast and she had

been occupied with much more serious things. Every day she remembered how lucky she was to be alive.

"You haven't been in mourning all this time for that ex-husband of yours?" Kathryn asked sternly.

"No," Gara said, truthfully. "But I was busy. Breast cancer is very time-consuming."

"But you're well now," Felicity said.

"And it's time to find you a boyfriend," Kathryn said. "Someone attractive and intelligent, with a sense of humor, with a nice summer house…"

"I *have* a nice summer house." Her little place on the beach in Amagansett had been part of her divorce settlement. She had bought Carl out.

"You're not like me, you don't need anything from a man," Felicity said. "You have a great deal to offer in a relationship. Not all men want twenty-three-year-olds."

"You should take an ad in the personals," Kathryn said.

"Fifty-five-year-old woman with one tit wants to get fucked," Gara said dryly.

She watched as they screamed with laughter. Felicity was doubled over, tears coming out of her eyes. Gara knew their laughter was partly in shock at her forthrightness, and partly in admiration for her spirit. She had chosen to keep her cancer an almost complete secret, even from her patients, and she knew the few friends she had told wouldn't tell. They didn't understand her secrecy—after all, she had survived—but they honored it. She approached her situation with unexpected humor, and her friends looked upon this with awe.

But behind the laughter was her secret realization that, without even knowing how it had happened, she had suddenly turned around to discover that she had become one of those women who'd already had her life. As a young girl she'd seen them: the widows, the mutilated, the card players. They seemed to be at the end of their lives as women, a destiny too far away to imagine. Now, except for her career, this dwindling away into invisibility did not seem so far away anymore. But it was still incredibly foreign and strange, and it felt much too soon.

"What are you laughing about?" Eve demanded, sailing

up to their table like the actress she was and glancing around to see if there was anybody in the restaurant she wanted to sit closer to. Her red hair was the color of fire, and she was wearing feather earrings and had a feather pinned in her hair, and her lipstick was almost black.

"Hi, Eve," Kathryn gasped, pulling herself together.

"Anybody here?" Eve asked. She pulled out a chair and sat down. "Not so lively tonight."

"It's still early," Gara said.

The waiter came over and Eve ordered a beer. "So how's Russell?" she asked Felicity.

"I have to call him," Felicity said, making a face. She pulled the cell phone out of her bag and dialed. "Don't sound like you're having too much fun." Her voice changed, became sweet, soft, and subservient. "Hi, Slugger."

"Great name for a guy who hits you," Eve whispered.

"We're here at Yellowbird," Felicity said into the phone. "Gara and Kathryn and Eve. That's all. How's the game? Uh-huh. No, I won't be late. Okay. No. Okay." She clicked off. "Yeech," she said.

"Such love," Eve said.

They ordered grilled chicken and salads. Billie kept a few simple items on the menu in addition to her regional dishes, for people who, like them, were always on diets. Aretha was singing on the sound system, in her gutsy voice, clear as a bell. *"Chain, chain, chain, chain of fools..."* That's us, Gara thought, and when do we learn? She thought that with the exception of Billie, and maybe Felicity, she was the only person who really listened to the music. Everyone else considered it merely background. The restaurant was full now, and so was the bar. People were still drifting in. Little Billie had finished his homework and was playing a computer game. Soft pops and pings of cartoon mayhem floated over from his corner.

Eve visibly stiffened. "Look who's here," she said, nodding at the door. She had a little smile on her face, but Gara could see she was upset.

"Isn't that Harvey?" Felicity said.

He was a successful manufacturer, middle-aged and big and sexy and handsome and blooming with heat and blood, a kind of male Eve. The two of them had dated briefly, and the other women had thought they were a perfect match, but it hadn't worked out. Looking back, it had turned out to be a flirtation and a two-night stand.

"Hello, ladies," Harvey said. He looked at all of them but Eve.

"Hello, Harvey," Eve said.

"Ms. Bader." And he was gone to a table in the back where some people were waiting for him.

Eve craned around. "Does he have a date?"

"What do you care?" Kathryn said.

"I don't care," Eve said, but she sounded hurt and angry.

Gara remembered their courtship. Eve had been in awe. His body is so warm, like a stove, she had marveled. I've never seen heat like that coming out of another human being. I think he's dangerous. Eve had liked that, the sense of danger. But then it had turned out he was the one who was afraid of her, and he had avoided her like the plague.

"I don't know why it never worked out with him," Eve said.

"You do so," Gara said. "You shouldn't have tried to tie him up in bed."

Felicity giggled. Whenever Gara was up front about something, which she often was, Felicity considered it outrageous, but she loved it.

"What was wrong with that?" Eve snapped.

Eve liked to tie men up in bed. Most of them wouldn't let her, but she tried all the same. When Eve had approached Harvey with her red silk scarves, he had said if there was going to be any tying up done he would do it to her, so there was none done, and after that he stopped calling.

"It's the power struggle," Gara said. "You can't try to dominate a man like him."

"Maybe he would have liked it," Eve said. "You know what's wrong with him? He can't have a relationship. Another one of those men who don't know what they want."

"He knew what he didn't want," Kathryn said cheerfully.

"No, no, he has problems."

How nice it would be, Gara thought, to be able to blame anyone else but yourself. Most of her patients blamed themselves for everything, especially the women. They came into their sessions asking, What did I do? What you did, she often had to tell them, was you picked him. That's what you did. Or you let him pick you.

The salads came and they ate hungrily. "I'm so upset," Felicity murmured. "I haven't heard from my friend all week."

She referred to her lover as her "friend," but they all knew what she meant. She had never told any of them but Gara his last name, but they had the feeling he was someone well known. He was married, too, and they had secret lunches in a pied a terre he had sublet.

"He'll call," Gara reassured her. "He always does."

"No, this time it's been longer than it ever was before."

"No, it hasn't."

"Are you sure?"

"If he wanted to see you all the time, you wouldn't want to see him," Gara said.

"I suppose you're right," Felicity said. "But when he doesn't call I think he's tired of me."

"You're obsessing again."

"I know."

"Why won't you tell us who he is?" Eve said.

"I can't. I've already told you more than enough. If my husband knew I was having an affair, he would kill me."

"Really?" Kathryn said.

"Probably," Felicity said. "Russell is a very angry man."

"You'd better watch out," Eve said. She was trying to sound solicitous, and perhaps she was, but Gara knew she loved the drama of it.

"I don't know why you need a husband *and* a lover," Kathryn said. "Why don't you get rid of both of them and start over with a man who makes you happy?"

"If I could, I wouldn't be neurotic," Felicity said. "The irony of it is that my friend is what's saving my marriage. After I see him is the only time I feel like being nice to my husband."

"And why is that?" Gara asked.

"I feel a sense of power. Being wanted by two men. What do you expect after my crazy childhood?"

"But after a certain time you just have to get off of it,"

Kathryn said. "If I let my childhood bother me, I'd be a basket case."

"Me too!" said Eve.

But we do, Gara thought. We keep making the same mistakes and passing them on to others. When does it stop? When can we finally put it to rest? Chain of fools...

THREE

Gara's parents called her "the miracle baby." After two miscarriages, years of infertility and worry, and six months lying flat on her back in bed, her mother finally produced the daughter she had been waiting for. After that, they never tried to have another child. This little daughter with the big blue eyes would have everything; on her tiny shoulders would rest the fulfillment of their dreams.

She was born in 1940. The Depression was not yet really over, the World War that would crank up the economy had not yet begun in America, although its presence in Europe hung over everything. It was not unusual to be an only child. Most of the children in Gara's class at private school had, at the most, one sibling. People couldn't afford more. Gara's mother told her that only the poor, who didn't know better, had a lot of kids. What she neglected to say was that her method of birth control was abstinence.

By the time the baby boomers were old enough to fill the kindergartens to bursting, Gara was twelve years old and ready to graduate from eighth grade. She had always been bright and precocious, and had been skipped twice. People were moving to the suburbs in search of a better life for their children, but Gara's parents were both second generation New Yorkers, and they had no intention of leaving the culture and autonomy of the city. Her mother couldn't even drive. Her father was a lawyer with an office in Manhattan, and he was not eager to commute. Their six-room apartment in a 1930s Deco building was spacious and filled with reproduction English antiques. It was a good setting for Gara to receive the boys who would come courting her when she was older.

Gara was delighted that they were going to stay, and that she would be going on to an all-girls' private high school that was supposed to be very difficult academically. She was too young to date boys anyway—in fact they sort of scared her—and her main ambition at the moment was getting into college so she could have some kind of career. Her mother was a college graduate even though she was a housewife. Her college psychology books were on their living room bookshelf, and Gara had read them all. She loved reading about real people who had weird problems. Her mother hadn't gone on to a career, but Gara could. Maybe she would be a clinical psychologist. The case histories made her think about her own family.

Her mother, May, was a pretty woman who had let herself get much too heavy. Although she did not cook, and the food prepared by their housekeeper was mediocre at best, she ate all the time. At dinner Gara had seen her mother eat half of an entire cake for dessert. In her well-tailored dark clothes, and her corsets with their hooks and zippers, May had a chunky, tubular look. It was when she was alone at home with her daughter, walking naked to and from the bath, that Gara saw the rolls of fat cascading down her mother's ribs, the giant dimpled thighs tapering to tiny aching feet, the cellulite, the varicose veins and broken capillaries that astonished and repelled her. Somehow she was aware, if her mother was not, that her mother had put herself into this state to stay away from sex. Gara wasn't sure how she knew, but she did.

Astonishingly, her mother still had beautiful breasts. They were smallish and well-shaped and didn't sag. Women in those days wore bras that made them look as if they had two ice-cream cones on their chests. But her mother confined herself in rounded brassieres with heavy wires underneath, not to attract attention but to avoid it. Those perfect, banished breasts and the abused body seemed to Gara to be the choice she herself would have when she grew up—she could be attractive or repellent, and it was up to her, as it had been up to her mother. She could exercise and diet and not be like her mother. They had the same build; she would have those pretty breasts. They would be a start. They would be her sex appeal. She would never not have sex.

May thought Gara was beautiful, told her so often, and lived through her vicariously. It was important to her that her daughter be at her best all the time. So at twelve, Gara had high heels, makeup (which the students were not permitted to wear at school), a permanent, shaved legs, a bra with nothing to put in it, braces on her teeth, and a mouton coat. The quest for perfection had started the day she was born, but it was only on the day of her graduation that she became fully aware of it.

At the graduation ceremony the girls would wear evening gowns, the boys would wear suits. Gara's gown was peach-colored. The graduates would each have their name announced and receive a diploma from the principal. It was the most grownup thing Gara had ever done. She had also won first prize in the essay contest, "What Graduation Means to Me," and would receive an additional certificate for this.

"Ritual and recognition," she had written. "Acknowledgment of what we have so far achieved, and a step into the future to become who we will be." She thought it had a nice ring to it.

May was applying makeup to her daughter's face—painstakingly, delicately, slowly—as if she were a child star about to go before the camera. Or as if she were a painting. Her mother was painting a picture. "We're not allowed," Gara said. "I'll get killed."

"Just a little. You're too pale."

Powder, rouge, lipstick, a touch of mascara. Gara scrutinized the mirror for any sign of a pimple or regrowth of the dreaded mustache her mother had made her have removed by painful electrolysis. She hoped no one would ever know she'd had such a disgusting thing as facial hair. She imagined the worst thing that could possibly happen to her. She would be arrested for some crime, and put into prison, and her mustache would grow back, and people would see it. She was relieved that such an event was unlikely.

Graduation was in the school auditorium, and all the parents, siblings, and grandparents were there. Gara and the others were waiting behind the red velvet curtain to make their appearance. Her family was already sitting down front. She wondered if she and the other kids would still be friends when they went to different schools, and she also wondered if she would miss any of them. Maybe two—the others she didn't like at all. Suddenly the principal, Mrs. Wexler, swooped down on her, glaring from behind her bifocals, grabbed her by the arm, and dragged her into the girls' bathroom.

"What's that on your face?" Mrs. Wexler demanded. But she already knew. She wet a harsh paper towel at the sink and scrubbed off all the makeup. "Does your mother know?"

"She did it," Gara said. She felt relieved. She had always hated being different. She also felt humiliated and insulted because the principal, who should have treated her with respect on her graduation day, had manhandled her like an object. She also felt damp.

"I can't imagine how your mother could do such a thing," Mrs. Wexler said, and pushed her back to where the others were already filing on stage to their places.

Gara received her diploma and her award and felt happy again. She was on her way to becoming an adult. It didn't matter that next semester she would be only a freshman, a beginner: right now she was at the top of her school, a graduate, and it was a heady feeling. She left the stage with the other kids who were all joining their proud families, who were showering them with joyful hugs, kisses, and congratulations.

Her mother rushed up to her looking indignant. For a fat woman she could move very fast. "Who messed up your hair?" she cried.

"My hair?" Gara touched it. "I guess Mrs. Wexler."

"Why?"

"She was mad because I had on makeup, and she washed it off."

"That's why you're so pale. But she spoiled your *hair*," her mother said. She smoothed it, pursing her lips.

Say congratulations, Mom, Gara thought, but she didn't say it. She had already learned that it was pointless to pick a fight she could never win, and she particularly didn't feel like it today. She knew that both of her parents were proud of her academic record; congratulations were implicit. It was just that brains were not the important thing; physical appearance was. As she and her parents left the auditorium she began to wonder if she had looked really bad, and if it would show in the class picture, for ever and ever, that Gara Bernstein was the ghostly one with the terrible hair.

When she was little, Gara had adored her mother. They were inseparable. But by the time she was in high school she was ambivalent, which she read was natural, and by the time she went away to college she felt her home was an unacknowledged battlefield. Her father had abdicated his power over both her mother and herself long ago. Gara was still afraid of him though, in an odd way. She felt the anger in him, the hidden rage of the vanquished. She was sure he didn't even know he felt like the side that had lost, but sometimes he seemed on the verge of hysteria. She supposed that was what happened to men who didn't have sex. She knew he didn't have a girlfriend. The very idea of being such an immoral person horrified him.

Gara had already decided what kind of husband she herself would have. He would be charming and funny, he would never try to dominate her, but he would never let her push him around. She didn't even want to try. They would have mutual respect. And although he would have to be the son-in-law, he would protect her from her mother.

Her mother seemed to have an instinct about the kind of men who would protect Gara from her, and she hated them. It had taken until her daughter went away to college to allow her to have a key to the family apartment, because there was always someone there to let her in, wasn't there? Now that Gara was dating, and it was embarrassing to have one's mother waiting up to unlock the door, her mother hovered in the bedroom hallway, making little pretend-clumsy noises, waiting for the boy of the evening to leave so she could find out everything. The boys her mother approved of respected the presence of this chaperone; it meant Gara was a nice girl. Gara sometimes wondered if it was the daughter, not the mother, whom they were afraid of.

She was, of course, still a virgin. It was the late fifties, and the only man a nice girl could go all the way with was the one she was engaged to, officially engaged, with a ring. The two worst things that could happen to you if you were single were gossip and pregnancy. There were pleasurable acts dating college couples did in cars that Gara was sure her parents hadn't done even when they were married, but that was her own business. She pretended to be as naive as she was supposed to be. Everyone did.

May was fatter than ever, and when Gara was home for vacations she persisted in revealing her body to her daughter even though Gara wished she wouldn't. She liked to have Gara keep her company while she was having a bath and getting dressed. Gara didn't know what to do. In a way she was mesmerized. She looked at her mother (the only middle-aged woman she had ever seen wearing less than a bathing suit) with a kind of morbid fascination. This was what could happen to you if you didn't watch out. Didn't May have any shame? But it was almost as if her mother, who was ordinarily extremely modest, considered Gara invisible, or perhaps so much a part of her that she was not an onlooker at all.

They continued to have their mother-daughter talks in the bedroom, and shared things, mostly Gara's life. When May was wearing one of her nice bathrobes it was actually a rather cozy situation.

"I learned how to use Tampax at college," Gara said. "A girl in my dorm taught me." She was seventeen, and quite proud of this new step in her independence. "Thank God, no more itchy pads."

May was alarmed. "But you're a virgin!"

"It says on the box, 'Good for Virgins,' " Gara said. Actually what it said was that they were suitable for unmarried women and girls, but that was the same thing.

"Well, if you like them I want to try one," May said.

"You do?"

"Why not?"

"All right."

"I mean now."

Gara brought her the little blue box and May went into her bathroom and shut the door. It was sort of a nice surprise,

Gara thought, that her mother was so open-minded and wanted to join the modern world at her age. Her mother opened the door.

"Help me," she commanded.

She was standing there, completely naked, the soft, white tampon hanging out of her. She had apparently thrown the applicator away. Gara stared at her, horrified.

"Put it in," her mother said.

She just stood there.

"I can't do it," her mother said. "Push it in."

"If that place is big enough for me to have come out of, then it's big enough for you to put in a tampon," Gara said coldly, and walked out of the room.

She didn't understand why her mother needed to have so much control over her. It was as if they had meshed into one person, with no boundaries between them. Sometimes Gara felt herself disappearing, being eaten away. She began to be repelled when her mother kissed her, just as she felt violated and squeamish when a boy she found unattractive tried to kiss or grope her. The choice of who would touch her skin, her body, had to be hers alone.

On the first date you weren't supposed to kiss a man good-night, on the second you didn't have to but you certainly could, and on the third it was impolite not to. So by the third date you had been bought. Ideally, if you couldn't stand him you wouldn't have put yourself in that position in the first place. If Gara didn't like a man at college, she never went out with him more than once, but at home, with her social life supervised by her mother's constant nagging, it was a different story.

"He called three times. Why won't you give him a chance?"

"I gave him a chance."

"It takes a while to get to know a person."

How could she explain about chemistry, about how one man made her want to nuzzle warmly into him while another made her feel cold and ill? "He's not my type."

"Maybe he has a nice friend," her mother would always say. It was the reason of last resort.

Gara had met a boy at college whose mother, it turned out,

was a friend of her mother's. Not a close friend, but someone she knew socially. His name was Marvin Wink, formerly Winkelstein; he was going to learn to be a stock broker after he graduated, his family lived in a nice house in the suburbs, he had his own car, his father was a rich doctor, and his mother was a hypercritical harridan of such proportions that her son had developed a stammer that became much worse when his mother was near. He was too tall and soft and heavy for Gara's taste, and when he was with her he was unable to say her name because he liked her so much. He called her "G-G-G-Gary." Whenever he danced with her he got an immediate erection, and she always pulled away. For some reason May considered him a suitable boyfriend for her.

She was in love with someone else. His name was Luke, he was handsome and funny, and he lived in California. She hadn't mentioned him to her mother because he wasn't Jewish, and she knew her mother would say he would never marry her, and that if, unfortunately, he did marry her, they would forever after fight over the children's religion. Gara didn't want to marry him because she considered herself too young to know whom she wanted to spend the rest of her life with, but she was in love with him all the same, and they had as much sex as they could, as often as they could, without going all the way, although they had talked about that, too. She was going to be a senior in the fall, and the thought of choosing her own lover, without even the mandatory ring, was beginning to seem quite tantalizing.

But in the meantime it was spring vacation, Luke was with his family in California, and Marvin Wink was here in the suburbs of New York. He called Gara constantly, and finally, because he had gotten theater tickets and her mother was nagging her, Gara said yes.

She started to worry immediately. She didn't much like him, he made her nervous, and after spending all that money for a Broadway musical and taking her to dinner and driving in and having to drive back again, she knew he was going to try to kiss her goodnight, and she was expected to let him do so even though he made her feel sick. She felt manipulated and twelve years old.

What would be so terrible if he put his warm, possibly wet

mouth on hers? She didn't know. All she knew was that she couldn't, she just couldn't, and she was going to have to. When Marvin picked her up she could barely be civil to him, and her father had to make all the conversation until they finally left for the show. They would eat afterward at Sardi's, where there were supposed to be celebrities to look at.

Their seats were in the mezzanine. Gara didn't even know what she was seeing. The lights seemed too bright on the stage, the colors too garish. She began to feel lightheaded, and nausea rolled through her.

"I'm going to faint," she whispered to him. She put her head down on her lap because she had heard that if you did you wouldn't black out.

Marvin was frightened. "Are you?"

She supposed she had fainted, because when the lights went up after the first act she noticed everyone near them was staring at her. People were murmuring with concern. She's sick. Are you all right? Is she all right?

"I have to leave," Gara said.

"G-G-G-Gary, what's wrong?"

"I don't know." She hoped she wouldn't throw up.

"Do you have a doctor?"

"It's the middle of the night. I'll be all right. I just need to go home. I'm sorry I spoiled your evening."

"No," Marvin said. "I'm taking you home with me. My father's a d-doctor. He'll look at you. You're very pale."

"I'm always pale."

"I'll take care of you." At least since she was sick he wouldn't try to kiss her. She let him lead her to his car and drive her to the suburbs, to his parents, while she half-dozed.

She hardly knew his parents and was ill at ease. By the time they got there she wasn't feeling faint anymore. His parents were so tiny—how did they have such a big marshmallow of a son? His mother, who had unreal-looking dyed black hair, glared at her. His father was concerned and kind.

"Polio," his father said.

"Polio?" That was absolutely ridiculous; she'd had a shot. People didn't get polio anymore.

"You never know," his father said.

Gara wondered why, if she had such a contagious disease,

none of them was avoiding her. She decided that his father would have diagnosed her with the Black Death rather than think that she just didn't like his son.

"We'll take you home now," his father said, "and tomorrow you get your mother to take you to your own doctor."

His father insisted on driving the two of them back to New York so he could keep Marvin company on the return trip, and feeling protected by her "polio" and the presence of his father, she actually had a pleasant time.

The next day her mother took her to their family doctor, and waited outside while she was being examined. Dr. Spear was a kindly, middle-aged man with thick white hair. He looked like an actor playing a wise doctor on TV. Blood pressure, temperature, heart, lungs, blood. There was a nurse. Then he asked for the speculum and gave Gara the first pelvic examination she'd ever had in her life. Girls had them only if they were going to be married. She wondered if Dr. Spear thought she had fainted because she was pregnant.

"Are you in love with this boy?" he asked.

"In love? No!" She was insulted that he could even think it. "I'm in love with someone else."

"So why were you out with this one?"

"My mother made me."

She got dressed and met him in his office. "There's nothing wrong with you except that you have low blood pressure," Dr. Spear said. "Under stress it's possible to feel faint. Do you often go out with people you don't like?"

"When my mother makes me," Gara said. She wondered what he must be thinking of a girl so dominated.

"Well, tell her you won't. Go out in a group if she wants you to go out. You work hard at college, and when you socialize you should have fun."

What a nice man he was, and so understanding. She wished she had a father like him. "Thank you, Dr. Spear," Gara said.

Her mother was alone in the waiting room, looking anxious. "I'm fine," Gara told her. "He said I have low blood pressure and I shouldn't go out with anyone I don't like." But she knew the truth was that she had fainted from fear.

"What did the doctor do?"

"A complete exam. A gynecological exam, too."

"He didn't break the hymen?" her mother asked, her voice rising with alarm.

She hated her mother for caring about her virginity more than anything else about her. She felt, again, as if she were for sale. *No, he just pushed it aside, the way the boys do at college,* Gara wanted to say, but instead she said, "No." She had no idea if she even still had one.

They went home. "His parents are going to think you're sick," her mother said. "They think there's something wrong with you. You have to go out with him again and not faint."

"I can't do that!" Gara cried.

"You have to. His mother is a big bitch. She'll tell everybody you're not well and then no nice boy will take you out."

"I can't," Gara said.

"You will."

Her mother gave her a bottle of smelling salts that smelled pungently of ammonia and lavender, and so a week later Gara found herself having lunch on a banquette at an expensive French restaurant, with Marvin at her side and the little bottle of smelling salts under her napkin. Her head was reeling, and every few moments she sniffed at the smelling salts and wondered what he must be thinking about this strange behavior. She hoped he thought she only had a cold.

Cut, chew, and swallow. Talk a little when you have to. Don't faint. Soon it will be over. She wondered what would happen if she did faint; would she have to go out with Marvin Wink over and over until she didn't? Probably. Her mother was crazy. Who cared what his mother told her friends? If she was such a big bitch why did her mother care at all what she thought or what she said? Her friends couldn't have been anyone she'd want to know.

What could Marvin's mother say? That Gara was frail and prone to collapsing, the victim of some mysterious disease, possibly fatal, that would make her the wrong choice for the wife of their sons and the mother of their sons' children? May had often told Gara that she, and not the boy, had to be the one to call it quits. No matter how boring he was, how unsuitable, you had to make a good impression so that he asked you out again, and then you could refuse to go. What people thought of you was everything. You had to be perfect.

Was that true? Were people so judgmental and cruel? Gara supposed so. It was what she had been hearing, in one way or another, all of her life.

FOUR

Felicity felt safe at Yellowbird with Gara. Without being conscious of the progression she had begun to think of Gara as her "good mother" as opposed to the one she had actually grown up with. Gara was only fifteen years older than she was, but it wasn't an age thing; it was Gara's protective attitude and willingness to listen and to give good advice. She loved that Gara was a therapist—it was like having an extra free one of her own. On the sound system Minnie Riperton was singing "Perfect Angel" in her sweet, high, trilling voice like a streak of silver.

"Oh, sing it, Minnie," Billie said, at the bar.

"Perfect," Gara said, "is a word I never want to hear again."

"Who wants anything to be perfect?" Kathryn said. "That would be boring."

"Or any *one*," Gara said.

"I'm perfect," Eve said. She said things like that, and then she got a belligerent look on her face waiting for you to disagree. The other three women just turned and stared at her. "We're all potentially perfect," Eve explained. "It's how you feel about yourself. When I give myself the power, I have it."

"The wit and wisdom of Eve Bader," Gara said dryly. Eve smiled.

"I don't allow negative vibes," Eve went on. "This audition I did today, I knew I was in control because I was psyched up to *be* the person they wanted..."

Felicity tuned out and allowed herself to obsess about her lover, Jason. He was tall and black and handsome, he was a successful suspense novelist, he was intelligent and interesting, and he was a wonderful lover. They had a chemistry together that was obviously destiny. Why hadn't he called for a whole week? She had left him two E-mail messages in their private code and that was enough begging; he had to be the one to call now. _Master, please instruct your slave._ She knew how sick that sounded, but she also knew she was an emotional masochist, if not a physical one. That was just the way she was.

Jason went along with it and liked it. He would never hurt her body—physical pain was not her thing, it revolted her—but he tortured her mind. She didn't know when he would turn up next and when he would disappear. He was aware that she suffered when he stayed away, but he had no idea how terrible it was for her. It was as if everything they'd had together that was loving and good had simply vanished, with no explanation and no trace. She felt like a lost child. He couldn't imagine the depth of her fear...or maybe he could.

It had been so passionate and wonderful last week; maybe that was why he hadn't called. They had brought in lunch to their secret pied à terre and hardly touched it. She had closed the curtains and lit candles, and they had smoked a joint together, had a glass of wine. They'd had sex on the bed and in the bathtub, and she'd had three orgasms, leaving her exhausted and euphoric. He had finally said he loved her. How could she be so stupid? Of course he would never call her again; he was married and couldn't afford to fall in love.

Felicity knew there were tears in her eyes and tried not to cry at the table in front of her friends who were having a good time. Gara had said Jason always called eventually, but Gara was just trying to be encouraging. Love was the fatal word, and he would never see her again. He would find another woman to take her place, one who wouldn't threaten him by making him have emotions.

Or maybe it was just that he was tired of her and had found the other woman already. He could have been lying when he said he loved her. Maybe she'd been deluding herself and he had been seeing the two of them all along.

Felicity turned all the possibilities of abandonment over and over in her mind and tried to dismiss each one methodically, logically, as if she were laying out a case. Jason would never find sex with another woman that was as hot and good as what he had with her. He had told her that many times. And yes, she believed he did love her and that she had finally gotten to him. His face had seemed so pure, so clear, so sweet when he admitted it. She knew his marriage was not much better than hers, so she had never worried that he would give her up for his wife. But what would she do if he kept avoiding her and never came back? How could she survive her own arid marriage without him? The concept of being alone with Russell forever, of having him be the only man she leaned on, the only friend, was inconceivable. She felt so lonely when she was with him, and she had no idea why.

Kathryn snapped her fingers. "Wake up, Felicity, you're in dreamland. Here come the two cute guys I met at the bar."

Felicity looked up at the two white men approaching, not knowing what to expect because Kathryn was so friendly that she liked everybody. One of the men had a nice, craggy face and was well dressed, but he was way too old; and the other was wearing baggy clothes from J. Crew and looked like a nerd, but when he got closer she saw that he was quite attractive and looked about her own age. In a way his very casual clothes were charming; he seemed almost boyish, or perhaps it was the way he carried himself.

"The older one's in oil," Kathryn whispered cheerfully. "He's from Texas. He's the one I want." She gave them both a big smile.

Felicity glanced at Gara. She had her arms crossed over her chest as if she were protecting herself. Eve's hot eyes were bulging, and steam was practically coming out of her nostrils. She was probably psyching herself up with her power, sending them her magical vibes. As for herself, she sat back quietly and watched.

"Pull up chairs, you two," Kathryn said. "This is Stanley Stapleton, from Texas, and Eben Mars. Gara Whiteman, Felicity Johnson, Eve Bader, and you know me." Everyone said hello and the men got chairs from an empty table.

"What are you ladies drinking?" the oil man asked. He looked at the label on their empty wine bottle. "Another of those all right?"

"It's just fine," Kathryn said. He waved at the waiter.

"We've met before," Eve said to the younger one, leaning forward. "Do you remember? At a poetry reading at the Y last September. You were there alone. We talked. Do you remember?"

"I think so," he said.

"You'd just had your book of poems published," Eve said.

"Who published it?" Felicity asked, getting interested.

"Merlin Press. It's very small, and so was my advance."

"I've heard of them," she said. "I'm a literary lawyer, among other things."

"Are you! Well, then you know I have to do something else to survive, so I make my real living as a potato farmer." He smiled at her, and although meeting another man was not on her mind, she couldn't help noticing he had a very appealing smile.

"A potato farmer!" Kathryn said. "In Idaho or Maine?"

"In East Hampton."

"I can't believe you've never heard of Eben Mars," Eve said. She already had her hand on his arm, laying her claim to him. "He was very famous in mergers and acquisitions in the eighties, made a killing and got out when he was forty."

"Forty-two," Eben said. Felicity was surprised; he looked much younger.

"He was legendary. Now he's a gentleman farmer and a poet."

"Not exactly a *gentleman* farmer," he said. "Sometimes I actually get down in the earth and dig. But you might say I am: I do make a living in potatoes, but I don't need to."

"That's what I like," Kathryn said. She laughed happily, and turned to her oil man. "Now, Stanley, tell us about your life."

And he was telling them, total strangers. He'd been divorced twice, he had two grown daughters, a third had killed herself in a mental hospital when she was sixteen, back in the seventies, drugs. The four women gasped, but he went right on with his story, obviously used to gasps. He had been seeing a woman in Dallas, he said, but they had broken up recently, because she had wanted him to marry her but he realized she was not the one. It was not that he would never remarry, he said, but he didn't want a woman who wanted to have a baby with him. He didn't want to go through all that again, it was too late, he wanted peace. All this private information came pouring out of him, and Felicity realized that it was Kathryn he was telling, that this was his donation, his courtship.

"I never want peace," Eve said. "I wouldn't know what to do with it."

"Do you have children?"

"One," Eve said. "A daughter."

"Me, too," Eben said. His face softened at the thought.

Oh, how I crave a daughter, Felicity thought. A little me. I'd be a good mother, not like mine was. It would be like making up, somehow. And she should have a father whose face gets all soft when he thinks about her.

"So who else at this table is divorced?" Kathryn asked. "I am, Stanley is, Eve is, Gara is…"

"I am," Eben said.

"I'm the only one who's not," Felicity said brightly, "but I wish I was."

They all laughed.

"Marriage is a great institution," Kathryn said. "That's why we keep trying. It's the people we marry who aren't so great."

Gara looked at her watch. "I have to go home," she said. She signaled the waiter for the check. She seemed depressed.

"Why are you going?" Eve asked. "It's early."

"I have patients tomorrow morning."

"Well, I'm not leaving," Kathryn said. "I'm going to finish this nice wine with Stanley."

"That's what it's here for," he said, looking pleased. He poured her another glass and smiled at her.

Eve tugged at Eben's arm. "I want to go dancing."

"I don't dance," he said.

"I'll teach you."

"I don't think so."

"Come on."

"No."

"Then let's listen to music. You can sit. We'll go to the Café Carlyle."

He thought for a moment. "I guess I could do that," he said, finally. "Anybody else want to come? Felicity?"

"I have to go home to my husband," Felicity said.

The waiter came with two checks, one for the table and one for Eve. "What's this?" Eve asked. "My own check?"

"Well, you came late," Felicity lied. Eve shrugged. They all slapped their credit cards down as if they were in a card game, and Eve told the waiter she wanted to take the rest of her chicken with her, and to throw in a couple of biscuits while he was at it. It didn't matter if she was going to a nightclub or going to get laid, she never forgot her leftovers.

"Felicity, we can share a cab and I'll drop you off," Gara said.

They stopped at the bar on the way out to say goodnight to Billie. "Thanks for coming," she said in her strange, hoarse voice, and gave a little wave. If she seemed to notice Eve's fast work she didn't show it. Nothing ever surprised Billie.

"So do you think she's going to tie him up tonight?" Gara asked in the cab. They shrieked with laughter.

"They're not going to let him in the Carlyle in those clothes," Felicity said.

"She knows that."

"They won't even be able to get in without a reservation."

"She knows that, too."

"So I guess they have to go to her apartment to hear music."

"Or his."

"If he's that rich he must have a place in New York; he wouldn't commute to the potatoes." She wondered what his apartment was like.

"How did she nail him that fast?" Gara said. "I didn't even notice what he looked like and she was already pulling him out."

"Because you're not looking for a man."

Gara sighed. "I guess not."

"When you want one you'll get one," Felicity said. "But you're lucky you don't care. You have no idea how difficult it is to need a man like I do. You don't know the half of it. You should be thankful every day that you're not me."

FIVE

The American suburbs in the early 1960s...the dream. Tree-lined streets, happy children playing in safety, good public schools, a private house with enough room for the kids and the dog, a yard for barbecues in the summer, where you might even eat tomatoes you had grown yourself in your garden, good neighbors, good friends. A place so dark at night, so fresh and clear, that children could lie in their beds and see the stars and the constellations. In the fall there was the smell of wood smoke, and in winter Santa Claus came down a real chimney the way he was supposed to, the way it said in the stories. It was for this dream of a happy, comfortable family life that Felicity Johnson's parents had moved to the white suburbs outside Detroit when she was five and her younger sister, Theodora, was three.

They had a lovely house. It had been decorated by a professional designer in cheerful, contemporary colors, and each girl had her own room. There was a game room in the finished basement, with a television set in front of a comfortable couch, a Ping Pong table, and shelves of books and toys. It was hoped that the girls would entertain their friends there, but as they grew older it turned out there weren't many friends, and the friends' parents didn't want them to come to a black person's home. There was only one other black girl in Felicity's class, and although there were three in Theodora's, her sister was overweight and shy, and preferred to have her nose in a book to making an effort. Felicity was the sociable one. Her friends were white, which was fine with her. They were all she knew.

There were two kinds of white people, she had discovered early. There were the kids who liked her and she liked them,

just as if there were no real difference between them at all;
and then there were the other ones, who called her Nigger
and Burnt Toast at school, who made her cry and want to
disappear. Her mother told her to ignore the mean ones. She
told Felicity every day how lucky she was to be living in such
a nice neighborhood, with all the advantages that were her
right in this country no matter what vile and ignorant people
said to her. Her father was a doctor, commuting to the black
part of the city, where his patients were. He was successful
and respected, and they had enough money. She would go to
college someday. She had piano lessons, and ballet lessons
and riding lessons, and since her father was always working
and hardly ever around, her mother took care of the rest of
her education as well.

Carolee, their mother, was a beautiful woman. Felicity was
in awe of her. She was tall and slim, as Felicity was, her skin
was a creamy light chocolate, and she loved fashionable
clothes. She had chosen to be a housewife, because that was
an upwardly mobile middle-class thing to be, but Felicity
knew she was brilliant and could have done something else
if she had wanted to. On Saturday afternoons Carolee took
Felicity and Theodora to the sales—dragged them, rather,
because they found shopping incredibly boring. Felicity
would have rather been with her friends, and Theodora was
too roly-poly to look good in anything. At the department
stores, Carolee hunted bargains, and showed her two daughters the difference between good clothes and bad ones. It was
as much a part of their education as the piano and riding and
ballet, as using the right fork and arranging flowers to cheer
up a room.

"It's better to have one good designer dress than a closet
full of junk," she always said.

Felicity admired her mother's closet. She didn't have a lot
of clothes, but they were all elegant, arranged neatly with
their matching accessories nearby. This wardrobe signified
"grownup" to her, the kind of grownup she was destined to
be—someone who looked right on the outside, no matter
what else was secretly going on.

Their happy home in the tranquil suburbs was not what
people thought it was, and Felicity wondered if the Johnson

family was the only one in the neighborhood with frightened children in it. She thought they might be. How would she know? People knew things and minded their own business.

She was eleven now, and she and Theodora were walking home from school for lunch, as they always did. The neighborhood was a sea of children. Kids were hurrying down the block, the boys pummeling each other, the girls holding arms and whispering.

The trees on their street were so large that they arched over the sidewalk, making shadows. As they came closer she saw the big white Bombagaster Office Supplies truck, parked a block away from her house as if that could fool anybody. They had seen it for three years, almost evey day, and lately every time Felicity saw it her face heated up with embarrassment. Her mother's friend, Jake, was there again for lunch with her mother, and right at the start of their friendship, as soon as Carolee had told them his presence had to be a secret from their father, Felicity had known he wasn't supposed to be there at all. Even Theodora knew he wasn't supposed to be there, although she was still too young to figure out what was going on.

Felicity felt helpless, knowing there was nothing she could do about the situation anyway. She never wanted her father to find out. Her poor father, a victim—working so hard, loving her mother, trying to give them everything he could—she only wanted to protect him and save him from learning about something that would make him miserable and humiliated. In a way, keeping the secret made her feel less helpless, knowing she was helping to keep peace in their home.

Peace was important, and you had to get it where you could find it. She already knew that. If her father didn't know about Jake he wouldn't be angry at her mother. When Jake was there her mother wasn't angry at them. She was loving, kissy and happy.

"Hello, cherubs!" her mother trilled. She had her hair tied back and she looked radiant. She was making steak and potatoes and green salad for Jake—he always got a real meal—and there were peanut butter and jelly sandwiches on the kitchen counter for Felicity and Theodora, as usual. The two girls licked their lips like two little cats and exchanged glances, resenting Jake's delicious-smelling lunch and their mother's attention to him.

"Hello, Mom. Hello, Jake."

"Hello, young ladies."

Jake smiled at them. He was the most gorgeous black man Felicity had ever seen in her life. He looked like a movie star. He always wore a suit and a tie when he came to their house, because he sold office supplies to people in companies. But in their kitchen it also made him look as if he had come over all dressed up for a date with her mother; which this was. There was an open bottle of red wine on the kitchen table, and he had the bottle opener in his hand.

Carolee poured milk for her daughters, smoothed their hair while they ate, and kissed them when they were finished, smiling at them and at Jake as if they were one big cheerful family. Felicity loved it when her mother was so nice to her, but deep inside she was also slightly nauseated because her father was being left out and deceived. She felt so sorry for him. She knew it was a terrible thing to be trapped in an unhappy marriage—her mother had told her so often enough—but although she understood her mother, she didn't have to approve of the way she was supposedly solving her problem.

"Let's go," Felicity said to her sister as soon as they had eaten.

"It's still early," Theodora whined, but she knew it was hopeless and let Felicity drag her away. She liked these moments with her mother and wished they would never end.

School let out at three o'clock. There were extracurricular activities for another hour and a half for those who wanted them, or you could stay in the school library and study, which Theodora always did, gnawing on her stash of candy bars. Felicity usually went to a friend's house nearby or played in the street with the few other kids who would have her, and then she picked up her sister and they went home. Neither snow nor wind nor early darkness stopped them from staying away from home as long as they could in those afternoons, because they knew what their mother would be like when they came back.

Jake would have left. He had a job and, equally important,

he had a wife. The remains of lunch would be cleaned up, and the bottle of wine finished. Another bottle would be open on the kitchen table, and their mother would be drunk and morose.

"If it weren't for you two kids I could leave this marriage and be happy," Carolee would often say. "But your father would get this house and custody of you, and then I'd have nothing."

It confused Felicity when her mother said that. Were her children really that important? Sometimes she thought her mother hated them, like on these days when Jake had gone home to his wife.

Felicity and Theodora walked into the house and went directly to their rooms to do their homework before supper. Felicity heard her mother go into her sister's room.

"Is that *chocolate* on your dress?" her mother said angrily. "You've been sneaking candy again. I'm going to cut off your allowance! Who's ever going to look at you? Good thing you got all A's again this month. At least you'll be able to get a job when you're grown up."

Felicity hunched over her math. She was terrible at math; her mind went in hopeless circles and she wanted to cry. At least she was thin. Her mother came into her room then, and her heart sank. When she pulled a chair over to the desk to help Felicity with her homework, or grill her, rather, Felicity was already trembling.

"All right," Carolee said, tapping her pencil on the first problem, "show me the answer."

Felicity pointed wordlessly at the figuring she had done, praying it wasn't wrong. When she grew up, if she was too ugly for any man to marry, she would be a lawyer like Perry Mason. There was no math needed in the law.

"Wrong, wrong, wrong!" her mother said. "Do it again and do it right."

She tried.

"No, no, no," her mother said. "Why can't you do it right?"

"I *can't* do it right," Felicity said. "If I could, I would have."

"Are you back-talking me?"

"No," she mumbled, but it was too late. Her mother was already up.

"I'm going to my room and getting my belt."

It was always this way. Felicity was too stupid, or too fresh, or too obstinate. It was so unfair. If it wasn't a belt it was Felicity's riding crop or anything her mother grabbed. Felicity was crying with fear and outrage before her mother even came back with her leather belt. Then they began their usual chase around the house, her mother flailing the belt, hitting her on her arms, her legs, her backside, her stomach—everything but her face because Felicity always took great care to cover it. She didn't know what she would do if her mother struck her on the face and blinded her.

The belt hurt like fire, like licks of flame. Felicity ran and ducked and weaved, crying hard, and finally locked herself in the temporary safety of her bathroom. She leaned against the cool tile wall, sobbing. She's going to kill me, I know it, she thought. This time she will.

"Come out of there!"

Felicity just cried and shook. Dark welts were already rising on her legs. I can't take it anymore, she thought.

Her mother was hammering on the bathroom door. "Come out of there, I say!"

The door was shaking. She's going to break it in and kill me, Felicity thought.

"If you don't unlock that door this minute, you'll never go to the movies again."

Silence. Oh, please go away. I hate you. I won't be going to the movies because I'll be dead.

"If I have to break the door down, I'll beat you twice as hard. I mean it. You know I will."

The door was really shaking now. Felicity opened it. Her mother sprang in, grabbed her arm, and let the belt fly, striking her on the side of her cheek. Felicity heard it as well as felt it. It sounded like someone biting into an apple.

She pulled loose and ran into her parents' bedroom, where the phone was, slammed the door, as if that was going to make any difference, and dialed her father's office. "Doctor Johnson, please. This is his daughter and it's an emergency."

Her mother opened the bedroom door and just stood

there, the belt still in her hand. When Felicity heard her father's sweet, deep voice she started to sob so hard she could scarcely talk.

"She's going to kill me!" she told her father. "Make her stop! It's Mom, and she's beating me with a belt."

Her mother strode over and took the receiver out of Felicity's hand. When she spoke, her voice was reasonable and amused. "She's lying," her mother said. "You know what a liar Felicity can be. She'll do anything to get a little attention."

"I'm not lying!" Felicity screamed. Why wouldn't he believe her? He was supposed to rescue her, protect her. She had told him and told him, but he wouldn't listen. He didn't want to know.

"Try to come home on time tonight," her mother said in that same pleasant voice. "It would be nice if we could all have dinner together. Oh, well then, see you when you get here." She hung up. "You'll never win," she said.

Felicity wiped her running nose with her hand and her mother gave her a tissue. She didn't seem angry anymore, and although she was still drunk, she was rational. She touched Felicity's cheek with her cool fingertips, as if she were just realizing what she had done.

"Oh, my God," her mother said quietly.

She took Felicity back into the bathroom then and put alcohol on her welts, gently, tenderly, her eyes very sad. Felicity was afraid to look into the mirror at her face. "That will be all right tomorrow," her mother said, and brought ice wrapped in a towel and held it for her, cuddling her long-legged daughter on her lap. "Poor little girl," she said, and rocked her.

Felicity was safe again. She relaxed into her mother's arms, and slowly, slowly, she somehow remembered how it felt to love her.

Felicity didn't know what she would do without her friends. She was twelve now, and her sister was old enough to find her own way home from school, so most afternoons she stayed at her new best friend Jennifer's house until just before Jennifer's father came home from work. Jennifer was white, with blue eyes and straight light brown hair. She had a finished basement, as Felicity's family had, done like a game room, and the two girls spent a lot of time down there sharing secrets and talking about boys and sex and love.

They were romantic and yearning and nervous and giggly. They practiced kissing on their own forearms, to see how it felt and to learn how to do it right, pretending their arms were a boy.

"So if you're not married, how old do you think you'll be before you do it?" Jennifer asked. There was only one it.

"Old," Felicity said. Her mother had told her the facts of life many times, in her own way, and Felicity was scared of sex. "My mother says that I should stay a virgin as long as possible because once you start you can't stop."

"Do you think that's true?" Jennifer asked.

"That's what my mother says."

"I've heard that, too." The two girls pondered this. "You know Mary's mother?" Jennifer said.

"Sure." Mary's mother was divorced. She and her husband had lived in the neighborhood for years and had three kids, and then her husband had left her for another woman. It was sad. Her mother was still young and attractive, and in summer she wore shorts to the supermarket. The married men liked her and went out of their way to talk to her, and their wives disliked and mistrusted her, although no one had ever heard anything bad that they could prove. It was all couples where they lived, and the wives had stopped inviting Mary's mother to dinner parties. That was sad, too.

"I heard my mother talking to her friends about her," Jennifer went on. "Men always chase divorced women because they know they've had sex already, and they can't do without it."

"Is it because it's so good, or because you just need it?"

"Both, I guess."

Felicity thought about that. If sex could make you enslaved then that was why you were supposed to wait until you were married. But her mother didn't like to have sex with her husband, even though he was a very good-looking man by anybody's standards. That was confusing. Maybe they were incompatible. Her mother said it was because she had never loved him.

"I think you have to be in love to have good sex," Felicity said.

"Love makes it better," Jennifer said. "Everybody tells you that."

The idea of having sex purely for its own sake had never occurred to either of them as an option, and although they knew people did, they thought it was disgusting.

They put on the new lip glosses they had bought at the drugstore and compared colors, and then decided to go upstairs to the kitchen to find a snack. It was Thursday, the day Jennifer's mother went to the supermarket, so they knew there would be a lot of interesting things.

They were on the landing when Jennifer's father came down the stairs. Felicity had never seen him before and didn't know why he was home from work. He was dark red and ugly, or perhaps that was just the look on his face. He had a baseball bat in his hand.

"I knew you had that nigger in this house," he said, furious. He raised the bat and Felicity's stomach fell about seven floors. She actually felt the jolt. Her skin began to tingle as if it had a life of its own. "Get her out!"

"Daddy," Jennifer murmured weakly. She seemed, surprisingly, to be more embarrassed than afraid.

"Get that nigger out of this house!" he said again, and he came striding toward Felicity, brandishing the bat, and she knew if she didn't run he would hit her, so she ran out the front door and away.

She ran all the way home, her heart pounding so hard she heard it in her ears like the wash of the ocean, too terrified to cry, too desperately miserable not to. She was gasping and gulping air, and she heard a high, keening sound she knew was her own voice. *No...no...*

She had been taunted and left out at school and in the neighborhood, but that had been by white kids, and kids could be stupid and mean. She had never seen such hatred in a white adult this close before. The thought that grownups—her friends' parents!—could despise her that much was terrifying. She felt tiny and vulnerable.

Felicity knew that today was the end of all the good times with her new best friend. Jennifer would never be able to see her again, except at school. She would never have friends she loved and who loved her, never. She would always be alone. She hated that man for insulting her, for trying to hurt her, for treating her like a low, dirty thing that didn't even have a right to exist. She hadn't done anything. She was just a kid and he was a grown man.

She ran to her own street, past the Bombagaster Office Supplies truck that was still there, into the refuge of her own house, and finally was able to breathe again. Her heart slowed down to its normal pace. It was earlier than the time she always came home, so of course Jake and her mother were still having their date.

Felicity went into the kitchen, looking for them, but it was empty, the dirty dishes on the table. She looked into the living room, but they were not there either. Then she tried to go to the basement game room, but the door was locked.

She stood there for a moment, chewing her fingernail, afraid to knock because she sensed that's where they were. Then she heard the noises. A voice was moaning, a woman's voice...her mother's. The sound was not pain or fear, but something so open and vulnerable and primitive it was hard to believe it was her mother at all. She put her ear to the door. *Ah...Ah...* Then she heard the man's voice; deeper, almost guttural, but just as lost. *Ah...Ah...* It was Jake. Suddenly she realized what the sounds were.

She wished she didn't have to hear her mother moaning like this, like some stranger. She was both repelled and fascinated. All these years she had known and yet she hadn't really known. But she knew now. The bad, wrong, secret, embarrassing thing between her mother and Jake wasn't just a flirtation, or a series of forbidden dates, or a movie style romance, or even an easy-to-misunderstand friendship. Her mother and Jake were physical lovers.

Now she understood what her mother had meant when she told her sex made you enslaved—she meant good sex. She was probably enslaved to Jake. That was why she was always so happy when she was with him, so affectionate to her children, and so sweet. Felicity thought that she had always suspected in some dim way that they were actually doing it during those stolen afternoons, but first she had been too young to figure it out and then she hadn't wanted to know.

She ran quietly up to her room and locked the door. She had noticed a long time ago that her bedroom was on a direct line to the part of their finished basement where the couch and the TV were, and there was a common air vent. When she crouched down and put her head to the vent she could hear what was going on down there. She did now.

The sounds her mother and Jake were making were both shocking and irresistible. Felicity let herself float into them, imagining what was going on. Then, slowly, she began to feel a prickling between her legs. The sounds grew more intense, and she grew more strangely aroused. She grabbed her pillow and put it between her legs and rubbed against it, as if it were a lover of her own.

SIX

A cold, dark winter night in Boston. The woman is hiding in the backseat of the car, lying on the floor under the heavy raincoat, the man and the other woman in the front, the man driving. The woman in the back is trying not to tremble, hardly breathing. The man turns around. The woman in the back holds up the gun and blows his head off. This is what Kathryn had to live with. How could anyone live with that?

But what Kathryn O'Mara Henry knew when she grew up was that you are always judged by the most dramatic event in your life, when in fact that event is usually the culmination of a series of things, a natural progression, and while extraordinary and terrible, not as central as it seemed. This did not prevent her from offering up her secret from time to time to certain new friends; and they were always stunned, as she knew they would be. She was never a woman who asked for sympathy, but in a way their quick and certain sympathy was a relief, a kind of balm.

Kathie, as everybody called her then, was a stalwart, wild child, born in 1938 into a kind of aristocracy. Her father, Brendan, was a brutal, powerful Boston cop, from a family of feared cops—her grandfather and her three uncles—who held a great deal of power on into the forties and fifties in Boston. Even if they had not been frightening they would have been respected, because in those days everyone looked up to the police. Little boys wanted to grow up to be them. The police protected you, they were brave, benevolent blue figures in the neighborhood, with their weapons that would hurt only bad people, never the good ones. Kathie was proud of being a member of a police family.

The O'Maras lived in a nice, small house in Roxbury, in a neighborhood where all the houses were alike. It was not far enough away from the city of Boston itself to be considered the suburbs, but it was a good place to live. Her mother, Sheila, had a night job in a textile factory, but she was always home in the daytime to take care of Kathie and her three younger brothers, Colin, Donal, and Kean, getting her sleep in snatches between doing the household chores while they were at the parochial schools her job helped pay for.

Young Kathie liked to play cop, and at eight she was dressing up in her little blue shirt, her brother's pants, a toy gun in her belt, and her mother's rolling pin for a billy club, strutting around. Her father would watch her with a big smile on his face.

"Think you're as good as a boy, huh Kathie?"

She knew her father liked her and admired her toughness. He didn't like her brothers, though, or even her mother. She had always been aware of it. As long as she could remember, her father had violent, unpredictable rages. He was an alcoholic, and a mean one.

He was such a drunk that he was demoted from plainclothes detective down to uniformed policeman, but he was never actually fired because of the family's power. Whenever Kathie saw him drunk on the beat, she would pretend she didn't know him, but of course all the other kids knew he was her father.

In all those years the thing her mother had been the most afraid of was his gun. He said he always left the safety on, but he had shot up the house once (there were bullet holes in the walls to prove it), and she didn't want him doing it again, or even accidentally killing her kids. "Guns are serious," she would tell her children, but of course they already knew that.

Sometimes her mother's face was puffed and bruised, her brothers' bodies were black and blue, and nobody ever asked why, not even the nuns at school. At the factory her mother's co-workers had their own troubles to bear, and people minded their own business.

The neighbors didn't ask either, because they knew. No

one teased Kathie about her father. It was not a matter for ridicule. The neighbors were afraid of his violence, so they protected themselves by ostracizing the O'Mara family. Her mother had no friends in the neighborhood, and the few kids from school who were still Kathie's friends were so frightened of her father that they came over only when they knew he wasn't there.

At least twice a week her father would come home at dinnertime so drunk and enraged that just the sight of her mother would be enough to set him off. He would shove her away, and then he would rush for the food on the table and throw it out the back door, plates and all; then he would throw out the pots with the food in them; and then he would hurl out the chairs. All the time he was doing this, everyone in the family would be screaming—him with curses, the rest of them with hysteria. Kathie and her mother and brothers would run outside to get away from him. The families in the houses alongside theirs would lock their doors and stay inside, terrified. He was violent, and he was a cop.

Then when his temper was spent, he would calm down and her mother would cook dinner again, as if nothing had happened, even if dinner was only a can of soup.

Every single day Kathie's father abused her mother and brothers in one way or another, and there was nothing she could do about it. She tried, however, even though she was scared. She threw things at him—a plate, her schoolbook, his heavy shoe—and he laughed. At the same time he was hitting her mother, he was laughing at his daughter's anger, as if to say: She's a chip off the old block.

If she had to be a chip off any block Kathie wouldn't have picked him. But she wouldn't have chosen her mother either. She loved her mother, who was warm and good, who worked hard for them, who was always there when they came home from school, who made dinner for them before she left for work, and breakfast when she came home in the morning before they left for school. But she had no respect for her mother at all. How could she let her husband treat her that way? Why didn't she hit him back?—she was a big, strong woman. Why didn't she just take her kids and leave?

"Oh, how we used to dance at the Avalon Ballroom!" her

mother often reminisced. Who? Kathie thought. Not you and
my father. "He proposed to me there," her mother said. "He
was so dashing and romantic." Who is this person you're
talking about? Kathie wondered. *Him?*

"You ought to leave him," she told her mother.

"Where would I go?"

"Anywhere."

"You don't understand," her mother would say. "I can't."

"Why can't you?"

"I just can't."

"But *why?*"

"I love him."

Kathie never wanted to get married. What was the point of
it? The nuns at school said you got married to have children,
that marriage was a blessed union in the sight of God. When
you had a baby it was called a blessed event. So how come
her little brothers were subjected to their father's beatings
and rages? When the nuns started their nonsense, Kathie just
shook her head and daydreamed.

Something inside her was bubbling and simmering all the
time, and frequently exploded. All she wanted was a peaceful home life, but she might as well have wished to live on a
distant planet. Sometimes, when her father was so drunk
that she could duck his huge fists, her mother would pour
his liquor down the kitchen sink, but then he would only go
out to the bars.

"You stinking son of a bitch!" Kathie would yell at his re-
treating back.

Her mother would cast her a look of fear. "Don't call him
that," she would plead.

"Well he is one."

A weaker man would have died already from all the poison he poured into his body, Kathie thought wistfully. There
was something superhuman about him. His arm muscles
bulged, ripe with veins; his legs were like sculpted wood.
Brendan seemed indestructible, a force of evil that would
never go away.

At last, the police force suspended him. He wouldn't be allowed to work as a cop again for two years. After that, if he
had shaped up, well then...but if not...The family needed the

money, so in a career move of supreme irony her father, who had no intention of shaping up, got a job as a bartender. Unfortunately, it was only during the day.

"He's with his own," her mother said.

Even though he wasn't on duty, he still had his uniforms and his gun. The neatly pressed uniforms hung in his closet, and the gun went into a shoe box on the top shelf, a constant reminder of explosive death, even though it was not in sight.

On occasional Saturday nights her mother went to the movies with some girlfriends from work. It was a kind of vacation for her, a respite from the constant tension at home. When her mother came back, she would report every detail of her evening—the plot of the movie, which of her friends was there, what they had said, their little jokes—in that sad and desperate way of people who have so few happy stories to tell. It was a recitation that would have been boring under other circumstances, but Kathie especially loved her mother on those movie nights, when she had come home from something that was good and all her own, her face radiant. Her mother had so few consolations: She didn't even have the satisfaction of knowing her children were safe, although she could have saved them. At these times when her mother looked relaxed, like a normal person, Kathie tried to forgive her for being so weak, but it was still impossible.

She thought her parents were lunatics, both of them.

Sometimes Kathie wondered why her father never tried to hurt her. Despite his general rages, she knew she was special to him, that she traveled in a bubble of safety. It began to occur to her that it might be because her mother didn't love her as much as she did her brothers, who were so timid. Her mother was always trying to protect them.

Yes, her mother loved her, but not in the same way as she did Colin and Donal and Kean, because Kathie didn't need her like that. She had her life outside the house, and she even had a job, baby-sitting for Mrs. Henderson's kids down the street, and getting paid for it. The Hendersons were always kind to her, their house was nice and peaceful, and their children obeyed her.

She was hanging around with a different crowd now. Her new friends were the tough girls, the wilder ones. Her friends' mothers would let them congregate at their houses, which was not only fun but a sanctuary because it got her out on her own. While she was still eleven, her best friend, Mary, taught her how to smoke. They would stand around Mary's backyard, posing like glamorous movie stars, their cigarettes in their hands, heads held back to exhale.

"You've been smoking," her mother accused her when she came home smelling of it. "It's not ladylike, and you're much too young."

"Go blow it out your ear," Kathie said. It was her new favorite expression.

Her mother didn't know what to do so she did nothing. She just looked sad. She couldn't physically hurt her own child, even with a slap; lecturing got her nowhere, and she was basically a mild and stolid woman. Kathie had never even heard her curse.

Kathie knew that she was often disrespectful and mean to her mother these days, but she didn't know why, or how to stop it. It was just that she was so angry, and her mother was the only person who would take it.

"Why are you so fresh to me?" her mother asked once.

"Fish is fresh."

Her mother just stood there looking at her, thinking. "Maybe it's good for you to let it out," she said, finally. "It'll save you."

"Save me from what?"

"From our life."

In Kathie's opinion, what was going to save her was her own nonchalance. She had been working on not letting things get to her. She knew that in this respect she was like no one else in their family. It was possible to be both angry and happy at the same time, because she was both. There were plenty of things to enjoy. She was twelve now, and the boys at school were starting to like her and pay attention to her. She was studying hard and getting good marks, which made her feel proud of herself. Her mother couldn't control her, so she could do anything she wanted, within reason. If only her father were different, but he wasn't....

"You have to stop being so rude to your father, Kathie. It

was cute when you were little and yelled at him, but you're a big girl now and it isn't cute anymore."

"Says you."

"You don't understand just how crazy he is," her mother said.

Kathie ignored that. Her own adolescence had become the most interesting thing in her life. She was glad to find she was beginning to look more like a teenager than a child, and next year she would actually be a teenager. She knew she was pretty. Everybody told her so. She had silky red hair and very white skin with a cute sprinkling of freckles across her nose, and a tiny waist to show off the little bumps that had finally turned into breasts. Suddenly there were as many boys as girls in their group of friends. The boys had started hanging around at her house now, willing to take the risk, and suddenly their behavior was self-conscious and show-offy. Her father took it the wrong way immediately.

"What are those damn boys doing on my porch?" he would scream at her mother. "I don't want my daughter turning into a slut."

"Go blow it out your ear," Kathie muttered to herself. Since at the moment she was thinking of being a nun when she was old enough, she had no fear for her virtue, and besides, the boys were harmless.

"Get the hell out of here, you little shits!" her father would scream at the boys, lumbering out to the porch with his fist raised. "Kathie, you get in here!"

"We're going to Mrs. Cavanaugh's house," Kathie would scream back, and then she and her friends would stampede away.

"You don't understand anything, do you, Kathie," her mother told her. What was there to understand?

Her father didn't like boys, he didn't even like his own sons, he didn't want anybody to be happy. What else was new? But there was always something, just when she thought she had seen it all.

This time it was an event that changed her life.

It was St. Patrick's Day, a holiday Kathie both loved and dreaded. She loved it because of the parade, which some of her girlfriends from school were allowed to march in, and because the holiday celebration seemed to be the first real sign that spring was finally going to come again. She dreaded St. Patrick's Day, too, though, because there was so much drinking afterward, and it was an official chance for her father to get drunker than ever.

She had gotten to the parade route early to secure a good place to stand in the front just behind the wooden barricades so she could see everything. People were wearing green carnations in their lapels, green hats with white shamrocks on them, green clothes, and waving small Irish flags they had bought from street vendors. The big brass horns went *oompah*, the drums were banged loudly, the bagpipes wailed, and the onlookers raised their voices again and again in cheers as they saw people they knew in the parade. The police in their uniforms marched proudly in thick and formal lines, each group carrying a banner that announced the district it represented. It was very raw and chilly out, and the young drum majorettes who pranced in their short pleated skirts had bare legs, their knees red from the cold. Kathie didn't know how they could stand it. She herself was all bundled up. She waved at her friend Mary and several other friends from school, a few yards down the line on the barricade, who were watching with their families. Everyone was out on the parade route; parents had even brought their babies. Kathie was sorry her mother wasn't there for the fun, but her mother was too tired and had too much work to do at home.

"Your father," Mary mouthed, pointing. Kathie rolled her eyes. Since her father's suspension he could not, of course, march with the police officers, but he was marching with his social club, an organization he only attended because it was another place he could drink. She could see Brendan was drunk already.

Suddenly her smiling father scooped a baby from its mother's arms and held it aloft, taking the infant with him as he marched. The mother screamed. The baby, astonished, wailed. Kathie's stomach turned over. The crowd of onlookers: her neighbors, her friends from school, total strangers, did not at first seem to know what to think. Brendan, benevolently bouncing this child in the air, seemed only to be in good spirits, perhaps even exuberantly affectionate. But Kathie knew better. He could go crazy in an instant.

"Hey, there," a man cried out to her father. "Don't drop that kid, there."

The baby's mother, white faced, had ducked under the wooden barricade and was running to catch up with Brendan and save her child. "Stop!" she screamed.

Kathie's father was no longer bouncing the baby the way a normal person might; he was tossing it in the air like a ball. The crowd watching him had gone abruptly quiet now, realizing that something was not right. Kathie screwed her eyes shut, afraid to look.

Aaah... A collective sigh. Then the laughter of relief. Kathie opened her eyes and saw that the mother had snatched her frightened child from Brendan's arms and was holding it again, comforting it. The laughter trickled away. People were murmuring uncomfortably among themselves because it was very clear that the infant's mother was sobbing. Then friends and relatives reached out to her and she was drawn back into the crowd, and Brendan's lodge had gone by, and it was all over. Except for Kathie, who was left with rage at her happy day being spoiled and humiliation because everyone—not just a few neighbors and school friends, but *everyone* had seen. She hated him.

When she went home Kathie told her mother about the latest incident. "Someday that bastard is going to kill somebody," Kathie said.

"Just be careful it's not you," her mother said quietly.

"Me?"

"Yes, you."

Kill *her*? She couldn't believe it. When she had said her father would kill somebody, she had only meant it would be by accident, and she had never thought it would be herself. Maybe she was stupid, but he had never touched her. She was his favorite, she was charmed and safe.

That night he came home drunk and caught her smoking, just as she was grinding out her forbidden cigarette on the sidewalk in front of the house. "You stink from cigarettes," he said.

"And you stink from booze." The minute she had blurted it out, she knew it was a mistake.

"What did you say to me?"

"Everybody in Boston saw you throwing that baby around today," Kathie said. "When are you going to stop embarrassing me in front of my friends?"

He hit her on the side of the head with a force she had never imagined in her life. Her ear was ringing from the brunt of the blow, and she tasted blood in her mouth where her tooth had cut the inside of her cheek. In that one instant the bubble of safety in which she had spent her childhood suddenly burst, leaving her exposed and vulnerable. She was not Kathie anymore, the Kathie who could handle everything: She was someone she hardly knew. As her father raised his fist to hit her again, she screamed and ran.

She ran until she was in an entirely different neighborhood, a place of warehouses and abandoned buildings and rats and possible murderers. She stayed there for an hour until she was more afraid to be there than at home with her family and then she went back. Her father had drunk himself unconscious. Her mother took one look at her face and started to cry.

And so it was that in the middle of the spring semester, by dint of a special dispensation for the emergency of the situation and her own good marks, Kathie found herself being driven by her mother in the family car from Boston to the Lancaster School for Girls in Little River, Vermont, where she would live and study for the next four years, except for vacations. It was night when they finally arrived there, to a lawn and a stand of trees, and an ugly gray cement building that looked like an air raid shelter, where you would hide if someone dropped the atom bomb.

Kathie's mother helped her take her suitcases out of the car. As soon as her mother had seen the depressing building, she had started crying again.

"Don't forget to say your prayers," she kept saying, as if that would protect her. It was obvious her mother didn't want to leave her there, but she had no choice. This safe haven was what she had really been saving her money for, all those years inspecting fabric at the factory at night.

Kathie had known about the Lancaster School for years. Not being a Catholic school, it would never have been her mother's first choice, but it was the only one that would take Kathie at such short notice. It was where the spoiled, rich girls went. They were the ones with the nice clothes and parents who could easily afford an expensive education. She was a little apprehensive, but not scared. She had never dreamed she would be here in such a fancy place. She was thrilled and excited and happy, and she could hardly wait for her new life.

SEVEN

"Happiness!" Felicity said, raising her glass of wine. They were in Yellowbird and everybody was glad to be there.

"Happiness," they all agreed, toasting to what they wanted or, in Kathryn's case at least, what they already had. It was crowded in Yellowbird tonight, with many of the regulars plus one large table of people they had never seen before. Billie seemed in a good mood; she loved money. On the sound system Janis was singing. "*Down on me, down on me...*"

"Oh, I wish," Felicity said, laughing, and they all laughed.

Gara knew Felicity was bubbly tonight because she had seen her "friend." Tomorrow he would call to tell her how wonderful their meeting had been, and then she would have another week in which to obsess and imagine he had forgotten her. As for herself, she was glad to unwind after what had been a depressing day. She felt she should always be on the patients' side, since they trusted her, but sometimes it was hard.

She thought about the attractive young man, Conrad, who had been her last patient of the evening. For two years he had been trying to figure out why he couldn't find a woman he liked enough, and he had finally thought he'd found the right one. She was thirty (three years younger than he was), she was beautiful, bright, interesting, warm, had a great job in his own field...he was in love. They hadn't even been to bed together yet; he had spent time getting to know her, which was progress for him; but the sparks had definitely been there from the beginning. He had decided he wanted to marry her.

"At last," he told Gara.

He had taken her to dinner at a romantic restaurant. That

would be the night he would make love to her, he would tell her he loved her, and then afterwards he would propose. He invited her to his apartment and they both knew what that meant. But in the restaurant she said she had something she had to tell him before they went any further. She'd had cancer, she told him; she was fully recovered, but she had a colostomy bag. He laughed so hard when he told Gara that it took a few moments for him to control himself.

"Wasn't that just my luck?" he said. "And I loved her!"

"Loved?"

"Well, obviously I can never see her again."

She hated that he was laughing. It was tragic; that poor girl, so young, in a marriage market that was so competitive that it was almost hopeless for the women with only ordinary flaws. With none! What would happen to her? Gara knew she shouldn't be thinking this way; she should feel what he felt, and of course she did, something like that was hard to take, she didn't blame him for being squeamish; but she identified desperately with the young woman, too, having to reveal her secret and be rejected. She wondered how often she had been rejected and thought it had been a lot.

"Why were you laughing?" Gara asked.

"It's so funny."

"Why is it funny?"

"Just my luck."

"Just hers, too."

"You don't expect me to have to deal with that. It's disgusting."

"It's tragic," Gara said.

"Are you blaming me?"

"Of course not. It's just a comment on our lives."

"That's what I've said all along," Conrad said. "There's nobody out there. It's a tragedy."

"So you'll have to start looking again."

"I know. I have six blind dates lined up for this coming week. I'm going to throw myself into it. No time to get depressed."

"That's a good idea."

Gara sighed and looked at her friends at the table in Yellowbird. It was a good thing she'd given up on men. She was middle-aged, she'd had her life. That young woman would find someone some day, she decided, and hoped that in the meantime she was as happy as she was just to be healthy and alive.

"Tell us about your evening with Eben," Kathryn said to Eve.

Eve gave a self-satisfied smile. She was wearing a short, tight skirt and a see-through sweater with no bra, although it was a little late for her to get away with that. Since her surgery Gara had found herself obsessed with breasts; she looked at other women all the time, on the street, everywhere. She looked at the size and shape of their breasts, amazed at what a variety there were. She wondered if their owners were properly enjoying them, and wondered, when she looked at opulent, sexy breasts bouncing along on the chests of young women who were a little bit self-conscious, a little too aware, if sometime in the future they would lose them. But she was much less obsessive than she had been at the beginning when she had not even looked at their faces. She was getting better.

"*Two* evenings," Eve said. "There's nothing like a young, stiff prick."

"Women who are getting laid dress sexier than they did when they weren't," Gara said dryly.

"Is that true?" Felicity asked with some alarm.

"Well, you don't have to worry," Kathryn said. "You're married."

"I hardly ever have sex with my husband," Felicity said. "I hate him." She opened her cell phone. "I'd better call him."

"Eben Mars is very interesting and very rich," Eve said. "I like him. He's crazy, though. The second time he called me up at the last minute, said he was on my corner with his portable phone and said: 'Do you want to fuck?' "

"And did you?" Kathryn asked.

"Why not?"

"Doesn't anybody use a regular phone anymore?" Gara said.

"Nope."

"All those antennas sticking up out of people's ears, like bugs."

"Hello, Slugger," Felicity cooed into her phone. "Whatcha doing?" She put her hand over the mouthpiece and made a face. "As if I didn't know."

Gara listened to Felicity talking to her husband in that soft, wheedling voice, and knew Felicity had an ambivalence she might not yet be aware of. She wanted to get away from Russell but she still called him constantly, as if she needed him as much as he needed her. She said she hated him, but she loved him, too. Gara knew Felicity had been in therapy for a few years, and wondered if she would ever get to the point where she would either change her life or resign herself to it.

Felicity clicked off and folded her phone. "I hate him," she said.

"What did he do?" Eve asked, excited at the prospect of hearing something bad.

"Nothing. He was very nice for a change. He's probably glad I'm not there."

"If you can't stand him, why did you talk to him for a good five minutes?" Gara asked.

Felicity shrugged.

"You know," Gara said, "there are women who would be very satisfied to have a rich husband for the lifestyle and a sexy, discreet lover for the passion."

"And they all live in Europe," Felicity said.

"No they don't," Kathryn said cheerfully. "You should hear some of the stories I hear when I'm having lunch and playing tennis and going to the gym."

"I'm sure," Gara said.

"I don't want a rich husband or any other kind," Eve said. "I'm never going to get married again. I didn't even want to get married in the first place."

"Neither did I," Kathryn said.

"Then why did you?"

"I was young and dumb," Kathryn said. "What about you?"

"I was pregnant. You remember what it was like in the sixties. Abortion was illegal so you married him. I was still in high school."

"Ah," they all said, sympathizing.

"But I threw him out after the baby was born, and divorced him and forbade him to have anything to do with me," Eve said. "I wouldn't take a penny from him. He was not a person I wanted to have in my life. He was just a cute guy who walked me home from school and carried my books. He was a lousy husband."

"What did you expect from a kid?" Gara said. "Did your daughter still see him?"

"Sometimes. She can if she wants to. That one mistake ruined everything for me." She sounded very bitter.

"But you have your beautiful daughter," Felicity said. "I only met Nicole once, that time you brought her here, but I loved her."

"Yeah?" said Eve. "Sometimes I'd like to go to my daughter's funeral."

There was a stunned silence. "Well, I married for love," Felicity said finally. "That shows how much anyone knows about anything. I thought Russell was a god."

"I married for love, too," Gara said.

Their food arrived: the usual broiled chicken and salad, except for Eve, who had ordered the chicken fried steak. She had a metabolism in high gear and could eat anything. All that anger must burn calories, Gara thought. Too bad mine doesn't.

"Another bottle of wine?" Felicity asked.

"I don't know…" Gara said.

"Oh, come on," Kathryn said. "If we don't drink it, Eve can take it home."

They ordered the wine. "I tried to leave my husband once," Felicity said. "I hadn't met my friend yet; I was still a good wife. I came home late from the office with wine on my breath because my colleague and I had had a drink when we got through working. Russell slammed me against the wall and hit me three times, and when I got away from him he locked the door and stood in front of it so I couldn't get out. I was screaming; I thought he was going to kill me. He kept asking: 'Who were you with tonight?' He called me a slut. I had never cheated on him, never. The next morning I looked so bad I was ashamed to go to work, but I did because I wanted to talk to the divorce lawyer in our firm. He took photos of me with my bruises and said I had a good case. I made the mistake of telling my mother."

"And...?"

"She looked at the photos of me all beaten up, and she said: "What did you do to deserve it?' "

"Oh, no!" Kathryn said.

"She said I had to go back to him. She said without Russell I'd have nothing."

"But you know that's not true," Gara said.

"She said she'd lived in an unhappy marriage and so could I," Felicity said. Russell swore he'd never hit me again, so..."

"And did he?" Kathryn asked.

"Once. About a year later. By that time I had my friend, but he didn't know it. He was just jealous, as usual."

"So your husband really pushed you into your affair," Eve said.

"Yes, but not the way you think." Felicity sipped her wine. "Let's not talk about him anymore. I'm too happy right now."

"But you can still divorce him now if you want," Eve said. "Do you still have the pictures?"

"Oh, sure. In my safe deposit box at the bank. But they won't do any good. The statute of limitations has run out. So Kathryn, we never asked you what happened with you and that oil man you met last week."

"Oh, yes, what was his name?" Kathryn said. "Stanley. Was it Stanley? I'm getting middle-aged and forgetful."

"There's no more middle age," Eve said. "You're young and then you're youthful." The others laughed and Eve looked pleased.

"He called me every day, so I went to dinner with him one night last week and he was obnoxious," Kathryn said cheerfully. "So I told him to buzz off."

"Next!" they all said in unison, and laughed.

"Cute," Kathryn said, looking across the room. They turned to see Little Billie walking through the crowded restaurant to talk to his mother, who was sitting at the bar. Hands reached out from tables to pat him, women cooed at him, trying to get his attention, all of them admirers in the presence of such nonchalant beauty. He said hello to the people he knew well and ignored the rest.

"He looks like an angel," Felicity said. "I wish I had one like that. A little darker. I wouldn't keep him in a bar at night. I'd keep him home with me."

"He *is* with his mother," Gara said, although she wondered how much longer Little Billie would put up with a life that was so different from the lives of his friends.

She glanced over at the bar. Little Billie's posture was stubborn, and Billie was shaking her head no, looking annoyed. Then he went back to his booth, sulking, and after a moment or two in reverie, Billie came over to their table and sat down.

"How many of you have kids?" she asked.

Kathryn and Eve raised their hands, and after considering whether her former stepsons counted, Gara did, too.

"Pain in the ass sometimes, huh?" Billie said.

"For sure," Kathryn said.

"He's in my face about going home," Billie said. "We live in a high rise, the kids play in the halls. He wants to be with them. This is a new, unpleasant development."

"Well," Gara said, "a nine-year-old kid wants friends his own age."

"He has them in the daytime," Billie said. "This is a school night, and children stay at home with their parents, wherever home might be. You're a therapist, Gara; what do you think?"

"I think that's a good point," Gara said.

"You're a *feminist*, Billie," Eve contributed brightly. "This is where you work, and you have your child in the workplace. That's acceptable."

"Who asked you?" Billie said, annoyed.

Felicity and Gara slid their glances at one another and tried not to laugh. Billie didn't like Eve; they were both surprised she had come to sit with them when Eve was there. Billie must really be upset about this, Gara thought.

"He's such a good kid most of the time," Billie said.

They looked at Little Billie in his booth, his chin propped on his hands, giving his mother the evil eye. But then he stifled a smile. It was obvious he couldn't stay angry at her for too long.

"A darling face like that," Billie said, "it makes you want to bite his nose." She smiled at him and he looked away. "Hey, Pete," she said to the waiter. "Bring Little Billie a hot fudge sundae. He likes it with vanilla."

"You're a good mother," Felicity said. Apparently she had changed her mind.

"Well, I try," Billie said. She got up without saying good-bye and went to greet a party of four that was coming in.

"She should send us a free hot fudge sundae," Eve said. "For the free advice."

"Just don't ask for it," Gara said, but they all knew what was coming.

"Pete," Eve called to the waiter. "We get a hot fudge sundae, too, and don't put it on the bill."

"No!" the other three groaned in unison.

"With four spoons," Eve said. "I'm still hungry."

"You can't do that," Gara said.

"No?" Eve said in the brusque, belligerent tone she took on whenever anyone criticized her. "Why not? I can do anything I want."

The sundae arrived and only Eve ate it. Kathryn didn't like ice cream, Felicity was always on a stricter diet than the rest of them, and Gara was embarrassed. She also knew it would no doubt appear on Eve's check and if she took even one bite Eve would demand that she split the cost. That was Eve. She wondered if Eve was really that hard up for money, or if she just liked wheeling and dealing and getting something for nothing. Eve often said she had always had to take care of herself. It must have taken courage for Eve to tell her ex-husband she didn't want any money or help from him. Not that a kid his age would have had much cash to contribute, but still...

Eve licked up the last drop of ice cream. Felicity looked at her watch and pulled out her cell phone again and called Russell.

"I'll be home very soon," she said to him, reassuringly. "I miss you, too, Slugger."

"Check!" Kathryn called.

When Pete brought the bills they looked them over. The hot fudge sundae did not appear on either of them. "Free!" Eve announced triumphantly. "I told you I can get anything I want. It just takes the power. You all should listen to me."

"I like the power of cash," Kathryn said.

"I like *my* power," Eve said. "The power of belief in myself."

Can anyone really be that confident? Gara wondered as they paid the bill and prepared to leave. What must she think when she's all alone?

EIGHT

Eve Bader was born on a small, struggling chicken farm twenty miles outside of Miami. She literally was born on the farm, since her mother went into labor early and her father had taken the truck into town to get something fixed. It was 1950, and her parents had gotten the money for their house and their dream from the G.I. Bill. The house was falling down when they got it and the dream collapsed soon after, and by the time she was five her parents were divorced.

She was an only child in a neighborhood overflowing with postwar fecundity. Everybody had brothers and sisters and friends, a mother who stayed at home and car pooled, and a father who went to work. She had a father who was absent, a mother who could drive a tractor, a neurotic tabby cat named Mayhem, and a black and white TV that showed a test pattern most of the day.

When Eve wasn't helping feed the chickens or clean the house she was watching the test pattern blankly, lying on the modern brown and orange tweed couch, stroking her cat, and wondering if it could be possible to send oneself right through that geometric design on the little screen to the world beyond where the people who would fill the screen at night originated. The yellow school bus stopped on the corner to take her to school and brought her home, she did her homework, and that was her life. The other kids didn't seem to like her, but she didn't know why. She wondered whether it was her personality or her clothes. She was the only girl at school who arrived in jeans, like a boy. It was just easier that way, her mother said.

"The kids make fun of me," Eve protested. "They don't like anybody who looks different."

"You'd better be different," her mother would say. "Do you want to grow up to be like me? You don't want to get married; men are no good. You have to be independent and be somebody."

"Be what?"

"Pick something."

When she was seven Eve decided she was going to be an actress, go to New York City, and be on *Playhouse 90*. The programs changed and went off the air, a lot of the television shows began to be seen in color, and she had new, alternative dreams of stardom. Maybe she would go to Hollywood instead of New York. Maybe she would be on a soap opera and wear those gorgeous clothes. It was a good thing, not a bad one, that she had grown up different. You had to have your own style to become famous. She set out to develop one.

She was always in the school play. In high school it wounded her to have to be the Nurse, not Juliet, because everyone knew that the girl who played Juliet was prettier, and more delicate, and more tragic; but Eve got to be Lady Macbeth. That was her finest hour. On stage she had heat and intensity. When she did the blood-on-my-hands scene some of the kids in the audience tittered, but she knew it was because they were stupid. Her mother had told her to pick, and she had picked. She knew her destiny.

When cute John Hawke, who was in her class and who did lighting on that production of *Macbeth*, became her boyfriend, Eve never for an instant thought that she'd spend her life with him. It was nice to have a good-looking boyfriend, to experiment with sex, to have someone to hang around with, to seem popular; and that was enough, that was normal, that was for now.

When she got pregnant she was stunned. Everyone was afraid of pregnancy, but still, when it happened, there was something unreal about it. She was only seventeen years old! Abortion was illegal, and she didn't even know where to go to get one. There were only two choices for her: go away to a home for bad girls and then give the baby up for adoption, or marry John. Eve didn't want a baby, but she certainly wasn't giving away any child of hers to be raised by who knew what.

It was humiliating to have a rushed and almost secret marriage to a boy she didn't love, with his parents glaring at her; worse to have to leave school because she was showing; and worst of all to have to live with him in her mother's house, in her childhood bedroom with the pictures of movie stars on the walls, because there was no money for them to be independent and his parents hated her too much to let the young couple live with them. She didn't know if she was a kid or an adult. She wished fervently that none of this had ever happened. She was fat and ugly and tired and lonely, and to make matters worse, he was madly in love with her and thought all of this was real life. His parents and her mother insisted John finish high school, but he kept making plans for the job he would get after he graduated and where they would live when they had a place of their own.

Eve didn't tell him that she had been planning the divorce while she was standing in front of the justice of the peace.

When their daughter, Nicole, was born, Eve had to wait almost a year for the sake of propriety before she told him she intended to get divorced. You couldn't break up too soon after the baby came because it made the forced marriage so obvious you might as well not have gotten married in the first place. She had never been particularly happy, but she thought that was the worst year of her life. John was in his senior year of high school, having a good time the way she should have been, and her mother had to work. Eve had hoped her mother would help her with the baby, but everything fell to her. The infant was constantly demanding. She realized she was not maternal, and somehow that did not surprise her. Maybe those feelings would come later. Right now she was exhausted and miserable...and bored.

She never did go back to school, but that didn't really matter, since the public library was well stocked with what she wanted so she could read plays at home; which she did, hungrily, imagining herself on stage in various leading roles, the rapt audience out front sending her a generous wave of admiration. She wondered if she needed acting lessons and, if so, who would pay for them. She read biographies of actors and actresses, was particularly taken by the ones who hadn't needed lessons to become stars, and decided she was a natural, too.

It was oppressively hot and humid most of the year in Florida. The heat started in March, and went on until something even worse—hurricane season—came in the fall. Even the winter, when the tourists came pouring down to stay on Miami Beach, was too tropical for someone with Eve's intrinsic heat of body and personality. The sweet-rotten smell of chicken shit, of the birds themselves, which she had taken for granted and ignored in her childhood, now nauseated her. The dry flapping of wings, the greedy clucking, the tiny, almost prehistoric heads with mean beaks and stupid eyes mocked her. She dreamed of her career, of escape.

John's parents refused to come to see the baby whom they felt had ruined their son's youth, if not his life. They were hoping he would come to his senses and get divorced when a suitable time had passed, he told Eve. They had made him apply to college. He told her this not to hurt her but because he thought his parents were acting unnaturally, and he wanted her to agree with him that their marriage would only get better as time went by, and to stand by him. Eve didn't reply. She was secretly glad they were on her side.

No, she knew she was not maternal. There were girls only a little older than she who had married their high school sweethearts after graduation and were happily anticipating their first babies, surrounded by the love and approval of their family and friends. There was the crop from the year before, their infants in canvas carriers attached to their own bodies, wheeling their carts down the aisles of the supermarket, looking proud, buying paperback books on how to feed your baby while they scooped up jars of baby food and gallon jugs of milk. Those girls smiled shyly when people stopped to tell them their babies were cute. They would bend to kiss the downy head between their breasts, and then they would glow. When people told her Nicole was cute, and they always did, Eve just kept hoping they worked for a modeling agency so she could get the baby a commercial and make some money.

She had already started sending Nicole's pictures out to

the local modeling agencies. A couple of them wrote back telling her the baby was very promising but too young, and to send photos later on. She filed the letters and called an employment agency about getting a job as a cocktail waitress in one of the big hotels on the beach, since she had been dieting and had her body back. John had been accepted at three colleges, but he was looking for a job instead. Eve knew she couldn't wait any longer.

"I want a divorce," she told him. "I want you to go to college. I'm leaving this town anyway to get on with my sidetracked career."

He was appalled, upset, confused. He offered a compromise. He would go to the University of Miami and get a part-time job on the side so that nothing much would change. He couldn't understand how she could give up so easily when they had a future together.

"No, we have a future separately," she told him. "Go to college. You deserve it. Forget me." She did not add, although she thought it: I intend to forget you.

He begged, reasoned, even wept. Eve was adamant, and finally he caved in. His parents were happy. She got complete custody because she was the mother, and didn't ask John for anything because she didn't want him to hold it over her. She told him if he didn't come around butting in about her child care it would be easier for everybody, and to her surprise he agreed. Eve realized it had been her he had loved, not the idea of their little family. Another life lesson, she told herself philosophically.

Her mother was concerned about the divorce, but understood. After all, she had encouraged her daughter's independence all these years. She was only sorry Eve hadn't asked John for money. She herself had nothing much to contribute financially, but she agreed to act as a part-time baby-sitter now that Nicole was older and not so much trouble.

Every afternoon Eve left her mother with the baby, walked a mile and a half to the bus stop, rode the twenty miles to Miami Beach, put on her sexy little cocktail waitress uniform, and worked at the Queen of the Sea. It was a tourist hotel a little past its prime, where most of the male guests were too old and too married to pinch her, but rich enough to tip. This was God's waiting room, someone told her. Mine, too, she thought, but I'm not going to die.

She kept a strict budget and stole whatever she could from the kitchen to take home. The money she would have spent for food went into her bank account, along with the remainder of her salary after minimal expenses and what she considered an unjust withholding tax. Nobody dressed nicely anymore, so she didn't have to buy many clothes, and what she did buy came from thrift shops where she was able to cultivate her offbeat image. In a year she had enough saved for the down payment on a car.

"I'm going to drive to L.A., Mom," she said one day.

"For how long?" her mother asked, thinking she meant it was a vacation.

"I don't know. I'll send for Nicole."

"What are you talking about?"

"I'm going to get established in Hollywood and then you can put her on a plane."

"She's too young to travel alone, and you know it."

"She won't be when I send for her."

"Are you out of your mind?" her mother exclaimed, upset.

"Maybe I'll be rich and then you can bring her out. Wouldn't you like to see the studios?"

"I don't want to take care of my grandchild full-time at my age."

"You're young."

"What happened to your job?"

"It served its purpose."

"But what about your plans for Nicole to model?"

"She can model in L.A. later. I can't just sit around here."

"You never were a natural mother," her mother said. "You never picked her up when she cried, you never played with her. You liked to fuss with her hair, but that was it."

Eve shrugged.

"I understand your ambition, Eve, but this child is your responsibility. I took care of you, now you have to take care of her."

"It doesn't sound like you had too much fun taking care of me, either," Eve said matter-of-factly, but she was a little hurt.

"I never had that luxury."

"Well, neither do I."

"It didn't mean I didn't love you," her mother said.

"I love her," Eve said. Did she? She wasn't sure. She didn't feel the way other mothers did, that she knew. She wondered if her mother was just saying it, the way she was.

She looked at her mother: a strong woman in overalls with her gray-streaked hair cropped short, a baseball cap on top of her head, steel-rimmed eyeglasses, no makeup, her skin leathery and wrinkled from years of smoking and being out in the blasting Florida sun, looking older than her years. She was a no-nonsense woman who had done what she had to do, but she still had dreams, if not for herself then for Eve. Eve had never given much thought to whether her home life was less loving than anyone else's, or the same; it had always just been what it was. It was hard to blame her mother for much. She thought about her own nature. On the outside she seemed like a volatile and passionate person, but inside there was a core of coldness and probably it ran in her family. Her father had never even tried to keep in touch with her after the divorce except to send her a Christmas card with a dollar bill in it every year. He had obviously never heard of inflation. She got tips better than that. He also sent her a birthday card, but it usually came late. Everybody knew when Christmas was, but he couldn't remember her birthday. They were well rid of him.

"I promise it won't be for long, Mom," Eve said. "Just till I get an apartment and a job that pays enough for me to hire a baby-sitter. I know I'm going to be a star."

"I hope so, too," her mother said.

The next day Eve left.

It was an exciting adventure driving to Los Angeles, and when she got there she was very busy just trying to survive, as she had known she would be. She found a waitress job at the Confident Onion, a health food restaurant on the Sunset Strip, she rented a tiny one-bedroom apartment in West Hollywood, she got lost and angry on the freeways, she went to open casting calls, and she tried to meet influential people, or just anybody. She had been prepared for hard work, but what she had not been prepared for was the terrifying, gut-wrenching loneliness. She had never lived alone before. She had thought it would be a wonderful relief, but to her amazement, it wasn't.

It was the first time in her life Eve had ever been scared. Every problem has a solution, she told herself. Her apartment was noisy, and at night she couldn't sleep, listening to the cars going by and the people yelling on the street, congregating in front of the clubs and the coffeehouses. She put up with a few nights like that and then she was out on the streets with them. It was like a party, and she didn't need much sleep anyway. She talked to strangers and made them into friends. Everybody loved everybody during those California nights in 1969. They gave each other flowers and wore love beads, and there was as much sex as you could possibly want. Eve started on the Pill and assigned herself a new project: a boyfriend.

She met him at the Troubadour, a club where you could go to see acts. His name was Juan. John the Second, Eve thought, smiling to herself. She recognized a certain familiar passive streak in him that made her feel comfortable.

He was dark and gorgeous and sexy, he was an aspiring actor, as she was, and he supported himself painting people's houses. When he said he was a painter people often thought he meant he was an artist, but Eve knew right away what he meant. She didn't mind at all. House painters made a lot more money than artists unless they were Robert Indiana or someone like that. She knew because she had a cheap reproduction of Indiana's red, blue, and green love poster on her living room wall like everybody else did. A week after they met Juan was living with her, contributing to the rent, painting her walls (for free, of course), and he was just as smitten with her as John the First had been.

Juan was so good-looking that people sometimes wondered what he saw in her. Eve knew that and laughed to herself, because she knew what it was. It's my energy, she thought. I'm the local Esso station. They come to my tank to be filled up. It was the first time she had really become conscious of what she now began to think of as her power. There was flower power, and people power, and now there was

Eve Bader power. She was glad now that she had come to Hollywood, and felt more optimistic than ever.

She called her mother once a week, before eight o'clock in the morning when the low night rates were still on. It was three hours later back home. "Things are good," Eve would report. "I went to two go-sees this week and they liked me. I'm hoping they'll call me back to read. I may have to get an agent. My friend Juan has an agent and I'm going to see her."

"You mention this Juan a lot," her mother said, finally. "Is he your new boyfriend?"

"Yes, for now."

"Are you living together?"

"Of course not," Eve lied. "What would make you think that?"

"Somebody in your apartment coughs like a man and I know it's not you."

Eve laughed. She felt closer to her mother now, far away from her, having their weekly phone calls, than she ever had living in the same house with her. "He keeps me from feeling so alone," Eve said.

"You wouldn't be alone if you had your child with you," her mother said. "She's talking a lot now. You're missing her development."

It had never occurred to Eve that she was missing anything. "I don't have enough money yet," she said.

"Nicole keeps asking, 'Where's Mommy?'"

"Tell her I'm in Hollywood trying to become a movie star, and when I am I'll make her one, too."

"She's so cute," her mother said. "I'm sure you could get her a part in a movie."

"She's too young," Eve said. "For little kids they use identical twins."

"Twins?" her mother asked, confused. "I never see twins."

"Separately," Eve said. She had become more knowledgeable and liked to impress her mother with inside information. "Little kids can only work limited hours in front of the camera, so they take turns."

"My goodness. Then it's too bad you didn't have twins."

"I hope that's a joke," Eve said.

"It is." They chuckled at each other. "Just do me a favor and don't get pregnant again," her mother said. "And that's *not* a joke."

"I'm never going to be pregnant again," Eve said, and she meant it. She had quickly learned you could get anything you wanted in Hollywood, including an abortion, not that she intended to need one, but it was comforting to know about all the same.

"I have bad news," her mother said. "Mayhem Two died." Mayhem Two was the successor to Eve's childhood cat, Mayhem, who had run out into the road and been killed by a car.

"Died of what?" Eve asked, more surprised than broken-hearted.

"He ran under the tractor."

"Ugh!"

"I plowed him right into the field."

"That's disgusting."

"Nicole is very upset. She keeps asking, 'Where's Mayhem?' So many losses for a baby her age."

"I'm not lost," Eve snapped. Where were you when I had my losses, she thought angrily. A father is a bigger loss than a cat. "You should get her another kitten right away," she said. "A three-legged one, so he can't get far."

"You're still a character," her mother said.

"So are you."

Their phone calls always ended with her mother putting Nicole on the phone. "Mommy, come home," she would say, but she didn't sound sad. It was better this way, Eve thought. And it was temporary.

The Confident Onion was quite a popular restaurant with music and movie people, particularly at lunch, because it was conveniently located and the food was good. Eve read the trades every day and was now able to recognize the people who might help her. There was a hot young screenwriter named Sophocles Birnbaum who came there often. He was a nerdy-looking little guy with glasses and bags under his eyes. The first time she found out who he was she introduced herself and gave him one of her head shots, which she always kept with her for encounters like this. "In case you're writing a part that would be right for me," she said.

He put the photo into his folder of papers. "How's the soup today?"

"Good. It's curry lentil. What's your new movie about?"

"I'll have the soup," he said.

"Is it a comedy?"

"Why?"

"*Duck Soup*," Eve said. "Get it?"

"It's not a comedy. It's a road picture."

"I'd be great for a road picture," Eve said brightly. "I'm like somebody you'd meet on the road. A lot of character parts in there, I bet. I played Lady Macbeth in high school. I have a lot of intensity."

"If you're an actress," Sophocles Birnbaum said, "why don't you try playing a waitress?"

"I'd be a perfect waitress."

"Right now, I mean," he said.

"Funn*ee*," Eve said cheerfully, undaunted, pointing her finger at him like a gun, and went off to get his soup.

She liked that she had established a speaking relationship with him. He came in at least twice a week, usually alone. When he didn't sit at her station she would go over to talk to him anyway. If she wasn't busy she would perch on the banquette opposite him in his booth.

"How's the script coming?" she would ask. "Do you have a title yet? Are you writing a part for me? I don't care how small it is. I'm willing to start small."

She read in the trades that the script was finished and they were starting casting. "Don't forget me," she would say now when she saw him. "Eve Bader."

"I know your name."

"Just reminding you."

"I have to ask you something," he said one day.

"What?"

"Are you kidding? I mean, are you putting me on?"

"Why would I kid about something as important as this?"

"Do you think I could eat a meal in peace if every actor who's a waiter came over to ask me for a part? Think about it."

"If I didn't ask you, how would you know I wanted one?"

His regular waitress came over and glared at her, so Eve stood up. "I have an agent now," Eve reminded him. "Beverly Kensington. See you later. Next time sit at my station."

That afternoon the manager suspended her. "I'd fire you, but he said not to," the manager said. "He just said to make you leave him alone."

"I can't believe he would say that," Eve said, hurt.

"Well, he did. You're off for a week, without pay."

She used her free week to investigate acting classes. She didn't think she really needed lessons, but Juan had told her class was a good place to make contacts. She had some money saved by now to pay for them. She decided to go to the acting school where Juan went, which was in a rundown-looking office space in a small building that housed spiritualists, fortune tellers, and a head shop that had incense burning all the time. The teacher was a failed actor. The whole room smelled of fear. Juan didn't notice because he was so passive, but Eve thought there were negative vibes. She was sure of this when during the coffee break between people's scenes she overheard one of the other girls telling her friends she was up to read for the new Sophocles Birnbaum movie.

Eve called her agent the next morning and protested. "How could you not send me? He's a friend of mine. We talk at least twice a week. He told me all about his movie."

"They're looking for an ingenue type."

"What do you think I am? I'm not even twenty yet! Did you think I was old?"

"You have a...strong quality. Fiery."

"You never saw me read an ingenue."

"Well, as long as you're a friend of his," Beverly said, "I'll get you put on the list."

The Sophocles Birnbaum movie was casting in a small building on the Fox lot. This was not just a go-see but an actual reading. The part was small but interesting: a teenage hooker who freaks out on LSD. Eve was excited and nervous. She wore a plain blouse and miniskirt and had tied her hair back, but when she got there the girls in the waiting room were dressed all sorts of ways, so she didn't know why she'd bothered to disguise her real quality. She pulled the ribbon out of her hair and shook it free. She knew she could do the part and be great at it.

There were two other men, older than he, in the audition room with Sophocles. When he looked up and saw her he seemed startled. Each actress had to read at a table, sitting down, which was difficult because Eve wanted to move around and express herself. What was worse, they let her act only one page. They seemed to be in a great hurry. "Thank you," they said gravely when she was finished. "We'll let your agent know. Next..." She couldn't tell if they had liked her or not.

He came in to the restaurant a few days later, after she had been reinstated. "Why aren't you at one of *my* tables?" she asked him. "Don't you like me anymore?"

"One of those things," he said.

"Should I have your table changed?"

"No, no, this is perfect."

"So how did you like my brilliant portrayal?"

"It was fine," he said noncommittally. He picked up his menu and looked at it.

"Does that mean I got the part?"

"Your agent will call you."

"When?"

"She should have called already."

"Does that mean I got it or not? Don't torture me."

"Not," he said. "I'm sorry."

"Why not?" Eve asked.

"You weren't right for it. Do you know where my waitress is?"

Eve sat on the edge of the banquette opposite him in the booth and leaned forward. "If you tell me why I wasn't right, next time I can be right," she said.

He sighed. "Do you know how many people read for that part? Only one of them was right for it and it wasn't you. It's a matter of personal taste, of choices, of a vision. Okay?"

"Then the next time you should make it clearer what you want," Eve said. "I could have done it differently."

"All right," he said. "Waitress!" He waved at another waitress. "Could you find my waitress, please?"

"Isn't she your waitress?" the girl asked, nodding at Eve.

"No."

"I'm sure I could take care of this table if you like," Eve said, standing up.

"Eve...does nothing ever stop you?" Sophocles said.

Eve looked at him, confused. "Why should it?" she said.

The next day the manager fired her for harassing the customers. Eve thought that was outrageous. She insisted he tell her who had made such an unfair claim and he said, "Everybody."

It made her very angry for about an hour, and then she decided to get on with her life. She got another waitress job right away at the Great Earth, a block up the Strip from where she had worked before, which also had its share of movie business clientele. She realized it was just as well she'd had to move on. She had milked the Confident Onion of whatever contacts it had to give her, and now she had new ones to make. An ambitious person should never stay in a rut.

NINE

When Gara was in graduate school studying to be a clinical psychologist, one of the prerequisites was that she be analyzed herself. She had wanted to go into therapy for a long time, and it seemed sublime irony that her mother, whom she considered the root of her problems, was also going to be instrumental in the cure, since her parents would be paying for her therapy. It was 1961. In the fifties it had been suspect to be in therapy—you were thought to be either crazy or self-indulgent—but now it was a little more mainstream. At any rate, everyone she knew at school was being shrunk, which made her feel like part of a group instead of an eccentric outcast, and it also made her parents feel less guilty and suspicious.

Her doctor was a middle-aged woman named Dr. Ragozin, a Freudian therapist, who had been very well recommended. Gara thought that with her long face and dewlaps she looked like a Walt Disney dog. She called Gara Miss Bernstein, and Gara called her Dr. Ragozin. The office had an uncomfortable foam rubber couch with a sheet of paper over the pillow, an oriental rug, several pre-Columbian statues, dim lighting, a framed photograph of Freud on the wall, a cluttered desk with two chairs, and a chair behind the couch where Dr. Ragozin sat while Gara free-associated. Gara went there three times a week, and wondered if what she revealed about her feelings was shocking, or just boring. There was never any indication since Dr. Ragozin seldom spoke.

One afternoon, when she was just getting up enough courage to tell the Tampax story, Gara heard a soft thud on the floor. It sounded like a pencil. Then she heard another, more audible thud. This sounded like the therapist's pad. Then she heard a snore.

She turned around to see Dr. Ragozin's head bent forward on her chest, her mouth open, her eyes shut, and realized she was asleep. With her facial muscles relaxed she looked as if she had melted. And she had: she had melted away and left her patient embarrassed and at a loss what to do. If I put my therapist to sleep, Gara thought—someone who is *paid* to listen—what hope is there? It was imperative that she sneak out immediately without waking the doctor. She would leave this office with her trivial stories untold, and henceforth keep her selfish life to herself. Her face felt hot with the pain of how boring she felt. She got up quietly, but just as she did, Dr. Ragozin woke up.

"Where are you going?"

"I thought I'd let you sleep," Gara murmured, wringing her hands.

"I'm so sorry. I was tired. You're the last appointment of the day."

"Oh."

"I never do this."

"It's all right."

"Would you like to lie down again and go on?"

Should she? *Could* she? How could she trust Dr. Ragozin not to fall asleep again?

"I want to sit opposite you at the desk," Gara said. "That way I can see you."

"All right. We'll do that next time."

So now her therapist sat behind the cluttered desk, and Gara sat in the straight chair facing her. It encouraged conversation instead of monologue and the way of therapy changed. They investigated Gara's dependency upon her parents, the love-hate relationship she had with them, the kind of men she liked (ones her mother couldn't dominate), and the men she didn't like (ones her mother could). She wanted the man she married to represent her, to command respect, to protect her and at the same time nurture her independence.

It was a given that she would have children, and Gara was afraid to admit she didn't want to. What she really wanted was to marry a man who had children already, so she could be kind to them, like a good friend, and so they would never blame her for the traumas of their childhood. Let them blame their own mother for those. Dr. Ragozin never indicated that Gara's own mother had actually meant her ill, so Gara took that to mean it was so easy to hurt a sensitive child even when you meant well that being in charge of an innocent soul was just too dangerous. She could not believe her mother didn't really love her—she preferred to think her mother had loved her too much, as her mother often claimed—but sometimes she wondered how you could love someone and try to destroy that person so you could own her, without a thought about the other person's feelings. She knew there was a great deal she had to learn if she was going to be a good therapist.

Five years passed. Gara was still in therapy and working as a case worker for the city now, knocking on doors of families who didn't want to see her, who pretended they weren't home. She could pay her own bills at last. She had her own apartment, and thus was able to date the kind of men she liked. But there was always something withheld in these tightrope relationships, either from her or from them. She had been brought up with the morality of the fifties, and then the mid-sixties' morality changed everything, and she was caught in the middle. She despaired of ever being truly in love, or of being entirely able to trust a man. She also despaired of her therapy, since she had read that a Freudian analysis should work in five years, and there was no indication she was any closer to being "normal." She felt she was not pretty, that she had too many faults, and she knew that socially she was shy unless she had some drinks. She was still fighting with her mother and avoided her as much as possible. She dreaded her duty phone calls.

Then, that spring, a friend who had been going to another therapist, a jolly man named Dr. Gold, suggested Gara try him. She did, and then she started going to both of them. She told him, but she didn't tell Dr. Ragozin.

"You can't go to two therapists at the same time," he told her. "You have to choose."

"Then I'll go to you," Gara said. Five years was enough.

She didn't have the heart to tell Dr. Ragozin she was giving up and going elsewhere, so she simply said she felt she was ready to leave therapy and be on her own. A few days later a letter from Dr. Ragozin arrived in her mailbox. Gara was afraid to open it at first. She remembered that how you feel when you look at the envelope is how you feel about the person. In that case, Dr. Ragozin represented bad news.

"Dear Miss Bernstein," the letter said. "I agree with you that you are successfully finished with therapy. I wish you luck with your new life."

Gara reread it, amazed. She has no idea I'm not cured, she thought. And she's so well known!

She thought about her own abilities. She had gotten all A's at college and graduate school, the people who finally unlocked their apartment doors usually responded to her, and at last she was going to be given some mildly disturbed patients of her own in an office setting. People trusted her. Maybe she was better than she believed....

She continued with the new therapist for another two years, sitting across from him at his desk. She told him how she had put Dr. Ragozin to sleep, and he asked her why she hadn't felt angry. That emotion had never occurred to her. When she relived the experience now she felt angry and cheated for the first time, and began to realize that she had often delayed or repressed her normal reactions as a way of protecting herself from the no-win situation of her childhood home. Making a good impression was always more important than how you felt. But didn't everybody believe that? Her mother wasn't the only one; she was just more extreme.

Gara looked around her at what the world had become in such a short time. There were the hippies, the flower children, the young runaways, the people in communes. They had overthrown the rules of the fifties, but now they were conforming to something just as stringent in its own way. They all wore the same clothes, had the same hair, were bone-thin, smoked pot the way their parents had consumed martinis, slept around because you were supposed to. She thought the drugs were what made all this sexual freedom possible. How could you enjoy sex with someone you had no feelings for without some kind of chemical reinforcement? She rejoiced at the end of the hypocrisy that had governed her social life, but wondered what would become of her.

As for herself and her friends, their feelings against the war in Vietnam and the series of assassinations of men they had admired and relied on to bring them into a brighter future had made them all grow up. They felt betrayed and cynical. She was almost twenty-eight. By now her friends from school had gotten married and had children. More and more lately she felt that perhaps her self-doubt came from the daily struggle to exist all alone. She sometimes felt exhausted from it. It was abnormal to have to date forever, to be charming to strangers, to hide your neediness so they wouldn't run away, to pretend over and over to be perfect until they knew you well enough not to care. She needed a sounding board, a real lover, someone who would share her dreams and be on her side.

She never knew if she found Carl Whiteman because she was ready, or because he was the right man at last. On a spring evening a woman friend invited her to the opening of an art show in a downtown gallery, where she said they might meet men, and at the very least would get free wine and cheese. As soon as Gara got there a mousy-looking man of ambiguous sexuality whom her mother would have loved fastened himself to her and kept asking her personal questions, trying to strike up a friendship. She answered him absently, looking around the room. Give him a chance, her mother's voice said in her head, he'll grow on you. Like a cyst, she answered back. In all of her life her mother never knew if someone was gay or straight, and if you told her he wasn't available she refused to believe it. He could walk into the house in a dress and her mother would probably think he was in a play. Gara moved away and the man followed her. That was when she first saw Carl Whiteman.

She was immediately attracted to his strong heterosexuality and his looks. He was tall and well built, with long, thick, light hair, and a glow about him that she had seen in the photos of certain astronauts. He looked about ten years older than she was—a grownup. He was standing in the corner surrounded by shorter men and he was making all of them laugh.

"Excuse me," she said to the man at her side and went over to the man she wanted to meet. She stopped in front of Carl and, made brave by desire, she smiled. He smiled back.

"I know you," Gara said.

"Do you? I'm Carl Whiteman. Who are you?"

"Gara Bernstein."

"We've never met," he said, but not as if he were dismissing her. His glance still lingered on her face with a kind of anticipation, and he was still smiling.

"I know," Gara said. "I just said that because I wanted to meet you."

She had never done that before. She couldn't believe she was doing it now.

"My card," he said, and handed it to her. He was an art dealer here in New York, and the card was expensive.

"Mine," she said, and handed it to him. She had just had it made.

He introduced her to the other men, who had foreign names that she forgot immediately. Her rejected admirer, who had trailed along, not knowing he had been rejected, introduced himself. "Would you like me to get you more wine?" Carl offered.

"Yes, please," Gara said, and went to the bar with him.

"So you're a therapist."

"Yes, and I love it."

"I went to a therapist for a while with my ex-wife," Carl said. "But nothing could help that marriage."

"Oh, you're divorced?"

"Yes, last year."

"I'm sorry," she said, although she wasn't.

"Don't be," he said cheerfully.

"Do you have children?"

"Two boys, six and eight."

You're just what I want, Gara thought. "That part must be hard," she said.

"My ex-wife and I fight all the time, but I get along great with the kids. I'm the nice one they get to visit."

"Of course."

He's glad about it, she thought; he's not in pain anymore. Good timing. She was afraid to ask him if he had already found another woman to be in love with. She knew from experience that if he were taken he would eventually mention his girlfriend, if only out of guilt. Maybe he hadn't been ready for anything serious; maybe he was ready now. She smiled sunnily at him and prayed that he was available.

They sipped their wine, looking at each other. "You do look familiar," she said. "I just figured out why. You look like a lion."

"King of the beasts?"

"King of the jungle."

He looked a little embarrassed at the compliment but also pleased. Her male therapist had told her that you could say anything flattering to a man, no matter how outrageous, and he would believe it, but the fact was that Carl Whiteman had a leonine look. No wonder she thought he could save her.

Save me? Gara thought. Yes, he could.

"Are you here with anyone?" he asked.

"No, are you?"

"I have those Dutch art dealers you met, who I promised to have dinner with," he said. "We have a reservation in fifteen minutes. But would you have dinner with me tomorrow night?"

"I'd love to."

"Can I call you at the number on the card?"

She wrote down her home number. You just know, she thought. After all the looking and all the disappointments, when someone comes along with the right spark, you know.

He leaned down and kissed her lightly on the mouth. "I want to spend time with you," he said. "Eight o'clock. I'll think of a place you'd like and call to tell you where."

"Paris would be just fine," she said, and he laughed.

When Carl had left she went over to her friend Linda, who had invited her, and who was eating the free cheese and crackers and grapes. "Let's go to dinner," Gara said.

"Why? Are you finished with this party already?"

"I found what I wanted," Gara said.

"I noticed," Linda said.

"Dinner?"

"I ate all this. I'm full."

"Then I think I'll go home. I'm tired. Long day."

"Okay. I'll stay a while and keep looking."

Gara didn't tell her that she wanted to go home and think about him.

When Carl called the next morning, Gara told him he could come to her apartment for a drink before they went out to dinner, and after work she bought some red tulips. She already had a case of wine stored in the closet, and her one-bedroom apartment was always very neat so she didn't have to clean it for his visit. She hoped he wouldn't laugh at her art. She lit candles and then had second thoughts and blew them out because she didn't want him to think she was trying to create some self-consciously seductive ambiance. She was not nervous, only excited. She hoped he would kiss her hello.

When he came in the size and masculinity of him made her apartment look small and girlish. He kissed her lightly on the lips as he had the day before, and she felt in a strange way as if he were coming home to her. She thought of all the men who had paused in her bed and they no longer existed, they were gone.

"How nice," he said, looking at her framed prints and photographs.

"Really?"

"Yes."

"You are sweet, complimentary, and nonjudgmental," Gara said.

"No, I like them."

She asked him to open the white wine, even though she was perfectly capable of doing it herself, and let him pour it. It was a little quirk of hers, one of the only dependent things she still did when there was a man around.

He looked over her record collection. "How many people live here?" he asked, surprised.

"Just me."

"Your taste in music is very eclectic."

"I know."

Then he took her hand and led her to the couch. "Let's talk about ourselves," he said.

"All right."

They sat side by side, sipping their wine. He was still holding her hand. There was something cozy about it. "I need a lot of affection because my parents were very cold," he said. He made the statement so mildly and matter-of-factly that it didn't seem like a line and didn't make her want to laugh; it actually touched her.

"I need a lot of affection, too," Gara said. "But I put a barrier around myself unless I really trust the person. My mother was physically smothering."

"And your father?"

"He was afraid to hug and kiss me after I was little; he kind of abdicated his role as my first love."

"Afraid of your mother or afraid of himself?"

"Aha! A good point. I'll never know because I won't ask him. He wouldn't know what I was talking about anyway."

"I married my wife because she was so intense," Carl said. "Later on it turned into intense hatred toward me, but that's another story." He smiled and shrugged.

"Did you cheat when you were married?"

"Toward the end. We both did."

"Why did she hate you?"

"Anything, you name it."

"I can't imagine anyone hating you," Gara said.

"You haven't met her."

"I hate to fight," Gara said.

"So do I. I dislike even raising my voice. People should be able to discuss things."

"I agree."

"Were you ever married?"

"Not yet."

He told her about his travels and she imagined traveling with him. She had never been to Europe and he went there often, to buy paintings, as well as to the Far East. His work sounded like a great deal more fun than hers because it was combined with what sounded like a full-time holiday, while hers was based on people's pain. But she was helping people, in her way, and she hoped to help them more when she was more established, and that was what gave her pleasure.

When they had talked so long they were almost late for

their dinner reservation, they left her apartment and went to the restaurant he had chosen to impress her. It was in the Village, an upscale Italian cafe, and filled with important people from the art world whom he pointed out to her, and whom she had never heard of. She felt stupid and uninformed and hoped he didn't notice.

He didn't; he was much more concerned that she be comfortable and happy. Again, something about him touched her. I'm falling in love, Gara thought.

When they realized they were the last people in the restaurant and the waiters were eating their own dinner in a booth, Gara and Carl left. It was very late, and they both had to go to work in the morning. When he took her to her apartment she thought of asking him up, and then thought: It's too soon. He kissed her goodnight very gently, and she felt the flash of electricity shooting down her body. They hugged and held on.

He was more giving in that moment at her door than most of the men she'd had brief affairs with had been during the entire relationship. Why didn't more men understand about hugging? Her women friends complained about this all the time, and so did she.

"I had a wonderful time," she said. "Thank you."

"No, thank *you*. I'll call you very soon."

"Good."

She thought about him all weekend and wondered what he was doing and whom he was with. Maybe he had his children for the weekend and he wasn't with another woman. Then why hadn't he mentioned he would be with them? Was he secretive? Maybe he needed his own space. Maybe he wanted to give her hers. She tried to pretend she was her own therapist and reassured herself that she had been charming company and that he had obviously liked her and enjoyed himself. It was a beautiful spring weekend, so she ran in the park, hoping she might see him, since all the divorced fathers she knew took their kids to the park on weekends, but of course she didn't see him even though he might have been there. When another man she didn't much like called on Saturday night at the last minute to see if she wanted to have dinner with him, she said she was busy. She didn't have the energy to make conversation; she would rather live on the memory of that kiss and that hug.

Carl called on Monday, and said, as she had hoped he would, that he'd had his sons for the weekend, and Gara realized she had known all along that he liked her as much as she liked him and that he would call. He took her to dinner, and that night they made love and he stayed over. She had never known such a sensitive and passionate lover, and when finally they went to sleep he held her all night as if he couldn't stand to let her go. She was enchanted by his body, the size of him, the feel and scent of his tawny skin, his golden, glowing looks. He seemed exactly what she had wanted all of her life.

"I love you," he said the next morning, and somehow she was not surprised.

"I love you, too," she said, and meant it.

After that they were together every night, at her place or his, and spent all weekend together when he didn't have his kids. She did not even mention his existence to her parents yet because she knew her mother would grill her and then find things to complain about, as she always did when Gara had picked the man herself.

That summer Gara finally met Carl's two sons, Cary and Eric, who were well mannered and shy and very cute. She campaigned to have them like her. She conversed with them as if they were adults, and made it clear that she valued them as people. In short, she treated them the way she had not been treated when she was their age. They quickly became very fond of her and she of them.

Carl's apartment was dark and sloppy and he seemed not to notice. He was personally very clean, but in his living habits he was messy. Cartons, filled and empty, took up most of the living room, and there were books and papers everywhere. The walls were covered with art, some of which she liked and some of which she didn't understand. He had odd sculptures, too: a chair with water pouring on it, a fur-lined teacup. His battered bicycle leaned against the wall. There had been a leak, as there often was in New York apartments, and the bedroom ceiling was coming down.

"You need to fix this place up," Gara said.

"I know. I was thinking of moving."

"That might be easier."

"Will you help me look for an apartment?"

"I'd love to."

"We could decorate it together. Would you like to do that?"

"Sure," Gara said.

"And then will you live with me?"

She hesitated. She was so sure of him now, so comfortable in the knowledge of his love. Everybody lived together. And yet she didn't want to give up her apartment in case something went wrong. "I don't know about living together," she said.

"But I knew right away," he said. "The night I met you."

"That you wanted to live with me?"

"Yes."

But for how long, she wondered. Forever, a month?

"Would you ever consider getting married again?" she asked.

"I never said I wouldn't."

"To me?" she asked.

"Not to anyone else."

"I want to be married to you," she said.

This time he was the one who hesitated. In that instant, which seemed much longer, Gara thought she had made a mistake; she should not have been so aggressive, so demanding, in such a hurry to make him commit.

"Then I guess I'd better think of a romantic way to propose," he said.

They took a bottle of champagne up to the roof of his apartment house and watched the sun set. He asked her to marry him as if it had been his idea all along, and she accepted solemnly. Then they both laughed with surprise that their future had been settled so easily. They were both filled with joy. They went back downstairs and spent the rest of the evening in bed, making love, finishing the champagne, sending out for Chinese food. How lucky she was, Gara thought, to have found a man who understood her.

A week went by, and she still had not broken the news to her parents, protecting her happiness, the breathless feeling of perfect romance. Then her mother called. The building her parents lived in, where she had grown up, had gone co-op, and they had bought their apartment at the insiders' price. There were some other, smaller apartments available.

"We want to buy you an apartment in our building," May said.

"What?"

"It's a wonderful building, and then we can be close and see each other more often. It's time you owned something."

The thought of living in the same building as her mother again, to take up again the invaded life it had taken her so long to be able to flee, was bizarre. How could her mother even think she would want to do that? "No," Gara said. "Thank you anyway."

"Don't give up this chance," her mother said. "Then when you find a man to marry you'll have someplace to live."

Gara sighed. She had to tell her mother; it was time. "I have been seeing a man," she said. "We're going to get married."

"Oh." There was a silence. The offer had apparently been withdrawn.

"I want you to meet him," Gara said.

"Married?"

"Yes. We just decided."

"Who is he?"

"His name is Carl Whiteman. He's an art dealer. He's thirty-eight. He's divorced and has two adorable little sons. They stay with him on holidays and alternate weekends."

"Children?" her mother said, with obvious distaste. "You're going to take care of some other woman's children?"

"You're so full of love."

"They won't like you. They'll always compare you to their mother."

"And you're so encouraging," Gara said.

"Don't be sarcastic. Wait until you have to deal with reality."

"I thought you'd be glad that I'm finally getting married," Gara said. "And he's even Jewish."

"I am glad," her mother said distantly, her voice trailing

off. "Since you're probably going to have your own child, too, there isn't anything in this building right now that's big enough. When I die, you can live in this apartment."

"What about Dad?"

There was a pause. It seemed her mother had forgotten her father existed. "Men die first," she said, finally. "This Carl, he's a lot older than you..."

"Ten years. Hardly ancient."

"Well, you know best," her mother said.

Gara wondered why she ever bothered to speak to her mother at all.

Carl went on a quick trip to Japan, and came back with some art and two pearl-and-gold spray pins, one set in yellow gold, the other in white. He gave them to Gara, and he also brought a yellow gold ring that was set with a large, beautiful pearl, which he gave her for her engagement ring. She was thrilled. They were going to her parents' apartment for dinner because it was her mother's birthday. She would present her intended, with his ring on her finger, and that would be that.

She wondered what she should buy for her mother's birthday. It was so hard; May never liked anything Gara chose herself. But that pin set in white gold would be perfect. It was a little matronly, a little too conventional for Gara's taste, so her mother would probably love it. And it would be from Carl, too, from his business trip. It would make him look generous and interesting.

"Could we give my mother the white gold pin?" she asked.

"Don't you want it?" he asked wistfully.

"Oh, sweetheart." She was so touched her eyes filled with tears. "I just wanted us to make a good impression on her."

"All right."

"And I know she'll lend it to me. She lends me anything I want."

The birthday party, like all her mother's parties, was intimate, with only her aunt and uncle and their spouses, and her mother's two old friends with their husbands. Her mother didn't have many friends, preferring the company of her own family. May's sister and brother were both lean; it was only May who had an eating disorder. The table was covered with platters heaped with rich and extravagant food, and the sideboard was laden with creamy desserts. Carl towered over everyone, as if he had come from another world, and he had. Gara had never before realized how tiny her family was. Even her obese mother—how could she have been so afraid of a woman as small as that?

Carl did not seem at all nervous. He conversed easily with everyone, and they looked at him with approval, even respect. How could they not? He was so handsome, so interesting. Her mother thanked them both politely for the pin, and looked at Gara's engagement ring without comment. She was obviously disappointed that it was not a diamond, but Gara knew a diamond would not have pleased her either. Her father, however, looked at the ring and Carl with shy pleasure, and smiled. Gara remembered then, as she seldom did, how much she loved this invisible man, despite everything.

Her uncle took Polaroids of everyone, and gave some of them to Gara as a keepsake. She and Carl left as soon as they could.

"I like your mother," he said.

"You do?"

"Yes. She's very intelligent, and she's very unhappy in her marriage."

"She is?" But of course she was. No man Gara had dated had ever noticed that about her mother before, or certainly the subject had not been discussed. Either they had been fooled by the facade, or they had not even cared. As for herself, Gara had preferred not to think about her mother's marital unhappiness. It lurked there in her consciousness as a given, and then was ignored.

"You're so perceptive," she said. "I wonder why both my therapists let me graduate from treatment without ever having brought it up. It's really important."

"They probably thought that an unhappy marriage was an acceptable state for people of that generation."

"But not for us," Gara said. "We won't let each other be

unhappy, will we? We'll tell each other, we won't let it fester, we'll make it right."

"Of course we will," he promised. "We're not our parents, we're completely different people. We'll be happy."

She met his parents, who had been cold to him when he was a child. With her they only seemed diffident, but she knew how to see beyond that. She was determined to make it up to him for their lack of affection and nurturing, now and forever.

She and Carl found a new apartment on the Upper East Side for the two of them to live in when they got married and decorated it as quickly as possible, in the dark, masculine way that Carl preferred. Gara was willing to give in since it made him happy, and besides, with two growing boys it seemed practical. She told him she didn't want to have a baby for a long time and he said that was fine with him. She didn't want to say never. Maybe she would change her mind, and it was good to keep her options open while she could. Her gynecologist kept telling her to have a baby soon because it would be very difficult to have one when she was older than thirty-six, but Gara didn't care. That was eight whole years away.

They had wanted to get married in a hotel, but every place they liked was booked so far in advance they couldn't bear to wait so long, so Gara's best friend Jane, who was married to a rich plastic surgeon and already had a Fifth Avenue apartment and two children, volunteered her living room, which had a view of the park with its blazing fall leaves. The elegant room was a wonderland of flowers, and Gara wore a traditional white satin and lace gown. Jane was the matron of honor. Carl's brother, who had come in from California, was the best man. Jane suggested having Carl's two sons be ring bearers for the double ring ceremony, but Gara thought that would be rubbing it in since they loved their mother, so she let them be ushers even though they were so young, and they liked it.

Her mother had been jealous and displeased by the idea of Gara's being married in "some stranger's" apartment, but she came around and actually was happy by the time the wedding day came, probably because Gara had let her choose the food, the flowers, the wedding gown, the cake, the rabbi, and most of the guest list. The only thing Gara insisted on picking herself was the music.

She spent more time than usual with her mother, making these choices, and she noticed that May had never worn the pin she and Carl had given her for her birthday. "Don't you like the pin we gave you?" Gara asked finally. "You never wear it."

Her mother glared at her as if she had done something unkind. "You know I don't wear *silver*," she snapped.

"It's white gold."

May did not respond, and she still didn't wear the pin. Gara wondered why she even bothered to try to make her mother happy.

The wedding went flawlessly, and on their honeymoon they went (at last!) to Paris and the south of France, where every morning Gara woke up thinking her life had turned into a miracle. Her husband complimented her all the time, he constantly said he loved her, he told her she was wonderful. She had always worried about her imperfections, about not looking right, and now she felt beautiful. She knew it was not a good idea to give someone else so much power, that beauty should come from your own sense of self, but she knew that was sometimes unrealistic. When she was dressed to go out with Carl she admired herself, and whenever she looked into the mirror, at the naked body he was so aroused by, she admired it, too.

"I want to grow old with you," he told her.

She could not imagine ever growing old.

TEN

From time to time Gara had a fantasy. In it she had not been born yet and was waiting to begin her life on earth. God showed her the long, happy years of her marriage and its devastating ending. You can make the choice now, God told her. You can spare yourself all that pain and despair, but you won't ever meet Carl, you won't have the good years with him. Or you can go into it and play the whole story out. When you've made your decision you will forget we have ever had this conversation. You will not be able to protect yourself from the events of your destiny, you will only know the present as it unfolds, and you won't know the end until it happens. You choose. You decide if it was worth it.

And every time she had this fantasy Gara decided she would keep the good years with Carl, just as they were, despite what came later. She thought that was either the greatest tribute to love or the grossest stupidity, but given the choice she would have done it anyway.

So here she was, on Valentine's Day, 1995, facing another holiday that emphasized love and togetherness, and feeling as if the whole city were full of romantic couples and she was all alone and always would be from now on. Her husband was now her ex-husband, and she never heard from his sons anymore. For a while after the divorce Cary and Eric had tried to keep in touch with her. They had seemed rather ashamed of their father's behavior. But they were adults with lives of their own, they didn't live in New York and seldom came there, and they had drifted away, as often happened with stepchildren, so she had finally lost the whole family.

As much as Gara told herself most holidays had been created for commercial reasons—buy more greeting cards, give more presents!—she remembered how sentimental she and Carl had been about every one of them. He had always given her a present for Valentine's Day, usually jewelry, always some kind of heart, with a loving card.

"I'm so angry at him," Gara had told her friend Jane when Carl had disappeared forever from her life, "that I've stopped wearing any of the jewelry he's given me."

"That'll show him," Jane said, and Gara had realized how ridiculous she was being.

She missed her longtime best friend Jane, who had been with her through all her crises. She missed Jane's sympathy and her quick tongue. Jane's plastic surgeon husband had walked out on her ten years ago, leaving her with two children, several million dollars, thin thighs, and the breasts and face of a woman twenty years younger. She had quickly found another husband, a successful television producer, and now they were living in Singapore, where he had a hit television series. Who knew when they would ever be back?

So who should she see this Valentine's Day, where should she go? Should she hide and ignore it? No, it had to be faced...but she couldn't do it all by herself. Felicity was unavailable; she was celebrating with her husband. Kathryn had gone to Canyon Ranch in Arizona for a week with two of her women friends, since she said she was her own best valentine this year. Gara didn't really want to go out with Eve, wherever she might be, and anyway, Eve probably had a date. Eve's men never lasted very long, but she always had a new one.

There was only one man Gara felt comfortable enough to be close to: her gay friend Brad Kinsella, who had named himself Brad the Consoler. She hoped he was home. Brad was a bright, sensitive, funny comedy writer she had met after her divorce. He looked like everybody's nice younger brother. His function in her life was determined by his nickname, and she often recruited him as an extra man and date. Brad the Consoler never minded being put on hold if there was a party or function Gara might need him for, keeping himself free while she hunted for straight prospects she could invite first. They knew each other's friends, each other's lives, each other's secrets, and their friends' secrets.

Like Gara, Brad hadn't had a relationship in a long time and despaired of ever having one. Like her, he was afraid to be open, afraid to be made vulnerable and get hurt. "Men are scum," he told her frequently. Even though she kept telling herself her new breasts actually looked better than her old ones had, her long-dead mother's voice kept interceding: *They won't want you if there's something wrong with you.* Gara felt different and ugly, and kept men who might be interested in her at a distance because she was afraid they would discover her secret and reject her. Brad kept men who were interested in him at a distance because he was afraid of the darker part of his psyche, the hidden rage he repressed under his mask of agreeable sweetness. He was in therapy, she was a therapist, and they were both so messed up.

She called him. He sounded wary, waiting for disaster.

"So what are you doing for Valentine's Day?" Gara asked him.

"Don't say the V word!" he said. "I'm suicidal."

"We should go out then. Let's go to Yellowbird."

"I think I'm too upset. I haven't smoked a cigarette for a week. I've been on the patch again. But tonight I'm going to rip it off and smoke myself to death."

"Not in front of me. I *had* cancer."

"Did you get any valentines?" he asked.

"Of course not. Did you?"

"Are you kidding? I didn't even send one to myself."

"But that would be even more depressing," Gara said.

"When you were in school," he said, "did you have to make valentines for your friends in the class and make an extra one in case some of the other kids didn't get any?"

"Oh, my God," Gara said, remembering. "And then if you actually got one of the spares for the unloved, and people knew?"

"We always knew. We would look at each other and give those looks."

"Childhood is so painful I would never wish it on anyone," Gara said.

"Your patients shouldn't hear you say that."

"Who did you think I learned it from?"

"So are your patients miserable about Valentine's Day?"

"The ones who are single are."

"You should have had them make anonymous valentines for each other, like school. "To someone else who can't commit."

"How about, 'Better luck next year'?"

"'To someone I'd like to tie up,'" Brad said, and they both laughed. "I bet Eve has a date."

"I'm sure."

"I'd like to tie someone up," he said. "Just gently. Soft scarves, no real knots, gently...wouldn't you?"

"No."

"It's sensual," Brad said.

"Did you ever do it?"

"I'm not telling."

"You did," Gara said.

"Maybe."

"You did."

"It was very nice," Brad said. "It can be nice."

She wasn't sure if she was shocked or just surprised. It seemed so out of character to think of Brad dominating anybody. "You mean you're a top?" she said.

"Of course I'm a top," Brad said, insulted. "Did you think I was a bottom?"

"One can't go by looks."

"All these years you know me, you thought I was a sissy?"

"I never thought about it."

"It's the real macho ones who ask me to tie their hands," Brad said.

"I'm sure. The ones with the wives and kids."

"You got it."

"Don't you want to go to Yellowbird?" she said. "I'm feeling very lonely and unwanted tonight."

"What if it's full of happy couples? I'll want to kill myself."

"We'll pretend we're one of them."

"Remember Father's Day?" Brad said, his voice suddenly delighted. "We went to dinner at the Four Seasons with all those families and when we left the waiter said, 'Happy Father's Day,' and your voice dropped about three octaves and you said, 'I'm the father here.'"

Gara smiled. "I don't know what came over me," she said. "It just came out of my mouth."

"All right," he said. "We'll go to Yellowbird and shop for love."

Yellowbird was packed when they got there, but Gara had never seen any of the people before. As Brad had feared, they were Valentine couples feeding each other, drinking champagne, looking into each other's eyes. Many of the women were wearing corsages. Gara and Brad were given one of the good tables Billie kept for her regulars, even though they hadn't made a reservation. They looked at the room full of lovers and immediately ordered martinis.

On the sound system Janis was singing "Tell Mama." Billie was wearing a sexy red dress with a heart embroidered on the bodice, and cowboy boots. She liked to get into the spirit of holidays. "Where's Little Billie?" Gara asked her.

"My housekeeper took him to a Valentine's Day party," Billie said. "A kid from his class. Can you imagine, at his age? He doesn't even like girls yet. But he wanted to go. They sure start them early."

"We were just talking about that," Gara said. "Our hideous childhood memories of Valentine's Day."

"I like it better now," Billie said. She went over to the bar where a tall, good-looking man with long, clean dark hair and an expensive suit was sitting alone on the bar stool next to the catbird seat. He hadn't taken his eyes off her. She sat down in her place of honor and bought him a drink.

"Well, *she* doesn't have to shop for love," Brad said. "She has an inventory."

Gara sighed. "We should open a restaurant."

They were eating their fried chicken and collard greens when she saw Eve's millionaire poet/farmer, Eben Mars, come in alone. He declined a table, walked around the room slowly and deliberately, and left again. Gara couldn't tell if he was looking for someone in particular or just looking for anyone he knew. He either hadn't seen her or didn't recognize her. They had met only once. "What was that?" she said when he had left.

"Nice-looking guy," Brad said. "He's probably straight."

"I met him. He had a thing with Eve. Maybe still is. What is he doing all alone on Valentine's Day?"

"Better than being with her."

"I'm sure he must know a lot of women," Gara said.

"But maybe no one he likes."

"It was just kind of odd," she said.

"I don't think so."

"I do," she said. "But I don't know why."

Brad ordered a second martini and raised his glass in a toast. "Next year you and I will each have a loved one on Valentine's Day," he said.

Next year sounded far away and therefore easier to deal with than Kathryn's promise that they would find love by spring. Next year was a safe fantasy for both herself and Brad, and Gara had a feeling Brad knew it.

"I'll drink to that," Gara said.

Despite their marital problems, Valentine's Day was one of the occasions that Felicity's husband Russell always tried to make festive and romantic. So today at the office there had been roses on her desk with a loving card from him, and when she came home there was a bottle of champagne open in a cooler by the lighted fireplace, a delicate diamond necklace in a velvet gift box, and reservations for dinner at Arcadia. On Valentine's Day he did everything for her, as if he were making love—better, actually, than the way he made love, when she had to do most of the work.

Her lover Jason hadn't even sent her an anonymous card. He devoted Valentine's Day to his own wife. Felicity was used to that, but it still hurt. She wondered if she should try harder to improve her marriage. On a night like this, when Russell was so kind to her, she remembered how much they had loved each other during the good times, and what dear old friends they were. Wouldn't it be easier to forget the grudges and the harsh words and just try to be happy?

She knew she wasn't the sort of person who could trick him into becoming a father. She could lie to him in other ways, but she was afraid to get pregnant "accidentally." Russell might never forgive her or the baby for changing his life. Besides, she would have to stop seeing Jason if she were going to get pregnant, or else she would never be sure who the real father was. She was certain Jason would leave her some day, but she couldn't imagine having the courage to leave him now. She loved him too much. How was it that a sadomasochistic emotional relationship like theirs turned her on, while her husband's emotional abuse turned her away from him? Russell reminded her of her mother, or perhaps her father...she wasn't sure, but all she knew was that something felt incestuous about their relationship, that he had become her parent, not her husband, and she dreaded having sex with him.

She knew him too well; was that it? She didn't know what he would do next; was *that* it? Why would you want to have sex with a man who was mean to you? But then why did she yearn for Jason? There had been a time, years ago, when she would have done anything to make her husband want to make love to her, and she had, wooing him, almost begging. Now he was the one who had to woo and beg. She had been in therapy for a year and she still felt as if she hadn't learned anything. Maybe Russell should be going, too, but he always refused.

Therapy was one subject she certainly wouldn't bring up tonight. It always made him angry. He was sure she was talking about him with the doctor, telling his secrets, and worse, her own—and of course she was.

Arcadia looked like a jewel box. The long, narrow room was lit with a romantic glow, and tiny, perfect flowers were on the tables. Felicity and Russell sat next to each other at a corner table in the back and he held her hand. She was wearing a simple black dress, very expensive, which she had paid for herself, as she did all of her clothes, and the new necklace, which cost more than all of her clothes for the entire year.

"You look beautiful," he said gently. His eyes held love and admiration.

"Thank you."

He was a nice-looking man, even if he was short and so much older than she was. He was tough in a strong, no-

nonsense masculine way, he had presence, he was impecca-
bly dressed. Other women looked at him with interest. They
thought she was lucky to have him, and some of them
wanted him anyway. Felicity was sure Russell had cheated
on her from time to time. There were unexplained gaps in
their relationship, mysterious abstinences, convenient business trips away from her. She had known about cheating all
her life thanks to her mother, and considered it unusual if
someone *didn't* stray, not if they did. If she left him he would
be married again in six months.

"All the men in the room are looking at you, Baby," Russell said. Was he still being admiring, or jealous? It was hard
to tell which way Russell would go until he was already on
his way there.

"I doubt that," Felicity said.

"They always do." Was it a compliment or a reproach?
Perhaps both. There was nothing uncomplicated about her
husband.

"Maybe they're looking at you."

"Me?" he said. "Why me?"

"Maybe they saw your picture in the paper," Felicity said.
"Your new building. You're kind of famous, you know. I'm
thrilled to be seen with you myself."

He smiled with genuine pleasure. "You are?"

"Mm-hm."

"Well, if they're looking at me it's because I'm fortunate
enough to be with you," he said.

She smiled back at him. She was safe. They would have a
good evening. The tension left her shoulders and she stroked
his hand fondly, with gratitude for his generosity and
thoughtfulness and for not making her miserable tonight.

During dinner they discussed their plans for their spring
trip and for their summer vacation. Russell thought commuting was a waste of time so they neither owned nor rented
a second house. This way they could go wherever they
wanted and leave whenever they chose. Felicity thought his
disinterest in having a place they could go for weekends was
eccentric for a man with his wealth, but since all he did on
weekends was watch wall-to-wall sports events on television, she realized he didn't care where he was. On those

weekends with him alone in their townhouse she was usually so depressed and lonely that when she didn't take work home she slept around the clock. He resented the sleeping but was unwilling to offer anything to keep her awake. She realized he didn't know she was sad, but she didn't know how to tell him or how to explain it. She was looking forward to their vacation, was glad to be going away anywhere, just to get a break.

"I made our reservations at the Beachcomber Park Royal," Russell said. "I got us one of the over-the-water grass huts on stilts, like we had the last time."

"Oh, good," Felicity said, pretending to be delighted. The Beachcomber Park Royal hotel was in Tahiti, on the beautiful, sensual island of Moorea, and the huts were romantic. You were supposed to feel as if you were the only couple there, cozy and horny in paradise. She had only unhappy and humiliating memories of their last time there, several years ago, when he had refused to touch her even once, but she knew Russell had no idea.

"I'm thinking about us going to Aspen for our summer vacation," he went on. "They have a music festival. The scenery is supposed to be spectacular, and the music, shopping, and eating in good restaurants will keep us busy."

"That sounds like fun," she said.

"But I'm still investigating Lake Como in Italy," he said. "We could rent a villa for two weeks. The area is supposed to be very lovely, and very quiet and peaceful."

Peace was the last thing she wanted, alone with him for two whole weeks. "I hope it's not too quiet," she said mildly.

"We'll rent a car and explore, have picnics, walk. Maybe I'll hire someone to give us Italian lessons."

As he talked on about the things they could do Felicity felt a wave of depression and guilt come over her. Depression because being with her husband gave her so little pleasure, and guilt because she wasn't more grateful that he wanted to give them both such a good time. All of this could have been—should have been—so romantic. What's wrong with me? she wondered. I'm not even happy when he tries. Why are my emotions on such a roller-coaster? Maybe it's because I'm getting my period. I feel bloated. I will not think about Jason with his wife tonight. They can't be having as much fun as we are.

"So what do you think?" Russell asked.

"You're the most organized person I know," Felicity said. "You're amazing." She hadn't listened to the information that preceded his question, but she knew her answer would be acceptable, and it was.

As they shared a dessert she felt his knee against hers and knew she was going to have to have sex with him tonight. She couldn't say no after he had tried to make their evening perfect; he would be furious, and she didn't want to risk one of his rages. She would have liked to pretend she had her period, but the last time she had done that he made her give him a blow job. She was dreading the end of the evening already; a passionate vital woman who needed sex all the time, she was repelled by the one man she was supposed to want it with.

More and more lately she thought that she had turned out to be just like her mother, and she had never wanted it to be that way; she didn't even know how it had happened.

After dinner they walked home through the cold, quiet streets, because it wasn't far. Russell was holding her arm protectively. In the distance, lit up, they saw the top of a high-rise apartment house he had built just before they got married. It seemed glamorous and remote, as he had seemed to her then, when she was young and foolish and desperately in love.

"Remember that one?" he said.

"Of course."

They stopped for a moment to admire it.

"It bought us our townhouse," Russell said.

"I know."

"When I think about growing up in the worst part of Harlem, the fears, the difficult times, and now being here, our wonderful lifestyle together, what I've made of myself... And yet, despite everything that we have, I can never forget that the past is only a subway ride away."

"It's closer than that," Felicity said.

ELEVEN

Kathie loved the boarding school from the moment she entered its doors. She slept in a simple dormitory with the other girls in her class, and while they were weeping with homesickness, she was curled up in a little ball of coziness and peace. She loved the uniforms that made everybody equal, so she could pretend her home was just as normal as theirs. She loved the quiet, the calm, the feeling of unchanging, ageless protection as she walked through the old halls. She loved her classes, which were challenging and therefore interesting. Most of all, she loved her teachers, even the difficult ones. She respected them all because they respected education, they knew what they wanted and they had gotten it, and because they were willing to devote themselves to her. It didn't matter how late it was, if there was a classroom problem that had to be explained or solved, they would stay, and make the students stay. There were no hours here like in the real world outside, no other job but their girls. Most of them were single; old maids she supposed they would be called, but she did not feel sorry for them for not having a husband and children.

Since this was the start of a new life for her, Kathie demanded to be called Kathryn. It seemed more sophisticated anyway, now that she was twelve. The teachers called her Miss O'Mara. She loved that, too, because it seemed as if they respected her in return. In class they told her she should learn to think for herself. She took that to include that she didn't have to believe in the concept of religion the nuns had taught her in parochial school (not that she had agreed with it all in the first place), and so she began to make up her own mind about everything. She still believed in heaven because

it seemed such a pleasant place, but she did not believe in
limbo or in hell. She believed in miracles the way she had believed in children's stories when she was young—talking
rabbits, giants, fairy godmothers—you knew they weren't
real but you liked to pretend. On Sunday mornings the girls
were driven to their various churches; Kathryn continued to
go to mass because it was expected of her, but in confession
she never admitted to her skepticism. She had long since decided she didn't have the vocation to be a nun after all.

Kathryn made friends right away. She was drawn to the
outgoing, rule-breaking girls like herself, as she had been at
home. Here, though, the rules were different, stricter; and
harder to deal with than at home or school, because she lived
here and was being judged all the time. She realized her
mother had let her get away with murder. But what else
could Sheila have done in that chaotic house?

"Reading under the covers again, Miss O'Mara," Mrs.
George said, on one of her purposely unexpected bed checks.
Of all the teachers she was the harshest disciplinarian, and
the only mean one. She had one long black frowning eye-
brow that marched across her forehead, and steel-rimmed
glasses, and her late husband had been killed in the war. She
was, Kathryn thought, too crazy to be a teacher, but she was
able to do whatever she wanted because her parents, the
Lancasters, had founded the school and still ran it. Mrs.
George's dark, fleshy face registered disapproval as she held
out her hand for the offending magazine. "Home decorating?"

"I like it," Kathryn said.

"And where did you get this?"

"My mother sent it to me," Kathryn said. The truth was
she had sneaked out to town a few days before with her
friend Patsy, when they were supposedly at the school library.

"Well, if you like decorating so much," Mrs. George said,
"tomorrow morning at eight o'clock I want you to scrub the
auditorium floor with one of your cute little bobby socks. All
of it."

Kathryn stifled a smile. How could anyone expect her to

scrub the auditorium floor with a sock? It would take forever. "Yes, Mrs. George," she said politely.

After Mrs. George left, the other girls were whispering at her, appalled. "How awful that she's making you do that! I cried the whole time when she made me do it. Why aren't you upset?"

"I don't know," Kathryn said calmly, and she didn't.

The next morning after breakfast she was on her knees in the auditorium, the assigned sock and bucket of soapy water in hand, Mrs. George standing there to be sure she did a good job. This room is so enormous I'll be here for the rest of my life, Kathryn thought, scrubbing away, and smiled at the ridiculousness of her punishment.

Swish, swish, rub, rub. Before she knew it, she was humming under her breath. I'll be here until I graduate, Kathryn thought cheerfully. At least I won't have to study or take exams. I wonder if they'll give me my diploma right here on the floor?

"You're a hard one, aren't you, Miss O'Mara," Mrs. George said.

Kathryn recognized the expression in the teacher's voice. She had noticed it often before in her life, at home, and when she glanced up, she saw a look she knew on the teacher's face. It was admiration.

"All right, you can stop now and go to class," Mrs. George said, liberating her. "Dump the water in the utility room sink on your way."

As she walked to the utility room, Kathryn knew there was a lesson to be learned here. If you didn't let them get to you, they wouldn't try. She wondered how two people as different as her father and this woman could feel the same way. So there really was a way to stay safe.... For the first time she realized there was something special about her, and (although she didn't dwell on it) something not very nice about the world.

Unfortunately she had to go home for vacations. Because life at boarding school was so orderly, the chaos at home seemed worse, or perhaps it really was getting worse. Her father was an aberrant force of nature, like an earthquake or a hurricane, and they never knew when his anger and vindictiveness would strike. Because the times of terror were interspersed with times of calm, it only increased the family's anxiety. During her "vacations" Kathryn felt as if she would never be able to take a normal breath.

After his suspension from the police force was over, her father was taken back, despite the drinking. Kathryn thought the police were corrupt. She wondered if her family's power had anything to do with them letting her father stay a cop. Sometimes he was away all night working, sometimes all day, and they were always glad when he wasn't home. When he was sleeping off a hangover, they would leave the house so they wouldn't wake him and have to deal with him again.

She and her mother and little brothers were still trying to protect each other. They had no one else. Her father's family didn't think her mother's family was good enough for them, so Sheila and the children never saw them. Her father's brothers—her three tough cop uncles, Brian, Michael, and Patrick—were no help. They had families and problems of their own, and they didn't know what to do about their alcoholic brother. Her paternal grandfather had died in the line of duty when Kathryn was very young, and she hardly remembered him although she remembered his big funeral; and her grandmother, whom Kathryn saw as a warm and matriarchal figure, had given up on her prodigal son and didn't even want to lay eyes on him. When Brendan would go to her house to try to see her, she would lock her front door and draw the curtains. It was useless to call the cops in a domestic dispute. They would drive Brendan around the block "to cool down," which of course enraged him further, and then they would take him home again and leave. Kathryn and her mother and brothers were isolated on an island of fear.

The good part of vacations was that the boys she had known before she went away were again hanging around the house to see her, or to take her off to gatherings at other people's houses, and now some of those boys had turned out to be very cute. All the money Kathryn got for baby-sitting Mrs. Henderson's kids she began to spend on fashion and beauty magazines, clothes, and makeup. She started to have crushes and to date.

At seventeen Kathryn graduated and was accepted at the University of Massachusetts in Amherst. It was a state school her parents could afford, and they would also pay for her to live there. Once again she had been given a reprieve from that dangerous house. She liked college immediately. She was awed by so many new buildings and masses of people, on a campus so vast that at first she always got lost; but she was excited to be meeting other students from all over the country, and soon was warm and happy in her dorm with a whole group of new girlfriends, and was being pursued by boys.

She was aware she was very pretty, without making a big deal out of it. She was very outgoing, and she had lots of boyfriends. Although she let them kiss her, she never let them touch her, which made her even more popular. It was the mid-fifties, and a girl who teased boys by never letting them get anywhere was always very popular. Since Kathryn wasn't interested in sex, this was easy.

Then, that winter, on a cold and snowy night, her father, drunk as usual, fell into the Charles River. It was a miracle that he was rescued and did not die. Not all miracles, unfortunately, were good ones. But the police department had had enough. Sheila had always been afraid to commit him to a hospital to dry out—she had always been terrified to do anything to enrage him—but now his buddies did it.

When Kathryn came home for spring vacation, it was wonderful having her father locked away, even though they knew it was temporary. Then there was another piece of good news. As a condition of being let out of the hospital her father was made to join A.A. Perhaps they had a guardian angel after all. Her father came home from the hospital completely sober, and suddenly his new friends at A.A. were his life. He would be hunched over the telephone for hours, advising someone or asking for advice himself. He went to daily meetings, he went to church, he read his spiritual pamphlets, he drank endless cups of coffee, and smoked innumerable cigarettes with the men who had become his new friends and often came to visit at the house; and the whole summer went by and he never took another drink.

But no one had warned the family that his reformation would not change anything. He was sober, but his rage and violence became even worse. Before, when he had been falling-down drunk, they could trip him, or sneak away when he had passed out, but now that he was sober, he was invincible. If he had hated her mother before in some random way, now he seemed on a direct campaign to destroy her.

"The doctor says he's what's called a dry drunk," Sheila told Kathryn and her brothers. "Whatever that means."

"I think the alcohol turned his brain to mush," Kathryn said. "It's too late; he's got no mind left."

"No, I believe your father's deliberately trying to drive me crazy."

"I hate you, you bitch!" her father would scream. "I want a divorce!"

He left notes in her mother's pockets, in her handbag, under her pillow, filled with curses and obscenities. *Filthy slut! Go to hell you dirty bitch!* He would pull all her mother's clothes out of the closet and throw them on the floor; once he even urinated on them, too. "Useless piece of shit!" he would scream at her. "I'm divorcing you!"

"Divorce him, for God's sake," Kathryn told her mother. "You'll be rid of him."

"I can't. I have no grounds."

"You *are* crazy," Kathryn said. "Look how he treats you."

"Abuse doesn't count," her mother said. "I asked a lawyer. The only thing that's legal cause for divorce in this state is desertion or adultery. If I leave him, he'll take everything, even our house. I couldn't stand to lose this house. It's all I have, and I worked so hard to help pay for it all these years. All that night work..." She sighed. "Desertion or adultery. He's not going to leave me, no matter what he says. And he doesn't seem to be having an affair with anybody."

"Who would want him?" Kathryn said.

"Oh, you'd be surprised. There are a lot of lonely women in this world."

"Then let's hope one of them finds him."

"One that doesn't mind eating off paper plates for the rest

of her life," her mother said with a wry little smile. She had given up buying breakable dishes years ago.

Sheila was such a sweet woman. Sometimes Kathryn wanted to shake her for being so passive, and then these bits of lightness would come out and Kathryn would find herself filled with love. If she could think of a way to protect her mother she would.

"Often I wonder how you survived to be so well balanced," her mother said.

"I think about it, too."

"It's your fighting nature."

"It was also you."

"What did I do?" her mother asked, but Kathryn could see she was touched.

"Drove *me* crazy," Kathryn said, smiling.

None of the boys Kathryn dated at college her first two years were drinkers. She avoided those like the plague. The boy she had dated the most often was Mike Webster. He was as handsome as a movie star, tall, dark, and calm, and she thought of him as a friend as well as a date. He was older, a senior, and sophisticated: He took her to dinner at restaurants on Saturday nights, when most of the boys made you eat in your dorm because it was free and then only took you out drinking afterward. He also liked to take her out with his friends so they could see how spirited she was, how independent.

"I'm bringing you my socks to darn," he would say, teasing her. It was a running joke because Kathryn would do no such thing, although other girls were always knitting scarves for boys and auditioning to be dutiful little wives.

"Really?" Kathryn would say. "I was going to bring you mine."

"Other girls would be thrilled to darn my socks."

"I'm not like other girls."

Mike would then beam at her. "There's nobody like Kathryn," he would say.

She went out with his friends, too, and he never seemed jealous. After all, she was young, only eighteen, and expected to have a good time. She felt as if she had known him forever, in the best possible way.

The boy she had a crush on now this spring semester was a twenty-one-year-old senior named Ted Hopkins, and he was the best-looking boy she had ever seen, better even than Mike. He was tall and dark and well built, with navy blue eyes, chiseled features, and a wonderfully seductive grin. Kathryn thought that with his looks and charm he could become a politician after he graduated, and in fact he already was the president of his class. He was a big man on campus, and all the girls wanted to go out with him. She had chased and chased him, and now he was taking her out regularly and she knew he liked her at last; which was perhaps only a minor triumph, because he was still dating other girls, too.

She wasn't sure of him, but that only made him more appealing. It also made him safe. Her girlfriends wanted to find someone wonderful to go steady with, and then get married right after graduation, because that was what you were expected to do, but after all those restricted years at a girls' boarding school Kathryn just wanted to have a good time. She was studying enough to get decent marks, but she considered that she was now also studying social life, and that it was equally important for a well-balanced mind.

What did she and all those boys talk about on dates? What did it matter? They laughed, they flirted, they went to football games and to parties, they were happy. Did they really know each other? No, but who cared? Kathryn hardly knew herself, so how could she understand much about someone else, particularly a man? Life was heady, and spring held limitless possibilities. She went home for spring break.

To her surprise she found herself thinking about Mike, since she had thought she was in love with Ted. She decided she would write Mike a joke love letter; it would make him laugh and he would think about her, too.

"Dear Mike:" she wrote. *"I am thinking about you and what you always want me to do for you. I have decided that even though it's against my better nature, I will give in. I love you and I'm yours. So bring 'em over, and you'll see that I'm better at it than any of your other girlfriends. Devotedly, Kathryn."*

She smiled. She could just see Mike howling with laughter.

She folded the letter and put it into her dresser drawer. She would mail it later when she bought some stamps. Then she got busy and forgot about it.

She came back to the house that evening to find her father standing at the door to her bedroom, wild with fury. His fists were clenched, his face was red. He was in uniform, and his gun was in its black holster at his hip. Behind him Kathryn could see that her bedroom was a shambles, the dresser drawers emptied and all their contents strewn on the floor.

"What have you done?" she screamed. "That's my room!"

Then she saw that her father had her "love" letter crumpled in his huge hand. Kathryn felt her stomach lurch. He would never understand. She tried not to tremble.

"What are you doing at college anyway?" he demanded. "You're nothing but a slut! All the money I spent on school and all you want is to get laid?"

"It was a joke," Kathryn said. "Mike always wants me to darn his socks and I was kidding that I'd do it. It was his socks, that's all, his socks."

"Socks? I'll sock you. Brazen little whore! I'm not going to spend any more money on your schooling. Not for a worthless little parasite like you. This is your last term at college, you're out. And you're out of this house, too, as of today, for good. No more money from me, you're on your own. I'm not going to support you ever again. Get packed and get out before I throw you out myself."

Her mother had come quietly to the head of the stairs to listen; she was deathly pale and said nothing.

"It was a joke," Kathryn said. "A joke. He's a friend, like a brother to me." She stood her ground and stared at her father. But this time it didn't work. She supposed it would never work again. Her life as the favored child had ended years ago, the night her father had hit her. She pushed past him and went into her room and shut the door, choking back her angry tears so he wouldn't see her cry.

She didn't have time to pack much, but most of her things were at school. Her mother drove her to the railroad station. "That was a silly letter," her mother said. "But I trust you. Maybe he'll come to his senses and change his mind."

"I hope so," Kathryn said dubiously.

"What are you going to do now?"

"I don't know."

Kathryn went back to the nearly empty dormitory and brooded. Vacation ended, the girls came back, spring term went on, and then Kathryn's mother called with bad news. Her father really wasn't going to pay for her next year at college, and her mother couldn't manage it alone. The tuition wasn't so much, but room and board on top of it were prohibitive. Kathryn felt as if he had beaten her in a worse way than with his fists, in a way she knew would last.

She knew without asking that her mother hadn't defended her; she never stood up to him because she was too frightened. It wouldn't have done any good anyway. Now Kathryn would have to leave school, when she had been doing well and loved it so. Kathryn was devastated. She had always assumed that college would be her life and then she would graduate and go on into her other life, whatever that might be, but in a moment it had all been taken away from her.

But what was even worse, almost unimaginable, was that her father was adamant that she couldn't come home to live. She's eighteen, he had told her mother, let her get a real job. But where would she live? And how could she afford to live anywhere on the kind of job she could get? At the Lancaster School she had been taught secretarial skills, but a secretary started at sixty dollars a week, and menial jobs paid even less. Kathryn had never been alone in her life, and had not had time to prepare for this. She was terrified.

Mike, of course, was home free. Inadvertently connected to her disaster even though the letter itself was in no way his fault and she had been too ashamed to tell him the story, he was getting on with his life. He was graduating next month, and he was moving to New York where he would have his own apartment and a good job. Kathryn wondered if she would ever see New York, if she would ever be anybody, if she would ever be happy again. She could go to New York herself, she daydreamed, and become a model. To be a model was what pretty girls all over the country wanted to be when they couldn't think of what else to do, because it seemed glamorous and easy. But she knew in her heart that she could no more be a model than grow wings and fly.

At the dorm the girls were planning what they would do all summer. Some were engaged, some would be working, others just wanted to get a tan and meet boys. All of them would, of course, be going home to their families. Kathryn found it hard to join in. Her father had stopped sending money altogether, although her mother still sent a little for her expenses. She looked again in the newspaper at the low-paying employment ads for women. Girls lived with their parents until they got married, and married women were supported by their husbands. Why should companies bother to pay them much?

Ted took her out to dinner. He was graduating, too, and he had gotten a job at Filene's department store because he was interested in retail. But even though he would be living in nearby Boston, Kathryn knew she would probably never see him again because she was merely a part of his past and now he was going on to be an adult.

"I'm interested in fashion myself," Kathryn said, toying with her shrimp cocktail. This was probably the last shrimp cocktail she'd ever see.

"You could get a summer job as a salesgirl," he said.

She had already thought of that and discarded the idea. Girls who got summer jobs as underpaid sales clerks thought it was fun because they did not have to live alone. "Actually, I'm going to quit school and go to New York and be a model," Kathryn said. It was part bravado and part fantasy, but she didn't want him to leave her life thinking she was nothing.

"You'd quit school?" he said.

"You bet."

"I thought you liked school."

"Models have to be young."

He was looking at her differently, she thought. "I sort of planned we'd still see each other after I graduate," he said then.

"You did?"

"Yes. Well, date. Sure."

How ironic, Kathryn thought, both flattered and saddened. Yes, Ted would date a college girl, someone he could bring home to his parents. She shrugged. "Maybe you'll get to New York," she said.

"How do your parents feel about this?"

"They feel I should have my chance."

"You'll be a famous cover girl and you won't want to go out with me," he teased.

"Maybe not," she teased back.

"You know, modeling is a very hard job," he said.

"And well paying."

"Do you really want to be independent?"

You should only know how I'm going to hate it, Kathryn thought. She looked away, trying to appear mysterious, but he took her hesitation for ambivalence.

"If you don't like school, there are other options," he said.

"Such as what?"

"Well, you could stay here and get married."

"Marry who?" Kathryn asked.

"Me."

Kathryn just stared at him in amazement. She had never known he liked her so much, and she had never dreamed of this, especially not with him. Ted had such a short attention span with girls that she couldn't picture him as anybody's husband, and she had never wanted to marry anybody in the first place. Marriage had never been a solution she had even considered.

"Well?" he said.

She wasn't in love, not the way you were supposed to be to get married. A crush wasn't love. But he was so good looking, really gorgeous. It was very tempting.

"Well?" he said again.

"I could do that," Kathryn said. It was all totally unreal.

"We'll get married right after graduation," he said. "Tomorrow we'll pick out the ring."

"I'm getting married!" she screamed to her girlfriends when she got back to the dorm. "Ted just proposed!" They all started screaming, too, and hugging her, and her friend Barbara was jumping up and down, looking like a rabbit in her white bunny slippers.

"She's marrying Ted!" they shrieked. "Kathryn, you're the first one in our class to be a bride! This is so exciting!"

They all believed in romance and living happily ever after. As for Kathryn, she didn't know what to think. She didn't have much choice. It would be an adventure, she supposed, at least it would be that.

Her friends gave her a shower, with the usual joke presents: a how-to book about married sex, slinky underwear, and a baby bottle for when the inevitable happened. Her days were a whirl of plans. The wedding was a small one, held in Boston the day after graduation. Since Kathryn did not want her father to come, not that he would have, she and Ted went to City Hall with her mother and brothers, Ted's parents, and a few friends. She had invited Mike, but he had already gone to New York to begin his new job. A judge performed the service. Ted was wearing his good suit and Kathryn was wearing a little white cocktail dress she thought she could dye later and wear to parties. She still couldn't think of this as real; it was just an adventure. She had known Ted Hopkins for only six months. They had never had a revealing or intimate conversation. They had hardly even been alone together.

The wedding dinner after the brief ceremony was held at the Bull and Bear, and then the newly married couple went to the very nice Copley Plaza hotel, where Ted had booked a room for their wedding night.

"Mr. and Mrs. Hopkins," he said proudly to the desk clerk when they checked in.

Who? Kathryn thought.

Their room was not very large, done in dark furniture and wallpaper that were supposed to make it look antique. There was a painting on the wall of somebody's ancestor. "You can't get rid of me now," Ted said cheerfully.

"I won't."

She went into the bathroom to change into the nightgown and negligee she had bought for their first night together. She locked the bathroom door. I'm going to have to have sex with him tonight, Kathryn thought, shivering with terror, not anticipation. I'm *married* to him. For the first time she was beginning to comprehend. We are married. *I hardly know him.*

Six months ago I didn't know he existed, and now he's my legally wedded husband. I never wanted to be married!

Suddenly it was real. She couldn't breathe. Her heart was pounding and she felt as if she were choking. Sweat was pouring down her sides, and when she looked into the mirror above the sink, her face was deathly pale and covered with moisture. Her hands were trembling. She was gasping for breath. Her past and her life and her fear descended on her and she couldn't escape them, any more than she could escape what she had just done. She was married.

TWELVE

Billie Redmond was in a mellow mood. Business had been very good tonight, and now with the evening winding down she could relax with a real drink and a cigarette. During the course of an evening at Yellowbird she sometimes drank vodka, but more likely ice water, and no one knew the difference. She liked to keep control. It pleased her that at this point in her life, at forty-eight, she had a successful career that made her a good living, a little son who was her favorite companion in the world, interesting acquaintances, employees she could trust, and the ability to balance excess and sanity in all things. It was time for a vodka on the rocks and a chat, time to hear a few special songs, and then she would collect Little Billie, who was napping on his cot in her office, and they would go home. On weeknights she always made it a point to have him tucked into his own bed by eleven-thirty.

"Sammy," she said to the waiter, "put on the night tape."

All the tapes Billie played were specially made double-length tapes that were collections of songs she had carefully chosen for various moods during the evening. The one she called the night tape was the only one that included songs she had sung herself on tour, long ago, with her couple of hits, and her one big hit, "Texas Stars." She played that tape only when she felt like it. No one recognized the woman singing some of the songs on it as Billie. How could they? That robust and vibrant voice, its clarity and power, its raw energy belonged to a being who no longer existed. Or perhaps just to a voice that no longer existed—the woman was still here, wiser, stronger, a little worse for wear.

Sometimes when people asked who the singer was she told them, waiting for the surprised look that always came, the disbelief they sometimes tried to hide, the questions she knew they were afraid to ask.

What happened? How did you lose your voice? Did it have anything to do with that, well...you know, that scar? Yes, she would have said, if anyone had been brave enough to ask, yes it did, but not in the way you think. But no one asked. Only their eyes asked, always. They stared, they looked away, they did all the things people do when confronted with something different and a little frightening, with deformity hinting of violence.

She could have plastic surgery to get rid of it, they were thinking. A lot of times she doesn't even try to cover it. Doesn't she notice it anymore? How could she not?

I want to keep it, she could have told them, if they had been tactless enough to say anything like that, but they never did. I paid my dues, she would have said with calm equanimity, and I don't want to forget it. I'm a survivor. If you can't deal with it, that's your problem.

She looked around the room. At table four Gara Whiteman was still here, the therapist; with Kathryn O'Henry, or O'Mara Henry, or whatever, the rich one. Felicity Johnson, the black lawyer, had been with them for dinner, but she had gone home to her husband. That nice gay guy was with them tonight, Brad, who was Gara's friend. Eve Bader had not been here, obviously having other plans, but Billie knew Eve could show up late in the evening, alone. She would sail in with that wild-eyed look of hers, her hair crackling, nervous about being by herself and trying to hide it.

Too bad for Eve there were two big producers having dinner together here tonight, Billie thought, chuckling. And good for me she wasn't here to bother them.

Billie stubbed out her cigarette, picked up her vodka on the rocks, and went over to table four and sat in the empty seat. "Hey," she said.

"Oh, Billie," Brad said in a pathetic, pleading way, "give me a cigarette, just one, please."

"Don't," Gara said. "He's on the patch."

"I'll take it off," Brad said. "Right here at the table."

"Stop that, Brad," Gara said.

"Oh, come on..."

"You two are like a married couple," Billie said. "Bicker, bicker."

"We are a married couple," Brad said. "We're all either of us could get."

They all laughed. "Husbands are easy to come by," Kathryn said. "Friends are hard."

"Oh, for a hard friend," Brad said.

"Ooh, corny," Gara said. They laughed again.

"I'm flying to London tomorrow," Kathryn said. "The daughter of a girlfriend of mine is getting married to an Englishman. In a castle in the country. I'm going to wear a big picture hat."

"You have the life," Gara said.

"It's about time."

"Texas Stars" began to play on the tape. Billie closed her eyes and held her head back, listening to it.

"What a great voice," Brad said when it was over. "Who was that?"

"Billie," Gara said. The four women already knew.

"Really? Weren't you terrific!"

"Thank you," Billie said. "Those were the glory days. 'Texas Stars' was on the *Billboard* top ten. I was on the road having adventures."

"I remember that song," Brad said. "I was in high school. My parents went on a vacation as usual and didn't take me, so I had the whole house to myself. I gave a party. I invited boys *and* girls because I hadn't officially come out yet. I got kissed twice that night, once by a girl in my math class and once by a football player. Billie, you were a star."

"Yeah, well," Billie said, but she was pleased. She sipped her vodka. It tasted nice. "Can I buy anybody a drink?"

"Absolutely," Kathryn said. "White wine."

"Pete," Billie said, "White wine." The empty bottle of the expensive stuff they had been drinking stood upside down in the cooler next to the table, but they would, of course, get bar wine. They would have paid five dollars a glass for it; it cost her less than one, and it wouldn't even rot their teeth.

"Thank you," they all said, raising their glasses to her. She nodded graciously.

"Funny about music," Billie said. "When you hear an old song you always remember where you were. Nothing pinpoints a moment in your life like music. It just brings everything back, as if you were there again. In my opinion the only really good songs were written between the mid-sixties and the mid-seventies, with the exception of the blues. I can never figure out if that's because they really were so much better or because I felt everything so strongly then."

"Both, I would guess," Gara said.

"Do you think anybody remembers 'Polka Dot Bikini' with their heart pounding?" Kathryn asked.

"Nobody we would know," Gara said.

"I never met Janis Joplin," Billie said, "but I always wanted to. So many of the great ones died young. I sat next to Jimi Hendrix at a discotheque one night in the sixties, but the closest I ever got to Janis was looking at her from afar with about a million other people at the Monterey Pop Festival in 1967. She was with Big Brother and the Holding Company. She sang 'Ball and Chain.' I was twenty years old and I'd gone to California for a vacation with some friends. You know, San Francisco with flowers in your hair kind of thing. I was singing already, had for a long time, in my daddy's roadhouse in Plano. But when I saw and heard Janis, I said to myself: 'That's who I want to be.' Three years later she was dead."

She took a sip of her vodka, remembering, and sighed. It wasn't a sad sigh, it was more one of nostalgia, because the past was so far away. "Later on, when I was starting out, every dingy little club was full of screaming Joplin wannabes. I had my own style, but in so many ways she was my inspiration. Then I got successful, toured around, doing arenas, civic centers, rock clubs, the Fillmore East, the Fillmore West, the Troubadour in L.A., the Hungry I in San Francisco, had a couple of hits, and I thought I'd be her."

"Arenas!" Brad said, impressed.

"Well, it wasn't like today," Billie said, "where you have only one band, or one singer. You'd get six or seven people on each show, like a mini festival."

"Still..." he said.

"Yes, still," she agreed. "It was an amazing time."

She let some of the pictures come back into her mind, holding them away just a little so she didn't have to relive the feelings, remembering in tiny flashes the life, the sounds, the electric nights, the man she had loved, and the darkness of the soul. She was here, safe and mellow and looking at the past, that achingly sad and gloriously high and pathetically confused period of her youth that seemed to have happened to someone else. And then she said the same thing she always did, which everyone thought they understood and which, although they were wrong, she never explained.

"I could have been Janis Joplin," Billie said.

"You certainly could," Brad said.

Billie smiled calmly. Everybody always assumed she meant successful. But she meant more; she meant dead.

She concentrated on her drink and the song on the sound system, so the others would know she was finished talking about the old days for tonight. She never liked to talk about that stuff for too long. Maybe I'll tell them some time, she thought. But I don't think so. There's one thing I don't want in my life, and that's to be anybody's interesting story.

Billie Redmond was born in Plano, Texas, in 1947, after her father had come home from the war and opened the little bar and grill that turned into the successful roadhouse he ran for the rest of his life. She had an older brother, Al, whose musical talent consisted of playing a comb with a piece of tissue paper on it. But from the time she first heard music, Billie sang along with perfect pitch. She had a deep voice for a little kid, and people thought it was cute. Then when she got older she grew into it, and by the time she was ten she was begging to be allowed to sing with the band at the Saturday night amateur nights her father had started to hold once a month. He finally let her.

"You should have a kid's contest," Billie told him. "I can't compete with grownups, even though none of them are much good."

"Well, don't tell them they're not much good," her father said, winking at her. Les Redmond was a tall, strong man with a big mustache and a sunny disposition. He liked having a lot of people around, brought in the band to entertain

them on weekends, was generous with his customers both
with advice and free beers, and when any of them got unruly
he threw him out himself. Les was proud of the fact that he
didn't need to hire a bouncer.

Her mother, Wilma, gave piano lessons. They didn't need
the money but she loved music and she loved children. She
taught Billie how to read music and play the piano, and Billie
taught herself how to play the guitar. Billie liked to listen to
country music and gospel and the blues.

"Les, why don't you have a little amateur night for the
kids?" her mother said.

"They'll be even more painful to listen to than the adults,"
her father said.

"Their parents won't think so."

"You have a point, my love."

Thus began the kids' contests, with an independent judge,
and Billie won so often she had to stop competing. She heard
the customers whispering, "That kid should be a pro," and
she knew she was lucky to have her life all figured out before
she was even old enough to worry about the future. She
knew she would not marry anybody in Plano, that she
would go wherever her career took her, and that she would
have adventures. By the time she was in high school she was
singing every weekend with the roadhouse band, had demanded and gotten a salary instead of an allowance, and
was writing songs of her own, which she slipped in once in a
while among the hits the hard-drinking customers wanted to
hear.

Her social life, however, was not as good as the rest of it.
She was too tall for the current fashion, as tall as the boys and
taller than some, and as rangy as a cowboy, so although she
had male friends she'd never had a real boyfriend. She concentrated on being dramatic-looking. She had great legs so
she wore tight jeans and cowboy boots. She had no cleavage,
which was a disaster for a would-be country singer or a high
school girl, so she turned it into an advantage by wearing a
man's shirt unbuttoned to the waist and then tied securely in
a knot. It was curiously seductive. She wore an armful of silver bracelets, a silver ring on each finger, and while every
woman and girl in town who could afford it went to the

beauty salon to have her hair teased and sprayed into a bee-hive, Billie let her straight brown hair grow down to her hips. When she sang she tossed her head and her hair flew like rib-bons of silk. When she bowed after her number her hair touched the floor. Men started to want her.

Onstage she seemed to be the woman they wanted offs-tage, so after her set they offered to buy her drinks, and sometimes she said yes. She liked the yearning look in their eyes and the remarks they made, the way they leaned to-ward her and pretended it was an accident when they touched her.

Good, she thought. When you could do the picking you didn't want me. Now I do the picking. She was seventeen and already in charge.

Sometimes they touched her deliberately, but if she didn't want to be touched she could be fierce. A man she didn't know pinched her on the ass once, and she hit him so fast and so hard that she knocked him off his bar stool. She hadn't really meant to, it had just been a reflex, but when she saw what she had done she was glad. After that the word got out that she was a little weird, that she didn't act like a nor-mal woman. You had to be polite to Billie Redmond or else. Some of the men called her a dyke, or a ballbuster, but the ones who didn't only wanted her more.

"I have as much faith as you do that you're going to make your career in music," her father said to her that year. "But I want you to have something to fall back on. The entertain-ment business is unpredictable and crazy. I'm teaching your brother how to run a bar and restaurant, and I'm going to teach you."

"You mean you want me to run this place someday?" Bil-lie asked, aghast. She wasn't going to spend her old age in this town, that was for sure. She couldn't imagine being any-thing but a singer. Besides, what her father did was too hard, it gave her a headache even thinking about doing it.

"Consider it summer school," her father said.

So there she was all summer long between her junior and senior years, learning how to understand and keep the books, how to order food and booze from the suppliers, why to put certain people at certain tables, how to watch for waste and stealing. He even made her waitress. At least he paid her for that, and there were also tips. She saved her money with a vengeance, for her escape into the music world.

"I'm never going to have to do this," Billie protested.

"You'll hire people to do whatever you don't want to do, but you have to know how to do it yourself so you don't get cheated."

In spite of herself she started to find it interesting. Her father acted so affable at work, but it was clear that he was always aware of everything and in control. In a way, Billie realized, what her father did was not so far from what she was doing. He, too, had to manipulate an audience. Les Redmond worked hard, but his roadhouse was also a social thing. He was not home for a single evening of the week. If his wife and children wanted to see him for dinner they would have to come to him, which they sometimes did, and he always gave them a table near the bar with a good view of the room and people treated them with respect. Billie thought it was kind of neat.

She would never end up here, though, she promised herself that. Her father's work might be his art, but it was still only his job. Hers was her soul. When she sang she often entered an altered state, close to ecstasy. It was clear to her that she had been given her voice for a reason, and not to take advantage of her talent would be bitterly self-destructive. Besides, she couldn't help it. Being able to sing was what gave her entire life purpose and made it bearable.

When she graduated from high school Billie let her parents talk her into temporarily working full-time in the roadhouse as the hostess while she saved more money. They knew she planned to leave home, but they wanted her to be able to take care of herself for at least a while when she was pursuing her career. She was not a hippie, they said, despite the way she had taken to dressing; she was a person with purpose. Life should be taken a step at a time. She thought they were right about the nest egg, but a stronger reason for delaying was that after growing up in a place where she knew so many people, the idea of going off to a city where she knew no one at all frightened her. She was only eighteen. Kids she'd gone to school with were getting married to their high school sweethearts, planning to have kids of their own. How much easier it was for them, Billie thought, to have a dream that was close to home. A few of her friends were off to college, and she knew they wouldn't come back. She didn't regret not having applied to college—college had seemed an impediment—but now she thought of it as another protected environment on the road to success, which was not for her either. Some of her friends had simply left town. The world out there was suddenly full of young people their own age, warm with love and drugs, making their own rules. They wouldn't be strangers to her for long if she ventured out there alone, she knew that. But she stayed poised on the edge of freedom, ready to step off, and afraid. She didn't want anyone to find out because it would seem so out of character, and humiliating.

She continued to sing at the roadhouse on weekends and sometimes she got a job singing at a party with the guys in the band, who liked her and treated her like a niece. Even they, these men she'd known for years, devoted musicians, had regular jobs during the week, and families to keep them anchored. She knew they had regrets and that everything was a tradeoff. She wouldn't let herself have their lives. She steeled herself for the loneliness to come.

It took two years for her to know she was ready, and it almost came by accident. She was twenty that summer. Her friend Lily Ann and Lily Ann's boyfriend Scooter wanted to see the West Coast. "If we don't go now while we're young we'll never go," they said, already afraid of being old. They invited Billie to come along to help drive, and she was glad to join them. She was afraid of being old, too.

They planned to see movie stars' homes in Los Angeles, and movie studios, and scenery very different from what they were used to, and palm trees and the Pacific Ocean; and in San Francisco they would check out the hippie scene, and at Billie's suggestion, the little coffeehouses where there were singers. But the highlight of the trip would be the Monterey Pop Festival where everyone Billie wanted to hear and see would be, the best of sixties' rock and blues: the Who, the Jimi Hendrix Experience, Aretha Franklin, Otis Redding, Johnny Rivers, the Byrds, Eric Burdon and the Animals,

Canned Heat, the Electric Flag, Quicksilver Messenger Service, the Jefferson Airplane, the Grateful Dead, and many more. They would stay in cheap motels along the way, and for the three-day-long festival itself they brought sleeping bags and blankets. Billie felt that in some way, at last, she was going to put her fantasies of her destiny together with the reality of what it could be.

When they got to the county fairgrounds in the little coastal town of Monterey she was stunned. She had never seen so many people in her life, a sea of people, an outdoor city of love. They wore love beads, boots, faded Levis, granny dresses, even stovepipe hats, and some had bells and tambourines. They looked just like her.

She and her friends joined the slow-moving, peaceful throngs strolling through booths selling paper dresses, underground pins, earrings, crosses, posters, and macrobiotic food. There were corn on the cob and pastrami sandwiches. Bright flags with astrology signs on them waved in the breeze. There were psychedelic movies and loud makeshift steel bands. When people were tired they put out their blankets in the warm California sunshine and played guitars, sang, socialized, or just slept.

"Somebody said there are fifty thousand people here," Lily Ann marveled. "That's three times as many people as in our entire town."

"Let's stay forever," Scooter said, grinning.

"But they won't...or I would."

There was a banner over the stage in the seven-thousand-seat arena that said LOVE, FLOWERS AND MUSIC, and onstage there was nonstop total volume sound. Delta blues, electric guitar, cool harmonica, acid rock, shaking and shouting, music that set the whole audience dancing. Day went into night. Dazed and gaping, drowning in music, totally happy, Billie knew she was on the verge of something important, but she didn't know what.

And then they saw Janis Joplin, a Texas girl, too, almost unknown, and Billie's life changed.

Janis Joplin with her band, Big Brother and the Holding Company, Janis Joplin, dressed in a gold knit pants suit, jumping and stamping her feet as if possessed, belting it out in a wild and passionate voice that sounded as if it would tear her throat apart... She was the best white woman blues singer Billie had ever heard. She was performing so far away from where Billie and her friends were standing that she seemed to be in miniature. But the sound was right there, and the energy, and the honesty, and the unabashed pain. It touched Billie in a way she had never been touched before. The sea of people receded, and Billie stood there hypnotized. For the first time, she understood that the future would be something she could deal with. This is who I want to be, she told herself. I would do anything to do this. She is me. *My God, she's not afraid to be afraid.*

Other things happened during the festival—the Who made their amplifier go wild with feedback and then Peter Townshend dropped smoke bombs and smashed his guitar to bits while Keith Moon kicked his drum to pieces. Jimi Hendrix's finale to his session was to burn his guitar onstage. But none of that violence impressed Billie at all. She had seen what she had come to see. All the rest was show business.

When she got back to Plano, Billie packed her things and left for New York City. She was still capable of being shocked by masses of people, tall buildings and traffic jams, but not for long. She rented a tiny apartment in Greenwich Village, slept on a mattress on the floor, and haunted the little Village clubs; and finally she began to get gigs playing there. She strummed her guitar and sang her own songs, doing what she had done at home in Plano, but this time she didn't have a band, not that it mattered since the stages were so small there wouldn't have been room for one. She had a lot more artistic freedom here than she'd had at home because the audiences were hip. They didn't demand she sing well-known songs whether she liked them or not.

Dark, smoky rooms that smelled of beer were familiar to her, and so were audiences, and so were admiring men. What was unfamiliar, although she had thought she was prepared for it, was the loneliness that touched her the moment she woke up in the morning and stayed with her all day like a creature with its claws in her heart.

She began to buy bottles of wine for her apartment, and kept a little buzz on all day. Wine, she told herself, was not hard liquor. It was just something to keep the creature at bay. She found out how to buy pot in Washington Square Park and from friendly neighbors. People were generous and shared. Pot was a social thing, like cigarettes, and it made you relax.

Everybody she knew took something. You could get pills in clubs, or at parties, and a prescription if you needed one and knew the right people. She started to take an upper from time to time when she was tired or sad, and a downer when it was hard to sleep. Everyone knew it was unnatural to try to go to sleep when the sun was already blasting in the sky.

That first summer in New York she lost her virginity at last, not that she hadn't had plenty of chances at home. At twenty she thought she was probably the oldest virgin in America. What had made her so cautious in Plano was that she was still living with her parents, and the men who wanted to have sex with her were the ones she met in her father's roadhouse. She didn't want anybody to talk about her, to say that you could get Billie Redmond as a kind of dessert after dinner and the show. As for the boys she had known at school, they had rejected her for so long that when they finally decided she was hot because of her performances, she already thought of *them* as rejects, and she wanted them to know it. She was haughty and mysterious, and all the guys simply assumed she was having sex with someone else. No one knew she was a virgin; it was her secret.

But in New York she was free. After she finished her gig she would go to the after-hours rock clubs, like the Scene, where the music greats came to jam all night, or to a hall like the Electric Circus to drink and smoke and dance. She slept late, often awoke with a beautiful man in her bed whom she had met only hours before, and sometimes she even saw him again. In the afternoons she wrote songs or took long walks around the city. She was still young enough to have short hangovers.

There were little record labels that came and went. You could get signed by one if they saw you performing in a club and liked you, and if you and they were lucky the little label might be bought by a big one. Elvis had started with Sun,

and Sun had later been bought by RCA. Or you might even
be signed by a big one in the first place. That was her dream.

Janis Joplin was famous now. Billie had followed Janis's
every career move because Janis had unknowingly changed
her life. After the Monterey Pop Festival, Janis and Big
Brother and the Holding Company had been signed by Co-
lumbia Records, where they made a terrific album called
Cheap Thrills. Then she left them and formed her own group,
the Kosmic Blues Band. But Janis was getting increasingly
bad publicity: she drank Southern Comfort all the time, even
onstage, and Billie had heard from people who were in a position to know that she was on heroin. It amazed her that
anyone could sing so well while indulging in that kind of
self-abuse, and she determined she would never do anything
like that to herself, no matter how lonely she was.

That winter, the last of the sixties, Billie was singing at the
Village Vanguard when she met Harry Lawless, the man
who would change her life again. She knew it the moment
she saw him, although she was not sure why she knew or
how he would do it. He sat alone drinking beer from a long-
neck bottle and smoking, and never took his eyes off her. She
kept glancing at him to be sure. He was older than she but
still young, and he had a craggy, scarred face that looked as
if it had survived many bar brawls, mitigated by long, soft
dark hair and velvet eyes. There was something familiar
about that ravaged face, a face she might have seen in her father's roadhouse, and it comforted rather than repelled her.
He looked to be a little shorter than she was, which she
didn't mind because she was used to it, and he was hard and
lean in his jeans, faded work shirt, and expensive leather
jacket. He was attractive in an odd way, and very sexy.

When her set was over he raised the bottle to her with a
nod of respect. She nodded back and smiled. When she came
down to look for the friends she was going to meet, he
stopped her. Billie let anyone stop her who looked as if he
might be someone in the record business, but in this case she
would have stopped anyway.

"You need a manager," he said, in an accent she recognized from all of her life.

"How do you know I don't have one?"

"I asked," he said. He handed her his card. *Harry Lawless* it read, *Outlaw Records*.

"Cute," Billie said.

"I thought so. Will you sit down and let me buy you a drink?"

"I'm meeting some friends here, but okay, just for a minute." She let him pull out her chair for her and she ordered a glass of wine. "So you're from Texas, too?" she said.

"Houston."

"Oh, the big city. I'm from Plano."

"How long have you been in New York?"

"Not long enough and too long," Billie said. "So who do you suggest I get to be my manager?"

"Me."

She thought about that. "If you have a record company, how come you're a manager? I never heard of anybody being both."

"Neither did I, but there's always a first time," he said. "Besides, it's a small record company."

"Well, I knew that."

"They're the best kind," he said. "I can sign harder edged artists."

"Anybody I know?"

"Pig Man and the Wanderers?"

She laughed. "What did they do, 'Oink'?"

He smiled. "Are you always this obnoxious to men who are trying to make you famous?"

"Is that what you're doing? Or just trying to make me?"

"A little of both. Seriously, Billie, you are very talented, and your voice is much too big for a room like this. I'd like to see you on a big stage, in an arena, strutting around, letting loose."

"Me, too," she said.

She wanted to touch him but she didn't. She could sense he felt the same. She had liked him right away, and now that she had seen him up close and listened to his voice and smelled his pheromones she liked him more. She felt safe with him, which did not reduce his physical attractiveness but made it stronger. She was so used to the courting antics of horny men that she could almost write the script for them, and the thing that had always been most apparent was that their attraction to her was impersonal. They didn't know who she was, only how she seemed. They didn't care to know. But she knew them very well. What she could sense about Harry Lawless, unless she was mistaken for the first time in her life, was that he and she were capable of digging into each other, right down to the vulnerable, trembling heart.

Her friends showed up then, and she introduced everybody. They were going to a club and she invited him to come along. While everybody else danced downstairs she and Harry sat at a little table in the corner of the upstairs bar and talked about music and their dreams, while the sound of the band downstairs came pumping through the floor.

"Every little independent record label wants to become another Motown," he said. "Motown proved it could be done. A little label doesn't have to be swallowed up as soon as it has a couple of hits."

"I thought that was what they wanted."

"No. And not me. For fifty thousand dollars I can finance a record. It costs ten cents to press a single that I sell to a distributor for fifty cents, and he sells it for a dollar, so I make forty cents a record. If I have a gold record that sells a million copies, I make four hundred thousand dollars."

"Whew," Billie said, impressed. "That's money all right."

"It could happen to us."

"Who is 'us'?"

"You and me. I'm in the process of putting together a band. It's going to be called Bandit. I want you to be the singer."

"Yes!" Billie said immediately. "Not to sound too eager."

They smiled at each other. "I'll put together a good mix of your songs and other people's, and we'll cut a record," he said. "Some of the band members have written some very promising stuff."

"Other people's songs?" Billie said.

"And yours."

"That's fine." Janis often sang other people's songs.

"I'll get you on the road. It's time for you to tour."

Billie thought about that, too. "If I'm going to do all this I guess I need an agent now."

"You can use a lawyer for the contracts. Why pay all those commissions?"

"You're going to be my manager and my agent and my record company?"

"You don't think I'll be fair to you?"

"I don't know."

"That's what you have your lawyer for."

"Then I'm getting my own lawyer," Billie said. "Not some friend of yours."

He laughed. "I insist on it."

The whole thing was very tempting. She couldn't keep on struggling forever the way she had been doing the past few years. She was impatient and itchy to make her mark, and besides, she had that feeling about him. She was an unknown and he was offering her a chance. Just for once in her life she might try letting someone else share the control.

"You'll be the artist and I'll be the businessman," Harry said. "I'll take care of everything."

It sounded familiar. It was what her father had done, and she liked it. Teach me what you do, Daddy, but don't make me do it. An artist should be free to soar.

"How much is this managing going to cost me?" she asked.

"Twenty-five percent of everything, but don't worry about it because I'll make you rich. I promise."

"I want to be famous," Billie said.

"You don't have a choice," he said. "They go together."

They fell silent.

"Are you going on the road with me?" she asked finally.

"Of course, whenever I can. You'll never feel deserted."

"Good."

"Any other questions you forgot to ask?"

"Yes." She paused, afraid of the answer. "Do you have a wife?"

"Not that I know of."

She was infinitely relieved.

"Do you have a husband?" he asked.

She smiled. "Not that I know of."

"A boyfriend?"

She shrugged. "Nobody special. And you?"

He shook his head. "Not at the moment."

"It's always good to know these things," Billie said.

"That's your next song," he said. "I want you to go home and write it."

"Now?"

"Not just this minute."

She started to hum and then to play with ideas and phrases as they came to her. "Do you need me now, do you want me now, do you have somebody else and will you want me anyway? Did someone find you first, is she waiting there for you? It's always good to know these things...not that it would have mattered."

"Not that it would have mattered," Harry said. They looked at each other and her heart began to pound.

"It's not a sweet song," she said.

"It doesn't have to be. It just has to be real."

"It's real," Billie said.

"For me, too," he said very quietly.

Their legs met under the table, and then their hands flew at each other and clutched, and then they kissed. They clung to each other and she ended up on his lap with her arms around his neck, necking wildly, thinking it was good the place was so dark and the clientele so stoned that no one noticed or cared.

"Come home with me," he said. "I want to make love to you all night."

If he can do that, Billie thought, I'm his.

He lived in an apartment that was clearly much more appealing than hers, although she didn't notice that until the next day. They did indeed make love to each other all night, a luxury she had seldom had, and finally fell asleep for two hours from sheer exhaustion. When they woke up he made very good coffee, and she drank it wearing his bathrobe. He had a bedroom and living room and full kitchen, and nice-looking funky furniture. He even had an upright piano. There were framed memorabilia on the walls of various groups, none of whom she had heard of, but that was normal because groups that didn't make it came and went like trains and changed their names all the time.

When she came out of the shower he was already on the phone. "Goodbye," she said when he finally hung up. "I'm going to go home and write that song."

"Good. And try to take a nap. I'll catch your show. Afterward we'll run over to your place and get some of your things so you can keep them here."

He was managing her already. She didn't mind; she sort of liked it. They lingered at the door, kissing. "If you don't go now I won't let you go," he said. "So go. See you tonight."

Billie hummed all the way home. They were a couple already. Neither of them had said they loved the other, but it was all right—they didn't have to, they knew. That would come next.

THIRTEEN

Felicity's mother and her mother's lover, Jake, had been seeing each other for five years. They had a little anniversary
celebration in Carolee's kitchen, and Felicity and her sister,
who knew how long they had been together, suspected what
it was because there was a bottle of champagne instead of the
usual wine. Then, in their domestic world that had long ago
ceased to make sense to them, they knew it to be true because
their mother told them, bubbly and happy, that she and Jake
were celebrating their "long and special friendship," while
warning them for the thousandth time that it was a secret.

Felicity thought it was disgusting of her mother and Jake
to make an issue of their illicit anniversary in her father's
house. Her mother was so open about it that Felicity wondered why her father was the only person in the world who
didn't know. But there seemed to be one other person who
didn't know: Jake's wife.

His wife's ignorance finally ended when she had Jake followed by a detective. After the detective told her all the par-
ticulars, Jake's wife called Carolee's husband, whom she had
never met in her life, and told him. Thus it was that on a
sharply cold and sunny winter afternoon Dr. Johnson, who
had always been the most mild-mannered of men, came
home unexpectedly from work with a gun in his hand and
confronted his wife and her lover in his kitchen as Jake was
finishing his usual delicious lunch.

It all happened so fast. Her father burst into the kitchen,
her mother screamed, Felicity and Theodora screamed, and
Jake stood up and knocked over his chair. Felicity could not
believe that this angry man brandishing a huge blue-black
gun was her father, the same man who had never had the

guts to protect her from her mother's beatings. His face was so distorted with anger and pain that she could not bear to look at it, but she couldn't look at the gun either. She and Theodora fled to their rooms in fear and locked their doors. But the yelling and screaming floated upstairs and through the walls.

Felicity's heart was pounding. She wanted to listen and she didn't; she wanted to know everything and she was afraid to hear her mother die. If Jake died she wouldn't care. She hated him and always had. But she didn't want her father to commit murder. My father is going to kill my mother, she thought, and he'll go to jail, and I'll be an orphan. The thought of being totally abandoned made her begin to sob.

"I ought to kill you both," her father's voice roared. "His *wife* had to tell me. That's how much I trusted you. You slut."

"Oh please...no," her mother was wailing.

"I'm sorry, I'm so sorry," Jake was saying. "Please forgive me. I'm so sorry."

"You were carrying on this disgusting affair for years, behind my back, while I was working so you could have a decent life..."

"I'm so sorry..."

"Get out of this house, you son of a bitch—now!" her father yelled. "And never come back!"

"Go!" her mother screamed. "Go!"

Felicity waited trembling for the sound of gunfire, which never came. What she did hear was the sound of the front door slamming, and when she went to her bedroom window she saw Jake running down the street through the snow, his suit jacket flapping. He had been in too much of a hurry to stop to take his coat. Felicity wondered if this was the end of it. She wished with all her heart that it was.

But of course it was not over. She could never underestimate her mother, and life was neither logical nor fair. The very next day her mother was on the phone with Jake, whispering and cooing and acting just as much in love as ever, making plans for a safer place to meet.

"I've made an arrangement with my friend Jeffrey," she was saying. "He's going to let us have his apartment in the afternoons. No, he's not an old boyfriend, he's a friend. He's totally gay. No one will think anything of it if I go to his place. Oh you're so sweet, but no you don't have to pay him. It's all taken care of. That's what friends do."

What friends did Felicity discovered a few days later. "You're coming with me today," her mother told her. She was in a decent mood—not happy, not angry, just matter of fact, almost resigned.

"Where?"

"To my friend Jeffrey's apartment."

"Is Theodora coming?" Felicity murmured.

"No, just you. She's fat and hopeless. You know you're my favorite. You're the one I love the best. You're getting to look like me already. You're going to be a beautiful woman. Come along now, cherub. We'll have a mother-daughter time."

Felicity didn't know what to think. She knew she was her mother's favorite daughter and she liked that even though she felt guilty about her sister. But she also knew that being the favorite, the one who resembled her beautiful mother (which she could still hardly believe because she knew she could never be as beautiful as her mother), was why her mother picked on her all the time. She didn't know whether Carolee wanted her to be perfect or whether she was jealous of her daughter.

Jeffrey's apartment was in a small building that had been divided up into six apartments. It wasn't near where they lived and it seemed private. The apartment was very cluttered but obviously carefully put together, with dozens of little knickknacks arranged in groups everywhere, fake flower arrangements on the end tables, and a beaded curtain at the entrance to the bedroom, as if a woman lived there instead of a man. A woman with no taste. Her mother had the key.

"Why are we here?" Felicity asked.

"I have to clean Jeffrey's apartment in return for him letting me borrow it. You're going to help me."

Felicity felt like crying. It was bad enough that her mother was cheating, but now she had to help her mother clean up the love nest. It wasn't fair; it was sadistic.

"Pick up a rag and that can of Pledge and make yourself useful," her mother said, nudging her.

Her mother vacuumed and put clean sheets on the large bed, did a big pile of laundry in the washer-dryer, and then she washed the dishes and scrubbed the bathroom. Felicity had her own little chores: she had to dust the tables and all those stupid fussy things on them, one by one, and wipe off the counter tops, and finally clean the greasy stove with Comet. She supposed her mother made Jake's lunch here the way she had done at home, and she hated them both more than ever.

Why do I always have to be a part of this, Felicity cried out silently to her mother. Why do I have to be a witness, an accessory to what you're doing to my father? It's a crime to do that to your own child. If I was your lawyer I wouldn't even defend you. I'd have the judge make you stop.

But no one made her mother stop, so for two more years Felicity had to help her mother clean Jeffrey's apartment so she could carry on her affair with Jake. Felicity felt like Cinderella with the wicked stepmother. But she didn't want the prince to come and rescue her. She was afraid of men.

Felicity was fifteen and looked like a young woman now, not a little girl anymore. She was tall and pretty, with her mother's slim, sexy body. The years of ballet lessons had given her slender, curvy legs and arms, a tiny waist, and perfect posture. But her sister Theodora still was so overweight that it was unhealthy, and she was getting bigger by the day, no matter what Carolee did to try to control her. They had thought that when she reached puberty she might lose weight, but that obviously was not to be. Whereas Felicity dealt with the tensions at home by becoming emotional, her sister sedated herself with food. Felicity cried when she was depressed, when she was afraid, when something or someone hurt her. The only time Theodora ever came near tears was when she was forbidden dessert. To her that was deprivation, pain, and ridicule, and something that Felicity didn't understand. If she had been fat like Theodora, Felicity thought, she would have been glad to have people help her stay on her diet.

Their father seemed to think that he had scared off Jake for good. A few times in the beginning he had come home unexpectedly just to check up, but when no one was there he was lulled back into his fantasy world where work took precedence over the needs of his family. He helped people who were sick or injured physically, whom he was not close to, whom he sometimes didn't even know, and for this he was treated with respect. Whatever happened at home he was able to ignore.

Then that spring, when the trees were just beginning to show their fresh new leaves at last, when the air was soft and the days were lengthening into mellow evenings, her mother fell apart. Carolee took to her bed for fourteen hours at a time and grieved and wept, she stopped leaving the house, she couldn't eat, and she refused to dress or comb her hair. She was a pathetic sight.

"Jake left me," she told her daughters. "It's over."

"Why?" Felicity asked.

"He found another woman who's single. She's single, so he can leave his wife for her. That's what he wanted. I couldn't leave your father. I would have lost you and this house."

You've told us that guilt-producing excuse often enough, Felicity thought. She was glad it was over, but still she couldn't help feeling sorry for her mother who was obviously suffering so much.

"I loved Jake," her mother said, in tears. "I never loved your father. I've refused to have sex with him for years."

"Why did you marry him?" Theodora ventured to ask in a whisper.

"I was young and stupid. I didn't know what I was doing. It was all a mistake."

That summer their mother became gaunt. Her cheeks were hollow, her eyes swollen, her hair hung in her eyes like a witch's hair. She told them she had lost twenty-five pounds. The weather was hot but she was always cold, putting on her bathrobe over the nightgown she wore all day, pulling it close, shivering. Her sharp elbows and knees protruded, her forearms and calves were just bone and ligament.

What power men have over women, Felicity thought. Having a man makes you happy, and not having one makes you miserable. Her mother, who had been a frightening figure, was now reduced to this wreck, too weak to chase her daughter around the house and hit her. Imagine losing twenty-five pounds from grief over a lover, Felicity thought. I hope she doesn't die....

But Carolee did not die, and when fall came she started fixing herself up and going out of the house again, and then she started to look better, and finally she was humming.

"I found someone new," she told Felicity. "He knows all kinds of celebrities. He's much more cosmopolitan and sophisticated than Jake was. I'll take you along to meet him. We'll have tea."

"You'll get caught," Felicity murmured, not wanting to go.

"Not if you're there," her mother said, smiling.

"How did you meet him anyway?"

"Through Jeffrey."

"Jeffrey?" Felicity said. "Is this one gay?"

"Of course not. I should know."

"You're not going to see him at Jeffrey's apartment, are you?" Felicity asked, dreading having to clean again.

"He has a place of his own," her mother said happily. "He's single. He belongs just to me."

So now began Carolee's elegant period, and every week Felicity had to join her mother and her mother's new lover, Ben, at Le Petit Grand tea room, where they pretended to be cultivated and English among the chink of china and the subdued conversation of old rich white people with nothing better to do. People stared at them and then looked away, pretending they weren't. Felicity had to keep reminding herself that they were staring because the three of them were black, and not because they knew her mother was having an affair.

Ben was very light-skinned, and he dressed as well as Jake had. Felicity had to admit that Ben was almost as good-looking as Jake, but she didn't like it when he pretended that her mother was his wife and that she was his daughter. Why don't you have a daughter of your own, she thought, annoyed and resentful. He told her he had never been married. He was obviously bad news, in any one of a number of ways.

She hadn't decided which way, because she hardly knew him, but she was sure it would reveal itself in time.

She was so on edge and tired of her life. She couldn't wait to go away to college, to law school, to get started being a lawyer, to get away from her mother and these domestic dramas. When she was accepted at the University of Michigan in Ann Arbor, she knew that at last she was on her way.

It was the time of rebellion in America, and nowhere more than on the college campuses. It was also the time of emerging Black Pride. Students, more than anybody, hated Nixon, because they felt he was a tyrant; because he was against liberals, blacks, Jews, and students; and mainly because of the war, which they were convinced was immoral and wrong. They were against the pig government, and the pig cops. When the National Guard killed four unarmed students during an antiwar demonstration at Kent State in Ohio the other students all over the country thought, "It could have been us."

Felicity's school was very politically active, with a large black student union. Now, for the first time, she began to look for her own racial identity. She went to meetings every week, to lectures on unity and Black Pride, read books to raise her consciousness, complained with the others about the lack of books on black history, and felt free to resent and speak against the white oppressor, the Man, instead of trying to be like him so he would accept her.

When she left home Felicity was still being forced to dress like her mother's little clone: matching bag and shoes, white gloves, pearls, every hair in place. As soon as she got to college, all that changed. She wore nothing but beat-up jeans and sexy little tops, and bought a few dashikis so she could dress like her African brothers and sisters. She tried in vain to grow a suitable afro. It was just soft curls, when she wanted impressive ethnic topiary, but no one seemed to mind. For the first time in her life she was popular, she had started to fit in somewhere at last.

She still had white friends, but now that she had started to date she dated only black men, holding fast to her emerging sense of herself. She was aware how immature she was when it came to men. Given her sexually precocious childhood it

seemed to her she should have been less uncomfortable and
frightened, but it apparently didn't work that way. Along
with their own voice her generation had delightedly discovered sexual freedom, but she had not. She couldn't help
thinking about her mother, who was so unhappily obsessed
with sex and love.

However, because without even being aware of it she had
absorbed a certain body language from watching her mother
all her life, Felicity was naturally seductive and charming
with men. The tilt of her head, her pout, her smile were all
Carolee. Felicity listened to her dates talk as if what they had
to say was the most important thing in the world, even when
it was idiotic. Although she hadn't done it purposely her
way of dressing was provocative, and she was curvy and
pretty. Her dates could hardly keep their hands off her. But
when she got frightened, which always happened when they
tried to get physical, she withdrew. She quickly got the reputation of being a cockteaser. That was the last thing she
wanted to be, but she didn't know how else to handle her
fear. Her freshman year she remained a virgin.

The college meals were starchy, unbalanced, and abundant. For the first time in her life, Felicity started to overeat.
At breakfast she broke the sweet, crumbly muffins apart, noticing the streaks of grease they left on the plate, and ate
three. No matter how bad the food was, she devoured it. At
night when she was studying she was always available to go
out for pizza with her friends, who had rejected dinner although she hadn't. Suddenly she was hungry all the time, a
strange sort of hunger because it was more like an emptiness
that sighed through her body, something less akin to appe-
tite than to fear. Chewing and swallowing sedated her.
Wasn't everybody scared their first year at college? So many
choices, all that freedom... Felicity looked in the mirror, trying in vain to close her jeans, and knew she was getting fat.
She thought: Theodora.

When she went home for Christmas her jeans were a
larger size and she was wearing baggy sweaters outside
them so her mother wouldn't notice. The dashikis she had
bought at college made a good disguise, too. She was afraid

to weigh herself because she knew it would make her depressed.

"You look a little chubby," Carolee said, eyeing her.

"I always blow up when I'm expecting my period," Felicity said offhandedly.

At the end of her first year at college when she came home for summer vacation she was even fatter. There was cellulite where none had existed before, and she felt heavy and logy. She got on the scale for the first time since the previous September, with trepidation, and discovered she had gained twenty-four pounds.

"What have you done to yourself?" her mother cried. "You look like your sister!"

Theodora sulked and turned away.

"I'm on a diet as of this minute," Felicity said.

If her mother could lose twenty-five pounds in a few months without even trying, surely she could lose twenty-four over the summer when she was trying very hard. Her sister turned back to look at her with a sardonic expression that said: Join the club, and Felicity thought: Never.

Felicity had learned about syrup of ipecac at college, from her roommate, Iris, who was slender and popular. She bought a bottle, and all that summer, no matter what she ate, she made herself vomit afterward. Ipecac had the nastiest taste imaginable, and after she threw up particularly violently her eyeballs were red and she was afraid they might bleed, but the extra weight began coming off fast. The ipecac also made it possible for her to binge whenever she felt so empty she couldn't stand it anymore. She stuffed herself only when no one was around. Full or empty, her stomach hurt all the time.

She never talked to Theodora about it because somehow Theodora seemed to represent the enemy. But Felicity thought about her sister gnawing constantly, like some kind of huge, neurotic woodchuck, and for the first time she thought she understood her sister's pain. She also wondered if Theodora had *chosen* to become the outsider in that family, rejecting her mother's ideal of womanhood and thus rejecting her mother's unhappy life. She didn't discuss that with her sister either. They had never clung together when they were threatened by danger, they had never been close. Each in her own way had been too busy trying to survive. It was sad, but at the bottom of her soul each of them knew she would turn on the other one if she had to, because that was the way it was.

By the fall Felicity was thin again, even thinner than she had been before the episode, and her mother was so relieved she bought her a new wardrobe for her second year at college—letting her pick the clothes herself—and a small scale for her dorm room. When she got back to school, Felicity went to a doctor her friends knew about who gave her a prescription for diet pills. Everyone was taking diet pills, and everyone knew they were full of speed, but nobody thought there was anything bad about that including the doctor who prescribed them for her. The pills and her willpower kept the gorging at bay, and whenever it overtook her Felicity knew she had the disgusting ipecac. It was no big deal; it was just what you had to do.

Her junior year she was finally ready to have a real boyfriend. His name was Lincoln, and she met him at a school party. A friend had brought him because he didn't go to college anymore; he had dropped out as a way of rebelling against his successful parents. She identified with that; she was rebelling, too. He was dabbling with writing, with painting. He was sitting on the floor, next to the window, his dark chiseled features outlined by the glow of the setting sun, his fingers long and sensual the way she thought an artist's should be, and the first thing she thought when she saw him was, That's for me. He was good-looking, smart, and fun to be with. He was the man who taught her about sex. When they started going together she was so timid she wouldn't even let him put the lights on when they made love, but he was very gentle and persistent, and eventually Felicity was able to relax. She was a child starving for love, and Lincoln made her feel safe, made her understand that lovemaking could be a generous thing, a sharing and giving of love. Soon they were living together off and on, in her off-campus apartment, for which she paid the rent.

She and Lincoln stayed together while she finished college. When they talked about their plans for the future Felicity didn't know how they would ever work it out. She wanted to go to law school; he didn't know what he wanted. He was very bright, but she was beginning to think he was much too unfocused about life. He wasn't even serious about his art. None of the things he wanted to do fit in with her own middle-class upbringing and her upwardly mobile ambitions, which had solidified through her new sense of entitlement. When Felicity brought him home to meet her family, her mother at first couldn't cater to him enough, under the guise of encouraging the romance (but Felicity suspected she was flirting, and watched helplessly); and then when Carolee realized he was really very interested in Felicity she became violently opposed to him as a good-enough husband for her daughter. Now she didn't want Felicity to see him at all.

"If you don't break up with him you'll get trapped," her mother told her. "Listen to me; I know."

Felicity tried to persuade Lincoln to go back and finish college and consider going to law school afterward, but he didn't want to. Then she got into Harvard Law.

As a woman and a black she felt she had two extra reasons to be the best she could, and she studied long hours; and while she studied, Lincoln played. It was obvious by now that they were drifting apart, but she didn't know what to do about it. Then one day he simply didn't come home. He stayed away for three weeks, and she was frightened and miserable wondering where he was while her mind wandered in class and she worried about keeping up with the work. Sometimes when she was trying to study in the library she found herself dissolving into tears instead, in front of anyone who cared to look. And then he came back. He told her he had been with another woman all that time but that it was over and he was back now.

Felicity didn't know why he had told her about his affair, but when she discovered he had been cheating on her something inside her went cold and dead. It was over, and there was nothing Lincoln could do to make things the way they had been before. She made him move out.

I shouldn't settle for a man like him, Felicity thought to console herself, and concentrated even harder on her studies.

Her mother was delighted they had broken up, and gave herself the credit for showing Felicity what a bad mistake she could have made. They both finally agreed on something, that a much better man would come along.

After all, look what had happened to hopeless Theodora! A brilliant student, she had gotten into Radcliffe, and in her junior year, Theodora became engaged to Calvin Longman, a black Harvard Medical School student with a great future and who didn't mind how enormous she was. This happy ending for her was a complete shock and a wild stroke of luck. She was so secretive that no one in the family had even known she had a boyfriend. Felicity thought Calvin was unattractive, not that it mattered; Theodora was in love.

Theodora and Calvin were married in the family's church in Detroit the day after her graduation. Felicity thought they must have bought all the white tulle in the whole city. Theodora looked like a galleon in full sail coming down the aisle, and she had a long train that hadn't been seen since royalty. The radiant couple were hoping to have four children and live in Cambridge, where he would do research. It was also the day after Felicity's graduation from Harvard Law School, but she attended the wedding alone.

Felicity was pleased for her sister, who had never had much happiness, but she was also bewildered and—she had to face it—jealous. How is it that she picked the right one for her right away and I have such bad taste, she wondered. Am I stupid? Maybe it's because Theodora knew to grab her chance, and my chance just hasn't come yet.

Thinking this made her feel better. When the right man comes along, I'll know, Felicity told herself over and over. If it can happen for Theodora, of course it can happen for me, too. And my husband will be a winner. I feel it, I know it. Someone wonderful will come along for me soon.

FOURTEEN

Eve had been struggling in Hollywood for four years. When she looked at her friends, who were also trying to be actors, she realized she wasn't any worse off than they were, but that was not what she had intended for her life. She knew she was special. She had an agent who still believed in her, although Beverly hadn't gotten her any movie roles or, in fact, anything but go-sees that seldom turned into auditions, and she had begun to wonder if her agent was any good. She still had faithful Juan, who was doing so well as a house painter he had put his dreams of being a star on the back burner for now. She had never been a woman who needed a man to represent her in the world, so if Juan didn't want to be an actor that was his business, although she thought it was a waste. As long as he paid his share of the rent....

But Eve had known all along that she had never been in love with him, and now she began to wonder if it was time for her to move on, go East. Friends she had made were telling her the work was in New York. There was theater in New York, and off-Broadway, where you could be discovered, and there was television, and longterm work in soap operas. Los Angeles was a one company town, in some ways a very small town, and while this was good for developing contacts, it was also limiting.

Nicole was still with Eve's mother, who was getting impatient now that the baby had turned into an active little girl. Eve had hoped she would get so fond of her granddaughter that she would want to keep her, the way you read about from time to time in those custody battles, but no such luck. Even though Nicole wasn't actually living with her, Eve had to pay most of her support, as well as take care of herself, and she was always looking for ways to make extra cash.

Another waitress who was also an actress, her friend Joanne had been moonlighting as a clown at children's birthday parties. That summer she talked Eve into trying it. The pay was very good for only a couple of hours on a Sunday afternoon, and she would be in a billowy clown suit, a red wig, and white face paint, so no one would know her. Besides, there wouldn't be anyone there she knew. They were rich movie executives and stars, and their wives, and the little brats she was to entertain. The husbands probably wouldn't even be there, except for the birthday father. She would blow up balloons, keep up a clever patter, do rudimentary magic tricks that she had learned from Joanne, give out party favors, and generally make a fool of herself. Joanne told her she could think of it as another kind of acting experience, but Eve was dreading it anyway. She didn't even like children. But money was money.

It was a hot day. The party was in a mansion in Beverly Hills, on Crescent Drive, or more precisely outside the house, where the kids couldn't do much damage. In the driveway there was a pony wearing bows in his mane and ribbons on his saddle, and there was a man dressed in white holding his halter so the kids could take turns riding around. Eve left her car with the valet parking guy who had been hired for the event and, in her full clown costume and makeup, carrying her knapsack filled with magic tricks, went out back by the swimming pool.

The birthday girl and her friends were already there, some with their mothers or governesses, and the lone father, who had nothing to do because there was a professional cameraman taking the home movies. Most of the parents would come back later to pick their kids up. Some of the kids were all dressed up, and others had changed into bathing suits. Eve looked at the pool longingly, and at the lucky brats jumping into it. She was bathing only in sweat. She could tell this would be a long party.

"Hello, hello," she said with a fake chuckle. "I'm Yahoo the Clown, and we're going to have a good time."

"Are you a boy or a girl?" one little boy asked, poking her.

"You'll never know," Eve snapped. She saw the mother looking at her peculiarly. "I mean, I'm just a clown person," Eve corrected herself. "You can call me Yahoo."

The first part of the party she had to wander around and be sociable, and then, before the ice cream and cake, she had to do her act. It must be over ninety out here, Eve thought resentfully. The little brats were the age of her own daughter, and her daughter had never had such an expensive party with a clown and a pony.

Sometimes she thought about her daughter and her feelings surprised her. For instance now, when she had to act like a clown for the extra money so she could send it to her mother to buy Nicole just basic clothes to replace the ones she'd grown out of. Part of her felt embittered when she thought of the burden of another person in her life, but another part felt badly that her daughter couldn't have any of the advantages these kids had. Nicole was getting cuter all the time, and she would have looked wonderful in one of those party dresses from Bambola that cost as much as the whole check Eve was going to receive today, the dresses the little girls here were rolling in the grass in. What did they care when they probably had a closetful at home?

She was so tired of scrimping and saving, of being poor, of having to parade herself in front of strangers who rejected her before she had a chance to say more than a sentence. Once she had even been rejected at an audition because she "stood out too much." Wasn't that what they wanted? You always noticed the person with star quality.

Eve blew up a balloon and deftly shaped it into an animal, bowed, and presented it to the birthday girl, who smiled. She made a camera appear from her sleeve and gave it to the kid, too, then another camera for someone else, and another. Some party favors. Where she came from you got gum.

"Me! Me, Yahoo! Me next!" the kids were clamoring. A few more years and they would be so jaded she would have to produce car keys for them.

Eve helped herself to some lemonade. She couldn't perspire through the white greasepaint on her face and she felt as if her skin was burning. In New York it would be cool, and there would be seasons. Her old car needed expensive re-

pairs almost constantly now. In New York she wouldn't
need a car. She would sell the heap. Beverly could probably
get her more work in New York than she'd had here, because
Hollywood actresses all looked so bland. Eve began to feel
she had an Eastern energy, which is why she had never fit in
anywhere, not in Florida, and not here.

"Showtime!" she announced.

The little kids all sat down on the grass to watch her. Their
mothers and governesses were under the cool roof of the
patio; they were no fools. Eve sang some kids' songs, told
some jokes, and did her magic tricks, but the kids were not
impressed. They had seen clowns before. All they were interested in was more presents, and the chance to play and be
wild. It was time for the Mickey Mouse watches. That got
their attention again for a few minutes. While Eve was dis-
tributing this bounty she automatically kept track of how
many cameras and watches she had not yet given away,
since she was planning to appropriate one of each for her
own daughter. By now she was an expert at filching, having
done it on a minor level in restaurants for years.

When her act was finished the kids raced for the birthday
cake. The adults had canapés and champagne. Eve took a
break to go to the bathroom, which was a major project since
she had to take off the clown suit, and on her way there she
picked up a couple of watches and cameras that the kids had
already abandoned and tucked them into her knapsack with
her magic stuff, along with the watch and camera she had
kept back. She might as well take souvenirs for Juan and herself, too.

When she got out of the bathroom two of the kids were
crying. "Somebody took my camera," one of them wailed.

"Where's my watch? I want my watch. I want my watch,
Mommy. Mommy, I want my watch."

"Yahoo, give her another one," the birthday mother said.
She was all dressed up in tight silk jeans and high heels and
a ton of diamonds, and Eve knew her for one of those young
Beverly Hills matrons who had to drive a Bentley into town
to have lunch and go shopping when she lived three blocks
away. Well, how could a woman like that carry a package, or
walk in those heels? She never had to hike to the bus stop

twice a day the way I did, Eve thought, resenting her and her money and privilege and fancy house.

"There are no more," Eve said, opening her eyes wide.

"That can't be. I bought extra ones."

"Yahoo took them," a little girl said. "I saw him."

Eve turned and glared at the little girl, who was three feet high and standing there with her tiny hands on her hips and her button eyes filled with smug malice. "Yahoo is neither a he nor a she," Eve said. "Yahoo is a clown."

"Well, do you have more?" the mother said.

"No."

"You do, too. I saw you," the kid said.

"You are very short, and you are mistaken."

The kid kicked her in the ankle.

"That's it," Eve said. "I'm leaving." She turned to the mother. "Give me my check and I'm out of here."

"We need to talk privately," the woman said, taking Eve by the arm. She led her to the kitchen, where a maid and a caterer were fussing around. "You are not to take the party favors for yourself," she said.

"I wouldn't dream of it."

"Do you mind if I look in your bag?"

Rage filled Eve like a fever. She wanted to tear the woman's teased, bleached blonde hair out by its stringy roots. "You dare to accuse me?" Eve snapped.

"I just want to see. If you didn't take them you'll let me look."

"What do you think this is, fucking Customs?" Eve said, having seen movies about smuggling although she had never been anywhere. "Are you the fucking government?"

"You don't have to be obscene."

"You don't have to be such a bitch."

"Get out of my house."

"Give me my check."

"I'll give it to you in the driveway."

"You'll give it to me now." Sweat was pouring down her body even though the kitchen was air-conditioned, and the itching of her sensitive facial skin under the greasepaint was almost more than she could bear. Her red clown wig felt like a hornet's nest. Eve pulled off the wig and grabbed a handful of paper towels and rubbed at her face. Her hair was wet and matted, and she was sure she had a rash. "You've given me a fucking allergy attack from this stupid costume," she screamed. "I ought to charge you hazard pay."

"I ought to call the police," the woman screamed back. She grabbed Eve with her slim, muscular arms, iron-strong from tennis, and pulled her out of the kitchen, through the back door, and out to the driveway. The little kids who had been lined up to ride the pony were giggling their heads off. This was the first thing about the party that they really liked.

"My check!" Eve said, holding her knapsack closed with one hand, the other hand outstretched.

The woman took the folded check from the pocket of her silk jeans, where she'd had it all along, and finally gave it to her. "You'll never work for my friends again," she said.

"I don't intend to."

A man was standing there, having come to pick up his kid. A skinny guy with glasses. Eve recognized him. It was Sophocles Birnbaum, from her long ago waitress days at the Confident Onion, and he recognized her, too. She'd read in the trades that he had gotten even more successful since she had last seen him. It had never occurred to her before that he had a private life as well as a professional one, that he had a wife, and a kid who went to birthday parties, like a normal person. She didn't know if she should say hello to him or pretend she was someone else.

She didn't have to choose. He cringed away and sidled into the house, his face turned away, as if he had never seen her before and was not seeing her now. She wondered if it was tact or if he really didn't want to know her.

Eve's rage abated and she suddenly felt terribly sad. The valet parking guy had come with her car and she got into it and drove away. As she drove down the clean quiet streets under tall palm trees, past mansions that seemed uninhabited, all the things she had once dreamed would someday be hers, Eve's eyes filled with tears, and she realized with a vengeance how much she hated this phony town.

When she left for Florida to see her mother and daughter for Christmas, it was with all her belongings, on her way to move to New York. She had parted from Juan with more nostalgia on his part than on hers, and from Hollywood with none. She knew Juan would find another girlfriend in fifteen minutes. People left other people and places all the time. If she ever came back here it would be as a star, or not at all.

Eve had not seen Nicole since last Christmas, and she was surprised at the change in her. She was five years old, almost ready to start school. She was bigger than she had seemed in her pictures, which anyway were six months old. Nicole looked just like Eve, as if all Eve's genes had been dominant. Her posture and body language were just like her grandmother's, which was not surprising, so she gave the appearance of being a tough little kid, but she smiled all the time. Eve could not imagine from whom she had inherited this sunny disposition. Her wardrobe consisted of jeans, just as Eve's had, but times and fashions had changed since Eve was a child and everybody else dressed like Nicole. She did not have to feel out of place and ugly the way Eve had.

"You did a good job with her, Mom," Eve said. She gave Nicole all her presents but forgot to give her a hug. Nicole didn't seem to care.

"Thank you," her mother said. "And Nicole, what do you say to your mommy?"

"Thank you, Mommy."

"She has a Southern accent," Eve said disapprovingly.

"What do you expect?"

Eve hadn't even thought about what she should expect. She had gotten rid of most of her Florida accent over the past years through her own hard work, feeling it would limit her choice of roles, and now with this difference between them the child seemed even less like her own.

"How long are you staying with us?" her mother asked.

"I'll leave the day after New Year's. I sublet a friend's apartment in Greenwich Village, and later I'll get something of my own."

"Then you're planning to settle in New York City?"

"You bet. I'm finished with Horridwood."

"Horridwood!" Nicole said, and laughed.

"She has your sense of humor," her mother said.

"I didn't think you'd noticed I had one," Eve said.

"Oh, I noticed."

Christmas dinner was just as dismal and lonely as it had always been. There was her mother and her daughter and herself, the scraping of fork and spoon on plates, the sparse and forced conversation, the hole of sadness in the pit of her stomach when she thought about other families having raucous and jolly Christmases full of people. At least with Nicole there, obliviously chatty about the events of her little life, it gave her and her mother something to talk about. The holiday dragged Eve back to her isolated and frustrating childhood, all those years she had dreamed of getting out, and she reminded herself that she was on her way, that she wasn't a helpless little girl anymore.

She helped her mother wash up while Nicole went out to play with her loot. "Next year," her mother said, "I'm going to have Christmas dinner at a hotel, in the hotel restaurant."

"We could have done that this year," Eve said.

"Well, this was a farewell."

"To what?"

"To Nicole. To you. You're going to take her with you to New York and pretend to be a real mother for the first time in your life, and I'm taking Logan Bewstar in as a partner and letting him run the farm while I get myself a nice job in Miami Beach and see some of the high life."

"A job as what?" Eve asked, incredulous.

"A bookkeeper. I've been doing all the paperwork around here forever, you know. A farm is a business just like anything else."

"But…"

"But nothing. You think you're the only person who has a right to be free? I sacrificed my whole life for you, and now it's my turn to have some fun before I'm too old to notice I'm having it."

"What sacrifices did you make for me?" Eve asked.

"Who did you think I did all this for, myself? I did the best I could. If you don't like it, that's just too bad. How did you think you got to be so independent? Because I taught you how. I made you special. Now, go out and do whatever you're supposed to do with your life. I've got all Nicole's clothes washed and ironed, and I bought her a new suitcase for her toys. She hates eggs, you ought to know, and she likes to sleep with a night light on. She sleeps with her teddy bear, and you have to read her Dr. Seuss before she'll close her eyes."

"Who is this Logan Bewstar?" Eve demanded.

"You remember him."

"No I don't. Is he your boyfriend?"

Her mother laughed, a deep happy laugh that came from a place inside her that Eve had never known existed. "Boyfriend? God, no. If you saw him you wouldn't have to ask that question. He's a twenty-eight-year-old hippie with long hair and a girlfriend, but he loves the idea of a chicken farm and he's going to do a good job. It's funny, isn't it? I thought my way of life would become obsolete with the new generation coming along, but kids like Logan want peace and quiet and I'm the one moving on."

"Miami Beach is hardly the high life," Eve said.

"It is to me."

"What is Nicole going to think about all this?"

"As if you care."

"I do care," Eve said, insulted.

"I'll tell her tonight, and it will give her a week to get used to the idea. She knows you're her mother, and she knew you were coming back someday to get her. I've always told her that. She was looking forward to her adventures in Hollywood, but now she'll look forward to the ones in New York."

Nicole was going to live with her. Eve felt as if her mother had dumped an eight-hundred-pound gorilla in her living room, but this was not a joke. "How am I supposed to pursue my career when I have to take care of a child?" she asked.

"You and only a million other people have that problem," her mother said cheerfully. "I suggest day care."

That night Eve couldn't sleep at all. She went outside and walked down the dirt road, in the humid tropical night, under the full, silky moon, cursing John Hawke's dick and testosterone and romantic teenage heart. She cursed herself for having been young and stupid on nights like this one, when she thought sex was innocent pleasure. If she had ever thought she could escape from her past she was mistaken, because Nicole would always be there to remind her.

She went back to the house where she had grown up. In a way, she thought, it was right that she take her child, even though she was dreading the responsibility and the added financial burden. It would be cruel to make Nicole live the lonely life she had lived. At least with her the kid would have some fun.

Eve looked up at the second-floor bedroom that had been hers. Now it was—for a few more days anyway—her daughter's. Well, Eve thought, it's you and me, kid. She had heard the line in a movie when the curmudgeonly man didn't want to take the spunky orphan, but was stuck with him. It's you and me, kid.

The house was lighted by moonlight, with a bright, glossy sheen. At the window she saw her daughter's small face, looking out at the only world she had ever known. So she couldn't sleep, either. There she was, probably wide awake with excitement, finally fulfilling her wish to be with Mommy at last, in show business. Eve walked closer. She didn't know if Nicole saw her or not; she seemed lost in a daydream of her own. Then she got close enough to see that Nicole's face was wet with tears.

Tears were pouring out of Nicole's eyes and dripping off her chin. Believing herself to be unobserved, she made no effort to wipe them away. Her mouth stretched into a miserable sideways figure eight and her shoulders began shaking. What Eve was looking at was not a fellow adventurer off to see the wizard but a terrified, sobbing child.

Eve suddenly realized that her mother had either deceived her or deceived herself. Nicole didn't want to go away with Eve any more than Eve wanted to take her. What had her mother expected? Nicole hardly even knew her. And there was nothing either of them could do about it. Eve knew how her mother was when she had made up her mind. Nicole looked down and saw her then, and looked startled; then she turned away quickly and went into the private darkness of her room.

She was stuck with the kid. And the kid was stuck with her.

FIFTEEN

Gara and Carl had been married for ten years, and she was always surprised that she had been happy for so long. It was as if marriage to him, although it involved some inevitable compromises that she really didn't mind, was a vacation from the pain and self-doubt she had lived with all of her life before he came along. The years were a kind of healing. When she passed the magic cutoff year her gynecologist had warned her about, Gara realized that unless she now made a great effort to get pregnant, which she did not want to do, she was probably unlikely ever to have a child of her own, and she felt much more relieved than nostalgic.

Carl was a welcome barrier between her and her mother, and her father seemed to like him. She had been saved from ten years of dating. She felt as if she fit into a place where her parents finally accepted her—at least, as much as her mother was capable. She was a happily married woman with a flourishing career and two nice stepchildren. Cary and Eric were in prep school and college now; they were sixteen and eighteen, tall, well-built, healthy, good-looking boy-men. She saw them much less often these days, but when the four of them had dinner in a restaurant she felt proud at the family appearance they must be making, and warm in the knowledge that they all got along.

Every day of their married life Carl told her at least once that he loved her. At night in bed he held her in his arms until one of them fell asleep, and when he woke up in the middle of the night he always reached for her. She knew how unique all that was. She heard about marital problems from her friends, and from her patients, and everything she read told of broken promises, changed goals and expectations, and loss. It seemed the divorce rate was climbing every minute. She was constantly aware of how lucky she was, and worried that her husband would die.

Carl's father had died unexpectedly a few years earlier of a heart attack while running for a commuter train, the year before his planned retirement. Gara imagined—briefly, because it was much too frightening—what it would be like never to see Carl again, to have him leave for work on an ordinary day and then not come home, and after this terrified moment she always flung herself into her happy, loving marriage with more consideration, more affection, more gratitude. She did not yet think of her parents growing old and sick or even dropping dead; the mystical power they still had over her made her think they would live for a very long time.

It was her husband she brooded about, his health and welfare, the muggers, murderers, accidents, plane crashes, all the varied terrible things that could happen to him. Sometimes she wondered if this was her secret way of keeping excitement alive—by imagining him snatched away from her and then miraculously restored. She knew you had to shake yourself up from time to time in order not to let a relationship grow stale, and if her method was morbid, at least it worked. She wondered why she needed it. It was unrealistic to expect things to be perfect all the time, but that was the way she was, even now.

Carl's way of keeping the excitement in their marriage seemed to be the brief business trips he took to Europe without her. When he left her it was never with more than one or two days' notice, and she was never sure exactly which day he would be back until he appeared, although she always knew where he was. He called her every day from his travels, came home laden with presents and funny stories and anecdotes, and as soon as he came back into their apartment he made love to her as if he had been starving for her touch.

"Don't you ever worry that he might be cheating when he's on a trip?" her friends sometimes asked her.

"No. I'm sure he's not, but if he is, it obviously makes him want me more." She really meant that, but she thought her calm acceptance of the idea of his perfidy was possible only because she knew he was faithful.

When Carl was in Europe and she was in New York Gara never told her parents he was away. She knew her mother would nag her to come for dinner every night, as if she were incapable of being by herself, and try to insinuate herself under her grown daughter's very skin the way she always had. There would be too many questions, too much clutching, too much criticism, too much worry. May could never comprehend that Gara actually liked to be alone, or more likely May just didn't care what Gara wanted.

Sometimes Gara and Carl were able to travel together, and it was like another honeymoon. Gara loved being part of his art world, which she thought was glamorous, and she enjoyed listening to his friends talk about new painters and new paintings, and hear their gossip about people she now knew. He had such a capacity for enjoying life, so much enthusiasm, and he wanted her to share it. He was only ten years older than she was, but sometimes she felt like his child because he was so protective of her happiness. She saw no conflict between being the independent woman he admired and her total reliance on his love. In fact, she thought, his love gave her the wings to fly. He was the good parent she had never had.

One night when Carl was away, Gara took her old family photo album out of the bookcase and leafed through it, trying to figure out the past. There she was, a shyly smiling child at the beach with her parents, having been told to smile for the camera, her mother's camera smile too large, too fake, her father's a little diffident, a little proud. They were just an ordinary family on vacation in the late 1940s, the hardworking husband and father, the housewife and mother, the child for whom they would move the world. Gara remembered then the other pictures she had only in her mind: her father teaching her how to ride a bike, holding the handlebars while he trotted beside her; taking her to swim in the waves, his hand under her stomach, telling her not to be afraid because he was right there. When had she lost him?

He was an ordinary father of the period, away working or at home silent behind his newspaper, abdicating control of the home and the child to his wife because the child was a daughter. He echoed May's edicts and opinions like a vice-president. If it ever occurred to him that May was too close, too smothering, that she was recklessly trampling down every possible boundary in order to be closer to her child, who was her dream and her little lover, her image in a better mirror, the object of her unacknowledged jealousy, if it really ever occurred to him he pushed the disloyal thought away. He was no worse than any man of his time, and better than many. Men were not supposed to be able to understand women. Had he known his beloved daughter was unhappy? Had he thought that was normal?

Maybe she should have told him if he didn't know. In an odd way Gara had always protected her father because she wanted him to approve of her. But there was more—what if he did know how unhappy she was, and he simply didn't care?

She had asked him once, years ago: "Why don't you ever defend me against Mother when you know she's lying?"

"Because you're going to grow up and go away," he had answered, "and I'm going to be with Mother forever."

Well, she thought, that's an answer. She had been touched by his simple, childlike honesty, the acknowledgment of his weakness in this family struggle. It had not occurred to her to be angry that no one would take her side. She knew that was her problem—she lived in the same body with her anger and didn't even know it was there until afterward when she pulled out the events again and looked at them. But she *had* gone away, and the fights didn't matter now; she had escaped. She put the album back on the shelf.

The next day she told her mother that Carl had a meeting—which was not true, he was still in France—and accepted an invitation to come to her parents' apartment for dinner that night. Gara supposed the ambivalence and the fantasy would always be with her: yearning to visit her kind, interesting, supportive parents, missing them, making the phone call, not able to accept that the parents she would visit were the ones she'd always had.

"Didn't Mother prepare a delicious dinner?" her father said. He looked at May with tenderness. Actually it wasn't delicious, it was strange: a watery brown gravy with small cubes of mystery meat and carrots in it. Perhaps he was worried that she would die; perhaps they were all obsessed with death.

"Yes," Gara lied. "What is it?"

"Steak and bologna stew," her mother said. "I made it up."

This is the last time I eat here, Gara thought. She wished she could keep the vow. Her mother had always done strange things with leftovers, but lately it had been getting worse. The only thing you knew for sure was that it would be fattening.

"I bought a new fur coat," May said.

"Oh? What kind?" Gara asked.

"*Seal*," May said. Her tone was defiant, waiting for a comment. She knew what she had done.

The animal rights movement was a growing new issue in the country. Pictures of adorable little white seal pups being clubbed to death were shown on television news or came in the mail; their dark-eyed, whiskered baby faces appeared on stamps, and were shown in ads in which their blood soaked the snow. You were ashamed to wear a seal coat and you would never buy one. You bought a mink. Minks were still considered nasty ferrets.

Gara said nothing, but she was shocked. I should have known, she thought. Only May would do that. She probably wanted to buy the last one before they got banned.

"I'll leave it to you in my will," May said. "You can have it taken in."

"I was thinking of getting puppy," Gara said.

"Getting a puppy? You want that mess around the house?"

"A puppy coat."

May peered at her, trying to figure out if it was a joke. "You always pick on me," she said. "You always misinterpret me. Why are you so hostile?"

"Please don't argue," her father begged mildly, but, as usual, he was saying it to Gara. They ate their coconut cake in silence, and drank their coffee, and when he had finished her father excused himself to watch the news on television.

Gara cleared the table quickly so she would not have to watch May eat the rest of the large cake, and then she excused herself, too, to go home. As she stood at the door, her mother's lips sucked hungrily at her cheek.

"Ah," May said, enraptured, kissing her, eating her. "Yum yum yum, delicious. My first-born and last-born baby girl."

That was the last time Gara ever saw her father alive. He had never been sick a day in his life, and a week later he was found slumped over his desk at his law office, having quietly bled to death of an ulcer no one had known he had. Her mother called to tell her, choking back tears she should not have felt ashamed to shed. How could you be a hysteric and a stoic at the same time?

Gara had felt death in the air that last night at dinner, but it had never occurred to her that it would be her father's. She had not hugged or kissed him when she left, because they never touched. She had never even had a chance to say goodbye properly; as usual he had left her to her mother, and now it was too late. Gara felt her heart breaking. *I saw a man upon the stair, a little man who wasn't there...* She had lost him years ago, and now she had lost him again before she was able to make the connection they both would have wanted.

It was her mother, she sensed, who would live a long time and surprise everybody. A perfect textbook candidate for a heart attack or a stroke, May didn't even talk about dieting, much less try it. She never exercised, never had. Gara had long since stopped trying to win a discussion of any kind with her. Her aunt and uncle—her mother's brother and sister—were both in therapy, had been for years, but it had never occurred to May that she had any problems having a nicer daughter wouldn't fix. Once, a few years ago, worried about May's unhappiness, Gara had had the temerity to suggest she seek help.

"You're the one who needs a psychiatrist," May had snapped, "not me. A girl who can't even be friends with her mother."

"I'm not a girl anymore."

"You're my little girl. You always will be. No one will ever love you as much as your parents do."

And if they don't love me enough, or in the right way, or for myself, Gara thought, is this the best I can expect from anyone? The mixed messages twined around her like smothering vines, and even now, although she was someone who was considered capable of solving other people's problems, Gara knew she had many of her own she had merely pushed aside. My husband loves me more than you do, Gara thought, but of course she would never say it.

SIXTEEN

The songs were sweet that year, in 1970. The Carpenters sang the mellifluous "Close To You," Simon and Garfunkel harmonized on "Bridge over Troubled Water," Diana Ross promised "Ain't No Mountain High Enough" in her velvet voice. And in the midst of all this loving niceness Billie Redmond entered the music scene with a shriek of raw energy and sexuality and lyrics that were unafraid. People didn't necessarily like her, but they had to notice her.

Harry Lawless had put together the band, Bandit, as he had planned, and Billie was the singer. There was gangly, red-haired Andy on bass; frog-faced Toad on drums; scrawny, twitchy Lenny on keyboard; and even scrawnier, twitchier Legs on guitar.

"I guess you must have picked the four ugliest musicians in the world to make me look better, huh?" Billie said to him.

"They're great musicians, though," Harry said. "And they always have plenty of women on the road, so they can't be that ugly."

"Oh, hey," she said, and shrugged. "Music is an aphrodisiac. We all know that."

It was the most exciting, happiest time of her life. The songs she wrote flowed out of her as if she weren't even writing them herself. Sometimes they were very good. It was as if finally she was really free to say whatever was in her heart and soul without worrying what people would think. What she didn't say in the lyrics she got across in the agony and energy of her singing. She stamped across the stage, her long hair flying, mike in her hand, her head back, her slender throat arched, her voice soaring out, her voice that was always too big for the room, even now. Sometimes she picked up her guitar and played along with the guys—her guys, her band, and everybody knew it.

They were touring all the time, booked in a variety of places from the pits to quite decent, with their own bus. Billie discovered what made Lenny and Legs so skinny and twitchy, and Toad so taciturn: drugs, which they offered to share with her. Cocaine and dexamyl to get up, Seconal and Placidyl to get down, grass and alcohol to stay even.

She and Andy took very little. He was the youngest member of the band, and still read the Bible and wrote to his parents. Billie treated him like a sweet younger brother. Bored on the bus, she and Andy shared a joint, they drank wine together, they split the scored blue dexamyl tablets with their thumbnails and each took half, saying, "Just a nibble," while the other guys laughed and said, "What are you, rabbits?"

"You're the rabbits," Billie would laugh. "How many dumb girls have you fucked so far, are you keeping a list? I'm sending it in to the *Guinness Book of Records*."

They loved it when she flattered them that way. She didn't know if they liked her much or not, and she didn't care, because they got along with her and they played the music that made her come alive, and that was enough for her. They were just guys to her—nothing special, neither family nor friends, just people she worked with—because the backbone of her life was Harry.

When she wrote a love song the man she was writing it to was Harry Lawless; when she sang of ambitions and past grief, it was about the sad time before she had met him. The physical attraction they had for each other was constant and electric. He didn't take the bus with them, he flew, because he needed the time to manage his business. When he knocked on her motel room door their clothes were on the floor in a matter of seconds, they had to come before they could even speak, and then they spoke business and love mouth to mouth, entwined. His natural place was inside her. The lyrics she wrote were as explicitly sexual as she could get away with, considering the tenor of the times when love songs spoke of being near and looking for a friend. When a phrase was not about sex Billie saw it that way anyway; it was always Harry, "Like a rock..."

The end of that year they made their first album, on his Outlaw Records label. Harry named the album *Billie and the Bandits*, even though the band's name was still Bandit. He said the title had a nice ring to it. While they were cutting their album, Janis Joplin was cutting hers: *Pearl*. But before she finished it she died of a heroin overdose in a Hollywood hotel room. Billie cried when she heard about it. She thought it was terribly sad, and that Janis was foolish to have treated her life so casually. She was much too young and talented to have died and deprived the music world of what could have come afterward. Now Billie began to think that they were not alike at all, that their natures were actually very different.

Billie and the Bandits came out in the spring of '71, and out of it came her first hit single, "Texas Stars." She wrote the song for Harry, for their lives in the same place before they met, their lonely, ambitious yearning under the same Texas stars, and for their success and sad parting when they became stars in the other way. It was pure fantasy, but so were most love songs. It was also her most commercial song to date. Making it commercial, even when she had to stretch the truth, was her gift to Harry, and her gift in return was that it became a hit and she became, for the moment, a star.

When "Texas Stars" got on the charts that spring, Janis's song "Me and Bobby McGee" was number one. Again she and Billie were together, although again Janis didn't know it. She didn't even see her song become such a great success. Nevertheless, Billie thought it seemed a strange and fitting coincidence that she and Janis should be on the charts at the same time, as if one of them was saying hello when the other said goodbye.

Although she thought "Texas Stars" was a good song, Billie didn't believe the lines she had written about her and Harry parting. Everybody was writing songs about being gone in the morning. Have to wander, don't count on me. She didn't worry about tomorrow. Today was so excellent it could only get better; they were all on a roll. They even had money now, and what they made, they spent.

Harry bought a little townhouse in New York, in a mews, and the two of them lived there together whenever they had time off. It was also his office. They decorated their love nest together, in velvet and gilt and excess. An ashtray made from an amethyst geode shaped like a bowl hung from the ceiling on a gilded chain; unfortunately, though, they discovered that when you tried to put your cigarette out in it, it swung away. They got a good laugh out of that mistake. Their sheets were white satin, custom made. They gave parties, and they went to other people's parties in a limousine. People they didn't even know came to their parties, and they never saw them again. It didn't matter. They were rich and they wanted to look rich...or perhaps they only wanted to look it. In the seventies in New York you could live like royalty on less than one would think, and they did.

It was a narcissistic time. Youth, beauty, and sexuality were everything. Billie and Harry had all three, plus talent. He was running the business and she was the artist. Even though she knew something about business she let him take care of everything that had to do with money, except pay her taxes. She was a working woman and she wanted to know what she made. She didn't own anything herself in the way of tangible property, but she didn't care. She had everything she wanted.

She had a few days off so she went home to Plano to see her family. As a favor to her father she sang one song— "Texas Stars," of course—in the roadhouse. The place was packed because people knew she was in town, and the customers went wild. It was worth the whole trip to see her parents' faces while they watched that. She was a local hero now, and everybody made a big fuss over her. But it all seemed unreal, and she missed Harry. She couldn't wait to get home again, to New York, for New York was now her real home.

"You ought to know," Toad said, when she got back, "Harry's been fooling around."

"Why are you telling me this?" Billie asked. She didn't know whether she should believe him or not, but she didn't want to know, and she didn't want to give in to the hurt she was starting to feel.

"I'm a friend."

"Who is she?"

"Nobody. It was just while you were away."

What should she say? Harry's a sexy guy, why wouldn't he give in to temptation? I'm enough woman for any man and you're a liar? Did you ever hear of "Kill the messenger"?

Toad mistook her silence for devastation. "It wasn't any big deal," he said. "I know Harry loves you."

"I know he does, too," Billie said.

"Toad says you were cheating on me while I was in Plano," she told Harry. She was sorry she had said it. It was as if the mention of anything sordid touching, even momentarily, their perfect world tarnished it forever; they would always be in love but it would be a little different. Everybody cheated eventually, especially men, and especially in the music business. Sex was one of the perks.

"You'll hear a lot of lies," Harry said. "He'd like to get you for himself."

"Well, that makes him even stupider than I thought," Billie said. "But don't lie to me and don't cheat on me, Harry. It makes us ordinary."

His eyes gleamed for a second and she knew she'd gotten him where he lived. By now they both knew exactly how to win. "We'll never be ordinary," he said. "We love each other too much."

They were making plans for a second album. Billie and the band were writing their songs, but this time most of the ones Harry chose were hers. The one he thought had the greatest chance to take off was the one she had written after their brief confrontation, called "Don't Cheat on Me." Basically, what she said in the song was what she had said to him. The woman in it was not teary-eyed, not weak, just realistic. Helen Reddy had had a number-one hit song, "I Am Woman," and feminism was getting a foothold in America. But Helen Reddy's voice was sweet, and when she sang "Hear me roar," she sounded less like a lioness than a pussy-cat. Billie's strong voice and commanding concert image was still a step ahead of anyone else's.

Harry called the new album *Life Games.* When it came out in '73, "Don't Cheat on Me" became a hit as he had predicted. He bought a sleek, black Jaguar car and had his and Billie's initials painted on the door, entwined, in gold leaf. By summer "Don't Cheat on Me" was her second gold record,

Harry had made another big chunk of money, which was good because he had spent the first one, and they went to Paris on a lavish trip to celebrate. They stayed at the Ritz and drank martinis in the bar, all dressed up; they bought a lot of expensive clothes, and he bought the two of them matching eighteen-karat gold Tank watches at Cartier, which was near their hotel. Billie was not wearing silver bracelets anymore.

They never discussed marriage, although sometimes she thought about it. They were as good as married already, and Harry didn't seem like the kind of man who would take to being tied down in the conventional way. She thought if he proposed she would accept; if he didn't propose she wouldn't be the one to try to change things. As for children, married or not, the last thing she wanted at this point in her life was a baby.

On each of her albums there had been one single that took off, and the other ones didn't. This often happened, and people bought the albums for the song they liked, but it cost a lot more to produce an album than a record, and without more than the one hit the album didn't have such a long life, so Harry decided to start releasing Billie's new songs separately, hoping to get a hit each time, or at least more often than not, maximize his profit and cut his losses.

"But I thought we made all that money anyway," Billie said. "We sure lived like we had it."

"This will be better," he said. "An album is just an ego trip. You've had two. When we have enough hits I'll release a greatest hits collection."

"But how will we know which song will make it?"

"I was right the first two times, wasn't I?"

She nodded. She didn't feel it was a good idea to mention that the success of "Texas Stars" had been as big a surprise to Harry as it had been to her. She began to write with renewed vigor. Then Andy came up with a song she and Harry liked a lot, called "Dance to Death." It was more upbeat than what Billie was used to, but it had a great deal of appeal, and they cut it. It was an immediate hit, Andy's first. They were all jubilant, like people who had won at roulette. There was money, there was fun, and Harry was euphoric.

"You see?" Harry said. "I know what I'm doing." He
bought her a diamond bracelet.

Billie was happy for Andy, too. He had a steady girlfriend
now, and he didn't want to go on the road anymore after
they pushed "Dance to Death"; he wanted to be with a studio band and settle down. Studio musicians got more than
road guys, and he was planning to be a family man. That was
okay, too. These days you would go into a studio and cut a
record with one band, then go on the road and perform live
with a different one. The audience who came to a concert
didn't notice as long as the original band wasn't famous, like
the Beatles, and Bandit never had been so well known that
Andy would be missed. Band members changed all the time.
Andy promised he would keep submitting his new songs to
Harry for Billie to sing, and everybody was happy.

The next record they cut was a song Billie had written,
called "No Questions, No Answers." She thought probably
it was her best to date, more mature, more polished. She
could see herself growing creatively and she waited for the
recognition. But nothing happened to it—it bombed. Billie
and Harry couldn't figure out why. They hadn't really
known what people would take to and they were as mysti-
fied about what people rejected. If they knew what the public liked every time out they would have been as rich as the
Beatles. They decided to do another record right away and
make everything right again.

The next record they released, Andy's second, shocked
them by dying, too. Billie was depressed but not scared, because Harry hadn't changed their lifestyle so she knew they
were still all right. They had become too successful too fast
and were spoiled. This was closer to reality. This was the
way everybody else in the arts had to deal with a career, and
although it was disappointing you just had to keep going.

Then one night she woke up because Harry wasn't in the
bed with her, and when she went downstairs he was sitting
alone in the living room drinking bourbon.

"What?" she asked gently.

"I couldn't sleep."

"Is it business?"

"No, just thinking."

She stroked his hair. He didn't respond to her touch so she
knew it wasn't sex he needed at this moment, and she stayed
quiet.

"We hardly ever use that pool table," he said.

"I know. Just people do at parties."

"Want to play pool with me?" Harry said.

"Sure."

So there they were in the middle of the night, alone and
sad, playing pool under the yellow light, the click and skitter
of the balls the only sound. Billie realized then that it was one
of the only times they hadn't had music in the background.
Suddenly she got scared that he didn't love her anymore.

"Are we in trouble, Harry?"

"Why would you think that?"

"I'm worried. Shouldn't I be?"

"We'll be fine," he said.

"Are you tired of me? It happens."

"Not to us."

"If it isn't business or me, what is it?"

"Neither one," he said. "But if it was, it certainly wouldn't
be you and me."

Could it be business? Billie wondered. Three strikes and
you're out. She had seen so many little record companies go
bust after having had several hits, and she knew there was
always that possibility. But not to them. Not to Billie Redmond, whom everybody loved, whose fans screamed and
reached out to her, all those raised hands, all those admirers.
Not to Harry Lawless, who was the bravest, smartest man
she knew. There was something comforting about playing
pool with him, stark naked in the middle of the night, in their
own luxurious house. He had a right to be moody once in a
while; who wasn't? She let him win, and then they went upstairs and lay in each other's arms, and he entered her almost
in his sleep, as if she was his comfort, his safe haven, and she
knew they would be just fine.

She was still on the road, more than she would have liked
because Harry wasn't with her as much as he used to be.
They had been together five years, and the honeymoon mad-
ness had changed to something that was still good but not
the way it was the first two years. Billie wondered if he was

having affairs when she was away, but this time she was afraid to ask. She kept bringing back to memory the night they had played pool together and the way he had seemed in bed afterward, and her confidence then that whatever the problem was he would be sure to fix it. Now, as the months went by and spring went into summer, then to fall, she watched Harry withdrawing into himself.

"We have to start to economize," he said one day. "I'm having a little difficulty with my cash flow."

"Okay," Billie said. She wondered where they should start. They hadn't had a party in a very long time, and they didn't even have friends over anymore. The hotels and motels she and the band stayed in on tour were always second rate. Harry had gotten rid of the bus and driver, and now she and the band rented cars when they had to, or took planes, always going coach. She and Harry hadn't bought clothes recently; they had enough to last them forever. They still ate out, but not at any place particularly expensive. They hadn't had a vacation for a long time either. Harry had no plans to cut another record for anyone at the moment, not her and not any other artist. After Pigman and the Wanderers had bombed several years ago he had concentrated everything on Billie.

"Do you need me to lend you money?" she asked him.

"No. Don't be silly."

"Hey, you don't have to act like my cowboy hero. Money is just money."

"Keep your money," he said, in an abrupt, closed-in tone that made her drop the subject, but now she wondered about everything.

Winter was coming. There was a different chill in the air, the days were short, and the leaves had fallen off the little trees in front of their house. Billie hated how every time she came back from a trip things were so different. She was alarmed about the passage of time, and about the way Harry seemed to be keeping her farther and farther away from him. If in fact his problem was financial, there was a straight line from Harry's bank account to Harry's dick. It was something Billie knew about men in general, but she hadn't expected it would happen to Harry.

"I'm always here," she said when he called her. "If you need me, I'm available to listen. I love you."

"Well, I love you, too," Harry said. She heard coins drop and realized he was using a pay phone.

"Where are you, anyway?" she asked.

"Some bar."

"I'll be back tomorrow and you won't have to go out to any bar."

"Goodnight," he said softly, and hung up.

He had called her from bars and friends' houses and parties before, but this time after Harry broke the connection Billie sat there on her bed in the stuffy motel room for a long time, feeling like crying because their goodbye had been so unsatisfactory and she didn't know where to call him back.

The next day she took a cab from the airport alone because she didn't want to wait to drop off the others. She had to get home soon, she needed to see Harry, even if he didn't need to see her. When she got to their house she saw a piece of white paper taped to the front door.

It was a marshal's notice of foreclosure. The bank had taken back the house. She was so surprised she was numb at first, but she had the presence of mind to pull the embarrassing thing off so no one in the neighborhood would see it, and then she put the key into the lock, and the key didn't fit. She looked at her key chain to be sure she had tried the right one because she couldn't believe someone had changed the lock, and then she tried the key again to see if it wasn't just stuck, but it wouldn't budge. Then she looked at the notice more carefully and read, "To Whom it May Concern, the contents having been taken to ABC Storage..."

She ran to the first-floor windows and peered in. The house was empty. No furniture, no rugs, no chandeliers, no pool table, no phone; nothing but a few motes of dust floating in the wan afternoon light. It looked as if they had simply moved away. She knew it was her house, but she looked at the number on the familiar front door again just to be sure. It was like a bad dream and she wanted to wake up, but she knew she wouldn't.

Harry! Where was Harry? She hadn't any idea, and he wouldn't know where she was either, so maybe she should just stay until he came for her. She thought seriously of kicking in a window, but what good would that do? There was nothing inside that house, not even a phone.

She went to the store down the street and got change and used their pay phone to call her answering service and then Harry's. There were no messages for her, and she left one for him when the service said it didn't know where he was. "Tell him I'm at the house."

Then she went back to the stripped and vacant shell. She sat on the front steps with her suitcases and her guitar beside her and wished she had a drink or just a glass of water to take a pill to make the trembling stop. Was he so broke he couldn't even have come to the airport? Was he hurt somewhere, in a hospital?

Billie waited for an hour, until she was cramped and chilled and going crazy, and then she went back to the store down the street and got more change and began using their pay phone to call everyone she could think of, including the guys in the band, to see if Harry was there or had left a message for her. She told everyone she had lost her keys. Then she started calling all the hospitals.

Nobody knew anything.

It was dark now, and cold, and she was exhausted. She needed a place to stay for the night. She was reluctant to call any of the guys from the band again. They'd been on each other's necks for two solid weeks and needed to get away from each other. But she didn't have any choice. She called Toad and he said to come right over. She pretended to be calm. She needed to keep the band from finding out how broke Harry was until she found out what was going on. She was surprised to see herself so cool and rational, but you just had to put one foot ahead of the other or else you would have time to think and get scared. She still couldn't let herself believe for one moment that Harry had left her, but what else could she believe?

"Harry's probably out getting drunk," Toad said. He gave her a joint and a glass of tequila.

"Some welcome from my old man," Billie said, pretending to be miffed, not terrified.

"Well, you two have been together for a long time."

"It doesn't seem long to me," Billie said.

She slept on Toad's couch, and the next day she started looking for Harry again, every hour plunging her deeper into depression and fear. That night, when she still couldn't find out anything, she knew she should go to a hotel, but she couldn't stand to be alone; she was too upset. She told Toad the whole story, finally, partly because they were both stoned. She told him he shouldn't get any ideas that she was available on the rebound. All she wanted was to find Harry and get things right.

"Me, too," Toad said. "I'd like to know what's going to happen to the rest of our bookings, if there are any."

He called the other musicians and they got together at Toad's apartment and decided Harry was gone for good. Billie refused to admit it.

"This must have been going on for a long time," Legs said. "I got kicked out of a place I owned once; they kept sending me letters and notices and putting things on my front door for months. Harry just didn't tell you."

"Harry handled the business," Billie said, to defend him.

But she couldn't sleep and the days were endless. She called her answering service every half hour and kept leaving Toad's number on it, too. She also called Harry's service several times a day to see if he had picked up her messages, but they wouldn't tell her, apparently at his request because he was hiding, and finally his service told her they had been discontinued. Her insides were churning, and she felt lost. Outlaw Records was gone, too, without a trace. The record company office had been in the house, and that had been their answering service.

She knew she would have to start all over again, knock on doors, go see the record companies with her songs, see if they wanted her voice on someone else's song, and she didn't know how she could when just going through the motions of living were all she could handle. All she could think about was Harry, so how could she ever pull herself together enough to write a decent song?

She kept looking at the notice that had been on their door, and finally she decided she should go out to Long Island City and get back her clothes and her jewelry. She rented a

U-Haul truck because she knew she needed something big; she had a lot of stuff. But when she got to the storage place she was greeted by a stubborn little creepy man who said she couldn't have her clothes or jewelry without presenting all the original sales slips, which of course she hadn't kept; why would she? Some she had never had; they were gifts from Harry.

"But they're mine!" she said. "I'm Billie Redmond, here's my driver's license, my credit card..."

"I know who you are," the man said. "I just don't know who owns the property. How would it look if I gave it to you and then tomorrow his other girlfriend showed up and she had all the sales slips because it was hers?"

"He has no other girlfriend," Billie said, although now she wasn't sure. "The clothing was in my house. I'll tell you the labels. I'll describe my diamond bracelet in detail. How would I know what it looks like and that it was even there if it isn't mine?"

"Get me a notarized letter from Harry Lawless that the women's clothes and jewelry that were in the house were yours and you can have them. That's the best I can do."

He didn't even say he was sorry.

Billie cried from helpless rage all the way back in the truck. She felt her property had been stolen from her, and it had. She knew Harry would have wanted her to have her things; he had bought some of them for her, and she had bought some for herself. They were not only expensive but they had sentimental value. Some of the best were from their wonderful trip to Paris. They represented hits, they were her happy memories of love. All she had now was what she had taken with her on the road—her Tank watch, her rings, some earrings—not much because she had been afraid of being robbed in a motel; but now she had been robbed by the law.

When she got back she told Toad what had happened and he said Harry probably didn't know she would need all that proof to get her things back. She knew Harry hadn't even thought about it. She was finally beginning to understand there was a more serious reason he was on the run.

Two long weeks after she had come home to find she had

no home, Harry finally called her. Her heart flipped up with relief and she felt as if the lights had gone on again.

"Where did you go?" she asked him. "I missed you so much."

"I'm not in New York," he said. "I have some problems with my taxes."

"What does that mean?"

"I didn't pay them for a couple of years. It's all my accountant's fault."

"That bastard!" she said.

"I know."

"Didn't you notice you weren't signing any forms?" Billie said. "Didn't you ask?" Immediately after she said it she wished she could take it back because she sounded like a nagging wife. That was the one thing she had never intended to be.

"I'm going away," Harry said.

"You are away. I want to go with you."

"You can't, honey. I'm in trouble."

"But you can pay back what you owe little by little," Billie said.

"They're calling my plane," Harry said.

"Where are you going? When are you coming back?"

"It was fun, honey," Harry said, "but it's over. As the man says, that's all she wrote. Take care of yourself." Then he hung up. He was gone.

Billie sat by the phone for a long time without moving. So deep was her grief that she could hardly breathe, and she wished she wouldn't have to. Later she remembered that she hadn't asked him for a letter about her property, and although she was so depressed that she no longer cared about material things, she thought it would have helped if Harry had written it to show he hadn't totally deserted her, and now she would never know.

After that she moved slowly, as if she were walking underwater, and she seldom spoke. Harry hadn't made any more bookings for them and the band was worried about money. Unlike her, they had an agent, and when a gig turned up to back another singer on the road in a bunch of crappy little clubs, they took it. They had no other choice.

The job was available and immediate, and their agent wasn't interested in representing her at the moment. Billie didn't think she could have gotten up on a stage right now anyway. She was too depressed. She stayed in Toad's apartment and paid his rent while he was away, drank, and stared at the wall, and finally one day when she felt slightly better she tried to pull herself together as much as she could considering her mental state and started going around to record companies.

None of them wanted her, not even the little ones. Then she went to agents. None of them were interested in taking over her career.

The last agent who was willing to see her was in a hurry and brutal. "Singers like you," he said, "who were stars in the early seventies are over. You've had too many bombs. Disco is in now. You have the wrong songs, the wrong sound. You're finished."

She couldn't believe he was saying that to her. How could this have happened so fast? "I could keep on touring," Billie said. "I just want to sing."

"Well, maybe little clubs in college towns or something. People who remember you might let you be an introductory act. I wouldn't be bothered to represent you for that and neither would any other agent when we can start out with a new young artist and make her a star."

"I just want to sing," Billie said again.

"Trust me," he said. "Go get a normal job."

If she could sing, get up on a stage again, she knew she would heal. But none of them cared what she wanted. They were telling her she was a twenty-eight-year-old has-been. What was she going to do with the rest of her life? She went back to the apartment and sat in front of the television set, the blinds down, a glass of vodka in her hand, smoking. She should never have let Harry run her whole life, she was thinking. But then she thought that perhaps if she hadn't had Harry no one else would have wanted her. Now she would never know.

There was an old movie from the fifties called *Sunset Boulevard* on in the middle of the night and she watched it. It was about a has-been movie star named Norma Desmond who went crazy. Billie identified completely with her pain. When the glory days were over, you were just ridiculous.

That was when she began thinking seriously about suicide.

SEVENTEEN

Kathryn and her new husband, Ted, had rented a room and bath and kitchenette-in-the-wall in a cheap apartment house—a newlyweds' first apartment—to stay in until he would get a promotion and maybe she got pregnant and then they would find something bigger and better and get on with what they spoke of as their *real* lives. They were collecting their dishes and flatware, setting by setting, and his parents had bought them a convertible bed, which later on when they had a real bedroom would become their living room couch. She had been Kathryn O'Mara Hopkins for a while now, but it was still quite unreal; she felt as if she were pretending to be another person with another identity and that underneath this person was her actual self, hiding.

A few nights a week the young couple went to dinner at his parents' house. She liked his parents very much because they were normal and were kind to her. Kathryn would clear the table with his mother after their pleasant, peaceful dinner, and wash the dishes with Ted, while he spoke longingly of a roomier, nicer apartment, and she thought how she could happily move in here with these good parents and stay forever, or at least until she grew up. She had no interest in being alone with him.

She had remained a virgin on her awful wedding night because she was so upset, but afterward they had gone to the Berkshires for their honeymoon and consummated the marriage. Kathryn was so scared of sex, so tight, so virginal, so resistant that the first few times she reluctantly let Ted take advantage of his marital rights, she was not even sure they had gone through with it. Every time they had sex she froze and it hurt. Nothing in her upbringing and experience had given her any reason to think this should be fun.

She was working now, too. She had gotten a job giving Tupperware parties for the other married women in the area, and because she was an extrovert, she was good at it, although she was bored with the lack of mental challenge. Why not have a baby right away, Kathryn thought; I'm going to have one eventually and it would give me something to do. She stopped dreading their nightly grappling, because now at least it had a purpose. By the time she was getting to like sexual intercourse a little and thinking it was something she might eventually be able to put up with on a regular basis, she was pregnant.

The pregnancy was easy. Ted got his wish for a pleasant garden apartment, he and Kathryn had a good time decorating it, and their son, Jim Daniel, was born right on schedule. Jim Daniel was an adorable baby, alert and healthy. Kathryn hadn't really thought about whether she would be maternal or not, but the appearance of this tiny, needy person unleashed a wave of warmth and love greater than anything she had ever felt for anyone. She was very busy and very tired, but content.

She had not seen her father since he had thrown her out of the house two years ago. She spoke to him only if he answered the phone when she called her mother, and then only to say, "May I speak to Mom?" They had nothing to say to each other. He was still not drinking, but Kathryn was convinced that the damage had already been done and he was crazy.

Then one afternoon, for no reason, her father appeared at her apartment with the worst-looking dog Kathryn had ever seen. It looked like he had gotten it in a junkyard.

"This is my new best friend," her father said. "He's rabid, but he won't bite if I tell him not to."

In a flash Kathryn imagined the dog mangling her child, and stood in front of the door. "Don't come in," she said. "Go away."

When they left shortly afterward, she was shaking. She told her mother of the bizarre happening a few days later and her mother said, "Your father never had a dog."

When her father did not come back again, Kathryn was relieved. She knew that if he did, she would not let him in.

She wanted to have another baby right away. It had not occurred to her how much more work two babies would be than one; all she thought was that two would be a family. When you got married, you had children. Besides, she had always had enormous energy. She got pregnant again easily. When her second son was born they named him Charles and called him Chip. He was sweet and happy, smiling all the time, and she and Ted felt lucky.

Kathryn could hardly believe how much Ted had changed from the popular, fun-loving, fickle college boy she had married by accident. He was the most devoted of husbands and fathers. She hardly ever saw him without a baby on his hip. He came home from work and helped around the apartment, he never made her wait on him, he always shared the care of the two kids, he even did the laundry. She had never stopped working, because boring as it was, she could make a hundred dollars a night giving her Tupperware parties, which she did several times a week, and while she was out Ted willingly baby-sat. She had no previous experience with the example of a father who enjoyed his children and his home, but nonetheless she suspected Ted was unusual. He liked being married much more than she did.

She had really nothing to complain about, but she still didn't like being married. She felt somehow betrayed by the way her life had turned out. She didn't know whether it was because she was too young to be so settled, or because she wasn't in love with her handsome, thoughtful husband, even though she was fond of him, or because she had never wanted to be married in the first place, never. More and more often lately Kathryn found herself thinking about how she could manage to get a divorce. Then she wouldn't be a wife, and she wouldn't have to live with a man. She would keep the apartment and the babies would live with her. She was not afraid of being alone; she had the children. She would take care of them. She had saved her Tupperware money and she was making more all the time. When she didn't have Ted around anymore she would hire a baby-sitter.

Her mother came to visit quite often. "Your father has a girlfriend now," she said. "She calls the house all the time asking to speak to him."

"What kind of woman keeps calling a married man's house?" Kathryn said.

"He won't tell me who she is, but I know *what* she is. We fight about that woman all the time. The last time I asked him who she was he came after me with a chair."

"I'll bet his friends know."

"His friends are no help. They probably do know, but they won't tell me. Those men stick together."

"Now will you leave him?" Kathryn said.

"I'm beginning to think about it."

"Better sooner than later."

Then, her father in one of his fits of rage threw her mother down the stairs and injured her back. Sheila was in such unbearable pain that she had to be taken to the hospital, where she was kept for a few days and put in traction.

Kathryn went to visit her mother in the hospital while Ted stayed home and baby-sat. She brought flowers. Of course her father was not there. The room was dim and peaceful and there was no one in the other bed. Her mother was in her cubicle with the curtains open, her own domain, with her I.V. and her hospital paraphernalia, pulleys and weights attached to her legs; full of painkiller so she nonetheless looked happy and rested; the nurse's station was right outside, and Kathryn thought how few these hours of peace and safety were in her mother's life. What a pity that she had to have been brutalized to be able to have what should have been her right all the time.

"When I get out of the hospital your father will get me a nurse's aide at home," her mother said.

"You're letting him get you the nurse's aide?"

"He will. I've given him the money for her."

"Why would you have to give him the money?" Kathryn said, annoyed. "Why can't he do even that for you? He was the one who threw you down the stairs."

"How can you even ask that by now?" her mother said.

Her mother went home to finish recuperating and Kathryn didn't think she had anything to be concerned about. Her brothers Donal and Kean were working in other cities now, but her little brother Colin, who was sixteen, was still at home, and of course there would be the nurse's aide. Between taking care of the two babies and her job Kat didn't even think about it.

Then, in the afternoon, Colin called her. His voice was high with fear. He told her he had come home from school to discover that her father had taken the money her mother had given him to hire a nurse's aide and had not hired anyone. They didn't even know where he was. Her father had also not bothered to get her mother the painkiller she was supposed to have, and her mother was helpless and out of her head with suffering. She couldn't walk or even get out of bed to go to the bathroom or get food or water, the slightest movement caused her agony, she was screaming and moaning, and he didn't know what to do. Kathryn grabbed her kids and rushed over, wild with rage at this latest betrayal.

"That bastard!" Kathryn kept saying between her teeth. She wished her father was dead. She called her mother's doctor, who wrote out another prescription for painkiller, and also some Valium, because her mother was now so agitated, and Colin ran out and got it.

Kathryn stayed by her mother's bedside, trying to make her sip juice for her dehydration and weakness, holding her hand until the painkiller and tranquilizer kicked in. It was frightening to see her mother reduced to something so elemental and vulnerable. Somehow it was worse than the beatings, or the household violence, because this time being a victim was not her choice. In fact, she had prepared not to be one.

"This time you've got to leave him," Kathryn said, although she wasn't sure if her mother could understand her. "Leave the man. Don't think about it anymore, just do it. You deserve a decent life."

Her mother looked at her. It was hard for her to speak, but anger gave her strength. "This time I will," her mother said.

It was a long recovery. Then, when her mother was able to walk again, Kathryn and Ted went with her from lawyer to lawyer trying to get one to take her case. She told them about the bullet holes in the walls, about the beatings through all those years, the violence, the abuse, about Brendan not getting the nurse, how he was trying to drive her crazy, how she was convinced he was going to kill her. She told them about the woman who had been calling the house every day, calling her husband, asking to speak to him when his wife answered, without any shame. She was sure it was his girlfriend, that he finally had one now. Who else could it be? Her mother said she was sure he was going to kill her or leave her now that he had another woman, and take the house that she had worked so hard all these years to help pay for, and she wanted a divorce so she could keep what was hers. None of the lawyers would take her case.

They all said she needed proof of adultery or desertion. She was so upset when she told them these terrible stories that most of them thought she was unhinged. One of the lawyers was even afraid of Brendan, because he knew him and what he was capable of. Kathryn was getting an education in the way women were treated under the law. There was no help emotionally either. When her mother went to her priest he told her if she got a divorce she would go to Hell. She was trapped on every side.

Since Kathryn was not afraid of Hell, she decided to pursue her own divorce from Ted. She did it in the only way she now knew was open to her within the restrictive, archaic laws of their state: deviously and with lies.

"I need some time to be by myself," she told him. "I have to be alone to think. So many things have happened so fast that I don't know who I am anymore. Why don't you stay with your parents for a while, just a couple of months?"

He felt sorry for her and he understood her stress, although it took her a lot of convincing to get him to agree to leave. When he did, he offered to take the babies with him if it would make this period easier for her, but Kathryn said no, she could handle them.

When Ted had left and moved in with his parents, Kathryn hired a divorce lawyer and sued him on the grounds of desertion. Since he had been such an exemplary husband and father, there was no one who would or could testify to his alleged mental cruelty, so she had to give her lawyer an additional five hundred dollars to hire "witnesses" to lie.

She thought the whole thing was unjust and corrupt, she knew what she was doing to Ted was unfair, but she blamed the laws and the men who made them, not herself. She was a victim, too. All she wanted was to be free. She did not ask him for a penny in alimony or child support.

When Ted was served with the papers he was stunned and devastated. It was all over before he even knew it had started. Kathryn had obtained an interlocutory decree, a six-month cooling-off period, and after the separation they would be divorced and there was nothing he could do about it.

"How could you do this?" he kept asking. "I don't understand. I thought you loved me. Why can't we work it out, whatever it is?"

"I just don't want to be married to anyone," Kathryn said. "We can be friends. You can see the babies as often as you want. You've been a good husband. It's not you, it's me."

Ted finally gave up trying to reconcile with her, but he still mourned his lost love. Kathryn was relieved by their new relationship, as she'd known she would be, but she hadn't realized how difficult it would be to pay her bills without the help of his job, too. And even with baby-sitters, everything was twice as much work without Ted around. He was over at her place every weekend to see the kids, and took them out with him for the day, but when he brought them home the two little boys would cry all night. "Daddy!" they would sob bitterly, "I want my daddy!" She had not realized that they had become daddy's boys. She could see that the older one, who was a toddler now, understood what had happened and resented her for taking his daddy away from him. In many ways this was worse than her marriage had been, but she knew she would just have to live with it.

It was deep winter now. It was cold, it snowed, it rained, the wind howled, it seemed they never saw the sun. Kathryn's mother called. "I've talked to the lawyer who got you your divorce," she said. "He told me if I can find out who that woman is and where she lives, he can make her the correspondent and can serve them both with proper papers. Then I can finally get my divorce."

"How are you going to do it?"

"I'll just have to follow him," her mother said.

"How are you going to do that? You're no detective."

"I'll find a way."

Kathryn went to sleep early that night, as soon as the babies were asleep. On the nights that she could stay home and didn't have to go out to work she was exhausted and glad for the rest. She was twenty-one years old and part of her felt like a kid who didn't know anything, while another part of her already felt ancient with responsibilities. The rain was peaceful outside her windows and her comforter was warm. When the bedside phone shrilled in her ear she was disoriented at first, and even more so when she looked at the clock and saw that it was one o'clock in the morning.

There was a woman on the phone, a voice Kathryn did not know. "Your mother's in trouble," the woman said.

"Who is this?"

"She's at the Roxbury police station." And the woman hung up.

Kathryn fumbled for the light and turned it on. She called the Roxbury police station, a number she knew well. "My name is O'Mara," she said. "My mother is being held there. Sheila O'Mara. Can you tell me what this is about?"

"Hold on." A pause. "Nobody here with that name," the cop said.

"Are you sure?"

"I'm sure."

Kathryn hung up. This was so weird. Who was that woman anyway? Was this some kind of practical joke? She wondered what kind of trouble her passive, law-abiding mother could possibly be in. Now she was wide awake. Maybe she should call all the police stations, but the woman had clearly said it was that one. Kathryn put the radio on to soft music and tried to figure out what she should do now, if anything. She knew the one thing she wouldn't do was sleep. The song ended and there was a news flash.

"A Boston police officer was brutally gunned down tonight outside the Avalon Ballroom. Officer Brendan O'Mara was killed in his car while off duty. The suspect is his own wife. She was taken into custody and brought to the Roxbury police station for questioning. More news later."

"My God!" Kathryn said, and jumped out of bed.

She dressed and ran upstairs to the neighbors, the Fiorentinos, whom she knew slightly, and leaned on their bell and banged on their door. Finally Mr. Fiorentino appeared, his face crumpled with apprehensiveness and sleep. "Please will you take my kids for a couple of hours," Kathryn said, "my mother's in trouble."

She left her babies with the Fiorentinos and drove as fast as she could to the Roxbury police station. On the way she finally realized, for the first time, that her father was dead, and that she felt nothing about her father's death; not remorse, not grief, only—if anything—relief. Her mother should have killed him years ago. But the one she was concerned about was her mother.

"That's O'Mara's daughter," one of the cops said. They knew her family, of course. She wondered if the woman who had called was her father's girlfriend, and if she had known about the murder even before her mother got to jail. Her mother had said she was to follow them. Just follow them…something had obviously gone wrong.

Her mother was sitting in a room, at a desk, surrounded by four people in uniforms. The two men were cops, the two women were police matrons. Her mother looked as if she was in shock. Kathryn felt sick. She stood at the doorway and watched as a cop shoved a paper at her mother to sign a confession; her mother signed, and the matron grabbed it and tore it up.

"Don't sign anything until you get a lawyer," the matron said.

"I killed him," her mother said dully, "and I want to die."

The cop gave her another piece of paper, and again her mother signed it and the matron tore it up. It was obvious to Kathryn which sides the men and women were on in the case.

"I took his gun with me," her mother said, "because I was afraid he would kill me. I thought the safety was on. I only wanted to find out who his girlfriend was."

"Don't say any more," the matron said.

"You stalked him," the cop said. "You hid under the back seat of his car. You shot his head off. There was a woman witness in the car who escaped, and she saw the whole thing."

Her mother covered her face with her hands then and her shoulders shook. "I want to die," she said again, but this time she was sobbing. Kathryn knew she meant it. Her mother had killed her father and was suicidal, and the only lawyers she knew handled divorces. Her mother would need someone good.

"Mom, I'll call Uncle Brian," she said. She turned to the cops. "You know my uncle, Captain Brian O'Mara, don't you?" Of course they did, they all knew her uncles, she was just reminding them that she came from strength and authority, that she was one of theirs. "And Captain Patrick O'Mara, and Sergeant Michael O'Mara?" She was pulling as much rank as she could. Her uncles, powerful and feared, were the only ones she could think of who could help. "Don't sign anything, Mom, until they get you a lawyer," Kathryn said. "They'll know what to do."

But would they do it? Her mother had killed their brother. They would not be able to forgive that so easily and help her—Kathryn was sure of it.

Maybe her uncles, too, would want her mother to die.

EIGHTEEN

The four friends were having their usual weekly dinner at Yellowbird. That winter, the winter of 1995, had been unusually warm, and because tonight was one of those rare evenings with damp and chill and the hint of snow, they had decided to drink red wine instead of white. Kathryn, impatient for dramatic weather, was trying out the designer Eskimo outfit she had bought for a trip to Scandinavia, but after the first glass of wine she started to peel it off. The others were in New York black, a color that went with everything else in your closet and didn't show the grit that flew through the city air and settled on everything. As always, the conversation came around to the subject of men.

"What is it about us and men?" Felicity asked. "Why do we give them so much control?"

"It's the social system," Kathryn said. It was the first sign of anger any of them had ever seen her show. "Women have children to take care of and support, they have to work, they're at the mercy of men. I would never have gotten married if I didn't need to. I didn't love any of my husbands. Well, one."

"But I give away my own autonomy for love," Felicity said. "I did it when I was young and I do it now when it has nothing to do with economics. I have no children and I make a big salary."

"I used to give it away, too," Gara said. "I needed a very strong man, the sense of power that would be on my side, because I felt vulnerable. I thought Carl would save me...and actually, in a lot of ways, for a lot of years, he did. I look back and I seem like such an idiot, but love makes idiots of most people. When I met Carl I thought he looked like a lion, the king of the jungle, and I told him so." She smiled wryly. "The Lion King."

Felicity gasped. "When I went out with Russell on our first date I told him he was like a king! I did! I thought he was going to save me, too. No wonder you and I are friends."

"I would admit a man was a king," Eve said, "only if he was a real one, with a country."

"Right," Kathryn said, and they all laughed.

"I would never give up my power to anybody," Eve went on. "Man or woman. My power is what makes me always win."

They ignored that.

"But Russell fooled me," Felicity said. "He fooled me on purpose, he wanted to. He was actually a despot."

"Maybe that was what you wanted," Gara said.

"I didn't want it. I was a naïve kid. Whatever was wrong I thought could be fixed."

"When are we going to learn we can't change anybody?" Kathryn said. "It's enough trouble just trying to survive."

"The next person I'm going to try to change is me," Felicity said. "I'm tired of being miserable."

"Hear, hear," they all cheered. But they had heard her say it before.

Felicity was twenty-five years old now, and she was working in a law firm in New York as she had dreamed she would; she had her own apartment, she had a life of her own. Her firm, Friedland, Jordan and Samm, was small enough to give her a degree of autonomy, she was making decent money, and she was able to work with authors. Her apartment was a one-bedroom in a doorman building on the East Side, and she often gave Sunday brunches or Saturday evening cocktail parties there for the many single friends she had met in the city, both black and white (although more were white), all young, upwardly mobile professionals.

Her college militancy had gone the way of her afro and dashikis. She worked in a white law firm. She lived in a white apartment building, although she had a few black neighbors who were just like her. She wore corporate little suits now, with high heels to show off her good legs, and her hair was long and pulled back for work in a ladylike bun. On weekends, when she went out with her friends or gave parties, she dressed to look sexy. Finding men was not a problem; finding one she would like to see twice was.

She thought about love all the time, although she had very few lovers. Everyone she knew worked harder and longer than they wanted to, went to the gym faithfully after work, went out on pathetic blind dates, and nearly fell asleep in the cab home because they were so tired. Her younger sister Theodora, who was living in Cambridge, had already had her first child of the planned four, and was working, too, doing something or other with statistics. It was the era of the overachiever.

Felicity met Russell Naylor at a cocktail party given to raise money for a black political candidate. He was there with a beautiful young woman. He was older than any of the men Felicity had ever been out with, but not too old; just sophisticated, she thought. He had a presence: the look of a man who enjoyed his success, and also of a tough guy who had come up the hard way, smoothed off the rough edges, and never forgotten his warrior heart. She knew he was a self-made millionaire building contractor because she had heard of him and read about him in the newspapers, but she had never thought of him as a possible romantic interest, just a role model. But now that she had met him she was fascinated. She liked him right away. This was what she wanted—a pillar of the black community with pizzazz.

She watched them carefully. She knew he wasn't married, so the beautiful woman was just a date, or, at the worst, his girlfriend, although he hadn't treated her like a girlfriend. Felicity spoke with him for a few minutes and she made sure he knew where she worked...just in case there was some chance he liked her.

The next morning at the office she looked him up in *Who's Who* and was interested to discover that he had apparently never been married and had no children. She remembered then that Russell Naylor had always been known as quite a ladies' man. Of course he would be; he was a catch. Why would he want to settle down? She let herself fantasize about him a little.

One reason he would want to settle down, she thought, was his age. He was forty-five. It was time. She was twenty years younger, at the prime of her fertility, innocent enough to be influenced, attractive and intelligent enough for him to show her off. But then her lack of self-confidence took over and she decided he wouldn't want her anyway. Why would he want her when he could have anybody? She doubted if he would even call.

He called her that same day, before lunch. She was stunned and flattered. "I just found myself free for lunch," he said. "Would you be free, too, by any chance?"

"Well, yes I am," said Felicity, in a tone that implied surprise at this fortunate coincidence. Actually, she never went out to lunch unless it was someone's birthday, and was therefore almost always available, but if she hadn't been she would have made herself so.

"How about '21' at twelve-thirty?"

"That would be lovely. See you then." When she hung up she stifled her shriek and giggle of triumph. "All right!"

He had assumed she knew where it was, that other successful men had taken her there, but since she had never been there she had to look for the address in the phone book: "21" was such a famous restaurant that even she had heard of it. Her boss ate there sometimes when he had an important client to entertain. It was just lunch, she reminded herself, but it was a beginning. Suddenly she felt sensual and attractive. Who knew what would happen?

It turned out that "21" was in a townhouse with a line of jockey statues going up the side staircase, and when she got inside it looked like a men's club, all dark wood and horse pictures. She was on time and Russell was late. When she told the man at the door whom she was meeting he obviously knew who Russell was, but he wouldn't let her go to the table; he made her wait in an anteroom with a big television set in it and a view of the front door. Felicity couldn't decide whether she had to stay here in limbo because she was only a woman, a young woman at that, and therefore suspect, or because she was black. But they knew Russell Naylor and seemed cordial, so it must just be her. She was aware again, as she often was recently, of how women were often treated as if they were nothing unless they had a powerful man on their arm, and how sometimes that made it even worse.

When Russell came in they all made a big fuss over him, greeting him as if they knew him well and were glad he was here, telling him there was a young lady waiting for him, noticing again that she existed. Russell beamed at the sight of her and Felicity felt better. He took charge immediately, and as they went into the bar where their table was he was shaking hands, greeting and being greeted by name by what looked like every tuxedoed man who worked there. He was like royalty in his castle.

They sat side by side at a small table with a red and white checkered tablecloth, under a profusion of boy's toys hanging from the ceiling. The place was full of white businessmen, with a few older white women who looked like society types, and a picture flashed through Felicity's mind of the tea room where she had to go years ago with her mother and her mother's lover. But she didn't know why, since this was certainly more like a men's club than a tea room and she was grown up and with her own date.

Her mother was watching her, she supposed, always in her mind even when she least expected it. Her mother would have been pleased to see her today.

They ordered bottled water and swordfish. "You certainly are important," Felicity said. "You're like a king."

He laughed. "The great acting teacher Stanislavsky was once asked by one of his students, 'How do you play a king on the stage?' And Stanislavsky answered, 'You don't have to do anything to play a king. The audience knows you're a king by the way the other actors behave.' That's why there are certain restaurants where I like to go regularly."

She digested that and was impressed. "You must read a great deal."

"Some," he said. "Not really. I used to go out with an actress and she told me that."

"The education of the bachelor comes from all the women he went out with," Felicity said, pretending to be teasing him.

"And you?" Russell asked. "How is your education?"

"Unfinished. I'm still pursuing it."

"I hope I can help."

"I'm sure you can."

They smiled at each other and she felt the spark. I could learn a lot from him, she thought. She asked him about his work and his life, she hung on every word, she was as pliant and seductive as she had been taught, which was by now almost second nature to her, and she even pretended to be as interested in sports as he was. Why were men so devoted to watching other men trying to take a ball away from each other? She told him nothing about her dysfunctional and crazy childhood because he had obviously liked his own parents, and poverty had been his only, albeit great, problem growing up. As they talked she was aware that he was sizing her up and that he liked what he saw. All she wanted was for him to save her. She was not sure from what, but she thought perhaps everything.

He told her about his travels, his vacations to exotic places—Tunisia, Morocco, Egypt, a cruise down the Nile; Hong Kong, Singapore, Bali—always with one woman or another. Felicity wanted to be that woman.

"I just got back from two weeks in the French wine country," he said. "I had a date with me and we had a car and fold-up bicycles. We would go into a little town and stop at a wonderful inn, and then we would ride our bikes for miles out into the country and have a picnic of charcuterie and cheese and fresh bread and good local wine, and then we would ride back in time for dinner. The next day we would be on to the next town. The scenery was so spectacular."

He's middle-aged but he's in good shape, Felicity thought. All that bike riding lets him eat things I would never eat, and look at him.

"I think you met her," Russell said. "She was with me at the party."

Felicity nodded. "'Date' or girlfriend?" she asked. She was jealous already.

"Was my girlfriend, now is a date. We're winding down."

"Maybe I could become her replacement," Felicity said flirtatiously.

"Maybe," he said, smiling. "You have beauty *and* brains. I'm very impressed."

"Thank you."

And although she was determined she would never give up her work, luckily her work was part of what made her appealing to him.

She knew her life with him would be so different from anything she had ever known that she felt like an innocent little hick with her fingers and nose pressed against the window to a magical world. I must be in love, Felicity thought. She wondered if it was success itself that was such a turn-on, or the fact that he had been able to achieve it. How could you separate the two anyway? She wondered what she could possibly do to keep from becoming another one of Russell Naylor's social statistics.

They had to go back to their offices then. The next day Felicity wondered if she should call Russell to thank him for the lunch, or if that would be too forward and if maybe she should write him a brief note instead. She wanted to keep the connection. While she was pondering this dilemma flowers arrived.

Thank you for brightening my day, the note read. *Russell.*

All right! Felicity shrieked to herself, and hugged herself as if she were her own best friend.

Then she didn't hear from him for a week. She hoped he was out of town on business, but she knew he was with the girlfriend, "winding down," if indeed he was. Why is dating torture, she thought, why can't people just have an arranged marriage to someone perfect and avoid all the bullshit? Then he called and invited her out to dinner. She took an unaccustomed lunch hour and rushed to Saks where she bought a sexy black dress she couldn't really afford, to wear for him.

Russell took her out to dinner three times, always to an expensive restaurant where he told her stories of his sophisticated adventures. His stories made her yearn for him with a feeling that was like pain. Finally he invited her to his apartment. Felicity knew what the invitation meant and she was ready.

She was overwhelmed by his apartment, a small penthouse in the sky, with the glittering city spread out below them, and a view of three bridges, strung with lights. Then when they went to bed she was even more stunned by what a good lover he was. Nothing in her experience had prepared her for this. He started at her perfectly pedicured toes and worked up slowly, slowly, teasing her until he gave her the best oral sex she had ever had. He didn't even let her do anything to him. He was hugely endowed, the biggest she had ever seen, filling up the emptiness of her body, her heart, her life, replacing it with pleasure. When he had finished with her she was besotted and lost. Older men are the best, she thought, the best. I want to marry him and live with him forever.

She chased him for a year, happy and serene when she was with him, anxious and miserable when she was not. She attended sports events with him and pretended to be as enthusiastic as he was; on the weekends that he was in the city she cooked wonderful meals for him in his apartment and helped entertain his friends; she played wife, she became, at least, good friend and confidante. He finally told her he was falling in love with her.

After that first night in bed together he had begun to let her do to him whatever he did to her, which made her feel more equal, but then later on he became the passive one, letting her do most of the work. But Felicity didn't mind; she loved him, she wanted him, and she didn't want him to get tired of her. She knew he was still seeing other women and she wanted to be better at sex than they were—better at everything. She wanted him to love her more and more, until he had to have her in the way she wanted—as his wife.

By then Russell was calling her Baby and she was calling him Slugger. Her nickname for him had a kind of sports reference, although Felicity was not unaware that in their choice of nicknames she was the little mild one and he was the big tough one. He was only her height, but he outweighed her by fifty pounds. He was as muscular and chunky as a bull; if he had wanted to he could have thrown her across the room, but he was Ferdinand the Bull who smelled the flowers. Secretly she named their unconceived children.

In June of their first year together he took her on their first trip, a ten-day cruise to the Greek islands and Italy. They flew to Nice, took the boat to Catania and drove to Taormina, looking down on the gorgeous Mediterranean seascape below. The tiny ancient town was hanging off the side of a cliff, with lemon trees and olive trees and flowers everywhere, the air redolent of their mixed perfumes. Their hotel was a twelfth-century monastery, where they made love laughing at the incongruity of tourists like themselves indulging in carnal pleasures in the former dwelling place of the celibate. The narrow, cobbled main street of the town was full of restaurants and trattorias, and shops with chic, expensive designer clothes and leathers. Russell bought her almost anything she admired.

There were a great many unfinished houses. He told her that when a girl child was born the family began to build a home for her, as her dowry, but since they had seventeen or eighteen years to finish it the men of the family worked on it only on weekends or whenever they felt like it. He liked to plan trips, and did extensive research on everything; he knew as much as a tour guide. Every day she was with him Felicity became more convinced that he was the most exciting man she could ever hope to meet, and she wanted his life, she wanted him, and she couldn't tell the difference.

"Are you happy?" she asked him.

"I've never been so happy, Baby."

"I'm happy, too. Do you know what I wish for most in the world?"

"What do you wish for? I'll get it for you."

"That you and I get married."

The happy smile disappeared from his face in an instant and was replaced by a look of cold and superior amusement as if he had shut a door. It made her feel stupid, and it hurt.

"Don't you think there's a reason why I've never been married?" he said.

"Is there? What is it?"

"I'm used to a lot of women," Russell said. "I don't know if I could be satisfied with only one."

"I know you've been seeing other women," she said carefully. "That's why I hate dating so much. You tell me you love me but I still have to share you."

"If it makes you feel better, Baby, you're the only woman in my life right now." She didn't believe it, but she nodded and pretended she did. "Marriage, though," he continued, "is very serious business. Marriage means committing to an emotional and sexual connection of years and years."

"Why don't you give me a chance?" Felicity said. "I know how to really work on making it exciting. You'll see."

"You used the word 'work'. That's the trouble with marriage. Why should it be work?"

"Because it is. But so is even one date. You and I try to please each other. Is that so difficult?"

"It's easy. Right now."

"It would be easy, too, if we got married," Felicity said. "Then maybe we could have a baby. I'd love that."

"A pretty little baby who looks like you," he said, smiling.

"I've always wanted children. Couldn't we just live together and see how it works?" Felicity asked. It made her feel humiliated to have to beg him like that, but she couldn't help trying.

"Oh, look there! Isn't that beautiful?" he said, grabbing her arm, pointing, changing the subject. Felicity did not pursue it because she didn't want to spoil their vacation.

At the end of their first year together, as if she had passed a test, or perhaps because he finally loved her enough, Russell finally let her move in with him.

"This is not a prelude to marriage," he warned her.

"Oh, I understand." But of course she paid no attention to his protest because she felt enormously encouraged. Time was not her enemy yet; she was still young and he was not.

The following year when she took her vacation they went to London and Paris for two weeks because she had never been there. He wined and dined her, he showed her the sights, he paraded her through museums, and one night, walking hand and hand with him along the Seine, high on champagne and melting with love, she proposed again—and again he said no. Felicity was beginning to realize that living with him didn't make her feel any safer than dating him had, although she'd thought it would. She knew he was still seeing other women—how else could he explain the weekend absences for "business" when he could easily have let her come along? They had been together for a long time, for him, and she wondered when he would finally decide to abandon her. If he married her it would be harder for him to leave.

She was still trying to get her mother to love her, even though she was an adult now, living in a distant city, with an independent life of her own. In spite of everything that had happened between them she wanted her mother to be her friend and confidante, the good, wise mother who had always popped up briefly to tantalize her but then suddenly turned on her, the stable mother who existed only in her dreams. At Christmas when she went home to Detroit to visit for a few days, Felicity asked her mother what to do about Russell.

"Cater to him in every way," her mother said. "Make his life so convenient he won't be able to live without you."

"I'm trying," Felicity said in despair.

"Try harder."

"I can't think of anything else to do."

"You just have to know how to play the game right," her mother said. "It's your fault if you can't get him."

Why is everything always my fault? Felicity wondered. The pain in her heart was overwhelming. She shouldn't have gone home at all.

NINETEEN

It is said that four o'clock in the morning is the time when most suicides occur. At four in the morning in that black night that was only day on the clock and certainly not in her life, Billie stumbled half-drunkenly around Toad's apartment looking for something to help her die. Pills were of course her first choice, but whatever he had collected he had taken with him on the road, and whatever she had collected she had already consumed over the last weeks of her deep depression. She was in no condition to go out anywhere tonight to score more.

She had grown up with guns around and was comfortable with them, but she didn't have one or it would have been easy. Knives made her sick. She could cut her food, but a knife slicing into living flesh in a movie made her turn away her eyes and shudder, and the thought of it happening in real life was more horrifying. She could much more easily have put a bullet through her heart than open an artery. She was not even confident that she could do a good job with a razor and a vein, and besides, Toad had taken his razor and hers was electric.

She thought of jumping off the top of his building. He lived in an apartment in a four-story brownstone in the Village, on a street of similar small houses, and if she missed the fire escapes and the trees that could break her fall she supposed she could do it. She had not been out of the apartment in two weeks. The liquor store and pizza parlor delivered, no matter how bad you looked, as long as you had the money. Somehow the thought of going out now, even if it was to meet her welcome death, was off-putting. She wanted to burrow into her hole and disappear. Fatal accidents happened to people all the time at home. The kitchen and bathroom were dangerous places. But the stove was electric, like her razor, and she didn't know how to drown herself. She was afraid some last moment of survival instinct, or perhaps just the agony of exploding lungs, would make her rise and gulp the air.

If you read the newspapers or watched television it seemed it was easy to be mugged, to die in a drive-by shooting, to be pushed onto the subway tracks by a lunatic, to be run over by a car, but when you wanted to commit suicide peacefully at home it was harder than she had thought.

Toad had cartons and cartons of old LP records, every one he had ever owned, tied up with rough, scraggly rope, pushed into closets, into corners. Billie blinked blearily and realized she had found what she had been looking for. Hanging would do just fine.

She went into the bathroom and pulled several times on the shower rod to be sure it would support her weight. Then she got the kitchen shears and sawed through the packing rope from several of the boxes and fashioned herself a nice noose. It was more like twine, but it would do. People hung themselves with neckties, with shoelaces. That was why when you were in jail and were suicidal, or even if you weren't, they took such things away.

She thought for a moment or two about leaving a note, but she had nothing to say to anyone anymore. Her songs would speak for her. She just wanted to be dead, to be out of this pain and humiliation, and finding her body would make that perfectly clear to anyone who had a question.

Billie stood barefoot on the cool bathtub ledge, the rope around her neck. She was taller then than the rod she would hang from, but she would leap. Unconsciousness would come quickly. She tried to think of an appropriate last thought, but the only one that came to her was inappropriate: it was of her parents, who had loved her and been good to her, and how sad they would be. I can't help it, Mama and Daddy, Billie thought. You couldn't protect me from this.

She flew out into the air to become an angel, and that was all she knew.

* * *

When she woke up she was on the tile floor in a pool of blood, and it was still dark. She didn't even know where the blood was coming from, although she knew she was bleeding, and she knew she was alive. Her head hurt so much from where she had hit it that she didn't even notice her neck. She slept there, on the bathroom floor, until wan light came in through the edges of the drawn blinds, and then she got to her feet and managed to get to the sink and the mirror.

She almost didn't recognize the woman she saw there. Her hair was dark and matted with blood, she had a black eye, and her neck was so swollen it went down from her jaw to her shoulders in a straight line like the enormous necks she had seen on some wrestlers. There was a ragged tear on the skin of her throat where the rope had wrenched it before everything came down, and she was afraid to touch it. It was scabby now and turning purple. Stupid bitch, she told herself. You couldn't even get that right. She leaned over the sink and threw up.

She didn't know if she should wash off the blood or try to get to a hospital. St. Vincent's was not far away. Now that she was alive, hung over, and sober, the attempted suicide and any thoughts of trying again seemed behind her. Maybe having survived was a sign. At least, having tried was a gesture of great drama and importance, a catharsis of a kind. She looked and felt so battered that her feelings about Harry and the agent and the music world that had betrayed her were numbed.

She put on her shoes and coat and went out into the street to get a cab. It was not until the driver turned around and asked, "Where to?" that Billie realized she could not answer him. She tried to speak and no sound came out at all.

The driver took her to the hospital anyway, she looked that bad. In terror and with no command of sign language and no inclination to write, she was not able to answer any of the questions they put to her in the emergency room of St. Vincent's, so they let her show them her identification and fixed up her wounds. It was too late, the resident said, to stitch her neck. There would be a scar. A cut like that had to be stitched right away, he said, or not at all. She was unable to talk because she had fractured her larynx. It would heal, and she would be able to speak again, although he wasn't sure if she would sound the same.

"Just don't try to sing," he said, with a pleasant laugh, and Billie realized he didn't recognize her.

Just don't try to sing....

She stayed in Toad's apartment and healed, being good to herself. She cut down the drinking to a normal amount, although for a while she didn't feel like drinking at all, and the only drugs she took were aspirin and a little grass. She hadn't been this healthy since she was that kid who had just come to New York, before it all started—the bad times and the good times and the bad. She had the shower rod repaired. She cleaned the apartment and kept the refrigerator stocked with nourishing food. She took walks around the city the way she had when she was twenty, but this time she couldn't think of any lyrics for her songs. Instead, she thought about her life, what she had done to herself and what she would do now. She waited for her speaking voice to come back and it finally did, but it was unrecognizable. She knew she would never sing again.

When you've reached the depths and paid your dues, Billie thought to herself, it's as if God has given you a second chance. If I give in to despair again I'll only be that foolish woman who was in love with Harry Lawless and lent him her life. At least I had my career when I could. That's something I'll always have: the experience and the glory and the memories. I destroyed any hope of having a singing career again when I killed my voice instead of myself, so all the worst things I could have imagined have already happened to me. Now I'm going to be happy. Now I'm going to be brave.

She thought about ways to make money that she might enjoy at the same time, and always her thoughts came back to what she had learned at her father's roadhouse. He had taught her well. She could open a small bar and restaurant here in New York City, and she would attract interesting people, maybe people in the music business, and when she was working there she wouldn't ever be alone or lonely. So now when she took her walks she looked for available spaces to open her place. She would call it Yellowbird, because that sounded hopeful, and it would be a monument to her mentor, Janis Joplin, because she didn't want it to be a mausoleum to her own past; that would be too morbid, and besides, most people hadn't ever known who she was, and she was sure that of those who had, plenty had forgotten.

She would need a loan, and for that she would need her father's advice. She was not ready yet to face her parents in her condition and have to make up lies. She would do that when she was better.

Toad came back between his road tours and she practiced her first lie on him. Her swollen neck had gone back to normal and she put on a turtleneck sweater to cover what she knew was going to remain an ugly scar. "The worst laryngitis," Billie told him. "Shit, was I sick! I was in bed for a week."

"It's going around," he said. "You sound like hell."

And I'm going to continue to sound like hell, Billie thought, and for the first time her throat hurt from chokedback tears, not injury, and she had to fight the wave of emotion that almost overwhelmed her because she had not been ready for it. I have a right to grieve, she told herself. It isn't weakness, it's natural. When Toad went out to the clubs with the rest of the band she pleaded illness so she wouldn't have to go with them, and when she was alone and safe she sobbed all night, deep, hurting sobs that left her well again. Even the timbre of the sobs sounded strange, but she was just going to have to get used to it.

A few steps forward, a few steps back, Billie thought. From now on I'm going to be nice to myself.

When she found the location she wanted for Yellowbird she flew back to Texas to see her parents. Her second lie was ready. "I had nodes on my vocal cords," she told them. "The surgeon took them off. I'm still healing, but I won't be what I was. I don't want to be mediocre, I'd rather retire and do something else." She told them her plans. "Daddy, the one thing you didn't teach me was how to get a loan."

He took her to the bank where he had gotten his own financing, where he had done business all his years, and they trusted her. She knew it had been a good move to get the money here, not back in New York, not that she would have been turned down in New York, but here she was still a star.

"Aren't you hot, honey?" her mother said when Billie kept wearing her turtleneck.

"No," Billie said. Of course she was hot, Plano was hot, but she never wanted her parents to know how she had betrayed them and their love by trying to kill herself instead of asking them for help. She was still their daughter and they would have thought they could have done something, but the truth was there was nothing they could have done. If she had been sane enough to take her grief home to the place where she was still cherished, she would have been too sane to get up on the rim of that tub with a shredded piece of packing rope around her neck.

"Well, I sure am," her mother said, fanning herself.

Billie flew back to New York, rented herself her own cheap apartment, and got to work on her new career. When Yellowbird opened, her parents came to New York—their first trip to this city—to celebrate with her. Billie was wearing a black chiffon dress with a matching scarf wound around her neck, which was fine because it was autumn. Her speaking voice, of course, was still the same.

"You ought to sue that surgeon," her father said. "He should have done a better job."

"I'm sort of grateful to him," Billie said. "I'm going to like my new life."

"That is true," her father said. "You can take it from me, that is so true."

Yellowbird did well from the beginning, and Billie didn't know why any more than she had known why about the ups and downs of her music career. She was still dealing with the fickle public, but they liked her. People dropped in because it was a neighborhood place and was different, and then they told their friends. Out-of-towners came in, and a lot of men. They liked to talk to Billie and get occasional free drinks. Sometimes celebrities dropped by. They liked that it was hard to find. Night birds came because they liked the ambiance. The restaurant critics, when they got around to reviewing Yellowbird, gave her mediocre reviews for the food, but that was okay because one star for a convenient neighborhood restaurant really meant two because people were lazy. Besides, Billie had grown up on that food and she didn't know what they were talking about. Obviously her regulars agreed with her.

Yellowbird was everything she wanted. It was small and manageable and income-producing, and she was able to rent a nicer apartment in a new high rise around the corner so she could be close to work. After a while Billie felt confident enough about herself to have her first affair, with a man she met at the bar, and when that was over she had another. She realized she could still pick and choose. She doubted very much that she would ever fall in love again—she was too wounded and too independent—but sex and romance were fine, too. She felt she had lived an entire lifetime in the decade that had just passed, and she could hardly wait to see what the next decade would bring her.

TWENTY

Gara was glad that her mother had always been very close to her aunt and uncle and their spouses, because after her father's death the burden of becoming her mother's constant companion would have fallen to her by default, and she didn't know how she could continue to be kind to and supportive of May when what she really wanted to do was fight with her. It was unconscionable to fight with the bereaved, Gara thought, although occasionally she reminded herself that she, too, was bereaved and deserved some consideration.

It was easier when she and Carl took May out to dinner at a restaurant, because her mother had good manners and even seemed a little cowed by Carl—after all these years!—and they were able to talk about a variety of things. Carl loved to hear her mother talk about how cute, how smart Gara had been as a child and was even now. Sometimes at these dinners the two of them clucked over her talents and foibles as if she were their child. It was a strange bond, but Gara liked it when they started their little routine. It made her feel warm. I may have married my good father, she told herself, amused, but it hasn't stopped me from sleeping with him.

But despite the encouragement of her aunt and uncle and their spouses, and her own greatly increased filial attentiveness, her mother did not want to try to have a life of her own, did not know how to, and Gara felt both resentful and guilty. There were the many phone messages from May when she knew perfectly well Gara was with patients and had turned on the answering machine, and there were the calls that reached Gara too early in the morning and too late at night, and there were the times when, knowing she had not been attentive enough, Gara had to put in the call herself and talk for an hour about nothing, and somehow always ended up defending herself about something anyway. They were in touch constantly now. It was not the calls she minded but their content. Her mother still managed to make her feel as uncomfortable as she had when Gara was growing up.

She knew her mother was lonely, but sometimes she wondered if her mother was that much lonelier than she had been before she became a widow. Gara wished she had not been an only child. If she'd had siblings they could have talked to her mother on the phone, too, on these empty evenings, watching their egos slipping away under the assault; they could have taken May out to dinner, her sisters could have gone shopping with her and asked for advice, and reluctantly—or perhaps willingly—accepted complete control.

Would these never-to-be-born sisters and brothers have gotten along with May better than she did? Would the configuration of the family have happily lightened the burden on her as the one, or would there have been rivalry, competition, even resentment? What if May had alienated them even more than she had Gara, and Gara had been left alone with her anyway? She pictured a selfish sister living in Europe (a sister who had fled for her life to a different continent), forgetting to call; a wandering, wastrel brother (a vulnerable boy struggling against his own parent-child bond that had been too strong) vanished somewhere on the West Coast, surfacing only to ask for money and introduce another grandchild they wouldn't see again for years. She would never know.

She talked to her best friend Jane about it. Jane's father had also died comparatively young, and Jane's mother, like Gara's, had never worked and didn't know how to fill her time. "Well, it's easier for me to deal with my mother," Jane said, "because I have sisters and we share her."

"I wish I did."

"I know, it's hard for you. I really understand. You know, my mother is difficult but not nearly as difficult as yours is. Mine never really brought us up. She let us do whatever we wanted. So in a way she's always been the child. I mean, she's harmless."

"Harmless..." Gara said wistfully. "How I would love and protect a harmless mother."

"It's hard anyway," Jane said. "Even with the grandchildren, although they do help amuse her. They adore visiting her because she dotes on them and lets them do just what we did when we were kids, run wild and have Twinkies for breakfast."

"I could not imagine my mother being a good grandmother," Gara said. "I always pictured her scaring them about all the perils in the world."

"Oh, mine does that," Jane said, and laughed. "We ignore her."

Gara was surprised. "It never occurred to me that if I had children they and I would become a 'we' to gang up against my mother. That doesn't sound so bad."

"They gang up against me, too," Jane said. "You only discover these things after you've had children."

"So where were you to tell me this before it was too late?"

"It's not too late. You and Carl can still have a baby. That doctor who told you thirty-six was way off. Things have changed. Women are having them now when they're thirty-nine. You have a whole year to get on it."

Gara smiled. "We're too content with things the way they are."

Five years went by. May was her mother and May was the child Gara had never had, demanding constant gratification like an infant, suffering from separation anxiety like a four-year-old, insisting on winning every minor skirmish like an adolescent. When Gara and Carl went to Europe for their brief vacations May would panic. She kept calling, asking when they would be coming back, and because she wanted to be sure not to miss Gara she called in the middle of the night. It was not night for her in New York. Of course as soon as she telephoned, Gara was wide awake.

"Will you remember Passover?" May said for the third time. "It's going to be at Aunt Laura's this year, and she wants you and Carl specifically to know you're expected."

"We'll be home next week," Gara said, annoyed. "Passover is next month."

"Just so you don't forget. Maybe you should bring her something nice from Paris. She likes Lalique."

"I think I'll do Passover and then you can all bring *me* Lalique," Gara said.

"Why are you always so nasty to me?"

"I don't know," Gara said. "Do you think it's so ludicrous that I might have a family event at my place?"

"Go ahead," her mother said, in that voice that meant: *You wouldn't know how.* Gara didn't know if she knew how or not, but she knew she would never do it as long as someone else wanted to.

"What kind of perfume do you want me to bring you?"

"Something we can share. Get a big bottle and we'll each take half. What about Shalimar?"

"I hate Shalimar," Gara said. She didn't want to smell like her mother. "Is Shalimar what you want? I'll get you your own bottle."

"That would be nice. And you know what else you should get? My friend Gertrude likes to buy a Hermes scarf and cut it in half and stitch the hem, and then she and her daughter share it. They're too big anyway. Gara, buy a Hermes scarf and then you and I will share it," May said in all seriousness.

"Motherrr!" Her voice sounded to herself as if she were still fourteen years old. "People don't cut Hermes scarves in half! That's destroying a work of art."

"Gertrude and her daughter don't mind."

"I'll buy you your own scarf. What color would you like?"

"You don't know by now what my favorite colors are?"

"All right, I'll surprise you and you won't like it."

"I always like it," her mother said, offended.

Gara remembered the "silver" pin but said nothing. She also remembered the scarves, the bracelets, the gloves that were never worn, not exchanged, simply put away like a reproach.

"Put Passover in your calendar," her mother said.

"It's there," Gara said. "The calendar comes with it."

"With Aunt Laura?" May said, and laughed.

Then, the night before Gara and Carl were to leave Paris to

return home, a phone call came from her aunt herself. Her
voice was grave. May, the immortal goddess, the thorn in the
side, the immovable object, the national monument, the well-
spring of guilt, the adored and hated mother, the piece of unfinished business of the heart, had been struck down by a
stroke and was in New York Hospital in intensive care, paralyzed and in very serious condition. So the food had finally
won. Despite understanding that this had been inevitable,
Gara was still in shock. She and Carl went to the hospital directly from the airport.

To her vast relief May seemed much farther away from her
demise than Gara had been led to expect. She was having
great difficulty moving and speaking, with one side useless
and a thick tongue, but she was very angry, and she was able
to make her needs known.

"Your mother is amazing," the nurse told Gara. "I've
never seen such determination."

"Ah, yes."

"I want a knife," May mumbled to Gara. "I want a knife."

"Who do you want to kill?"

"Myself."

"You almost did. When you get well, and you will, and
home, I'm taking you to Pritikin."

"You think I'll get well?"

"Yes," Gara lied. Actually she had no idea, but she knew if
May had to live in this helpless state she would rather be
dead. "Listen to the doctor," she said. And to the nurse, "Be
careful, she might try to hurt herself."

She spoke to the doctor. He was an eminent specialist
named Dr. Green, and he thought May was the sweetest
woman who had ever lived. Gara wondered what her
mother had done to him, but then she knew. This was the
way May affected anyone who was not her daughter and
who hadn't known her for a long time.

"This is a critical period," Dr. Green said. "She could have
more strokes. She's extremely overweight, and her heart is
not good and her cholesterol is high."

"I know," Gara said.

"She could be gone tomorrow, but if she has her way she'll

live forever. An amazing woman. Still, I must warn you, none of us are masters of our fate."

"I was hoping you were," Gara said.

At home that night, exhausted and jet lagged though she was, with resentful patients coming in the morning to remind her she had abandoned them, not knowing they might soon be abandoned again, and May possibly living her last hours on earth, Gara couldn't sleep. All her life she had wanted to be away from the spell of her magical mother, the bad witch; and now that the fulfillment of her wish was at hand, she wondered how she would be able to live with the guilt. It's not as if her stroke was my fault, she reminded herself. I am not the magical child, not the all-powerful; my anger doesn't kill.

She crept out of bed quietly so as not to wake Carl and went into the kitchen where she drank water from the refrigerator and thought about her mother. The worst part, Gara thought, is that she's going to leave me before we ever make peace with each other. I never wanted a different mother; I just wanted the one I already had to behave differently. I was as stubborn as she was. We all are; we never give in, carrying the struggle into relationships with people who represent our mothers without our knowing it; and if we do give in we are more than defeated, we are lost to ourselves.

People who have had happy childhoods with accepting, happy parents, have no idea what it's like for the rest of us. They just know they love and are loved.

I hate May for leaving me, and I hated her for tearing me down all those years, but if I ever let myself feel the love I have for her hidden somewhere inside my infant heart, I don't know if I can stand the pain.

My mother and I will never have our epiphany. We will not have our dramatic last act, our tearful confrontation with forgiveness and understanding. Not this mother, not with this daughter. I had to become the way I am to save my life, and so she lost as much as I did.

Yes, Gara thought, May lost, too. That's the tragedy and, if I want to think of it that way, the revenge. We will spar and bicker for the rest of our time together, and she will claim she is being cheated of the daughter she wanted, but because she doesn't know me she will never really know what a loving daughter she could have had.

Gara found pieces of time to go to the hospital every day to sit with May and listen helplessly to her rage on about her helplessness and complain about the hospital food. At the end of the week they moved her out of intensive care into a private room. Things seemed better, so Gara told Carl she would slip out of the hospital early, meet him after work, and they would have dinner together in a neighborhood restaurant.

"Oh? Where are you going?" May asked.

"Just to get some Chinese food with Carl."

"Comb the back of your hair."

"I'll be back tomorrow," Gara said.

"Enjoy your life," May said. Gara didn't know if it was meant as a benediction or a complaint.

The slip of paper in Gara's fortune cookie read, "All great losses are also great gains." At approximately the same time that she was reading it aloud to her husband in the restaurant, her mother died of a massive coronary, alone in her room at New York Hospital. It seemed a bizarre and frightening coincidence, and Gara wondered if it would have been easier if her fortune had been, "All great gains are also great losses."

She was an adult now, irrevocably. She had no parents, no siblings, no children. She stood alone, the oldest and youngest of her most direct, intimate bloodline. And she was only forty-three.

Afterward, whenever she had to talk about May's death, Gara would add sentimentally, "You know, the last thing my mother said to me was, 'Enjoy your life.'"

"Oh," everyone said, "May loved you so much. She was always so considerate. Always thinking about you, wanting you to be happy."

"It's too bad she didn't enjoy her own life," Carl said to Gara when they were alone.

"I know." She played her mother's last words over in her head. There had been bitterness in May's tone, whether because Gara was deserting her or because she knew Gara's life was and always would be happier than hers had been. "Enjoy your life." A complaint or a benediction?

Perhaps the whole point of their mother-daughter struggle was that the message had always been mixed. It made Gara feel better to understand that. It was no one's fault, it was just the way it was.

TWENTY-ONE

Eve was living in New York with Nicole now, in a small apartment on St. Mark's Place in the Village, a neighborhood Eve considered sleazy and too reminiscent of the Sunset Strip in L.A. where she had started out. She wondered when she would ever be able to afford to live somewhere decent, in a big apartment overlooking clean streets, where everyone in the building was an adult and wore nice clothes, instead of here where they looked as if they dressed from pushcarts and were young and druggy. Nicole was in first grade at public school, and after school she was in day care at a nearby church. Even though Eve was half Jewish and half Baptist, she had never been brought up in any religion, and neither had Nicole, and Eve couldn't care less, church or synagogue, as long as it was affordable.

"Baby Jesus loves me," Nicole said.

"That's nice."

"I can talk to him when I'm lonely."

"Yeah, well, just don't start hallucinating," Eve said.

She was working as an office temp all over the city, going to casting calls and auditions on the side. She wished it had been the other way around: pursuing her career and working part time to pay for her subsistence, but having her child with her was a great deal more difficult, she was realizing over and over again every day, than sending money to have Nicole live with Grandma.

There were clothes, books, toys, doctors, the dentist, and groceries. It was necessary to hire baby-sitters. A child was as expensive as an adult, except that an adult did not grow out of things the way a child did. At least Nicole didn't need much food. She had strange eating habits: she refused to eat anything for supper but graham crackers soaked in a bowl of milk. Eve hoped she wouldn't get malnutrition. She sneaked children's vitamin drops into the milk, the way you would with a kitten, and felt maternal for having thought of it.

A child also demanded time. After crying for her grandmother and her former life for two solid months Nicole adjusted and seemed like her old self, or the part of her old self Eve knew about. Nicole was irrepressibly chatty, and she didn't like to be alone. She wanted Eve to help her with her little homework. She wanted to sleep in Eve's bed. She wanted to have play dates. As often as she could Eve parked her in front of the television set, the way she had spent her own time as a child.

"Watch this good movie," she'd say. "*Godzilla*, made in Japan for two cents. See how phony the sets look? This is from the genre of el cheapo horror movies."

"Like *King Kong*, Mommy?"

"No, *King Kong* was the best they could do at the time. They thought it was terrific."

"I'm going to be an actress like you," Nicole often said, although she had never seen her mother work.

"No, you're not. You're going to be a producer and hire me."

In her spare time Eve was looking for a kind and sexy boyfriend to replace Juan, to help with the rent and be around for sex and company so she wouldn't have to hire a baby-sitter so often and go out. So far the men she had met were unreliable, unemployed, unattractive, and unacceptable. The four U's. It was a vicious circle, Eve thought; if you went to a lively local bar restaurant to drink and meet people, you met the kind of men who couldn't afford to go anywhere better, and she didn't have the money yet to go to places where she could make the contacts she wanted.

New York cost too much. The prices on the menus sent her into shock, and now that she had sold her car she spent so much on taxis she could have rented a car instead, but where would she park it? If she put it in the street it would be wrecked, vandalized, or stolen, and a garage cost as much as her apartment. Baby-sitters charged so much they must have thought it was a real job. She had been in an off-off-

Broadway show, but it paid so little it was as if she weren't working at all. In some irrational way she blamed Nicole for everything that was frustrating or difficult in her life, even though a lot of this was in no way Nicole's fault.

Her mother sent her a picture postcard of a luxury hotel on a beach with palm trees, whereon she wrote that her new life was everything she had hoped. Eve felt like sending her one back of Times Square, saying that her new life was everything she had dreaded.

But despite everything, Eve loved New York. It was exciting, it was composed of many different little villages, and you could walk. She bought a ratty fur coat at a thrift shop for the cold winter and didn't mind the weather at all. She was basically a hot-blooded animal, and she had found her place. Even the sticky summer didn't really bother her. This was better than where she had grown up.

I'm a New Yorker, Eve thought, after the first year. The city and I have the same energy. I belong here. This is where I will become a star. For all that the city beat you down it was also a place where it was possible to be an optimist. She was pleased to see that her daughter, still at the adaptable, imitative age, had finally lost the speech patterns of her roots and had become a New Yorker, too.

Eve met her next live-in boyfriend, Mack, in a way that she considered typically New York. On a pleasant spring day she had stopped in front of Rockefeller Center during her lunch hour to watch a street mime. He was tall and thin and supple, with curly red hair, dressed like one of the usual Marcel Marceau clones, in whiteface with a daisy in his hand; but he had a sense of humor about him and an inordinate gracefulness that set him apart from all the others she had seen. She thought he was good enough to be professional. He was also very cute.

Although she never wasted money she was moved enough to drop a dollar into the hat he had placed on the sidewalk. Then she continued to stay, while passersby stopped and went on again, some of them leaving money, and to amuse herself she tried to make eye contact and rattle him. He was her age, and she wondered what he was like in real life. Then he finally gave in and started making eye contact with her.

"Coffee break," he said, stopped still, and then shook himself as if he were shaking off a dream. "Want to have coffee with me?"

"Real coffee or make believe?" Eve said.

He swept up his earnings and they disappeared into his pockets. Then he bowed and offered her his arm. "Real."

"All right."

He led her to the corner where there was a street vendor. Since there was no coffee he bought her a Coke. "My name is Mack."

"I'm Eve. I'm an actress."

"Well, I'm an actor, in case you didn't guess."

"Do you *like* being a street mime?"

"Actually it's fun."

"I was a clown once," Eve said. "I hated it."

"In the circus?"

"In Beverly Hills. Same thing." She smiled at him. She wondered what he would look like without his makeup.

They talked for a while and then he made a dinner date with her. He went back to his miming and she went back to her office. That night she recognized him without his makeup and liked what she saw. He was straight, single, serious, and from Maine. He was attending acting class and his family sent him money. They had pizza, and afterward Eve took him to her apartment and let him stay all night. It was the first time she had done that with Nicole living with her, but she couldn't live her life for her daughter forever.

"Slack Mack," Eve said to him, laughing. He was completely boneless except for the bone that counted. They had sex three times. At breakfast he mimed for Nicole and made her giggle. He said he had a little niece just like her. That weekend he moved in.

It had always been that way for Eve where men were concerned: instantly or nothing. They either liked her energy and power or they didn't. Since she had no idea how to tell the difference, when she wanted something she went after it, and her scattershot technique had worked often enough for her to feel she had a certain irresistible appeal. Now that she had Mack to share the responsibilities of her life she could concentrate on her career.

It was during her relationship with Mack that Eve found out she liked to tie men up in bed. She was just kidding around with him one night and it came to her that it would be fun, and the next thing he knew he was spread-eagled on her thrift-shop four-poster bed with his hands and feet tied to the bedposts with her scarves. Loosely, of course, at first, but later she began to tie him with knots he couldn't get out of. She was good at it. Slack Mack was supple, but he wasn't Houdini. She liked to sit on top of him and ride him when he was helpless like that, and obviously he enjoyed it, too, because he got very hard and went insane. Sometimes Eve wouldn't let him move.

"You're mine!" she would hiss at him, impaling herself on his penis with such force it seemed she was impaling him. "You can't get away, you'll never get away. Stay still!" She always came with greater intensity when she enacted this little scene than she ever had in the boring missionary position.

She bought pretty silk scarves to tie him up with. Her favorite was red, the color of fire, her color. She anointed him with oils. She dribbled Nicole's Yoo-Hoo chocolate syrup on him and licked it off.

"My hands are falling asleep," he sometimes complained.

"That's the only part of you that is," Eve would answer.

Once Mack jumped on her, pushed her down on the bed, and insisted on being the one on top. He held her wrists with his strong hands and Eve remembered that whatever she had done to him had been with his implicit permission and therefore she was not as in control as she had thought. She felt as if he was raping her. When he tried to kiss her she bit him.

"Don't *ever* hold me down again," she told him afterward.

"You're very sick, do you know that?" he said, looking in the mirror at his lip where it had begun to swell.

"Oh, am I? Well, I have news for you. You're the sick one."

She didn't like to admit that she hated men, but she knew in a way she did. What did they expect? Look at the way my father behaved, Eve thought resentfully. She had never known a nice man growing up who could be a role model, who would care about her. Even her teachers had been women. But the funny thing was, even though she didn't like men, she needed one anyway. She was trapped by her heterosexuality. Or perhaps just by her sexuality.

"Why can't you be like other girls?" Mack asked, a little plaintively.

"I'm a woman," Eve snapped. "Not a girl."

"Why can't you be like other women?"

"It takes two to tango," she said, and turned her back on him.

She knew he would never go away until she was ready to dismiss him.

The next year, at long last, after all her miserable part-time jobs and penny pinching and rejections and humiliations, both their careers turned around. Both she and Mack got jobs on soap operas in New York. Her soap was called *Brilliant Days*, and she played Xenia Braddock, a villainess. Xenia was always doing inventive terrible things to the women she was jealous of, and taking their husbands or boyfriends, or even, in one story line, their baby.

Eve was excited because it was steady work with a contract and promise of publicity and millions of viewers and fans, but she was also somewhat displeased because a soap wasn't what she considered art. The stage was art. Even some movies were art. Close-up head shots in little bitty scenes with almost no time to rehearse and work on her character was not art, and she thought most of her lines were stupid and the story was worse; and of course her part wasn't big enough.

But there was real money coming in for the first time. Eve and Mack and Nicole moved to a better apartment, on the Upper West Side near work, where a lot of theater people lived. They both worked long hours, and had different days on the set because of their characters' different story schedules, and they had pages of dialogue to learn overnight, so she hardly ever spent time with him anymore even though they were still together.

From time to time Eve took Nicole to the set. It was a very family-oriented atmosphere, and if you wanted to you could bring your small children and they were welcome. One actress even nursed her baby in her dressing room. Eve was one of the younger members of the cast, and the other actors were surprised to see she had such a big daughter. They made a fuss over Nicole, who knew her place and never made trouble, smiled at everybody, and was growing up to be a very winsome-looking child. Eve kept hoping Nicole would be discovered.

"You ought to write a part for my daughter," she told the producer, Ira Stebbins.

"Tell the writers, don't tell me," he said lightly, to get rid of her. Eve knew enough to be aware that if they had a part for a child they would only hire a professional child actor, but how was Nicole supposed to get to be a professional if they wouldn't give her a part? Eve had already made it her business to become friendly with the head writer, Anna Malkovit, an ancient but adorable little woman with crinkly bright eyes, who always wore a hat at work; Eve wondered if she was bald. Usually she wore a baseball cap (which reminded Eve of her mother), but unlike Eve's mother she had a fondness for the Yankees.

"Xenia should have a daughter," Eve told her.

"She can't have children. That's why she stole Susan's baby."

"Well, what if a doctor fixed her up and she could? Or if a miracle happened? Things like that go on all the time in soaps."

"I know," Anna said. "I make them up."

"Well, I think Xenia should have a long-lost daughter who shows up already seven or eight years old, and she thought the kid was dead but she isn't, and then you wouldn't have to hire any babies, who are a pain in the ass to work with. What if her little daughter was living all this time in South America?"

"South America is a last resort for when a soap is running out of plot," Anna said. "Kindly don't tell me how to write my own story lines."

"I'm just trying to be helpful," Eve said. "Actually, I'm too young to have a daughter her age. No one will believe it. Maybe Nicole should be my half sister, and now she's an orphan, so she comes to live with me. If I was mean to her the fans would hate me even more."

"They hate you enough," Anna said. "Go away."

Since her good ideas fell on deaf ears Eve went to the producer. "Ira, my part is getting to be just peripheral," she said. "You aren't even using me. I have so much more to give. I think you should have a story line with me and my daughter."

"What daughter?"

"My real daughter, Nicole, who you know and love. Everybody likes her; she has real charisma. She should be Xenia's long-lost little sister in the show."

"I don't think your part is peripheral," Ira said. "You have a very strong personality. If Xenia's role was too big it would overshadow the other characters and skew the show."

"Did you say 'screw'?" Eve asked, annoyed.

"No, I said *skew*. As in tilt, make unbalanced. A little of Xenia goes a long way."

"That's only because of the way I play her," Eve said.

"That's what I just told you."

She backed off for a while, trying to think of new ideas to present to him and Anna. Then, one morning, as she was approaching the coffee and food table, Eve overheard Ira Stebbins talking to Patsy Marlin, the actress who played Susan, who was his best friend. Eve had often wondered if they were having an affair, or if they once had.

"The thing about Eve," he was saying quietly, chuckling, "is that she doesn't even have to act. There's something about her that's so intrinsically annoying that she could play Xenia in her sleep."

"I wish she would," Patsy said.

They don't like me! Eve thought in surprise. Why don't they like me? They must be jealous. These people are such hypocrites. They all pretend to be a big happy family and act like they love each other, but way down deep I bet they're all out for themselves. Well, they're all scared for their jobs, that's what it must be. They know if I had a decent chance I could run away with this stupid show, and they don't want that to happen.

But it still stung that there were people she had to work

with who disliked her. Eve didn't know what to do about it so she willed herself to forget about it, and after she had turned her power onto her own well being for a while she found she was able to put them out of her mind.

This didn't mean she gave up trying to have Xenia become a bigger part, or that she didn't approach Anna Malkovit from time to time with new ideas she'd had (which were always rejected), or keep after Ira Stebbins with the hope of wearing him down. It only meant she was able to do it with calm and confidence. Everybody really likes me, she told herself, as much as they can considering how scared and jealous they are. If I had to make the choice I'd rather win an Emmy than have them invite me to the dinner parties I know they have because they talk about them the next day. Nobody ever said this wasn't a tough world, and it takes the strong to win in it. I have always been strong.

After she had been on the show for a year Eve had her own small fan club and answered all their letters herself. People started recognizing her on the street—or at least they recognized Xenia Braddock. "Xenia!" they would call after her. Her fans were mostly young women. Sometimes they knew she was an actress and told her they watched her faithfully, but sometimes they told her she was a bitch. Eve understood that was a compliment, even though they didn't.

Mack was a success, too, on his show, with his own coterie of young women fans, who told him they loved Farley, his character. "Don't marry Larissa," they would warn him. "She's cheating on you." He and Eve would laugh about it.

She knew they didn't spend much time together anymore, but the sex, when they had it, was still good and a bond between them, so it didn't occur to her that anything was wrong until the night she came home from work and found him packing his things.

"I'm moving out at the end of the week," he said. He looked nervous and creepy, as if he was getting ready to dodge some physical violence on her part. "I've rented my own apartment."

"What?" Eve screamed.

"I'll leave you my share of next month's rent because I

didn't give you any notice," he said meekly. "You can keep all the furniture and the stereo."

"I should hope so," Eve said. She wasn't upset because she loved him—because she didn't love him—but she was furious at this unexpected betrayal. "Why are you leaving me?"

"I've wanted to for a while," Mack said.

"Why?"

He hesitated. "To tell you the truth, I'm afraid of you," he said finally. "You're a dangerous woman."

"How am I dangerous?" Eve demanded, knowing it was true.

"You just are. There's an anger and violence in you that scares me."

"You love it," Eve said.

"No," he said. "I don't know if I loved it. But I know I don't anymore."

"Where are you moving to?" she asked. She had never been ditched before and she began to feel a little nauseated.

"The East Side."

"Couldn't get far enough away, huh?"

"I'll miss Nicole," Mack said. He was packing his rolled-up balls of white socks in neat rows in his suitcase as if he were packing eggs.

"Sure you will. You don't know she's alive."

"I spend more time with her than you do."

"Then why don't you just take her?"

"Will you tell her goodbye?" Mack asked.

"Do it yourself."

"She's not my daughter, you know," Mack said. "She's the daughter of my...ex-girlfriend, I guess you are. It's your place to explain to her what happened. I know it's going to be hard on her, but you can explain that I was a transient date and things didn't work out."

"Don't you tell me what to tell her," Eve snapped. "You have about as much insight as a frog."

"I really feel badly about her," Mack said. "I know she likes me."

"She doesn't like you," Eve said coldly. Actually, she thought Nicole was very fond of him. "She's an actress, like her mother."

"Have you been acting, too?" Mack asked.

"Which means what?"

"Do you love me?" He had asked her that before, from time to time, and she had said yes, but it had been the necessary reply, since he had also said that he loved her.

"You should know that I do," Eve said. "Although now I'm beginning to change my mind."

"You always said you did," Mack said. "But somehow I never really believed it."

"Why not?"

"I don't think you're capable of loving anybody but yourself."

"Why would you ever think that?" Eve said, insulted.

"It's just how I perceive you."

"You've been saying those trashy lines too long on your show," Eve said. "You're beginning to turn into your character."

"Maybe I am," he said.

"You're weak."

"I guess I used to be."

She drew herself together and marshaled her inner resources. "So now you're going to leave me *and* insult me?" she said. "You don't have to wait until the end of the week. You can get out tonight."

"Okay," he said, and he sounded relieved.

When he got to the front door with his suitcases Nicole came out of her room. Her face was streaked with tears and Eve realized she had been listening. She had always been a sneaky little thing under all that sunniness.

"Your mother and I have decided to break up," Mack said to her. "It's in no way your fault. You have nothing to do with it."

"I hope you come back," Nicole said softly. They hugged each other. He did not hug Eve and she made no move to touch him. He gave her one backward, inscrutable look, and then he was gone.

After Mack left, for a few angry weeks Eve felt as if he had trashed her life. She took over his closet space and drawer space as quickly as possible so she would find an advantage to his absence, and she told Nicole she was not to mention his name because he was a liar and a bad person. Since the party who is cheated on is usually the last one to know, it took Eve that long to discover that Mack had been having an affair with an actress on his show, the one who played Larissa. She was a totally plastic-looking blonde, and Eve was sure she wasn't very good in bed. They had apparently moved in together after he left; so that was the apartment on the East Side. Eve wished them both a miserable early-morning commute across the park and a rotten life.

Whether or not she had loved him didn't matter. Mack had been her boyfriend and another woman had taken him. But Eve felt that because she had been with him before he met the interloper she had put her mark on him forever, as if she had branded him, so that no matter where he went, no matter who he ended up with, he would be roaming with her name of ownership on him. He should have waited until she got tired of him before he tried to go away. Now she would always hate him, and hate was a negative vibration that hurt the hater as much as the hated, perhaps more, so she had something else to be angry at him for.

It also rankled that she had to pay the full rent herself every month now. It was a lucky thing the apartment was rent stabilized. Of course, she was making a lot of money, and investing it wisely and conservatively, but half the rent was half the rent. She tried to look at the good side. Although it was true she would never have chosen such a nice apartment if she thought she and Nicole would have to be living in it alone, it was also true that as a woman on her way up in the world she deserved a pleasant place to live, and to have it without being dependent on a man's help was even better.

At Christmas, as they always did, Eve and Nicole went to Florida to see her mother, who was now living in a pink-painted Art Deco building near the beach. Every year Eve swore to herself it would be the last time because she was so bored and the visit brought up so many unhappy memories. But Nicole was happy. She liked seeing her grandmother and she loved swimming in the apartment's small pool. Her grandmother had treated her to swimming lessons the first year they came to visit.

Eve's mother, who had always looked like a man, had

been reincarnated as a Miami Beach matron. She had let her hair grow and dyed it a reddish blonde, and had it set into a stiff, petaled shape that made her head look like a spun-sugar artichoke. She was wearing makeup now, and it got into her wrinkles and made them look worse, and her no-nonsense steel rimmed eyeglasses had been replaced by fanciful oversized sunglasses with glittery rims. The overalls had been replaced, too, by pastel-colored polyester pants suits, worn with floral or psychedelic printed blouses. Her nails were manicured and painted red. She had a lot of friends, for the first time in her adult life, all widows or divorcees her own age, and her social calendar was always full.

"Val," the other women would beseech, "we need a fourth for bridge; Val, we want to go to the Flamingo for happy hour, come with us!" Eve had not heard her mother called by her first name by anyone for years, not since her father had left, and she sometimes thought that whatever had happened in her home when her father was with them were only fantasies, not memories. Her mother's new look and name made her seem more distant than ever.

"So where's Mack?" her mother asked.

"Gone."

"No loss. You didn't need him."

She didn't ask who had left whom, and for that Eve was grateful. Now that Mack was out of her life she sometimes thought she loved him after all. Sometimes, walking on the beach alone at the end of the day, when the sunset made gold and silver streaks in the sky above the eternal waves, she felt a sad, sweet longing that was like pain. Maybe it was just being in Florida and missing her father—another memory that was probably a fantasy. Mack had been kind to Nicole. But these warm nights made Eve miss Mack more than she ever had in New York.

She thought about the good times, the way he had made her laugh, how he had clowned around, how he had listened to her sympathetically whenever she complained. She remembered holding his long, slim body while they slept and thinking how that very act always made her drowsy. She had picked on him and yelled at him and he had never gotten mean about it. He had loved her. Other men had, too, but Mack was different. She had never known that until now when it was too late and he was gone.

Why hadn't she noticed how lovable he was? What was wrong with her? They could have been happy together.

After she got back to New York, Eve began to watch Mack's soap again on the days she wasn't working, hoping to get a glimpse of him. She hated watching his love scenes with that bitch he was having love scenes with in real life, too, but she missed him, and having him on her television set made her feel closer to him. She was beginning to wonder why he had really left her. He had said it was because she frightened him, so maybe they were ill-fated from the beginning after all, but still, she found that hard to understand. What Mack was really afraid of, Eve decided, was not her but himself, not her control over him but the fact that he secretly liked it. One's own weakness was always terrifying.

She had to believe that or else she would just feel too sad. But despite everything she did to console herself, whenever she thought about losing him her eyes would fill with tears.

TWENTY-TWO

Kathryn's mother had been languishing in jail for five months. Bail had been denied because she was suicidal. Although Kathryn had asked her uncles to help her find a good defense lawyer, she had not heard from them again in all this time, not even to tell her if they had hired one, and by now she and her brothers were sure that they had deserted them. She knew their uncles had to be angry about the murder, even though they were well aware of what her father had been like, and she was afraid to call them, hoping they might get over the worst of it with time. It was bewildering and upsetting, but she realized she would have to face the fact that they not only probably wanted her mother to be electrocuted, but they didn't care what happened to the rest of their family either.

It had been a strange funeral; everyone acting proper and sad and hypocritical. Her father had had very few friends at the end, and this nearly empty church was what he deserved, Kathryn thought.

Her brothers Donal and Kean had come home for the funeral. Afterward Kathryn talked with Donal in the kitchen. She was pouring coffee with a steady hand into a row of cups on a tray for him to take out for their visitors. "You're glad he's dead, aren't you?" she said.

"I don't know. I mean, he was my father."

"Oh, come on," she said. "Bullshit."

"We're going to have to live with this," he said.

"So what?"

"You've always been this way," Donal said. "You make up your mind and you just *know*."

Kathryn shrugged.

"What makes you so sure of everything?" Donal asked.

"I'm not sure of anything."

"But then what makes you so strong?"

"It's just the way I am," Kathryn said. "Dad picked on you three boys because he could tell you were weak."

"I guess we're all glad he's gone," Donal said. "Might as well admit it. I look in the mirror sometimes and I see his face, but it's me. I hate that I look like him."

"Don't dwell on it," Kathryn said. "You don't act like him, and that's what matters. Don't forget the cream."

Kathryn realized that if she didn't start looking for a lawyer for her mother on her own, the court would give her a public defender, and Kathryn was sure that meant a death sentence. You could not kill a cop and expect to get away lightly, even if you were his abused wife. Once a week she went to visit her mother in jail. Her mother was in the psychiatric ward now, and looked terrible.

"I'll never forgive your father for not getting me a nurse when I was so sick," her mother kept saying. "That was the worst thing he ever did to me. It was the Valium that made me shoot him. If he had gotten me a nurse, the way I wanted him to, I wouldn't have been so sick, and I wouldn't have needed a tranquilizer. I'll never forgive him for the Valium. I wasn't myself. It was just an accident. I took his gun because I was so afraid of him. I thought the safety was on. I wasn't thinking right. It was the Valium."

Kathryn had found out the whole story. Her mother had followed her father for eight hours, and finally had hidden in the backseat of his car, under his policeman's heavy raincoat. She had taken the gun. She knew he was going to pick up his girlfriend, and she figured that way she would be able to find out who the woman was and where she lived. But Brendan picked up his girlfriend, Dorothy, at the coffee shop where she worked, and then he took her to the Avalon Ballroom, the scene of his long-ago romantic evenings with Sheila. Those evenings when he had been an attentive suitor seemed so long ago now that the Avalon Ballroom had no special meaning to his battered wife; it was simply one of the places one went on a date.

It had been very cold that night, and Dorothy was chilly.

Brendan had told her there was a warm raincoat in the back-seat and she should put it on, so she had reached back to get it and had discovered Sheila. Dorothy screamed. Brendan stopped the car with a screech of brakes. Dorothy jumped out of the car and ran away, still screaming. Brendan turned around and saw his wife. Sheila raised the gun with trembling hands and shot him, and because she was so close, she shot most of his head off, showering the inside of the car with brains and blood.

After the murder, Dorothy went into the Avalon Ballroom, where they called the police, but after that, the story became unclear. She was definitely the witness. She was probably the unidentified woman who called Kathryn to tell her that her mother was in trouble. Until the police came, Sheila apparently stayed beside the car with her husband's body in it, in a state of shock. When the police and the ambulance came, she was so covered with blood that they thought at first she was another victim, until they saw the gun in her hand.

Sheila did not remember anything between the time of the shooting and the time she was taken to the police station, and given something else to wear because her clothes had become state's evidence. It occurred to Kathryn that her mother's mug shot, a staring, terrified face covered with blood, was not unlike the way her mother had sometimes looked during those long years of her marriage, but this time the blood was Brendan's, not her own.

Fortunately Kathryn was not completely alone during this dismal time of waiting to see what her mother's fate would be. Ted and his parents rallied around her and the two babies. They were there to help, to shop for food, to baby-sit, to be family. This was comforting since she no longer seemed to have much family of her own. Kathryn still wanted her divorce as much as ever, but she let it slide for now because everything was such a mess, and let them take care of her.

Then finally, five months after the murder, when her uncles had made up their minds what to do, or when they had decided their brother's children had suffered enough, or when they had pulled the strings that had to be pulled—Kathryn didn't know which and certainly wasn't going to ask—her uncle Brian called and said he was coming over to see her.

Her three uncles arrived at the apartment together. They were handsome, dark-haired men, broad shouldered and fierce, intimidating in their policemen's uniforms, and equally so in the civilian clothes they were wearing for their visit, and they seemed so large that their presence filled the entire living room.

"The problem of your mother is taken care of," her uncle Brian said. "We have a lawyer for her and the trial will be a hearing in front of a judge, which is a lot easier and shorter than a jury trial. She'll plead not guilty by reason of insanity. The judge is our man, Linwood Budgie. He'll do what we told him to do. She'll get some time in a mental hospital and that will be that. The trial is next month. We'll tell you when."

"Thank you," Kathryn said. She breathed a sigh of relief. She had known they could fix it with just a word. The world of the powerful blue men was back in place. "Thank you so much," she said again.

Her uncles nodded.

"How are the kids?" her uncle Patrick asked. He had always been the nicest and friendliest of her three uncles.

"Fine. They're sleeping. How are yours?"

"Still hell-raisers," he said proudly, and smiled.

"Mine, too," Kathryn said.

"They take after you, then," her uncle Michael said. "As I remember it, your mother had to send you off to boarding school to keep you under control."

"I guess so," Kathryn said.

"Yes, indeed, she did," her uncle Brian said, but he looked pleased. Now they were all smiling at one another. "I guess we'll be going now," he said.

"Would you like a drink, or some coffee?"

"No, no. We're off. I'll call you." And they were gone.

The trial was held on a gorgeous day in spring, the kind of day that makes you feel impatient and cheated to think of wasting a minute indoors, not to mention years in a mental hospital. Kathryn's only previous experience with a murder

trial had been what she saw in the movies, so she wore a demure black dress with a white collar. She thought for a moment that she looked more like the murderess than the
bereaved in that outfit, because that was what the accused always wore to look like a good person, and she particularly
thought so when she saw that her mother was wearing the
same thing. But of course it was too late to change.

Even though she had been reassured by her uncle Brian
that everything had been taken care of, Kathryn was a little
nervous. Their lawyer's name was Wilson. He looked innoc-
uous when she had wanted someone fiery to really convince
everyone that her mother was not guilty because she had no
comprehension of what she had done. Kathryn wondered if
he knew the trial was fixed. The prosecutor looked pompous
because he probably thought he was going to win. She knew
he was going to ask for the death penalty. The judge who
would be on their side and save her mother, Linwood
Budgie, was a jolly, little, old, white-haired man who looked,
in his black robes, like an overage choirboy. Their choirboy...

Kathryn glanced around the courtroom. No one in the
family was there except herself and her three brothers. Her
father's family had never liked her mother and now they
liked her even less, and her mother's family had been
estranged from her for years. There were, however, some re-
porters and several rows of scandal-hungry strangers, because the murder had been given quite a run in the press.
Her alcoholic father, who had only managed to stay on the
force all those years because of political corruption, had been
changed overnight into a hero cop. Her pathetic mother was
now a cold-blooded killer. Kathryn could hardly wait for the
whole thing to be over so they could disappear back into
their anonymous lives which were far too dramatic to begin
with.

Her father's girlfriend, Dorothy, was there. Kathryn recognized her from her picture in the newspapers. She, too,
was dressed in black, with a big picture hat and dark glasses,
and she was sobbing. Kathryn wanted to shake her. It annoyed her that her father's girlfriend was feeling so sorry for
herself, when it was partly her fault that this had happened
in the first place.

The hearing began. It took less than two hours. Unlike murder trials Kathryn had seen in the movies, there were no surprises, nor had she expected any. Everything had been well rehearsed, well planned. Dorothy was an important witness. Her mother, who had been tranquilized, was not allowed to testify. It was as if everyone but the prosecutor had already decided she was incompetent. She looked a little dazed. Once in a while, after her moment of glory on the stand, Dorothy continued to give a muffled sob and honked into her handkerchief. Colin was chewing his lip, and his eyes were big and round. He'd been through a lot for a kid, but at least this would be the end of it.

Behind the bench the judge was scribbling away, taking notes. He didn't have to go away to deliberate. "I'm ready for sentencing," he said. "Please rise." Kathryn's mother stood up and everybody looked at her with interest. The end was always the good part. "Sheila O'Mara," he began. "The court finds—"

"I did it," Sheila said. Everybody gasped. Kathryn's heart nearly leaped out through her throat. "I killed him," Sheila said, "and I want to die."

My mother is going to die in the electric chair, Kathryn thought, stunned. The courtroom was in an uproar.

Judge Linwood Budgie was banging his gavel to try to get the courtroom back in order. He looked a little as if he would like to leave. Kathryn could clearly see the confusion on his face. He was supposed to pronounce her mother innocent, but the defendant herself had said she was guilty. How the hell was he going to deal with that?

The judge cleared his throat. The room had gone silent. There was a long pause, or at least it seemed long to Kathryn. "The court finds the defendant guilty," he said, finally. "And I am putting her on probation for five years and remanding her to the custody of her daughter."

The people in the courtroom exploded with astonished gabbling. Kathryn just sat there in shock. She couldn't believe what had happened. Since the bewildered judge obviously hadn't known what to do, this was what he had done. Nothing like this had ever occurred before.

She's safe, Kathryn thought. It's a miracle. Thank you, God, for this astonishing last-minute rescue.

But then she realized what it meant. I'm just a twenty-two-year-old kid with two babies to take care of, she thought, and now I have custody of a suicidal murderess. What am I going to do?

TWENTY-THREE

For Russell's forty-eighth birthday Felicity cooked him a lavish dinner at home with all his favorite soul food and French wines, and invited his ten best friends. She knew he preferred it when she did everything herself instead of hiring a caterer, because it made him feel taken care of. She filled the apartment with delicately scented flowers, tiny pale roses and stephanotis, the kind of flowers that one often saw in a bridal bouquet. This was a hint, although he wouldn't get it, and if he did he would probably be annoyed. She was having a hard time balancing her long hours at work with the attention he liked, but she enjoyed playing wife. This was as close as she was ever going to be to having the actual role, she was becoming sure of that.

Her relationship with her mother, which had its ups and downs, was fairly good at the moment. As long as she stayed away from home her mother couldn't hit her. It was easier to hang up the phone than run away. Her mother wanted Felicity to marry Russell as much as she herself did. Carolee kept telling her never to give up, and for this birthday party she had mailed Felicity some special, secret recipes of her own for some of the food. At Carolee's suggestion, for his birthday present Felicity had bought Russell a new, expensive video camera, so he could take movies of their next trip together. If we *are* together, Felicity thought....

In two years he would be fifty. Wasn't he afraid his life would pass him by? She would be thirty in two years, and she was afraid. She saw her dismal life ahead of her; waiting, waiting, waiting, no husband, no children, knowing Russell was still seeing other women because the two of them had no real commitment, putting up with it no matter how hurt and angry it made her, accepting his lies, too much in love to look for another man, and then finally dumped when she got too old. A man, she had discovered, could always find a younger woman to take care of him. A woman, no matter how intelligent and charming, still needed her looks and sex appeal. Her mother had taught her this, and even though she saw exceptions all the time, she knew it was the rule.

Russell's friends were his age. They were all married and they brought their wives. Everybody was black; Russell didn't really feel comfortable with white people although he dealt with them on various levels every day. Felicity looked around at the familiar faces. Some of the women were first wives, some were second, and one was the third. Some, she knew, were being cheated on. All of them were attractive, well dressed, trying. You couldn't win, she thought.

The birthday party was a success. After it was over and everyone had left, raving and complimenting her, Felicity initiated sex with him, using all her considerable skills, and was thrilled when he responded and then took over as a way of rewarding her for having made him feel special. She knew him so well now. He knew her. They were family. She would do anything to get him, but she didn't know what to do that she hadn't already done, except get pregnant, and she knew that would only make him furious.

"I love you, Baby," Russell said afterward. "Thank you for my party. It was wonderful."

"You're welcome," she said. "I love you, too."

"I know you do." She sighed and put her head on his shoulder. "I'm going to Washington on business this weekend," he said. "I'll be at the Hay Adams. Do you want me to get you some theater tickets for Saturday night and you can take a girlfriend?"

"You mean, in New York?" she asked stupidly.

"Yes. I can't take you with me. I have to meet some potential business partners. Investors."

This time her sigh was not contentment but pure frustration. He gave and he took away. She gave and gave and gave. If she was his wife—or even his fiancée!—he would take her, she was sure of it. Then she would be an asset instead of just an ornament, a diversion. She would no longer be considered a trivial woman. But then she thought how generous he was to think of getting her theater tickets so she would have something fun to do, and she thought how hard it was that he never did anything to make her really angry. If she could get furious at him she might be able to get the courage to do something else with her life.

"That would be great," she said. "I want to see a musical. I'd like to see *The Tap Dance Kid.*"

"No, I want to see that with you," Russell said.

"Then how about *La Cage Aux Folles?*"

"Mmm," he said doubtfully. "I wanted to see that, too."

"Then what about *My One and Only* with Twiggy and Tommy Tune?" Felicity said, beginning to be annoyed. "You won't like that."

"I won't?"

"No."

"Okay. I'll call my scalper first thing tomorrow."

He telephoned her on Saturday morning as he always did when he went away for the weekend. "Everything okay?" he asked.

"It's fine. How's the hotel?"

"Beautiful. Baby, do you know what I forgot? That blue suit I wore at my birthday party, it needs to go to the cleaner's. Would you take it?"

"Of course."

"Thanks."

"Do you have a room overlooking the White House?" she asked.

"The what?" He sounded annoyed.

"One of the men in my office said the Hay Adams Hotel overlooks the White House. I thought maybe you'd see the President taking a walk or something."

"Oh," Russell said. "No, I don't. I don't care about my view, I'm just here to work."

"Why are you mad at me?" Felicity asked, hurt.

"I'm not mad."

"It seemed like it."

"You go and have a nice day," he said. "I'll see you to-morrow night."

"Bye...."

She found it hard to concentrate on the show, even though she enjoyed it and it didn't take much brain power. Then when she got home that night after the show Felicity did something she had never done before. She wasn't really sure why she did it, but an instinct pushed her, and she didn't even know where that instinct had come from except that she knew Russell so well by now. She called the Hay Adams Hotel and asked to speak to him; and the operator said he was not registered there.

"Did he leave?" she asked.

"Just a moment." There was a pause while she looked it up. "No, he was never here."

"Are you certain?" She felt abandoned and deceived and tried not to cry. She had suspected something like this all evening while not wanting to admit it.

"Yes, there was no one by that name here. Are you sure you have the right hotel?"

"Maybe not," Felicity said. "Thank you." She hung up and burst into tears.

He had done it again; he was cheating. For all she knew he was right here in New York at some woman's apartment, holed up for the weekend. Maybe he was in Boston with that white bimbo he'd said he had broken up with a few months ago. For a man who wasn't comfortable with white people, Russell managed to make an exception when that person was female and young and pretty and stupid.

"Where are you?" she screamed, although there was no one in the lonely apartment to hear. His money and his generosity and his lies mocked her. How could he do this to her so soon after the loving birthday celebration she had gone to so much trouble to prepare for him? He had been planning to cheat while she had been planning his party.

She pulled his blue suit out of his closet and then she threw it on the floor. Was the bimbo sitting right there while Russell called her to tell her to take his suit to the cleaner as if she were the maid? Or as if she were the wife! Maybe she didn't want to be his wife after all. Maybe she already was his wife. Felicity had left a man once for cheating and suddenly she knew she could do it again if she got pushed too far. She thought about Lincoln, her college boyfriend, and how all the warmth she had felt for him had gone cold when he hurt her. She *could* leave, she could. She had never loved Lincoln the way she loved Russell—she was older now, more mature, surer of what she wanted—but when Russell came back, if he didn't have a good excuse for lying to her she would go.

And he'd better lie well. Because when he came back he would have credit card receipts and she would be able to find out where he had really been.

She couldn't sleep that night, and when Russell came home on Sunday evening Felicity's eyes were swollen with sleeplessness and all the tears she had shed. She put ice on them and thought how unfair it was that she was looking her worst at the moment when she should be looking her best.

"Well, how was Washington?" she said. "Did you get the investors?"

"No," he said. "The trip was a waste."

"Then I guess that was why you didn't go at all," she said.

His brows drew together. His face was angry but his eyes were scared. "What do you mean?"

"I called the hotel and you were never there. You lied to me."

"Well, I..."

"Were you in Boston with that creepy little thing again? Or is there someone new?"

The silence hung in the air for a moment. "Okay," Russell said. "I was cheating on you. But I told you right from the beginning that I could never be a one-woman man. It doesn't mean I don't love you, Baby."

"I'm leaving," Felicity said. The words just came out of her mouth on their own. She hadn't expected him to hit her with the truth like that, but now that he had she knew it had to end between them because there would never be any hope. She would have preferred to sound forceful, but her voice came out like a pathetic mew. Nevertheless, she meant it. She went into the bedroom, took down her suitcases, and began to pack. If she just concentrated on one thing at a time, on gathering her belongings, she wouldn't have to think about what would happen when she had gone and was all alone, missing him and their life together, nursing her broken heart.

He followed her into the bedroom. "Don't go," he said.

She didn't answer. She went into the bathroom and scooped up all her makeup and toilet articles and dropped them into a duffel bag.

Then he followed her into the bathroom so she pushed past him and went back into the bedroom again. She would never be able to get all her clothes into the suitcases. "I'm going to have to leave some things here," she said, "but I'll be back to get them when you're at work."

"You don't have to go," he said.

"Yes, I do."

"She meant nothing to me."

"So what?"

"I'll break it off," he said.

She shook her head. "You'll find another one." She was crying again. She headed for the door, dragging the suitcases and the duffel bag, and her purse and the heavy briefcase of her work from the office, with tears pouring down her cheeks and her nose running and no free hand to wipe it. Let his last sight of her be as this mess; it obviously didn't make any difference that she had tried so hard to be appealing to him.

"All right," Russell said. "I'll marry you."

Marry her! He would *marry* her! She put down the suitcases and gaped at him. He handed her some tissues and she blew her nose.

"We'll get engaged now, I'll get you a ring, and we'll be married in a year," he said. "I need a year to get my act together. This is going to be a very big life change for me. I have to prepare for it."

"How are you going to do that?" she asked mildly.

"For one thing, I'm not going to see any women but you."

"Do you promise?"

"I promise." He looked at her. "Well, do you want to marry me?"

To think that she had given up all hope that he would ever ask. Felicity rushed into his waiting arms and felt as if she had come home, but this was not the frightening home she had escaped from, it was the safe, warm and happy home she had always wanted. "Yes!" she said.

Russell took her to Tiffany's and bought her a big round diamond, set in platinum with two baguettes. Felicity couldn't stop looking at it, admiring the way it caught the light. Her mother was thrilled and her father was pleased that she was settled, and with such a good catch. To further convince her of his good intentions Russell put their engagement announcement in the *New York Times*. Felicity bought several copies and mailed them home to her parents, and sent one to her sister in Cambridge. Theodora had been blessed with twins and so she now had three of her planned four children, the easy way, but Felicity wasn't jealous. Now she was going to have what she had dreamed of, too.

There was only one problem, but it was a big one. From the time he said he would marry her and give up all his other women, Russell refused to have sex with her anymore. Felicity knew he was punishing her for making him change his carefree life. She was quite sure he wasn't still cheating, but she didn't know what he was doing about his sex drive, so she assumed he was secretly masturbating so that she would be the only one who suffered from deprivation. She had tried being seductive and he ignored her, she made advances and he shrugged her off. When she became more aggressive in bed and tried to do what he had always enjoyed, he pushed her away.

"Why don't you want me?" she asked him.

He was tired, he had a headache, he had work to think about. There was always an excuse.

"Let's go for couples counseling," Felicity finally said.

"Don't be ridiculous. There's nothing wrong."

At last, after three months, to keep her quiet, Russell had sex with her. She felt he was just going through the motions, that there was no passion there, and she didn't know what to do. She was wondering if he wanted to drive her away so she would break the engagement.

But I can never do that, Felicity thought. She couldn't imagine life without him, he was all she had ever wanted; she was madly in love with him, enslaved. She knew that if she didn't give up they would eventually get married, and then if Russell still kept her at bay she would get him to go for marital counseling because if they were trying to save their marriage he wouldn't be so embarrassed. Married couples had sexual problems all the time.

Somehow it seemed to her that being married would solve everything. Despite the disillusioning things she knew about marriage from her parents and her friends and Russell's friends, she still thought that actually being married would work some sort of magic. Their marriage would be different from other people's. He would get used to their union, he would grow to like it, and he wouldn't be angry at her anymore. He was the one who had proposed this time, in order not to lose her, so she knew he loved and needed her. She also knew that Russell always had to win, and because he viewed his capitulation into the world of the domesticated as a defeat, there now were war reparations to be paid. She was paying them. She was convinced she wouldn't have to pay them forever. He was not impotent, he was withholding; he was just showing her who was boss.

Felicity's mother came to New York several times during the long engagement to help her plan the wedding. Carolee enjoyed shopping with her daughter and staying in a hotel. Russell wanted to be married in New York because that was where all his friends were. Felicity didn't care. She just wanted to be married. She didn't say anything to her mother about their strange sexual situation because somehow it seemed too private to reveal to anyone. Besides, she knew that her mother, true to form, would only blame her.

She thought how fragile and ambivalent her relationship with her mother still was now that she was an adult with a life of her own. As in her childhood, they bought clothes together again, and Carolee was the arbiter of her daughter's taste. But Felicity was no longer bored and trying to get it over with as she had been as a child; now she enjoyed the attention and liked deferring to her mother's fashion sense. Those times were close and friendly for both of them. But even though they pretended to have a good mother daughter relationship, as if the past had not happened, or as if they had even discussed it and clarified it and Carolee had asked for forgiveness, Felicity knew how volatile every moment was. She knew her mother could turn on her, or make a hurtful remark, at any moment; and she also knew that she would do almost anything to make her mother love her, to be kind to her, to be uncritical, and at those times when her mother chose to be tender she always melted.

Felicity decided she wanted a formal church wedding. Since she had made no church affiliation in New York and Russell didn't care, she could pick any church she liked. She chose the Cathedral of St. John the Divine because it was so big and imposing, so medieval-looking, like an edifice from the age of faith and fear. She wanted Russell to really feel that he was being united with her in the eyes of God, and that he would have to behave himself forever after, and she felt she needed all the help she could get.

She and her mother chose a long, slim white lace gown with a small train and a long veil. Her four bridesmaids were friends from college and New York, no one from back home; she'd had no real friends there. She was forced by convention to let her sister Theodora be the matron of honor, even though Theodora was so fat after having her twins that she still looked pregnant. Both Felicity and their mother agreed on something for a change: that it was a shame they had to include Theodora because she ruined the composition of the tableau. But what could they do? Theodora would be so hurt to be left out. The reception would be at Tavern on the Green, in Central Park, with the fairyland lights in the trees, the banks of flowers, the colorful Tiffany glass.

Felicity and Russell went back to Tiffany's, where they chose a simple gold wedding band.

"This way you can look forward to more diamonds on our anniversary," he said affectionately.

He could be so nice, so sentimental, talking about their long future together as if he wanted it and believed in it as much as she did. But with their wedding day approaching, a year after they became engaged as he had promised, as her fiancé he had had sex with her only four times. After that first time, when he had seemed to be on automatic pilot, he was more passionate, but Felicity couldn't help wondering if he was being so proficient with the purpose of making her miss sex with him more.

Now she knew why it was called the battle of the sexes and why so many books were written to tell women how to get their man. She was becoming more and more convinced that the whole struggle of getting the man you were in love with to commit wholeheartedly to marriage was genetically ordained. The woman was on one side and the man on the other. She moved in, he retreated. She invaded, he fought back. Strategy was always vital. Once you had entered his camp and gotten him to sign the truce—the engagement announcement—you couldn't give him an excuse to break the engagement. Russell always kept her off balance. He was obviously a man who didn't want to be married, to be trapped and tied down, and yet he was so kind to her in other ways that at times she couldn't help believing he did want domesticity, and with her, the way he claimed he did.

In an odd way, sometimes he reminded her of her mother: charming, unpredictable, sadistic, generous, mysterious. She didn't know why the two most important people in her life had to be so complicated, so difficult to win.

At last, at last, it was her wedding day. In a few more hours she would be safe. Felicity was euphoric and hysterical with nerves all morning, and when she finally walked slowly down the aisle on her father's arm she was trying not to giggle from a combination of panic and joy. In five more minutes she would be Mrs. Russell Naylor, and there he was, waiting for her, solid and strong. As she approached the altar, beaming, her mother leaned forward from her seat on the front row aisle.

"Wipe that stupid grin off your face," her mother hissed.

Felicity's heart sank. She turned herself instantly into the picture of demure solemnity her mother wanted: the perfect bride doll. She felt foolish and sad. She would never know how to do things right, never. But she wished that at this moment, of all moments in her life, her mother could have managed to keep her bad-tempered advice to herself.

But then she looked up at Russell's dear familiar face, and she was tremendously heartened to see that he was as close to nervous laughter as she had been. In that shared moment of held-back hilarity she had never felt closer to him. He was her best friend. They were on the same wavelength. Now, finally, she knew everything would be all right. We'll make it, she thought, sending the thought out to him, willing it into his mind and his heart. We *will* live happily ever after. We *will* beat the odds. We *will* be different.

That night, their wedding night, back in their penthouse apartment, Russell consummated their marriage enthusiastically. She felt legal at last. The next morning he took her to Bora-Bora for their honeymoon, for a week, where they lived in a grass hut on the beach with room service. They had sex four times. She thought everything would be all right now. She thought she had survived the war.

TWENTY-FOUR

After her mother's trial was over, Kathryn and her kids had to move in with her mother and younger brother in her mother's house, since her mother was too depressed to be alone. They had been there for six months now. Her mother was living with guilt and grief, and Kathryn was living with low-grade anxiety. If her mother picked up a bottle of Lysol, Kathryn would wonder if she was going to clean the bathroom or swallow it. When Kathryn went out to fill her orders and left her two little boys with her mother, she wondered if her mother would decide to gas herself and take the babies with her, or cut her wrists so she would return home to find two hysterical children with a corpse. If her mother had been deranged enough to kill once, who knew what she might do now? People did all kinds of crazy things. The doctors at the mental hospital told her to take the locks off all the doors so her mother couldn't lock herself in and do something to herself.

Ted had escalated his visits. He was over at the house nearly all the time now, trying to help her with the kids. And, as always, every time he left to go back home his two little boys filled the house with their hysterical sobs. They didn't want him to leave, they wanted to go with him. "Daddy!" they would scream. Chip, the baby, would scream all night. "I want my Daddy! I want my Daddy!" Kathryn's mother, who was a nervous wreck anyway, would go into the kitchen and bang pots around in frustration. The house was in chaos.

Kathryn had never seen children so attached to their father, especially boys. The older one, Jim Daniel, seemed angry at her and at the world. Kathryn was convinced that if she didn't put a stop to these visits their father would do more harm to them than good. At the very least, he should see them less. She kept trying to explain that to him, but he loved his children and didn't want to be away from them. She just wanted to get finished with the divorce and find some peace.

Since he wouldn't listen she finally went to his parents about his visits. "You've got to tell him to stop upsetting the babies," she said. "They're too attached to him." Kathryn knew they had observed the pitiful scenes themselves. Ted often brought the boys home to his parents for the day, and when he had to take them back to Kathryn they knew he was going to desert them again and started crying as soon as he carried them out of the house.

His parents, who only wanted to be helpful, understood and reluctantly took her side, and told him he had to wean the children away from him because he was making them too confused. But Ted didn't understand. How could he, Kathryn thought. He had the fun of playing with them and she had the consequences afterward. She was the one who had to bring them up. He was only making it harder for her. She wished he would stay away.

The divorce came through. She was single again. It took a long time for his parents to convince Ted that his love and kindness was making his children unhappy, but when he did admit it he decided to leave town altogether because he couldn't think of any other way to handle the situation. He couldn't stand to be so close to them and not see them. He got a job as an assistant manager in a department store in San Francisco, and Kathryn hoped he would fall in love and marry again and get over the whole mess. She had never wished him ill. She had no feelings about him either pro or con. Leaving Boston had been his idea. She had only wanted to be left in peace.

Now that she was on her own, even though she could hardly afford it Kathryn almost always got a baby-sitter, but her mother never liked them and complained constantly. Her mother was so unstrung from everything that had happened to her that having a stranger in their small house was too much for her, and Kathryn would often come home from doing her deliveries to find that the newest baby-sitter had been fired, and the children were alone with her again.

Her mother had not yet returned to work and had no immediate plans to do so. For some reason she had been given her husband's pension, and his insurance policy with double indemnity due to his unnatural death. It was as if they didn't know what else to do with them. Kathryn thought the cops had always known what a brutal man her father had been and were on her side. So Sheila had her house, her savings, her insurance, her widow's pension of fifteen hundred dollars a month, and she was free on five years' probation. The newspapers had made a terrible fuss about it.

MURDERESS SET FREE, the headlines read. VICIOUS COP KILLER FOUND GUILTY AND RELEASED. In the eyes of the press Sheila had become a threat who was still walking the streets. Sitting at home in a state of mourning was more like it.

Kathryn and her mother did not talk about the murder anymore. Sheila didn't mention it and Kathryn didn't bring it up. Without asking each other what to do they had both decided to put any discussion of the past behind them. For Sheila it was too painful, and Kathryn, who couldn't care less that the brute was dead, just wanted to forget it.

Her mother was only forty-four years old and still had the rest of her life to live. And so do I, Kathryn thought. I can't go on staying here; we're driving each other crazy. The rules of her mother's probation in her custody did not stipulate that she had to live with Kathryn, so Kathryn took her two little boys and moved into a place of her own. She knew it would be better for everyone.

The new place was a small apartment much like the one she had lived in before, a twenty-minute drive away from her mother, and she soon was immersed in her own life again. The newspaper stories seemed long ago. Because she was still using her married name people didn't know who she was, and it would never occur to anyone even to imagine that something so dramatic had happened in her life.

Saturday night was date night, but Friday night was the social night in town, when the week's work was finally over. When Kathryn could get a good baby-sitter she would go out, too. She liked to drink and spend time with other young people her age, to laugh with her girlfriends and flirt with attractive men. She was still friendly, she still liked people, just as she had at college, before all these things had happened to her: the wrong marriage, the responsibility of babies, the murder and its aftermath. She had no interest in getting married again, and she never made plans for the future, so now she just drifted along enjoying everything.

It was summer. On weekend afternoons people rowed boats on the Charles River, couples walked hand in hand in Boston Common under the trees, or sat at little outdoor sidewalk restaurants. Sometimes on Saturdays Kathryn went to the public library to take out children's books to read to her kids because she couldn't afford to buy them. It was stuffy, hot and dusty in the library, but she never stayed long. She was there one day when she noticed, sitting alone at the wooden table bent over a book, the last man in the world she would have expected to see in a library on any day, not just on a beautiful Saturday in summer. He was gorgeous: tall and well built, with the kind of muscular body you never saw on most men, and thick long blondish hair; and the minute she saw him she wanted to know him. Kathryn walked over to him, her books in her arms, and sat down. He glanced up at her and smiled. She smiled back. She pretended to be reading the books she had with her, and then she looked at him again.

"*Huckleberry Finn?*" she whispered, peering at the book he was reading. "Is it good?"

He seemed embarrassed for an instant. "Yes," he whispered. "You never read it?"

"This is what I read lately," Kathryn said. "I have two kids."

She stroked the books so he could see she was not wearing a wedding ring. She didn't even know this man, but she was more attracted to him in two minutes than she had ever been to her ex-husband.

He looked surprised. "You have two kids already?" he said.

"I can't believe it myself."

"It would be worth your while to buy them those books,"

he said. "Kids like to have the same story read to them over and over."

"Oh, you have children?"

"No, but I have friends who do."

At the other side of the table, the few people who were wasting this beautiful summer day sitting inside a library reading, glared at them because they were talking.

"I guess we'd better shut up," Kathryn whispered.

"I could use a cigarette. You?"

"Sure."

They got up and went outside and sat on a bench. She noticed that he had greenish eyes that narrowed when he lit his cigarette in a way that made him seem worldly and very sexy. "I'm Alastair Uland," he said.

"Kathryn Hopkins. Where did you get such a nice name?"

"I'm half German and half English."

Good, she thought, not an Irish ancestor in sight. "And is Mark Twain your favorite author?"

"Actually," he said, "this is the first time I've read him. I was a real truant in school and didn't learn to read until I was sixteen. I just faked it. It's only now as an adult that I'm catching up on the books I should have read when I was a boy."

"And what do you do, Alastair?"

"I'm a construction worker."

"Brains and brawn," Kathryn said. He looks like a movie star, she thought.

"Well, if the guys at work knew I was sitting in a library on my day off reading a kid's book they would laugh me out of town."

"Their loss," Kathryn said. "Do you care what they think? I wouldn't care. I think it's admirable that you enjoy literature."

They finished their cigarettes and talked some more, and then they went back inside and Kathryn checked out her children's books. When she left, he asked her for her phone number, and folded it carefully into his wallet.

He called her the next day and invited her out for Saturday night. When he came to pick her up he was carrying a present for her boys: a brand new copy of *Pat the Bunny*. Kathryn was touched and impressed at the considerate gesture.

After that they began to see each other on a regular basis and they became a couple. Sometimes they went to the movies or out to dinner, but neither of them had much money so more often he came over to her apartment and they just stayed in for the evening and he read to her kids or watched television and she cooked. She liked being domestic and taking care of him. He took care of her, too, and of her kids. They took the kids places together, and on the evenings when Kathryn was working Alastair would come over to baby-sit. He enjoyed her two little boys and they took to him, too, because they missed having a father, especially Jim Daniel.

Kathryn told Alastair she hadn't gone to bed with Ted before she married him, and she wouldn't go to bed with him either, and he respected that. She knew by now that men actually preferred it when they couldn't have you. She and Alastair necked, but that was all. She found him incredibly sexy, but she restrained herself from doing anything she might regret later. She was a "good" girl, and it was the way she wanted it and the way society wanted it and it worked with him.

Kathryn was in love with him, though, and it was obvious that Alastair was crazy about her. She had never been introspective, but this time she thought carefully about taking the risk of becoming attached to the wrong man. She was aware that extraordinary good looks often filled in for whatever else was unknown or missing, so a man with great beauty seemed smarter, nicer, more perceptive, funnier than other people, and when he did have any of these qualities they seemed a wonderful plus. She could find no fault with him, however. His best quality was that he was so kind. Ted had been kind, too, but she just hadn't been in love with him. She figured she had a knack for finding men who were good to her.

After Kathryn and Alastair had been going together for six months he asked her to marry him. It was the natural progression of the way their relationship had been evolving, and she said yes. She knew they would be happy. This time around she was going to marry a man she really knew, not some stranger.

They were so eager to be together that they eloped, avoiding all the fuss of a wedding, and that night at last, after waiting so long, they consummated their union in his apartment, three times. Kathryn found him irresistible, and the act she had dutifully performed with Ted was suddenly magical. Alastair was her first real love, her first sexual passion.

The next day they left the babies with her mother and drove to Vermont to a ski chalet to play in the snow and sit by a roaring fire, and best of all, to be alone together. Alastair taught her to ski. What a wonderful, multitalented man he was, Kathryn thought, as she watched him skimming down the slopes; and so full of surprises.

It was a lovely, miraculous honeymoon. Yet she worried about her children, even though she called her mother every day. She had never left them with her mother for so long a time. On their way home, when she and Alastair stopped for gas, Alastair went into the restroom and Kathryn, impatient to be on the road again, began filling up the tank. He came out, and suddenly, oddly, he was in a rage.

"Why couldn't you wait for me to do that?" he yelled.

"What's the big deal?"

"You're my wife. *I* take care of *you*. Are you trying to make me look stupid?" The cords on his big neck were standing out and his face was red. What a temper he had—she hadn't suspected it, nor had she thought he would be such a protective husband. She was very surprised, but not afraid. He was probably coming down from his honeymoon euphoria, as she was; and was depressed to be going back to the real world.

"I'm sorry," Kathryn said. He seemed to calm down then. She was sure he would be fine as soon as they got back to her—no, their—apartment and christened the bed.

He was better at home, but not the way he used to be. The few times they went out—with the kids, or to the supermarket together, once to a restaurant—men glanced at Kathryn admiringly, and whenever they did, Alastair glowered at them like a dog watching over a bone. He had never seemed to notice other men's glances before, or perhaps he had even liked it. But now he was jealous, Kathryn realized. But what did he expect? Men had always looked at her, and she didn't really pay attention to it anymore and neither should he. She was a pretty, curvy redhead, and it wasn't as if Alastair had just discovered that. It was one of the reasons he had fallen in love with her. If he didn't want men to look at his new wife, he should have married someone ugly.

After they had been home for two weeks, she decided to have their nextdoor neighbors over to play canasta. They were a nice couple, Sally and Lou, about Alastair's age, and they had two little kids of their own. Kathryn served beer and pretzels and cheese, and coffee and cake. They laughed and joked, and Lou flirted with her a little, but certainly not in any way that was offensive, since Sally didn't mind. It was a very pleasant evening, and when their guests were leaving, Sally and Kathryn hugged and promised that the next time they would all have dinner together.

As soon as their guests had left, Alastair turned on her with a look of rage.

"Why were you flirting with Lou?" he demanded.

"I wasn't flirting," Kathryn said. "He was being his idea of charming and I was just being friendly. You know I'm friendly."

"You're too friendly."

"If I wasn't friendly," she pointed out, "you would never have met me."

"Don't think I don't remember that." His tone was angry, accusatory.

"What's eating you tonight, anyway?"

Without warning he punched her in the jaw. Kathryn fell on the floor. She was so stunned she didn't realize how badly he had hurt her until a moment or two later. She touched her jaw where it was beginning to swell, and then she got up slowly, warily, watching to see what he would do. She knew he wasn't drunk; he'd had only one beer all night. He was a social drinker at most, which was one of the things she had liked about him. She almost couldn't believe he had hit her, but she also felt that she could handle him. He was not her father, and she pushed the nightmare of that experience out of her mind.

"Don't ever hit me again," Kathryn said. "I mean that. You touch me again and I'll be out the door and you'll be married all of three weeks."

As she spoke, she heard herself slurring the words and realized her jaw was getting stiff. He noticed it, too.

"I'm sorry," he said.

His green eyes were sad and embarrassed and full of love and regret. Kathryn felt herself wavering. She had only just discovered he was a jealous man, so maybe she should have been cold to Lou; but that would have been rude and this was a free country and Alastair should know by now that she was ebullient and gregarious. She had been that way before they were married.

But she hadn't belonged to him then. Now that they were married, he thought that she did.

He helped her into a chair. "Stay here," he said. "I'm going to get ice. I'll be right back."

He returned with ice cubes, which he wrapped in a towel and held on her face until her swollen jaw felt a little better. He knows exactly what to do, Kathryn thought resentfully. I wonder how many women he's hit before? Or maybe it's only me.

"I won't do it again," he said.

She waited for a few moments and then she nodded. "Okay."

They made love slowly and then they slept in each other's arms, comforting each other, and she thought it was over. But the next day Alastair was jumpy and unhappy again as if he couldn't get the harmless little flirting incident out of his mind, and whenever they went out in public, he continued to be as jealous as ever. She realized that she would have to watch every little thing she did. This was not the way she had ever dreamed she would spend her married life, and she wondered how she could recapture the kind, gallant man who had won her heart and then had turned into this angry stranger.

They had settled into their married routine now: working, taking care of the kids, being a family. They had decided to live in her apartment for a year, because it was bigger than his, and for now it was good enough. Later, they thought, when they had saved enough money, they would put the down payment on a house. She got a new job, as a secretary, working for Morgan Life in an office building downtown. This would give her all her evenings free to be with him and the kids. The lovemaking between her and Alastair continued to be electric. Whenever Sally tried to make a date for the four of them to get together again, Kathryn made some excuse. She just didn't know how else to handle it.

It only took three weeks before Alastair hit her again anyway. This time he punched her several times, accusing her of being unfaithful to him while she was at the office.

What am I doing here? she thought. *I am not my mother.*

"I'm sorry," he said afterward.

"You're always sorry. Sorry isn't good enough."

That night she packed, took her babies, and went to stay with her mother, which was the lesser of two evils, until she could figure out what to do. But before Kathryn even had time to breathe and sort out who she was and what her life had become, Alastair was knocking on her door with flowers in one hand and teddy bears in the other, pleading.

"Give me another chance."

"I'm not a punching bag. If you have a problem, talk about it."

"I know. I'm not so good at talking about feelings."

Why had she not ever noticed that before?

But he was so gorgeous and appealing and sexy, and she loved him passionately, and he obviously loved her, too, in spite of everything he had done, so she let him come over to spend a few evenings with her, although she wouldn't move back in. And then it was just spending the weekend with him in their apartment. And finally she moved back in with the kids after all. Just to give him another chance....

But there was no safety anymore. He was jealous of everything she did, and things he only imagined she did. He was breaking dishes, throwing furniture. It was all too familiar. The next time he punched her and knocked her down, she made up her mind to leave for good.

Kathryn had a girlfriend at work, Norma Jones, who was divorced and had a little girl. Norma lived with her widowed mother, and when Kathryn confided that she was looking for a place to stay with her own little kids, Norma quickly offered that she move in with them and share the rent. "My mother will baby-sit," Norma said. "We could use the extra money and you'll have your own room." So that very day before Alastair came home, Kathryn and the children had moved in with Norma's family, without even leaving a note to say goodbye.

It wasn't as clean a house as Kathryn had hoped for, and her room was tiny, with just enough room for a crib, which her two boys shared, and a single bed for her. Sometimes at night the boys cried to get into her bed, so she let them sleep with her. They had both been toilet trained very early, but now her older one, Jim Daniel, had taken to wetting the bed. She put him into diapers at night and told him not to worry; she knew he was just scared to be living in this strange place, and he probably missed Alastair.

Then one day Kathryn came home from the office to find Jim Daniel sitting on his potty in the living room and Norma's mother bending over him yelling in his face. "Stupid!" Norma's mother was saying. "Bad boy! Stupid boy! Make peepee in the pot, not in the pants." Jim Daniel was not crying, but he was looking baffled and forlorn, and this hurt Kathryn more than his tears would have.

"Don't yell at him," Kathryn said.

"How do you expect him to learn?"

"Nobody ever yells at him," Kathryn said, "and you're not going to start now."

"Don't tell me what to do," Norma's mother said. "You obviously can't raise a child."

Kathryn held her temper in, but she was enraged and distressed and wondered if she should go to stay with her own mother. It couldn't be worse than this. When it happened again, she protested to Norma.

"Don't fight with my mother," Norma said.

Kathryn managed to stay there for ten days. She was always arguing with Norma's mother and she had no idea what the woman was doing to her kids when she wasn't there to see it. She knew that once again she had to figure out what to do—and quickly.

That night Alastair appeared at the front door with flowers. "I'm glad your friend called me," he said in a meek little voice. So that was how he had been able to track her down. Kathryn did not know how she felt. Part of her wanted to be away from him, but another part as strongly wanted him to bring her back. "Give me another chance," he begged. "Please. I'll be different. You'll see."

She went home with him.

But of course he was not different, and the violence continued. She knew she would never have stayed with him if she hadn't loved him so much. Somehow the more abusive he became, the more she was attracted to him. She didn't understand why her heart led her into such a wild and lonely place, why her body betrayed her by wanting the man she most feared.

She left him again, and took the boys with her to live with her mother. Her mother had not changed. She was as depressed and unpredictable as ever, but now she kept adamantly denying that she had ever been depressed at all. But at least it was home—for the moment. Whenever Alastair called, trying to convince her to let him make it up to her, Kathryn got off the phone as quickly as she could.

She had been living with her mother for three months when Kathryn finally allowed herself to deal with the fact that she could not be happy without him. She missed him and thought about him all the time. Now she had enough distance from the bad parts to be able to remember the good ones. When she thought about their warm family evenings together, she felt nostalgic, and when she thought about their lovemaking, she yearned for him and thought her life was passing her by. This time she let him persuade her to come back to live with him. Six weeks later she was pregnant.

They found a bigger apartment and moved in. They stopped talking about a house. "When he has a child of his own, it will mellow him," Kathryn told her mother.

"Don't you believe it," her mother said. "The minute I saw him I thought he was no good. He was too full of himself, showing off his body, all those muscles, how strong he was."

But that was what I liked, Kathryn thought. And still do...

At last her mother was feeling better, and had started going to beauty school so she could get a job. Kathryn was glad to see the change in her. But then something else happened at home. Kathryn had left Alastair with her two boys and gone to her mother's house for a few hours so her mother could give her a permanent. When she came back the boys were all alone, with black smoke issuing out of the bedroom. She ran in to see what had happened and discovered the cushion of the bedroom chair was on fire, shooting flames. Kathryn grabbed the entire chair and flung it into the bathtub and turned on the shower until the fire was out. Her heart was pounding. Where was Alastair? The whole apartment smelled from burned and wet feathers. She could see the forbidden box of matches the boys had been playing with, lying on the bedroom carpet. How could he have left them alone? Then he walked in.

"Where were you?" Kathryn demanded.

He looked at the wreckage and took in the situation in an instant. "I went nextdoor to get a fire extinguisher," he said. "To save them."

"Where is it?"

"They didn't have one."

The two of them stood there looking at each other. "You didn't need a fire extinguisher," Kathryn said. "You shouldn't have left them. The whole place could have burned down."

"He went to save us," Jim Daniel said. He looked up at Alastair as if to get his approval.

"He saved us," little Chip echoed.

Alastair shrugged and pulled out a new pack of cigarettes from his pocket and lit one. She suspected now why he had gone out, but she didn't want to believe it. He loved her children. He would never do something that stupid.

Alastair sat on the couch and put the kids on his lap. "You know you're not supposed to play with matches," he said to them.

"We're sorry." It was over and they were safe. For all she knew Alastair *had* panicked after the fire had started, not gone out for cigarettes before it happened. Why would the kids lie? She and her little brothers had never defended her father for an instant, and it never occurred to her that her little boys would want to protect the man who had now become the father in their lives. They were her children; she knew them.

The kids had learned a lesson and so had Alastair. She didn't mention the incident to her mother, who disliked Alastair enough already. Kathryn forgot about it, and to the best of her knowledge Alastair never left the children alone again.

Kathryn was already enormous in her pregnancy, and the doctor told her she was carrying twins. She had no idea how she was going to be able to take care of them, but she figured she would find a way. When the twins were born, they were girls. They named them Stephanie and Gaby. After the birth, Kathryn found out in earnest how hard life was going to be. Her oldest was still too young to go to school, so now there were four little kids at home and she still had her full-time secretarial job at Morgan Life. Luckily Alastair was able and willing to share the childcare and her mother pitched in, too, and there were the blessed baby-sitters. More than ever Kathryn respected the way her embattled mother had brought up four children alone, kept a job, dealt with her father, and survived it all.

A year went by. Jim Daniel was in first grade finally, and had learned to read. Ever since she'd had him, her first baby, Kathryn had understood the love for a child, but more and more she was beginning to understand what she considered the power of love for a man. She suspected very strongly that she would never leave Alastair permanently, no matter how many times he hit her; that they were joined together forever, not because she was afraid, but because she was so attracted to him, and the worse he was to her, the more she wanted to win him. The only explanation she had for why she was so perverse was that the heart was unscrupulous.

Then, after the worst fight they had ever had, she woke up on the floor and realized she had been unconscious. She didn't even know for how long. Her head felt like a watermelon and there was blood in her mouth. Her body hurt so much that she just wanted to stay there on the floor all night, not move, not think. She closed her eyes and drifted away. When the front door slammed, she heard it as a peripheral part of her waking dream. He was partly her husband and partly her father in this dream state of hers; it was now and it was then. *This time he didn't even apologize. My father never apologizes, but Alastair does....* It was not until the next morning, when her babies' wails made her come to attention and drag herself up to try to begin her day, that Kathryn realized Alastair was still gone.

The police came to her door later. Kathryn knew them and she knew their arrival meant something was wrong. The two cops took in her damaged face in silence, and then they told her, hesitantly, that her husband was dead. He had been shot in a bar. When they told her, Kathryn screamed, and could not stop screaming. She was free and she did not want to be free; she was safe and the loss of Alastair tore at her heart and she wanted him to be alive. She wanted to wake up and find that this news had only been part of her nightmare, but she knew she was already awake and it was over.

She grieved for him for two years, and remembered him for the rest of her life.

TWENTY-FIVE

The eighties were boom time. Yellowbird was doing well and Billie had enough money to support herself and someone else. Her apartment in the high rise around the corner from work had two bedrooms. She feared the jokes time played. At seventeen and unprepared to raise a child, you could make one in one shot in the backseat of a parked car. At thirty-eight, appreciative of and yearning for motherhood, you were likely to be going around to fertility doctors. She was thirty-eight years old, and if she didn't have a baby soon it might be too late.

Sex, she had realized, was in some insidious way imprinted in the genes really for procreation. It was all about having babies. No matter if you didn't want one or couldn't have one; the body hungered. It was why men were attracted to women who were still young enough to be fertile; their unconscious smelled the monthly blood growing in the nest, waiting to nourish their child. The womb called out to them, even when its owner was carefully buying birth control and thought this was just a date. Horniness was nature's trick.

Marriage, she decided, was out of the question for her. She had adjusted to living her life alone and independently, and she never wanted to be hurt again. Besides, to find a man she would be willing to marry and who wanted to marry her would take too long. She had been a single woman in New York City for long enough to know how slim the pickings were. This city, or at least Yellowbird, where she spent her waking hours, attracted too many losers, and she had become all too aware that where bachelors were concerned, interesting and emotionally available seldom went hand in hand.

She needed seed, not aggravation. A sperm bank was out of the question, too. She had her own sperm bank at Yellowbird. She could choose a different man to get pregnant with every month if she wanted to. She never wanted to tell a child of hers that she had bought him from an anonymous donor, even if the donor was a genius. She wanted to meet the prospect, see what he looked like, know about his family history, and conceive her child in the heat of passion so at least there would be a story to hand down, even if it was a fantasy.

But if she did it on her own there was the one great risk— AIDS. She had to interview the men carefully to find the right one, because foremost on her mind, since she was a sensible person, was always the fear of the risk of the plague that had equated fun with death and ended all their carefree days. He would have to be straight, square, and as safe as she could be sure of short of asking him to have an AIDS test for something that was never going to be a relationship.

She hoped the child would be a boy.

Now that she knew what she wanted she looked every night for the man who would be the proper father for her unborn son. Even though she would rather it wasn't a daughter, she knew that girls tended to look like their fathers, so his looks were important. She didn't care if he was married; in fact she thought she would prefer it. Married and from another state would be even better. She didn't want him, whoever he was to be, coming around to stake his claim or, even worse, tantalizing her child and constantly abandoning him.

Suddenly she became the perfect listener. She would buy each new, unaware, potential prospect a few drinks and ask him about his life, his childhood, his talents and dreams. Men loved to talk about themselves. What Billie wanted to know was everything about the gene pool she was thinking of jumping into.

"Oh, your sister had a nervous breakdown? How sad. Why?" *Next.* "It's so tragic that your father was an alcoholic. So hard to grow up with that." *Next.* "Twins run in your family! How convenient to get all your kids in one fell swoop." *Next.* "Are your parents still alive? And do you still have grandparents? I just love old people, don't you?" She felt that since she was not looking for love or commitment, at least she could try to have a shot at perfection.

When she saw Cal Fortune walk into Yellowbird in the week of her fertility her heart turned over. He had that rangy cowboy look: the jeans, the boots, the blue denim shirt under the expensive jacket—a look many of the men at Yellowbird affected—but on him it seemed natural. She hoped he wasn't taken, that he might be the one. It wasn't that he was more beautiful than any of the other men she had briefly considered, but that there was something about him both electrifyingly sexual and familiar. She wasn't sure what it was. He was her height and wiry, but the golden curls were reminiscent of no one she knew, and his calm, handsome face tantalized her into some kind of memory she couldn't place. It never occurred to her that he might not want to be seduced by her because it seemed predestined.

"Do you have a reservation?" she asked him.

"No, ma'am. I just came into town for a few days and I thought I'd try here."

"One?"

"Yes."

"It shouldn't take too long," she said, looking through the book.

She slid into her customary seat at the bar and gestured for him to sit beside her. "Welcome to Yellowbird," she said. "I'm Billie Redmond. I own this place."

"I'm Cal Fortune."

"You're from Texas."

"You could tell."

"Takes one to know one," Billie said smiling at him.

"Dallas," he said.

"Not Houston?" And then she knew whom he reminded her of. He was Harry Lawless if Harry had never been in a bar fight, if his life and past had been wiped clean off his face. Harry Lawless...so the pull continued, just when she thought she was rid of him, when she thought that the memories were dead.

Although she had had many lovers through the years she had not been so physically drawn as this to any man since Harry, and it occurred to her as she felt the warmth radiating from Cal Fortune's knee, which was not even touching hers, that it would serve Harry right if she had a baby with someone who looked just like him, only better.

"Buy you a drink?" she asked.

"Thank you."

He had a beer, she had a vodka. He didn't look like a man who drank a lot. They both smoked.

"And what are you doing here in town?" she asked.

"I've never been to New York. I thought it was time."

"It *was* time," she said. He didn't know what she meant, of course.

"I've been to some shows, a couple of museums."

"You just came alone?"

"I'm getting over a bad divorce. The decree came through last week. I thought I'd celebrate or commiserate with myself, as the case might be. She did take the house and the kids."

He put the house before the kids, Billie thought. He'd never come bothering me if he ever found out, which he won't anyway.

"How awful," she said. "Divorce is so difficult. How many kids?"

"Two. A boy and a girl. Three and five."

"Young."

"We should never have gotten married in the first place. People do stupid things sometimes, trying to make a marriage work."

"Better not to marry," Billie said. "I didn't."

He appraised her admiringly. "But you've been asked, many times, I'd bet."

"Oh, a few."

He glanced around the room. "You're an independent woman, and doing well, it seems."

"I am. And what do you do?"

"I'm a lawyer."

Intelligent. She approved. "Not a divorce lawyer, though?"

"Corporate. For the Dallas Oil Consortium."

She figured him to be her age, maybe a little younger. Virile. Well-rounded, since he was a lawyer who came to New

York to forget his troubles and went to museums. Everybody went to shows. "So you just found Yellowbird off the street?"

"It wasn't easy."

"It isn't supposed to be."

"I was wandering around. I must have walked ten miles a day since I've been here. It's new for me not to be in a car."

I hope you didn't walk in those boots, she thought. "You must be tired," she said.

"Not really. I run ten miles every morning at home. Different shoes, of course."

She smiled. "Did you take up running for health or fun?"

"I'm a pretty healthy person," Cal Fortune said. "Nobody in my family gets really sick and we all live to be ninety. I just wanted to be sure to keep the line going."

And so do I, Billie thought. "Another beer?"

"That's very kind of you."

"Hey," she said, "I'm sorry there's such a long wait for your table, but those empty ones are reservations."

"Of course, I understand."

They talked for another hour and then she let him eat. Since it was late and the restaurant was not full he asked her if she might sit with him for a few moments and she of course agreed. She sat there while he consumed a plate of fried chicken and everything that went with it and said it reminded him of his mother's cooking, which he meant as a compliment. Billie had a salad. She wasn't hungry. She wanted to run her palm across the oddly familiar planes of his face, devour his mouth, and, more to the point, open his fly. She imagined her fingers at Cal Fortune's heavy silver belt buckle and remembered the times when Harry met her on the road and their clothing was on the motel room floor before they even began to talk. It wasn't the same now, she knew, not really. Nothing would ever be the same as it had been with Harry. But this was close enough, and this one was nice. She was not a child anymore. She didn't need him to take care of her.

Just give her a son.

When it got late she told one of the waiters to put on the night tape, as she often did when she was feeling mellow,

and she told Cal about her brilliant career. He was impressed, as all of them were. Of course she didn't tell him
what had ended it.

"Nodes on my vocal cords," she said. "I started singing
too young and too loud and never had voice training. But
that can happen anyway, even if you protect yourself. It's a
risk singers take. I'm glad it segued into Yellowbird. I'd hate
to be still on the road."

"But what memories you have!" he said. "Most people
never have a tenth of what you had, and you're still so
young."

He put his hand on hers and all the little guard hairs on
her arm stood at attention. He looked into her eyes and it
was as if Harry were back. If I were a fainting woman, Billie
thought, I would faint.

She left before the place closed, as she often did, and she
took him with her. When she got him in her bed he wanted to
wear a condom and she was pleased that he was so careful.
She wouldn't let him wear one, of course. He didn't really
mind.

They were all over each other in the rush of their mutual
attraction. He wasn't afraid of her or of his performance; it
was as if his genes knew what she wanted even if his mind
deceived him. The accordion of her orgasm sucked him in,
and as she pressed her cervix to receive the warm gush of his
seed she felt this was both a sensual and a sacred moment.
After it was over she wouldn't get up, not to smoke, not to
pee, not to drink water, imagining the beginning of her
child's existence swimming toward the completion of it, like
a shooting star.

Cal brought water, he lit her cigarette. He stroked her skin.
She liked this tenderness, that he hadn't just gotten up and
tried to leave. It would be too poignant to have conceived
their child and be instantly abandoned; this was a moment to
be savored and shared. She was not as heartless as that, she
was still sentimental, because this was the story she would
have to tell:

I had a brief, passionate affair with a beautiful man. He was won-
derful in every way, but he was just passing through. I didn't know
until later that we had made you, and by then he was gone, like a

phantom, like a memory. If he had stayed it would not have worked between us. Our lives were too set in two different places. It was too late, and we were too unalike. But I will always be grateful that he left me you, because you will be better than both of us.

But maybe she wasn't pregnant after all. "When are you going back to Texas?" Billie asked.

"In three days. I know it's my vacation and you're working, but can you spend some time with me?"

"As much as you want," she said.

They spent three days and nights together. He had theater tickets and she had to run Yellowbird, but except for those hours apart they were inseparable, attracted, overwhelmed. They made love as often as possible and neither of them spoke of love or commitment. She realized he thought she was exotic. He told her New York was a great place to visit but he could never live here. He probably had a girlfriend picked out by now back home, maybe already in place and being cheated on here in the anonymous city, and many more women there waiting for the chance to snag him. Cal Fortune would be a catch for someone. Billie knew she would never let herself love him. He would remind her of Harry Lawless every day of her life, in some ways better than Harry, in other ways less than he, and Harry was someone she needed to forget. Or maybe that was only an excuse and she just couldn't love anybody anymore.

She knew she would love her child.

"Do you come down to Texas to visit your family?" Cal asked when he was leaving.

"Sometimes."

"You could come to Dallas. I'd like to show you around."

In maternity clothes? she thought. "Maybe I will," Billie said. "But usually my parents come up here. It's a treat for them."

"I wish I could think of some way to thank you for these wonderful days together," he said.

She stroked his hair, the golden curls that would be so remarkable on either a daughter or a son. "It was wonderful for me, too," she said.

Just before Cal Fortune left town Billie looked into his eyes for a long time. She didn't really know him, but maybe what she did know was all there was to know. She was glad she wasn't twenty anymore, willing to follow him anywhere, to give up everything for love. Even as she kissed him goodbye she felt him floating away from her.

He didn't send her flowers, and he didn't call. She was both glad and disappointed. You made a bargain, Billie told herself. You made the rules. Don't consider yourself cheated. Six weeks later when her period was late and she felt a little queasy, she went to her gynecologist.

"You're pregnant!" he said with false jollity, just in case she was glad about it, a single career woman, nearly forty. He waited for her to complain.

"Good," Billie said.

She didn't take another drink or smoke another cigarette from that day on through her entire pregnancy. Her concern for the fetus was even stronger than the pains of withdrawal. She ate what she was supposed to, she took vitamins, she made herself walk. When her customers at Yellowbird saw how happy she was to be pregnant, they were delighted for her. The amniocentesis showed a healthy baby boy.

The two transvestites, Gladys and Lucy, insisted on giving her a baby shower at Yellowbird, inviting her list of friends. Billie was a little surprised to see how small that list actually was. She had always been so busy it had never occurred to her. But then, she had never been a woman with many friends. She did not invite Toad or the guys from the band, from the old days. She hadn't seen them for years. Once she was a mother, she knew, she would have different friends. Her son would go to school, she would join the PTA. Or maybe not.

She investigated birthing centers, where no one would ask her who the father was, but in the end she was afraid of complications and opted for the more conventional way of having the baby in a hospital. Her doctor was pleased; a hospital, he felt, was more equipped for emergencies, a first baby at her age....

She was in labor for twelve hours with her son. When they finally laid the warm little person against her body, she felt the ripple of electricity go right through her, from her breast to her toes. You are me and not me, she thought. She had never felt so profoundly human in her life. I can't believe I did this, she thought in awe, I can't believe I made you. How can anybody possibly think having a baby is ordinary?

I will take care of you my whole life, Billie promised him silently. Or at least as long as you want me to.

When she had to fill out the birth certificate she named her son Billie Redmond. She would call him Little Billie. She wrote down her own name, Billie Redmond, for the mother, and when she had to write down the name of the father, she did not hesitate for a minute. William Redmond, she wrote.

Now, she thought, you are a hundred percent mine.

TWENTY-SIX

Felicity and Russell had been married for three years. She was sometimes surprised it had lasted that long. What she had misread as his sophistication and demanding good taste had turned into what it really was: the fear of a man who thinks he is a fake, and the constant critical barbs of a control freak. She felt as if he didn't like anything about her. They had sex once a month, if that, and only after she had bathed and perfumed herself to his satisfaction. "You smell," he often told her, turning away.

She was horrified, bewildered, hurt. Had he always felt that way? "Nobody ever said he didn't like the way I smell," she would protest.

"I don't like it when you talk about other men."

After their passionate honeymoon Russell would never perform oral sex on her again, although he always wanted her to do it to him. From a superb lover he became a cold and selfish man whose foreplay was minimal, whose barely repressed anger turned her angry in turn, so now his enormous penis was no longer a national treasure—now it hurt, and she wished it were half as big.

"Do you have to wear that dress?"

"What's wrong with it?"

"It makes you look cheap."

It was almost as if he and her mother had conspired to make her feel like nothing. Felicity was beginning to think there had been a horrible mistake and she had married her mother. She felt like an inadequate little girl again, still living at home, but this time she was in his home. She remembered when she was chasing him, thinking at that time in how many ways Russell's temperament was like her mother's, but she had been too much in love to understand what it would be like to have to deal with this.

When she was courting him she had made excuses for everything. When she married him she had thought she had won the war. Now she realized the war would never be over.

"I want to go to couples counseling," Felicity told him.

"Why?"

"Because I'm miserable and we're not getting along."

"It's your fault if we're not," he said.

She bought and arranged flowers for their apartment and he complained if they shed before she took them away. If she left the bureau drawer open half an inch he yelled at her and told her she was a careless slob. In the morning when they opened their eyes, the first thing he told her instead of good morning was, "Wash out your mouth."

He was still punishing her for making him give up his freedom, and she was thinking seriously of getting a divorce before it was too late.

"I'm leaving you," Felicity said.

Russell looked up from the TV. All he did now when they were at home together was watch sports events on television; he had nothing to say to her and didn't want to listen to what she had to say to him. But of course he had always done that, hadn't he, and hadn't she pretended to like sports as much as he did?

"You're what?" he said. He actually sounded wounded, mild.

"I can't be married to a man who hates me."

"Who said I hate you, Baby?"

"I do."

"But I love you."

"You have a fine way of showing it."

"Don't I support you?" he said, in that same innocently aggrieved tone. "Could you ask for a better life?"

"That's not the issue. You insult me."

"When do I do that?"

"All the time."

"I never insult you. You're crazy."

"You tell me I'm not attractive, that I smell bad."

"Baby, you're the most beautiful woman I've ever seen."

"That's not true," Felicity said. "I know I'm not so pretty, but I'm pretty enough. I try all the time. You don't care."

"When was the last time I brought you flowers?" Russell asked sternly.

"Two days ago," she admitted.

"Then how can you say I don't care?"

How could she, an intelligent woman, a trained attorney, be so helpless to put a cogent argument together when she was talking to him? He frightened her, and needing his approval she floundered and drew back. What could she make of a man who belittled her one minute and was unexpectedly sentimental the next?

"You're just working too hard," Russell said. "I see how much work you bring home from the office."

"I'm surprised you notice anything. You're always glued to the television set."

"I don't want to bother you."

Could that be true? She backed down, she wondered, she tried harder.

Two more years went by. She was promoted at the office to partner. She knew she was their symbol: a woman and a black, but she also knew she was good. She realized that for the moment Russell was right about not wanting a baby, that it was the wrong time. She continued to be the good wife, but now she didn't have time to cook for him so often, they didn't entertain as much. But every six months they had a party for his friends.

She and Russell had been to India together, to Hong Kong and Singapore and Indonesia, to Portofino and Naples and Venice, to Nice and Cannes. He liked to plan their trips with careful perfectionism, to take complete charge. On these expensive and exotic vacations he seemed to enjoy showing her off. He was kind to her and she felt close. Back home in New York they were always nice to each other in public. They were affectionate to each other, with their nicknames, with their coyness. People thought they were a happy couple. But now the sex had dwindled to the point where three and four months would go by without Russell's ever wanting to touch her. When she made overtures he drew away.

"Why?" Felicity asked him.

"You're just my wife," he said. "You're here every day. I told you I could never be satisfied with one woman."

It made her cry when he said that, but hadn't he told her before they were married, hadn't he warned her? She was sure that now he was having an affair again. He had to have someone, or a lot of women, if he wasn't going near her.

"I want to be more exciting to you," Felicity said. "Tell me your secret fantasies. Tell me what you like."

He shrugged. "I don't know."

"Yes you do."

"I want you to wear sexy lingerie," he said finally, but he was just throwing her a bone.

"That's easy enough!"

She dressed up for him: the garter belt and stockings and high heels with no underpants, the panties with the hole, all the black and red and ruffled things she could find in the department stores and the sex shops. It was a complete waste of time. Now she was just his wife in a pathetic costume. She felt unattractive and unappealing and foolish and wronged.

"You're having an affair, aren't you?" Felicity said.

"No I'm not."

"Of course you are."

"Believe what you like. You won't listen to what I tell you anyway."

Then one night she went out for drinks with a colleague from the office, a man she wouldn't be interested in in a million years but who made her laugh; and when she came home Russell was waiting up for her, angry and jealous and accusing her of being the one who was cheating, calling her a slut. He hit her three times and pushed her against the wall. She tried to run out of the apartment but he locked the door and stood in front of it so she couldn't get away. She was screaming. She hadn't been so terrified since the days when she was little and her mother had chased her around the house with the belt. Cheating had never even occurred to Felicity as an option for herself—only leaving had.

The next day she sneaked in to work embarrassed about the way she looked and desperate to change her life, and talked to a divorce lawyer at her firm who took Polaroid photos of her bruises, and that weekend she went home to see her mother.

"I'm leaving him," she told Carolee. "Look at these pictures of what he did to me."

"What did you do to deserve it?" her mother asked.

"Nothing! *Nothing!*"

"Where will you be if you leave him?" her mother said. "Who will you be? Just another lonely divorced woman looking for husband number two. I lived in an unhappy marriage and so can you. There are always compensations. Russell is a catch. Most women would think you're lucky to have him."

"I'd rather have a kind husband like my sister has," Felicity said, although she didn't actually mean Calvin.

"You'd never settle for a man that pathetic-looking and you know it."

"He's a catch for Theodora."

"And Russell is a catch for you. You're my beautiful favorite daughter. You deserve the best. He was only jealous because he loves you so much."

"Oh, Mom." She always melted when her mother was kind to her. "Russell doesn't even want to have sex with me anymore."

"Men want what they can't have," her mother said. "I know."

Felicity went home to Russell. He apologized and promised he would never hit her again, but although she finally forgave him she didn't really trust him anymore. They both agreed to try harder to make their marriage work, but as the months went by Felicity didn't see any difference. She thought he was possibly too old, too set in his ways, ever to change for her. Maybe she was too hurt and angry to try to change for him. After that she just coasted along, depressed and confused. Sometimes she pretended she wasn't interested in Russell at all, which was now more true than not, and once in a while, to catch him off guard, she tried to seduce him, just to see if she wasn't totally repulsive, even though she didn't enjoy it when she succeeded. He took her when he decided he wanted her.

She was still trying to figure out when that was. At first she had tried to find out so she could get him, but now she wanted to know so she could avoid him. He wasn't her lover, a lover wouldn't be so selfish. He wasn't her best friend, hadn't been for a long time. A best friend would not be so critical. She had to admit she still loved him, but now it was not as a husband but more as a dear and long-known member of her family with whom she had shared a past. She also had to admit she hated him.

She knew other people put up with sexless marriages, the way her father had, but she was too young and vital to settle for a life like that. How ironic that everybody thought she was so lucky to be Mrs. Russell Naylor, even her mother, who was supposed to love her.

How even more ironic that Russell said he loved her, too. Maybe he meant she was just a dear member of his family, the way she felt about him. He probably didn't even bother to figure out what he felt, as long as she continued to be conveniently there.

Her firm had a new client, the successful black suspense novelist Jason Collins. Felicity had met him once when they signed him. He was an attractive, youngish middle-aged man with a mischievous twinkle in his eye that she had liked. He had seemed to appreciate her as a woman and his attitude hinted he was prevented from flirting only by the office setting and their professional relationship. At the time she had been surprised and flattered. Despite his jealousy Russell had by now also made her feel no man could possibly be interested in her. Now Jason Collins's new manuscript was in, and she was to read it for possible libel, and then she was to have the usual meeting with him to ask him who each character was, whether they were real or imaginary or a composite. The publishers insisted on being protected when an author had as big an advance as he did.

She stayed up until four o'clock in the morning, reading and taking notes, and despite the fact that she had to read his novel for other than pleasure she found it well put together and engrossing. She found herself lingering over the sex scenes. You couldn't help picturing the author in them to some degree. Wouldn't she like to ask him, in their meeting, "Is this you?"

I'm really desperate, Felicity thought, smiling to herself, when I start daydreaming about an author because of the sex scenes he's written. That's how bad my life has gotten.

Her new office was furnished with English antiques and flowered chintz. Two spotted ceramic dogs sat on the corner of her desk and there was a wallful of law books. She was wearing a black suit with a short skirt and very high heels, and as always her makeup was perfect. When Jason Collins came in he looked at her appreciatively. She was flattered all over again, but she was also aware that they were both wearing wedding rings. She was sure his marriage was happier than hers. She supposed his lucky wife was the inspiration for those sex scenes, and wondered what she looked like.

Felicity sat on the small sofa and he sat on the chair, because she had decided quite a while ago that to sit behind her desk in situations like this was too intimidating to the client. After all, she was on his side. When they both had coffee at hand she went down her list. It was quite straightforward. Jason Collins was enough of a pro to know how to disguise characters who were real, and in this particular book, although he had done a great deal of research with the police, it had been mainly to verify or explain things he had made up and wanted to be accurate.

She looked up to see him looking at her legs. She would have tried to tug her skirt down to cover more of them, but it would have seemed too girlish, and besides, it couldn't be done. He smiled at her.

"Do you work out?" he asked. "You have incredible muscles in your legs."

"I used to dance as a kid," Felicity said. "And I still try to get to the gym."

"I can see that."

She thought he looked like he worked out, too, but said nothing. He was still looking at her in that same appreciative way, and suddenly, for the first time in a long time, she felt pretty.

"Well," she said, tapping the manuscript, "I think you're fine. And I would like to add that I loved the book."

"Thank you."

"You kept me up all night. I mean, it did."

He laughed, as if people didn't say that to him all the time, as if she were somehow seductive and clever. "Can I take you to lunch?"

"Today?"

"If you're free."

She only hesitated for an instant. "I'd like that very much," she said.

She let him choose the restaurant, and even though she had an expense account and it would be easy for her to take him, she let him orchestrate everything because he seemed to want to. He took her to a pub with photos of authors on the walls and simple but good food. He was known there, and obviously felt comfortable. She had never been there before. Jason seemed very pleased to be with her; he introduced her to his waiter as if she was going to become a regular there herself, and told the waiter that when she came back he should take good care of her. There was something fresh and new about going out to lunch with Jason Collins, as if it were a date, as if for this one hour she had no angry, critical, jealous husband to go home to at the end of the day; that she was free, her own woman, wondering if this charming, attractive man would be the one she fell in love with. And, of course, in the fantasy Jason was single, too.

"Did you always write?" she asked.

"Always. I starved for a few years, but then I hit it lucky when I was in my twenties. So I've been a professional writer ever since. My parents, unfortunately, never thought it was a real job. This is my twentieth book, and I think they're finally getting it, that I won't starve again. I'm glad they lived long enough to see that."

"Do you have children?"

"Yes, a boy and a girl. Both at Yale. I never went to college myself, so it's a thrill to have them there."

She supposed she should ask him about his wife. This was, after all, not a date, and he was not single, but she knew there were degrees of availability and she was curious to know more about him.

"And does your wife work?"

He nodded. "She's a teacher. She's five years older than I am. In fact, she supported me before we were married, when we were living together and I was still struggling. I think I married her out of gratitude. Now I often wonder if I did her such a favor. I didn't do myself one and she knows it. I don't like being married; I never did, except for the kids. They have always given me a great deal of pleasure."

"But you wouldn't get divorced?" Felicity said.

"What would be the point? I'm never going to get married again."

So he just cheats, she thought.

"Tell me about you," he said.

"I'm not supposed to tell the clients about my unhappy marriage," she said, smiling, pretending to be lighthearted about it.

"Then it's unhappy?"

"Yes. My husband is a lot older and very controlling. I've grown up since we were married, and the things I used to be impressed by...well, I made a mistake, too."

"So here we are," Jason said. "Two more statistics."

"I know," Felicity said. "It's so sad. There is no one who believed in love and happily ever after more than I did."

"But you could get divorced," he said. "You're too young and beautiful to stay in a loveless marriage."

Beautiful? she thought, surprised. "Thank you," she said.

He smiled at her in a flirtatious way. "And you smell so good. Is that your perfume or is it you?"

"Writers!" she said. Oh, God, he likes the way I smell, she thought. I'd like to record this moment and stick it in Russell's face.

"It's true," Jason said. "Am I embarrassing you?"

"No, I love it."

"And is there someone else in your life?"

"Of course not," Felicity said. Then she thought she had sounded offended and sanctimonious. "But if there were," she added lightly, "why would I tell you? You know enough about me already to put me completely in your power."

"Really?" he said, pleased, his tone as light as hers.

"Do you like that?"

"Actually," Jason said, "I do."

He called her afterward, and they met for lunch again, and then again, filling each other in on all the details of their lives before they had met, while Jason's compliments and flirtatious remarks flattered her and made her feel more and more attractive and desirable; and gradually Felicity began to feel aroused, like a sexual woman thinking about having a relationship with a man who was her equal. She never mentioned these lunches to Russell. It took a few months before Jason suggested seriously and not just in banter that they have an affair. She knew he understood her more than any man she had ever met, and she felt she meant the same to him. They were two kindred spirits. By then she was in love.

You could put me completely in your power. Do you like that? Yes, I do. Looking back on it later, when Jason was the emotional master and she was the emotional slave, Felicity remembered exactly when they had established their future relationship and laid down their roles, without premeditation, simply by instinct. It had started at that luncheon table, on their first date, with a chance remark; and she knew then that nothing is only by chance.

Jason had a little pied à terre where he went with women he was seeing, an apartment borrowed from an understanding friend. The first time Felicity went there she was nervous, but Jason was so passionate and appreciative of her body that he awakened her to her own sexuality at last, to a degree she had never dreamed was possible. She thought of him as her own private sexual revolution. Afterward she was glad she had gone, and knew she could not stop going, but she felt guilty and she never stopped feeling guilty.

I'm doing just what my mother did, she thought, reproaching herself for becoming what she had hated. It's immoral, it's unkind, it's unfair, it's bad. But the sex was so incredible with Jason, and it made up for everything she was suffering at home. Jason was affectionate and believed in foreplay. He complimented her. All the sexy romantic things Felicity had tried to no avail with Russell were now a part of her ardent lunchtime experiences with her lover. Jason made her feel attractive and sensual and wanted.

He also knew how to keep her off balance, to make her doubt herself and their relationship and want him more. That was the part where he was the master—master of his

besotted slave and master of manipulation. She didn't know
if he was seeing other women or not. He said he wasn't. But
then, so did her husband. Sometimes Jason said he loved his
wife, that it was only marriage he didn't like, not the woman
he had promised to live with forever, and that hurt. There
were long gaps, two weeks sometimes, when Jason really
wanted to torture Felicity, when he didn't call her at all, or
return the messages she sent him. She would give up and
mourn having lost him forever, cry secretly in the bathroom
so Russell wouldn't hear, and then Jason would call and
make three dates with her for the same week.

She bought a cellular phone and gave Jason the number so
he wouldn't have to go through the office receptionist. When
Russell saw it Felicity said she had bought it so he could always find her, and he was pleased and said it was about time
she joined the electronic age. How little he knew. She and her
lover had been sending each other coded messages on their
computers since the beginning.

Sometimes now Felicity and Jason were reckless. One
night they met each other after work. She told Russell she
was working late at the office, she turned off her cell phone,
and she didn't come home until midnight. That was the second time Russell hit her. He accused her again (but this time
he was right) of having a lover. She was reminded then that
he could be dangerous and easily incited to violence, and after that she became the most reassuring of coy little girl-
wives. She always remembered the day her mild-mannered
father had come home to threaten her mother and her
mother's lover with a gun. Russell had never been mild-
mannered on the best of days—he was more like an angry
bull—and now Felicity knew she could never be sure of what
he would do if he found out about her.

She felt it was worth the danger, though. The affair with
Jason was the first time in her entire marriage that Felicity
had felt alive, and she hadn't even noticed she was dead.

She hated Russell now and wished she had the courage to
leave him. She hated the way he screamed at her, the way
she never knew whether he would turn on her or not. But she
was sure that if she did leave Russell that Jason would leave
her in turn, because she would be too available. It was safer

for Jason the way it was; she was married and afraid of her husband. She had a husband and a lover, and she really didn't have either of them.

Now suddenly, for some reason, on some of the days she had been with Jason secretly at lunchtime Russell wanted to have sex with her at night. This was the husband who had belittled her, who hadn't wanted to touch her, who had pushed her away...now she was the one avoiding him. She never wanted to have sex with Russell again. Maybe that was why he was aroused by her, when nothing else had worked.

Sometimes she had to let him do it. And sometimes now the sex with Russell was great, not because he was any less selfish than he had ever been, but because she discovered having two men in the same day was an aphrodisiac; it made her feel powerful. It made her feel desired. It made her feel she had a buffer against either of them hurting her too much. It was not about Russell or Jason, it was all about her.

Felicity decided Jason was the only thing that was saving her marriage. Her marriage was the only thing that was keeping Jason. She was trapped in this triangle that made her feel guilty and frightened and unbalanced. If she left Russell and then—immediately, inevitably—Jason left her, she would be all alone.

She had learned the message from her mother too well: without a man she did not exist. Without having sex to fill her up Felicity felt empty, a kind of shrieking, hollow, yearning space with the shell of a person around it, walking through life pretending to be whole.

On Friday evenings when Felicity knew the long lonely weekend was ahead, when she was in their townhouse in solitary confinement with her husband, she bought vast amounts of prepared food, and then she ate it all, secretly in the kitchen, when Russell was watching TV or asleep. After she ate it she would make herself throw up so she wouldn't get fat. She was bulimic again, just as she had been when she was younger, trying to fill up that endless emptiness, quell the fear. Her life had gone out of control once more, and she couldn't think of any way to save herself.

TWENTY-SEVEN

Gara and Carl had been married for twenty years. She had never been able to believe their happy marriage had lasted so long, not at the beginning and not even now. She would count the years on her fingers to make sure she hadn't made a mistake. Twenty years—what a record, what an oasis of love and support and peace and friendship in a city that seemed filled with lonely people who had been betrayed by love, or the lack of it. Whatever had happened in her and Carl's marriage that had been difficult—arguments, forced separations, business worries—had been part of life, and she knew she was lucky to have avoided worse disasters.

His sons were grown and gone, Cary to Paris to work in an art gallery, Eric to New Mexico to be an architect. She and Carl visited them once in a while, or they came to New York, but it was clear that they were wrapped up in their own adult lives now. She always had to keep remembering that they had a mother, that she was only their father's wife, and nothing would change that. She didn't mind. Other women, she knew, had their own children who avoided them. That, she also knew, was what really hurt.

Carl's gallery in New York was not doing so well these days. He worried and brooded, and sometimes now he was short-tempered with her and wanted to be alone. She knew when he got home at the end of the day that he wouldn't call out his customary cheery hello that was part question to be sure she was there to make his life safe, that he wouldn't come to find her with his face alight with love; that instead he would pour a glass of wine and sit in front of the television set channel surfing and not watching any of it.

"Don't cook, let's go out to dinner," he would say finally,

his first words to her. She preferred that, too, because on the few occasions they had dinner together alone in their apartment now, he didn't say a word. At dinner out, in a small neighborhood restaurant where they were known, he would pretend for the waiters' sake that life was wonderful, and then he would tell her quietly how worried he was about money.

"I'm making enough money for both of us," Gara said several times. "You laughed when I saved it so carefully, but now we have it."

"I know," Carl would answer. "You're rich. You're lucky."

"*We're* rich. It's *our* money." But she could tell because she knew him so well that he couldn't live with an arrangement like that. He needed meaningful work and success, he needed to pick up the check, and he never intended to retire.

That summer, as always, they went for weekends to their little gray house on the beach in Amagansett, on the Long Island shore, and she took the month of August off as all the therapists did and she and Carl were able to go there for longer weekends. But this summer things were tense and melancholy. Carl walked on the beach alone and asked her not to join him, and sometimes at dusk she saw him on the deck looking out over the ocean with the strangest look on his face, as if he would never see it again.

He went to Paris more often, to see Cary and survey the art scene, but when he was there he called her every day. Carl was much nicer, more cheerful and affectionate, when he was away. Gara knew how difficult it was for him to be in his late fifties and feeling his life had jumped away from him, taking its own course, leaving him helpless just when he should be learning to be serene. She was as supportive as she could be, but she felt helpless, too.

"I've decided to open a gallery in Paris," Carl said finally.

"In Paris?"

"Yes. It's going to give me a fresh start. I have contacts there, and Cary is going to work for me and help me."

"Then he'll run it?"

"No, of course not. He's not as experienced as all that. I'll run it."

"You?" She realized she was blocking the painful reality of what the move would mean, that it was so far away they would see much less of each other. "What about your gallery here?" she asked, trying to sound calm.

"Lucie can continue to run it. I'll be back and forth." He smiled. "I feel young again."

"Yes," she murmured, knowing it was true. "You look younger." Carl looked completely different now. She finally felt chilled and afraid about what his life decision would mean. "But what about me?" she asked. "What will I do?"

"You can't desert your patients. You don't speak fluent French and you certainly couldn't start a new practice in Paris at this point in your career, even with Americans. Your work is here. You'd hate living there with no job, no language, me away all day. I'll be back and forth to New York all the time."

So it was that or bankruptcy? It still seemed like his fantasy, his living so far away so much of the time, his new life. If he were her patient she would join the resistance, tell him it was a wonderful idea, wait for him to express the doubts that had to be there because he was changing the entire structure of their marriage. But he was not her patient, he was her husband, and she did not want to act pleased. "I guess you've given this a lot of thought," she said.

"Of course. This will get me out of the financial hole I'm in. The new gallery will be a real opportunity for me."

"Carl, I don't want to dissuade you, but this is something we should discuss. I don't want to be apart from you for so long…"

"Neither do I, but I have no choice. Please understand."

What could she do? Argue with him and alienate him, destroy his confidence, make him stay against his will and feel so useless and frustrated that he would finally leave her? She knew she could never give up everything to follow him, because she had a life, too, and her life was here, and she would only end up resenting him. For a moment she wished she were a different kind of person, that she was a housewife, content to follow him, to make do with loneliness, to search for new friends, to create a home in a foreign place where he could be the one with the interesting career. But if she were, he wouldn't want her. That was not the woman he had married.

"I do understand," Gara said finally. "And I agree, I think it's a great opportunity for you." She forced herself to sound enthusiastic, to imagine it an adventure for her, too, an addition to her life, the excited American in Paris. She had always enjoyed their vacations there. "And I'll come to stay with you whenever I can," she said.

He didn't answer, and very briefly she thought it was odd he didn't concur, didn't reassure her that of course she would visit often, that she could afford it, that she could rearrange her schedule and take long weekends in the winter as well, but then she told herself that he didn't have to answer; he knew she would be there.

She talked to her best friend Jane about the move, on the phone several times a week. Gara realized she discussed her feelings about it much more with Jane than she did with Carl, but he seemed so fragile, so desperate, that she was afraid to tear him down. "What am I going to do?" she asked Jane.

"You have to let him go," Jane said. "You have a career here. What if you give up everything to be with him and then the Paris gallery fails? Then you'll both be out of work. It's different for me; I'm an old-fashioned wife. I don't mind being bicoastal, running the apartment here and the house in L.A., and if Eliot goes on location I go with him and bring the Porthault sheets. That's what I do. But you would hate that."

"I know. But he'll be lonely. What if he cheats? He's still attractive, he looks younger than fifty-eight. And men can be old and ugly, it doesn't matter, women still want them."

"If a tree falls in the forest and no one is there to hear it, did it really fall at all?" Jane said.

Gara had to smile. "I guess it will be more romantic to live apart for a while," she said. "Whenever we get together it will be fresh and new. After twenty years it's good to shake things up a little."

"Absolutely," Jane said. "Give him a giant box of condoms. Join the resistance, as you like to say."

"I wouldn't go that far," Gara said.

He left in September. It was not until Carl was packing

that the reality of the situation hit her. He was really going; this was a big move. Suddenly he was taking not just a small suitcase but almost all his clothes. He seemed in a hurry, and as she stood there watching him Gara fought back tears. Once he had made up his mind, everything happened very fast. A moving company appeared and took the art and the sculptures that had been in the apartment for years because Carl had decided to ship them to Paris so he wouldn't be so lonely, and, as he pointed out to her, she had never liked them anyway. She realized they had always been his, not hers, because he had chosen them and paid for them, and some of it had belonged to him before they had even met, but still she felt somehow betrayed that he was taking his meaningful things with him on this journey and leaving her behind.

He's taking his totems, she told herself reassuringly. It's okay. He needs them. He's frightened, too. But in an odd way she felt divorced, although neither of them intended it that way. She supposed this was what divorce felt like.

"I'll stay with Cary until I find an apartment," Carl said. "I can save money that way."

"In that little apartment?"

"He's hardly ever there. He has a new girlfriend."

"You're going to put the art in his apartment?"

"I don't know what I'm going to do," Carl said, and he sounded testy. She allowed the matter to drop.

He was gone then, and Gara was stunned by the empty, final feeling in their apartment. She wandered around looking at the new spaces, avoiding his barren closet. This was not another of his brief business trips with a foreseeable end; this might be a separation of a month or more, and the back and forth could go on for years.

As it turned out, it was two months before he came back to see her, and then he stayed for only five days, full of business talk and excitement.

"I'm so busy," he said. "Opening a new gallery is a lot of work."

"I want to come to see it," Gara said.

"You will."

"Why don't we plan that I come to see you this time? I'll come for the Thanksgiving holiday. I can take a week off."

"But I might be back here then," Carl said. "I'm going to close the New York gallery. It's costing me too much money."

"I'm sorry," Gara said, but she realized it was inevitable.

"Let's wait and see who visits who over Thanksgiving," he said. "My life is so unpredictable now. You have to be adaptable. You know I can never make plans until the last minute."

"You never could," she said. "I've always accepted that."

She was trying to settle into her new routine. In some ways she was surprised to find herself so content. Carl called her every morning, for only a minute because it was so expensive, but after he called and she knew he was all right and still loved her Gara would become absorbed in her work. At night she would read in bed or watch television, able to do what she wanted to do when she wanted to do it, without worrying about anyone else. The refrigerator was nearly empty now, with small packages of leftover takeout lingering until the end of the week when she threw them all out. She tried not to think about sex, and although she often pretended his arms were still around her when she slept, she was also rather guiltily relieved to have the whole bed to herself.

Their social life had formerly been couples. She realized that all her women friends were married, and so now she sometimes went to the movies alone when she had nothing else to do, and she discovered she liked it. There was no one else to complain that he wanted to leave in the middle of the movie, or to make her stay. The apartment was not so lonely anymore, but she still found herself counting the days until Carl might be back; doing magical numbers, alchemy, putting out her vitamin pills and thinking, He'll be back before these are gone, he has to be back before the bottle is empty. Somehow the little routine made her feel safe, as if things had not changed that much.

One brisk Saturday afternoon Gara went downtown to say goodbye to Carl's old gallery, since he was going to close it.

There was a new woman there at the desk, middle-aged, with dark hair.

"Where's Lucie?" Gara asked. "Off today?"

"Lucie?"

"You know, Lucie, the young Frenchwoman, the manager."

"I'm Martha. I've been here for two months. Lucie went back to Paris to work in Mr. Whiteman's new gallery there."

"You mean now?"

"No, when I came. Can I help you?"

Lucie went to Paris when Carl did? She had been there for the past two months and he had never mentioned it? He had said she was going to run the gallery here in New York. Had he simply changed his mind?

"No thanks," Gara said, and left. She hadn't even bothered to tell this woman, who didn't know her, that she was Mr. Whiteman's wife.

She walked all the way home, a distance of miles, through the blowing paper, the honking traffic, the shuffling crowds, numb and confused. It was probably nothing. She was reasonably sure there was nothing going on between Carl and Lucie. Lucie was twenty-eight, with a slender, long-legged young girl's body, and short, spiky, bleached-white hair. She had a pouting upper lip and a high, childish voice just this side of babyish, that went up at the ends of sentences as if they were all questions. Carl could not possibly take someone like her seriously.

Nevertheless, when Carl called the next day Gara said, "I went by the gallery yesterday and there's a new manager there."

"Oh, she's terrible," Carl said. "She's just temporary."

"I didn't know you took Lucie to Paris."

There was a tiny pause, as if she had caught him. "Well, she's so good," Carl said. "And she's French, which helps me."

"France is full of French people," Gara said mildly. "Why Lucie?"

"What is this about Lucie?" Carl said. "She's just a girl who works for me. People always take their staff with them when they relocate."

"But what about your son?"

"What about him?"

"I thought he was going to help you."

"He is. He does."

"Then when did you decide to take her?" Gara asked, carefully keeping her tone very neutral.

"I don't know. What difference does it make?"

"I just think it's odd you didn't mention it."

"Honey, there are many things about business I don't tell you," Carl said, sounding very irritated. The way he said "honey" was more like name-calling than an endearment. "I have a lot of financial problems and things on my mind."

"I wish you would share them with me."

"I do," he said.

"Don't get upset," Gara said. "I'm on your side."

"Then act like it."

"I am." There was a silence. "I'm sorry," Gara said, feeling foolish and guilty for being so annoyingly jealous. She wished for an instant that she could be Lucie: young, admiring, following the older man to make her future career, her whole life ahead of her. Lucie going out with young Frenchmen, smoking cigarettes, drinking in cafés, getting laid, not worrying about cellulite. And underpaid, insecure, worrying about AIDS, all the bad things about being young...

"It's just that I miss you so much," Gara said.

"I miss you, too."

"And I love you," she said.

"I love you, too. I'll see you soon."

As it turned out, it was Carl who came to New York for Thanksgiving, but only for three days. He didn't tell her he was leaving so soon until he had already arrived, and by then it was too late for her to try to rush back with him for a mere two days. He spent a lot of time on the phone, and they made love only once, and perfunctorily. They had Thanksgiving dinner at Jane's apartment with Jane and her husband and Jane's two children from her first marriage and their dates, and Jane's sisters and their husbands and children. Looking at all these contented people, Gara found it difficult to be joyful about her own life or to find thanks in her heart for anything but friends and food. She supposed that should be more than enough when other people didn't have even that, but she also felt Carl had ruined their eagerly anticipated holiday by cutting it so short and acting so distant.

There were so few holidays. Christmas would be here soon. Christmas would be four months since he had left, and so far they had seen each other only twice. At this rate they would be seeing each other six times a year. They should be taking turns visiting one another, but she hadn't even been to see him yet.

"For Christmas and New Year's let's all go to the Swiss Alps!" Jane said. "Eliot, don't you think you could manage that? Gara, you and Carl come with us. The advantage of living in Paris is it's so close to all those great things in Europe. We'll rent a house. A cheap one, and we'll all share."

"What about it?" Jane's husband, Eliot, said to them, looking interested.

"We'll see," Carl said.

Gara was sure that meant no.

What was she to think about a marriage in which they saw so little of each other? Was this just the way it was in the beginning when Carl was trying to get on his feet, or would things get worse? That night when they got home she and Carl had a fight, instigated by her, which ended with her in tears and him angry. The next morning she apologized and they made up, because they had so little time together. And then he was gone, with nothing decided, nothing promised, everything still on hold.

The next day Gara went out and bought a Supersaver plane ticket to Paris for Christmas week. When Carl called her she told him.

"But what if I come to New York that week?" Carl protested.

"Everything will be closed in New York," Gara told him firmly. "You can't do any business. I want to be with you in Paris for Christmas and New Year's. It will be romantic and fun."

"But…"

"My plane tickets were a bargain and they're nonrefundable. What you have to do is make hotel reservations at some little place for us, you pick it. Unless Cary is gone, and then we can stay at his apartment."

"Oh, you don't want to stay there," Carl said. "It's not civilized enough for you."

"Then get us a *pension*."

"They'll be full."

"Not in the winter they won't. Don't you want me to come?"

"Of course I do," Carl said.

"Then I'm coming," Gara said cheerily, trying to make it sound like the adventure they had pretended it would be...or she had pretended to herself it would be. "We'll buy each other Christmas presents when we're there, and we'll have a wonderful time."

After they hung up she cried again. There was only one reason she could think of why her husband didn't want her to be with him, and that was because he would rather be with someone else.

That night Gara couldn't sleep, and finally gave up and watched the clock. She had often told her patients when they were trying to figure out whether or not their spouse was cheating on them that if you have an instinct about someone you know that well, then you're probably right. Now she had to give that advice to herself, but she prayed that this time she was wrong and that there was a good excuse for Carl's behavior. She felt it was a fruitless prayer. When it was three a.m. in Paris she called Cary's apartment.

Cary answered, sounding as if she had awakened him, which was what she had intended to do. She was sorry about that, but it was the only way she could also wake up Carl—if in fact he was even there—and set her mind at rest. "I need to talk to your father," she said.

"Gara?"

"Yes."

"I'll see if he's here." He came back. "I guess he went out."

"Where is he?"

"I don't know."

"Well, is he coming back?"

"Yes, I'll tell him you called. Is everything all right?"

"It's fine. I'm sorry I woke you up. I forgot how late it is there."

"That's all right," he said. "Goodnight."

After she hung up Gara sat there for a long time thinking. There is still something not right here, she thought. What is Carl doing sharing a tiny one-bedroom apartment with his thirty-year-old son who supposedly has a girlfriend and is never there but was certainly there tonight? He and Cary were never even that close. And could Carl possibly be out this late with clients? He never did that at home. As far as she knew he never even did it on business trips. So now the new Carl is a night owl, unless he's peacefully asleep somewhere else, with someone else.

Merry Christmas, she thought bitterly. Happy New Year. I just hope it isn't Lucie, because that would mean it's been going on longer than I ever would have believed.

Gara packed her nicest clothes for Paris, although her heart wasn't in it. She felt as if she was going to a funeral. Carl called to tell her he had reserved a room for them at the little Hotel Lenox on the Left Bank, not far from his new gallery. He also told her Paris was cold and damp, and to bring warm things to wear. At a previous time in their lives that would have seemed romantic, but now it was only inconvenient.

He met her at the Orly airport on a chilly morning under a lowering white sky that seemed as unfriendly as he was. He had a little French car now, another thing he had neglected to mention. They drove to the hotel and he told her he would wait in the bar and have coffee while she unpacked because their room was too small, that she should take her time. What might have been considerate seemed distant instead. Gara was acutely conscious that although they hadn't seen each other for a month Carl hadn't even kissed her hello. He had every sign of a husband who is having an affair and is guilty and resentful. When she was putting away her clothes she noticed that he had brought only one change of clothing with him, and thought it was odd. Of course, Cary's apartment, where Carl was supposedly living, was not far away, so he could always get more, but it made her feel even more temporary than ever.

She unpacked and went downstairs to join him at the bar where they were still serving breakfast. The large comfortable chairs were far apart and the place was nearly empty anyway, which was almost as good as being alone. They drank cafe au lait neither of them wanted and looked at each other with inscrutable faces.

"Is it Lucie?" Gara said.

He reddened. "Is what Lucie?"

"The woman you're having an affair with. You can't fool me, I know you too well."

"None of this has anything to do with her," Carl said.

"Where are you really living?"

"Paris, I guess."

"I mean, where in Paris are you living, Carl?"

He looked at his hands, front and back, as if he had not seen them lately and was surprised to see them still attached to him. Then he looked at her. "I want a divorce," he said.

Her heart banged in her chest. Her throat felt as if she had swallowed ice. She had been expecting a confession, but not this. She realized she had been ready to let him have his fling and get over it. But now all she could do was stare at him, devastated, and ask, "Why?"

"I wish I still loved you the way I did in the beginning," he said, "but I don't."

Why did he have to say that? All she could do was fight for him in the best way she knew how. "You're not supposed to," Gara said. "You don't have to. Things change. We love each other in a different way. You always say you love me. You must love me in some way."

"I do," Carl said. "Like a friend."

He was twisting her soul and destroying everything she had believed in—that they were special, that they were above all this, blessed and charmed. "Couples go through these crises," Gara said.

"Don't use your professional voice on me, Gara."

"You've never heard my professional voice."

"I don't want to be married anymore," he said.

"Not married, or not married to me?"

He hesitated for an instant. "Both."

She wondered if bursting into tears would help, but she

was still too stunned to cry. Some survival instinct held her calm, but she was aware that her nails had been digging into her chair. A divorce? Just like that? Twenty happy years gone, forgotten? Maybe those years weren't as happy as she had always thought, but she couldn't believe that. At most only the past year had been bad.

"We need to have a separation," she said, in that same neutral voice she had found herself using more and more with him lately. "Not just this, where you sneak off and lie to me, but a separation with ground rules and an understanding that you're going through a period where you're trying to find yourself, and that I'm giving you enough time to get over this thing with Lucie or whoever you're living with. I'm willing to let it run its course. It will, you know. The other woman is the key that opened the door to your married life and let you out to freedom. But we weren't unhappy enough or bored enough for you to want to be married to her instead of to me."

"Don't blame it on Lucie," Carl said. "She's just a little girl."

So it was her, after all. "She's twenty-eight," Gara said. "That's not a little girl."

"But she's like one. She needs me."

"Of course she does. For a while. I see older men with much younger women in my practice all the time. They get married and then soon she's cheating on him with a man her own age. Then he comes to me to find out what happened."

"It's not your fault either," Carl said.

"Thank you. Just tell me, did I nag you or complain too much? The other things, like getting older, I couldn't help."

"You never nagged or complained."

"But I did get older." She heard her voice crack.

"So did I," Carl said. "You're still a beautiful woman, a wonderful person. But as you said, things change. I changed."

"I can change, too," Gara said. "What do you want me to be?" As soon as she said it she regretted it, because she knew she wasn't what he wanted, changed or not.

"Don't change anything," Carl said. "You always think

you have to be perfect. You're fine the way you are. I just can't be with you anymore."

How civilized they were being, when each of them knew they had the power to hurt, maim, and kill the other. But then she thought: He already has killed me.

They sat there in the bar, afraid to go up to the room, talking quietly, neatly clearing up the shards of their shattered marriage, making plans while the waiters cleared away the breakfast things and set the tables up for drinks. Carl agreed to separate informally for a year and see what happened, but only, he added, because they could get a no-fault divorce in New York after a year. He said he didn't want to be unreasonable about any of the things that belonged to them. He already had his art, and since Gara would probably want to stay in their rent-stabilized New York apartment he wouldn't try to take any of the furniture. He wanted only the rest of the art that was in both of his galleries and in storage, and he would give her the beach house in return. He said she could have the paintings that he had left behind in their apartment if she wanted them, and she said that she did. She knew he was taking too much, but she was too confused and numb to be vindictive.

There was no question of her going to see his new gallery now. Lucie would be there, and Gara never wanted to set eyes on Lucie again. Carl said he had to go back to work, that she should try to rest since she was jet lagged, and they could have dinner together with Cary that night. He had made reservations, he told her, at a nice brasserie he thought she would like.

And then am I to stay or go? Gara wondered. Will he see me, will he avoid me and spend the holidays with Lucie? I have a hotel room, but what will I do here? She could not possibly imagine herself shopping or sightseeing after what had happened. Then she realized that since they had agreed to separate, of course tonight was their farewell dinner, and after that she would be on her own.

She went up to her room and looked at his suit in the closet, his hypocritical piece of window dressing, and pulled it off the hanger and held it to her body and sobbed. It smelled of him, it had been next to his skin, he had worn it to

places that had so many memories for them both. How easily
her husband had been able to shed his old life, as if it were
simply another garment.

Why did he bring a suit here and put it into the closet in
the first place? Gara wondered. To fool me? To put me off?
Because he was really ambivalent? She had no answers; she
couldn't think. When she had cried herself out she walked
heavily to the chair and laid Carl's suit on it. She had pushed
away the pain for the moment, until it would come back with
greater force, and now she knew she had to start to deal with
the rage. She addressed the chair with the suit as if it were
him, the Gestalt method she made her patients use when
they had problems with people who were not there, dead or
alive.

"You're both ludicrous!" she screamed. "You and that
bitch, you're a fucking joke! She's the same age I was when
you married me, but *you're* not. You're thirty years older
than she is. You're not even rich. She's hideous. She has a
face like a duck and at least four too many teeth. Nee, nee,
nee, nee, she talks like Betty Boop. Her friends must be
laughing, and when our friends meet her they'll laugh twice
as hard. I hate you, I hate you both, I hate you for hurting
me!" When she was finished screaming she felt a little better.
She wondered what the people in the next room were making of it all and hoped they weren't there.

That night she and Carl had dinner together, with Cary.
Cary's girlfriend did not come along and of course neither
did Lucie. The brasserie was a blur of noise and light, and
Gara couldn't eat a thing or say a word.

When Carl went to the men's room she finally spoke, but it
was to his son, the stepson she had thought was her friend
for so many years. "Cary, why didn't you tell me he wasn't
living with you?"

"I couldn't," he said. "It was none of my business."

"I guess it was hard for you, too."

He shrugged uncomfortably.

It's his father, after all, Gara thought. "I'm sorry he put
you in that difficult position," she said. "You shouldn't have
had to lie for him."

"I don't like Lucie," Cary said, to make amends.

"You don't?" she said, pleased, grasping at anything that would make her feel less alone.

"I never did. But I only met her a few times."

"You don't work together in the gallery?" Gara asked, confused.

"Of course not. I have my own job."

Oh, Carl, Gara thought, stunned at what was one more lie. *I don't know you at all.*

There was no point to staying in Paris over the holidays anymore. What would she do? She couldn't bear to be alone there and she couldn't bear to be alone in New York. Jane and her husband had not gone to the Swiss Alps after all, so Gara gave up her Supersaver and bought a regular return ticket to New York. She spent Christmas and New Year's on Jane's couch, since Jane's children were in the guest rooms. During the day Gara was weak with grief; at night she could hardly sleep, and whenever she did fall asleep she had nightmares of Carl telling her he was in love with Lucie. When she was awake she kept telling herself it was not over, that he would reconsider, be sorry for the mistake he had made, and come back to her. Jane kept telling her he would, although they both knew she had no more idea what would happen than Gara did.

The week finally passed. When Carl called her to wish her a happy New Year, Gara felt briefly, idiotically happy. She knew it was not an attempt at reconciliation but simply his separation anxiety; but she took it as a sign of hope all the same, even though a part of her, the part that sought self-preservation, was dimly aware that she shouldn't even want him.

She wished she could cancel her patients for the first few days after New Year's, but she knew they had probably been going through traumas of their own while she was away from them, and it would not be fair. Yet she felt so disorganized, so numb and beaten, that she wondered how she could listen to them with her whole heart. Carl had even destroyed her work, she realized, and she felt as enraged over that as she had over his destruction of their marriage. But her work was also her solace—she knew that, too.

She sat in her office under the bright, happy primitive

paintings she liked and Carl didn't, with snow drifting down outside the window, listening to stories of loneliness, fear, and pain. She had done this for years, but now it was as if someone had pulled aside her skin and let her feel firsthand what her patients were going through. If a patient said her grief felt like a knife, Gara knew that knife. It had cut her, too. If a patient said the night felt like a prowling animal, Gara could see its shadow and smell its breath. "It hurts!" a patient wept, and Gara finally, truly understood.

For this insight at least, she thought, I can thank the son of a bitch.

TWENTY-EIGHT

Kathryn, at twenty-eight, had made up her mind that she was never going to be weak enough to marry again. Marriage, she had decided, was much too difficult. But after she met Rod Henry at the Morgan Life Christmas party and started dating him, it took only five months before he started trying to persuade her that if she married him her luck would change.

He, too, had been divorced, but he had no children. He was thirty-five, not handsome like Alastair had been, not sweet like Ted, but decent-looking enough (tall, dark, and lanky), and pleasant enough (he laughed at her witticisms and told her she was beautiful), and almost stereotypically normal. As a young man he had been a professional tennis player, traveling the circuit until his knees gave out, and now he was a vice-president at a company that supplied Eastern hospitals with medical equipment. He traveled a great deal for business, which meant he wouldn't be around too much. He had family money. He had a nice large house in the suburbs with trees around it, and a tennis court in back, where he was giving her tennis lessons, and a new Cadillac, and Kathryn knew if she accepted his proposal she would have a comfortable life for herself and her four young children. He could afford to send them to private school. She was overworked, overextended, and tired, and she would be able to quit her job and be a full-time mom. She would make a good home for Rod and help him entertain his friends. She didn't love Rod Henry, nor was she particularly attracted to him, but she was sure she could stand to go to bed with him after they were married. Naturally, she wouldn't let him touch her before.

She had married the first time because she had little choice, and she had married the next time for passion, and now she decided was the time to marry for good sense, for her children. The poor little things had been uprooted so much they had a bewildered look on their faces half the time. They had grown up with chaos, and they accepted everything. As soon as Rod started coming around regularly to take her out, they began to get attached to him. If they all lived together he could give them tennis lessons when he was home, Kathryn thought, and she could buy pretty clothes for her girls. The whole family could go on vacations together. She watched Rod turning the steaks on his outdoor grill on a warm spring night and thought how domestic their lives would be, how normal. Surely she deserved that, too, as much as her lonely little kids did.

Her mother was working in a beauty salon and doing well. People liked her, and it kept her busy. Sheila had had friends before but precious little time to enjoy them. Now she was free to do what she pleased, and although she was not particularly happy she wasn't miserable or suicidal anymore either, as if she had finally put the events of that violent night behind her. At least, she didn't talk about it. When her five-year probation was over and she could travel, she took a trip to Southern California, and when she came back she announced to Kathryn that she was going to move there.

"It's too cold here in the wintertime," Sheila said. "Those snowy, rainy nights bring back bad memories. I'm going to work in a hair salon in Santa Monica, near the beach. You can all come to visit me."

I guess I'd better marry Rod, Kathryn thought, and get on with my life, too.

They had a lovely little family wedding in Rod's garden, and went to the Bahamas for their brief honeymoon. The four children moved into their newly decorated rooms: The two boys in one, the two girls in the other, and Kathryn quit her secretarial job and became a full-time mother.

From the day she let Rod consummate their marriage, it seemed he could never get enough of her in bed. But her passionate love match with Alastair was a thing of the past; now she was merely a dutiful wife. She was sorry she didn't love Rod and therefore was not attracted to him, but she had made her bargain, and pretended to like it.

There were other disappointing things though, she found, that came with her bargain. Rod didn't want to spend the money for private schools, even though it certainly wasn't a burden for him, and so he sent the kids to public school. When it was time to buy school clothes, he was shocked at the cost and made her go to Pik-a-Penny. There were no fairy-tale party dresses for her girls. Rod complained that the children ate too much, and asked how a boy could drink an entire quart of milk at one meal.

"They're growing," Kathryn said, annoyed. "You never had kids, how would you know?"

"It's okay, Mom," Jim Daniel said. "We get milk at school."

"I hope you're listening to that," she said to Rod, but he didn't seem to care.

As the years went by, it turned out they never went on family vacations either, because Rod said hotel rooms for six people were too expensive, he had to travel for business so he was glad to be home, and besides, wasn't his house and tennis court just like summer camp? Kathryn was annoyed about the vacations because she had wanted to broaden the children's horizons and have adventures herself. Except for being so cheap, Rod was a good and affectionate father to her kids, and they were devoted to him. She supposed it was better that her kids not be spoiled, that they could be just regular kids, even though they lived in such a nice house. The boys went to Little League, and joined the Scouts; the girls took ballet lessons at the Y.

When they were very young, Stephanie and Gaby, who had never really known their father and did not remember him, kept asking Rod to adopt them, but he wouldn't. He said it wouldn't be fair to the boys, who had a father. "It's love, not legal things, that make a family," Rod would say to the twins. "Don't you think we're a real family already?"

"Yes."

"Well, then." After a while they gave up.

More years went by. Everyone was getting along the way

Kathryn had always hoped they would. People had told her how hard it would be to find a man when you had four kids, but she had done well, all things considered. Under Rod's tutelage, Jim Daniel was turning out to be a promising tennis player, and they discussed the possibility of his following in Rod's footsteps. Then, without any warning, a pointless, senseless tragedy struck.

Jim Daniel was fourteen and, as all children in the suburbs were, impatient to be old enough to drive a car. One afternoon he took Rod's car out by himself, lost control of it, and crashed into a tree. Kathryn rushed to the hospital, and by the time Rod had been located that night she had already heard the devastating news: Jim Daniel's right arm had had to be amputated below the elbow. She looked at her son, small for his age, and slim, with her red hair and pale skin, so vulnerable looking, and now with only one arm, and felt a combination of rage and grief. How could he have been so stupid? The fact that he had lost the arm he played tennis with so promisingly was of little consequence next to the realization that life from now on would be more difficult for him in so many ways.

After he lost his arm, Jim Daniel changed. Rod was still away on business a lot anyway, which Kathryn thought was probably for the best, because now for the first time he and Jim Daniel started getting on each other's nerves. She didn't know why, but try as she would to get them to make peace with each other it got worse all the time. By the time Jim Daniel was in high school there was hardly a day he and Rod didn't get into some kind of argument which Jim Daniel always started. Jim Daniel had turned into an angry and moody teenager. Kathryn told him to accept his childish mistake, that it was past, to make the best of what life dealt him, and he looked at her with an expression she could not read at all. He seemed totally ungrateful for the loving home Rod had given him. She was glad the three younger kids were having an easier adolescence. They were still devoted to Rod.

Kathryn had much too much energy to stay at home indefinitely, so she decided to go back to work. Rod was so stingy she knew her added income would help with four growing children who needed things all the time. She remembered the decorating magazine she had been caught reading at boarding school and realized she had always liked home decoration, so she took some courses in decorating, and got a resale license, and then she got a job at a small firm called Charming Interiors. She was so cheerful and enjoyed her clients so much that they found it a pleasant experience, too, and recommended her to their friends. It was like the old days when she gave her Tupperware parties, in a way, but now she was also decorating for men.

Her mother was happy in California. One day, out of the blue, she announced that she was going to marry again. His name was Arlo, he was the man who owned the beauty shop where she worked, he was a widower, and they had fallen in love. Kathryn was surprised Sheila wanted to marry anybody. She supposed this one would be kind to her, but why couldn't they just live together? If her mother married him she would have to give up her substantial widow's pension. Her father owed that to her, at least, for all her years of suffering, and Kathryn tried to talk her out of what she considered a reckless idea.

"I don't care," her mother said.

"You're making a big mistake to give up that money. I mean it. It's crazy. A steady income like that doesn't grow on trees."

"I don't care."

Her mother always had been a romantic. She married Arlo, lost her widow's pension, and was content.

More years went by. Kathryn's children were growing up to be very attractive, she thought proudly, and they were nice, too, even Jim Daniel when he wasn't in one of his odd moods. She wanted them to go on to college, and then become successful and happy, the dream all mothers have, but when Jim Daniel was a senior he dropped out of high school. Kathryn was confused and Rod was disappointed. Instead of getting his diploma he left home and began bumming around the country, coming back every once in a while, getting into a fight with Rod, and leaving again. She knew he was drinking too much and she knew he was taking drugs. Other kids his age did that, too, but there was a depth of anger and pain in him that she could not touch, and it frightened her. It would seem he had never gotten over the loss of his arm, although he said he was used to it, or the loss of his athletic career, although he said he didn't care, and she felt there was something more that she would never know and that perhaps he did not know himself.

Kathryn had never been an introspective person, but now that her son was so troubled she tried to figure out what she had done wrong. When she divorced Ted, Chip had been a baby and didn't understand any of it, but Jim Daniel had been old enough to blame her somehow for sending his father away from home, and she wondered if he still felt that way and if that was why in his teenage years he had turned so belligerent and unhappy. Maybe he even blamed her in some way for the death of Alastair. Young children had strange ways of explaining death, which they saw as a desertion or disappearance, and Jim Daniel had liked Alastair. Perhaps Jim Daniel had always felt that Rod didn't really want him, because he was so cheap. She felt sad and disturbed about the situation, but she didn't know how to rectify it.

Jim Daniel didn't come home for Christmas that year, and then she didn't see him for six months. He called her from Minnesota to tell her he had been arrested for drug possession and she sent him money for a lawyer, and then she paid to send him to detox. She wondered if in some way he took after her father, if all this was as simple as the fact that excess ran in her family and he had been the victim of Brendan's genes.

When Jim Daniel came out of detox he continued wandering, and after a while he called her for money, sounding drunk, and Kathryn knew he was in trouble again. She wondered how often she would have to save him, and when he would stop asking her to.

He was twenty-five years old and he still couldn't hold a steady job. His girlfriends never lasted either. He was so handsome and bright, but lost to her and she didn't know why. Kathryn finally tried to put it out of her mind. She had done the best she could, entering a compromise marriage to give her children a normal, decent life, staying at home with them once she could afford it, and the three younger ones were doing fine. She had been married for seventeen years. What was done was done.

Then, one fall day, Jim Daniel appeared at her office unannounced, carrying a pot of yellow marigolds in the crook of his good arm. She hadn't even known where he was, and had certainly not expected him to be in town. He was clean shaven and neatly dressed in jeans and a tweed jacket, and he looked thinner but sober and not ill. Kathryn gasped. She wanted to jump up and hug him but she didn't know what to do because she was so surprised to see him. She had not laid eyes on him for over a year.

"Hello, Mom," he said.

He held the pot of flowers out to her like a peace offering, and then he put it on her desk. She hugged him then, feeling his slight body under his jacket, breathing in the masculine combination of tobacco and after-shave, remembering the little boy she had hugged years ago and the little-boy smell of him then, musky, like a mushroom. Over it all was the acrid smell of the marigolds, flowers that were planted as borders to flower beds so their odor would drive away rabbits, a love-hate present, not to be understood, but she was grateful for them anyway.

"I'm so glad to see you," she said. "You look wonderful. How are you?"

"I'm fine. You look good, too."

"Well, where are you staying, Jim Daniel? When did you get here? Do you want to stay with us?"

"So many questions," he murmured.

"I'm still your mother."

"You know I won't go to the house," he said.

"I didn't know that."

"You know it now. May I sit down?"

"Of course," she said. She shut the door firmly so they could be alone. He pulled up the side chair and sat down facing her across the desk. "Are you staying in town for a while?" Kathryn asked.

"Just today."

"Well, can we have lunch at least? There's a cute little

place down the street that I've fallen in love with. I'll take you there."

"Sure," he said. "But I need to talk to you now. I don't want to say this in a restaurant."

Anxiety prickled. Maybe he was going to go away forever, and the flowers were a goodbye. Maybe, despite how healthy he looked, he had some terrible disease and wanted to tell her he might die.

Kathryn picked up the phone. "No calls until I tell you," she said to the receptionist. Then she turned to her son. "All right, tell me," she said, and tried to seem calm.

"I owe you an explanation," Jim Daniel said. "I know I've been difficult in recent years, but I couldn't help it. There was a reason. I've wanted to tell you for a long time, but I just couldn't. When I went into detox I started therapy, as you know, and then I continued it afterward from time to time. I started to face things. Now I've turned the corner, I think. At least now I finally need to tell you so you'll understand why I'm the way I am."

"If you're gay I don't care," Kathryn said.

"I'm not gay," Jim Daniel said with an ironic little smile.

"Then what is it?"

"I know you've been wondering why I hate Rod so much. I hate him more than you could even know. Well, you remember the accident, when I plowed his car into a tree."

"Of course I do."

"I wasn't driving," Jim Daniel said. "Rod was. He was drunk."

"He was *what?*" Kathryn said, stunned.

"No one knew. He begged me not to tell, he said he'd go to jail. He made me feel guilty because it was me that had wanted to go driving in the first place. Then he ran away, to get help he said, but he didn't come back. Remember, somebody in the street called the ambulance? Rod had been drinking at a business lunch and then he decided to let me take the car out with him because I kept pestering him. He was going to drive to a place where there was no traffic and let me practice."

"Oh, my God," Kathryn whispered.

From the very moment he had told her, she knew it was

true. Jim Daniel, no matter how troubled he had been, had kept one good quality: He didn't lie. He only covered up. He had covered up for Alastair, too.... She felt the scream rising and choked it back. "Why didn't you tell anybody later?" she said. "Why did you let us blame you and be angry at you?"

"Rod never wanted us," Jim Daniel said. "I knew that. We were too expensive. I guess I just wanted a father so badly, wanted him to care about me, that I didn't want to lose him. I didn't realize how angry I would feel when he let me get away with it."

Kathryn thought about how hard she had fought to give her children that normal, happy home, and she was over-whelmed with rage and pain. She had not been able to pro-tect her child after all. She had betrayed him. She had aban-doned him to a careless, selfish, cowardly adult whom she had thought was good. What kind of a mother was she?

"Oh, Jim Daniel," she said over the enormous lump in her throat, tears beginning to run down her face. "I'm so sorry, I wish you had told me."

He shook his head.

"Didn't you trust me?" As soon as she asked that she knew it was a stupid question. Trust had nothing to do with it. He had needed something she could not give him.

"So now you know why I preferred not to tell you in a res-taurant," Jim Daniel said, turning the subject away from his feelings to hers. He handed her a tissue from the box on her desk. "I was just a kid and he took advantage of me and my need to have him approve of me. I thought I loved him, but then I started to hate him and I guess I always will."

"Of course you hate him," Kathryn said. In one devastat-ing instant, she hated Rod, too.

"Are you going to tell Rod?" Jim Daniel asked.

"Of course. I want to see how he tries to defend himself."

"But you believe me?"

"Of course I do," Kathryn said.

After she had composed herself enough to go out in public they left for lunch. He was hungry and she was too shattered to think of what else to do. She took him to her new favorite place and asked for a quiet table in the back, so that no one would greet her and force her to pretend that she was all right. She was aware that Jim Daniel was relieved that he had finally told her. In that small way she had taken some of his pain.

She had a stiff martini. He had a Coke. Kathryn was glad to see he was dry again and hoped it would last. She couldn't eat. While Jim Daniel ate she tried to catch up on his life since she had seen him a year ago.

"Where are you staying while you're in Boston?" she asked.

"At a motel."

"Do you have a girlfriend?"

"Yes, but we're having some problems, so I came here alone. I got here last night. I wanted to see you and then I'll go home."

"Where is 'home'?"

"I'm back in Minnesota, but I don't think I'll stay. I'd like to try Alaska. It's supposed to be peaceful there."

"Lots more men than women, though," Kathryn said.

"She'll come with me if I want her to," Jim Daniel said.

"Your therapist is in Minnesota?" she asked carefully.

"Yes. Do you remember how when I was growing up we didn't know anybody in therapy? It was for weaklings and crazy people. I had to get arrested to go. But it helped."

"Maybe you should continue," Kathryn said, although she had never had any use for therapy either until now.

"We'll see."

"I'm going to divorce Rod," Kathryn said. "I can't live with him another day now that I know what he did."

"I always knew you stayed with him for us," Jim Daniel said.

"How did you perceive that?"

"I just did."

They stayed in the restaurant a long time. She called her office and said she was going to the showrooms and wouldn't be back that afternoon. After their lunch Jim Daniel drove to the airport. This time he gave her his phone number and address, but she felt a deeper ache at their parting than she ever had before.

"Don't wait so long to see me next time," she said.

"I won't."

When they hugged each other goodbye, she felt his prosthesis hard against her back.

She went to the house and waited for Rod to come home from the office, sitting in their den in front of the fireplace, next to the wall of books, the shelves of her children's school awards, their framed high school and college diplomas (except for Jim Daniel's, who had none), the family photos of holidays and happy occasions, in her perfect suburban home. She drank some wine and smoked half a pack of cigarettes. Then she heard Rod's key in the door.

"Hi, honey," he said, coming into the den and turning on the TV. She picked up the remote control and snapped it off. He looked annoyed. "What's the matter with you?" he asked.

"I saw Jim Daniel today," Kathryn said.

"Oh? He's back?"

"Yes. We had a long talk. He told me what really happened the day of the accident."

Rod didn't say anything.

"You aren't going to deny it?" Kathryn said, surprised.

He just looked at her, his face pale, his shoulders a little hunched as if guarding himself from a blow.

"What did he say?" he asked finally.

"That you were driving. That you were drunk. That you made him take the blame and you ran away. You left him alone! He could have died. You made him lie. He was just a *kid!*"

"Would you believe me if I said that didn't happen?" he asked.

"No," she said.

He poured himself a scotch with shaking hands and drank it. "You'd believe him, the bad seed, before you'd believe me?"

"You haven't said anything to convince me," Kathryn said. "And now a lot of things make sense that didn't before." Their glances locked.

"I knew someone would call an ambulance," he said finally.

"Well, whoop-de-do. What a hero."

He drank another shot of scotch and seemed calmer now, almost relieved. When he lit a cigarette his hands were very still. Kathryn looked at those large hands with their neatly manicured nails, imagined them on the wheel, thought of Jim Daniel's mangled body in the crushed car, and wanted to kill.

"You weren't afraid you'd go to jail," she screamed. "You were afraid you'd lose your insurance, you cheap bastard."

"Believe what you like," he said.

She realized then that he had been waiting for years for her to find out, and now whatever he'd had to fear was going to happen...or not. He knew she wouldn't tell the police about something that had happened over ten years ago; she wouldn't kill him. He thought she might not even leave him, although if she did leave him he wouldn't care. He didn't love her the way he had seemed to in the early years of their marriage, and she had never loved him at all.

"I want a divorce," Kathryn said.

"All right," he said, and he sounded relieved.

What he meant, she realized, was: Is this all? Am I free from any further punishment? She didn't want to let him off so easily, but she didn't know how to hurt him enough to make up for the way he had hurt her son, and her. "I want you to go," she said.

That night Rod went to a hotel, and the next day Kathryn hired a divorce lawyer.

She told Chip and Stephanie and Gaby what Rod had done and they were surprised. She thought they would turn on him, but they continued to like him, and see him, and she wondered what she had done to raise such desperate children who insisted on protecting whatever father figure came into their lives.

Jim Daniel quit therapy before he was finished and moved to Alaska with a different girlfriend. After a while Kathryn got a call from him, and he was drunk again. She was angry at him for backsliding, but, more strongly, she felt anger and pain over the cause. No matter what she tried to tell herself, she still felt it was her fault, that she hadn't been enough for him. The feeling never left her.

Finally she sought out a therapist for herself. The doctor, a youngish woman about her age, asked her about her own childhood, and Kathryn told her. As she did, unaccustomed feelings of rage and sorrow flooded her, and she began to choke. The therapist *wanted* her to feel sorry for herself! She never went back.

That was the end of therapy for her, as far as she was concerned. She was convinced that if she dwelled on the past she would be miserable. She had known too many people who did, and it never did them any good. She would pull herself together on her own.

In fact, she remembered less and less about her childhood, except for the good parts. There were whole gaps in her recollections these days, and she was glad. The one memory that never stopped haunting her, though, was one she had only gotten second-hand. Whenever she thought about how Rod had betrayed her son's love she still blamed herself, although she had no real reason to do so. A mother should not fail her children, Kathryn believed; what use is she on this earth if not to keep them safe?

After a while, she stopped thinking about that day when Jim Daniel had told her. If she did not put it out of her mind, at least she pushed it aside. She lived in the present. There were so many things in life to enjoy—friends, people she met, her work, a fine day, a strong game of tennis, a good meal, a long walk, a show. Anyone who met her would only think that she was an extraordinarily happy person.

But every time Kathryn smelled marigolds, her eyes filled with tears.

TWENTY-NINE

Eve sat at her daughter Nicole's high school graduation ceremony and looked around at the other parents. They were mostly in twos, like the animals in Noah's Ark, and she wondered if they were divorced couples who had reunited for this one day with the child they shared, or if they were still together after all these years. She did not like that she was alone. She knew it was her own fault, that she had never had any interest in finding another husband, but she didn't like that the men she had been involved with for a year or two or three had all gone away, thus leaving her uncomfortable and exposed on important occasions like this one.

Then she remembered that having brought Nicole up by herself was something to be proud of, so why should she even think of sharing this day of glory with any guy who had just come along for the ride? She was a single mother, she had worked hard, she was a feminist, if only by accident. She had been an independent woman long before it had a name or a cause.

Eve had not been able to talk Nicole out of inviting her grandmother to come to New York for her graduation. The truth was that Eve was ashamed to be seen with her mother now that she looked so flashy. So now her mother was sitting next to her, resplendent in a white beaded dress, her pink hair piled high, and a new, disgusting addition: her pink painted nails so long they curved under at the ends. Eve pretended she didn't know her.

Eve looked at the graduating class on the stage. Her daughter was definitely the cutest one, with Eve's small, even features, large eyes, and abundant hair, but not her heat or anger. She had no idea where Nicole had gotten her sweetness. Certainly not from anyone on her side of the family. Medusa's daughter had grown up to be a Pre-Raphaelite maiden.

Nicole had determined she really did want to be an actress, so now she was going to chase her dream full time. That meant Eve wouldn't have to pay for college, which was a great relief. She wanted acting classes, and Eve had told her she would have to get a job and pay for them herself. Eve didn't know why Nicole wanted them anyway, when she herself had done very well without any. Nicole had enrolled in the Lee Strasberg Institute, and hoped later on someday to get into the Actors Studio. Eve wished her luck. Her daughter had always had two sides to her; the winsome extrovert and the serious part, and Eve knew if Nicole took after her she would get what she wanted.

Not that she herself had really gotten what she wanted, or what she felt she deserved. After they had written her out of *Brilliant Days* she'd had to face the fact that she had been fired. No one had ever liked her there, not for a moment of the five years she had been on it. She was never able to get another soap opera role, and eventually even she heard the gossip. Eve Bader is too difficult. Eve Bader is a pain in the ass.

Of course she told everyone that she had left by choice to pursue more serious work in the movies and even, although she was better than that, in television. She said it so often that eventually people accepted it. They may have thought it was a stupid career move to leave *Brilliant Days*, but they understood her need. Actors had themselves written out of TV all the time to try to get into films. When Eve told people the story she wanted them to believe she actually believed it herself. Life was a kind of acting. And then, as it always did, the public forgot her, forgot Xenia, her character, who had died somewhere in the South American jungle, the venue of the soap-opera writer's last resort.

After the graduation Eve had offered to take Nicole to dinner with her grandmother, and after dinner Nicole's friends were having a party and she was going to go there and stay over with a friend. She had a lot of friends, far more than Eve had ever had. Nicole already had a job as a waitress, starting tomorrow night. She was going to continue to live with Eve until she could afford to get her own apartment.

"You can stay with me and pay rent," Eve had offered.

"No," Nicole said. She gave Eve a peculiar look. "Most parents would be glad to have their children live with them."

"Which means what?"

"Which means if I have to pay rent I'd rather live by myself."

Eve was annoyed at this ingratitude. "I never had it easy and why should you?" she snapped.

"I don't want it easy," Nicole said.

"That's not what it sounds like."

"No," Nicole said. "I just want to know I'm loved."

"Since when does freeloading mean being loved?" Eve asked.

"See, that's the way you are all the time. You never say you love me."

"I'd like to love you with a machete," Eve said.

"Thanks, Mom."

"I love you," Eve said reluctantly, because she didn't mean it.

"I love you, too," Nicole said, "but the only reason I can think of why is because you're my mother."

How extraordinary, Eve thought. Being a mother put you into an exclusive club in which you were loved just because you were there. "What about all the sacrifices I've made for you all your life?" Eve said.

"I know. You're always reminding me."

"I have to."

"I can't win with you," Nicole said. "If I try to tell you I respect you, you turn it into a fight."

"Nobody wins with me," Eve said, "and don't you forget it."

Who wanted children, anyway? She regretted the day Nicole was born, but sometimes, despite her resentment, she felt her unexpected love for her daughter coming through her defenses, a kind of leakage of the heart, and it made her feel so weak, so vulnerable, so frightened that she had to breathe deeply and meditate it away. What if something happened to Nicole? What if she died? If you let yourself become a victim of your feelings, loved someone too much, that person had too much power over you, and you could be devastated by a betrayal, by a loss.

I have the power, Eve thought. It was almost her mantra. Sometimes when she meditated, which was an activity she had begun a few years ago, she actually used the words. *I have the power.* It was infinitely reassuring.

She considered herself lucky that her own waitressing days were behind her. She had always saved her money carefully, even during the time that it was flowing in, and now when she went for an audition Eve knew there was no hint of desperation about her, only talent and ambition. She hadn't made it to Broadway yet, although she had done off-Broadway, and she had done quite a few small one-shots on various TV series, which she preferred to refer to as guest star roles. She supposed if someone offered her a recurring part she would take it, even though her mind was still set on her movie break, and she went to every audition her agent set up. Sometimes the agent sent her under protest but gave in because Eve wouldn't stop calling her.

"If they said I'm wrong for the part let them see me anyway," Eve would insist. "If they have their minds set on some stereotype then let them think of another part in the future that is right for me." Eve never thought she was wrong for any part. She knew she could do whatever they wanted, if they would only tell her what it was. Stay in there. Fight.

She was thirty-five now, too old to be considered young anymore in her world, but not old enough to have to complain the way the older actresses did that there was nothing for them. When she had to tell people that she had a daughter who had already graduated from high school she always added quickly that she had been younger than Nicole was now when Nicole was born.

"I was twelve," Eve would say, and laugh. She never told anyone how old she was, and thought how age discrimination was another burden women had to bear, and how unfair it was.

After Nicole had been studying acting for a year she got an agent, and quickly ended up with a small role in a Broadway play. Eve went to the opening night and to the party afterward, where she spent her time introducing herself to theater people she thought might help her own career. When the *New York Times* review came in, Nicole was singled out for her "luminous presence." Eve was proud of her, but she also couldn't help feeling jealous. It had happened so fast, and had been so easy for her!

Nicole had a boyfriend now, Eddie, and moved into her own apartment with him. Eve remembered her own early, struggling days in Hollywood, with the specter of her financially dependent baby always looming in the background, and although she felt she was above self-pity she nevertheless couldn't help feeling sorry for herself. When Nicole's show put up its closing notice after only five months she called Eve to tell her. Eve was concerned, but she also felt a little bit of vindictiveness sneaking into her heart. An actress was supposed to have disappointments.

"I told you not to take on the burden of your own apartment," Eve said. "Now what are you going to do? I hope Eddie has enough money to support you."

"I thought you were going to invite me back," Nicole said, and laughed in a phony way.

"Not with him. You're an adult now. I'm not running a hotel, unless you both want to pay rent."

"Oh Mom, you're so full of love."

"Well, what *are* you going to do?"

"I'll get another part somewhere," Nicole said. "In the meantime I'm a terrific waitress."

"You have a good attitude," Eve said.

"I got it from you."

"Oh?" She was flattered.

"I've always wondered why I'm so well adjusted with you for a mother," Nicole said. "You never brought me up; I had to invent it. But I always knew to take the good from you and learn from the bad. Grandma taught me that."

"About me?" Eve said, insulted. "She said that about me?"

"She said that about life."

"She never told me anything about life," Eve said. "All she did was plunk me in front of a television set."

"And widen your horizons."

"You are greatly mistaken if you think TV ever widened anybody's horizons," Eve said.

"You told me it did all the time," Nicole said. "When you had me watch."

Why did she and her daughter always have to get into these arguments? "'How sharper than a serpent's tooth is a thankless child,'" Eve said. "I gave up my career for you."

"Yeah, right."

"Do you think I wanted to be in a soap? I did it for the money, for you. I was never lucky enough to have just myself to think about, the way you are."

"I can't continue this discussion," Nicole said. "I only called to tell you the news about my show before you read it in the newspaper." She hung up.

The next day she called again, of course. Nicole kept coming back like a yo-yo with a very short string. They argued and hung up on each other more often than not, but afterward Nicole was always there, full of news, wanting to share her life, never apologizing for being irritating the day before. No matter how often Eve told her to get lost, Nicole was convinced that they had an unbreakable bond, and Eve began to wonder if it wasn't true, even though she wasn't glad about it.

Only a month after her show closed Nicole's agent got her a part in a movie. Just another thing, Eve thought, to make me feel how hard my life has been. Eddie didn't go to Hollywood with Nicole, because he was in graduate school at NYU, but when she came back to him after the shooting was over she was the same unaffected person she had ever been. Of course, Eve thought, the movie isn't out yet. Just wait.

It was a nice little movie, about four young friends, and although after it opened it didn't stay around very long, Nicole got excellent reviews. They called her "a refreshing newcomer." By then she was already in another play. Nicole was one of those lucky actresses who would always work, Eve decided. Even if she never became a star, which more than likely she wouldn't, she wouldn't have to worry either.

She stayed with Eddie for a long time. "I want it to work,"

Nicole told Eve. "It's very important to me that I have a relationship that lasts."

"Not if it's bad you don't," Eve said.

"There are problems, sure, there always are, but overall
it's very good. We're both working on it. Neither of us had a
normal home life growing up, so we have no example to follow, but we're making it up as we go and learning a lot."

"What do you mean you didn't have a normal home life?"
Eve said. "What did you want? *Leave It To Beaver? Father
Knows Best?* You watched too many reruns. Those were only
normal lives in people's dreams."

"You know what I mean," Nicole said.

Nicole stayed in her play for a year, and then her agent got
her another part in a movie. This time the publicity mills
started to grind. There were glamorous pictures of Nicole,
whose hair was now red, and interviews in magazines. They
mentioned Eddie, who was working for a publisher, and the
sheepdog named Melvin the young couple now had, and
they mentioned Eve, and referred to her years as Xenia in
Brilliant Days. Eve was thrilled to see her name in print.

"This will do it!" Eve told her when she called.

"That's what my press agent says, if I can believe him."

"I mean for me," Eve said. "People are going to see that.
Didn't you think it was a nice plug for me?"

"Sure, Mom. That's why I put it in."

"We should get parts in a movie as mother and daughter,"
Eve said, excited. The adrenaline was beginning to flow, as it
always did when she made plans. "I used to take you to the
set and try to get you written into *Brilliant Days*, and it would
be a great publicity gimmick if we worked together now that
you're grown up."

"It would," Nicole said, but she didn't sound excited
about it—more neutral, as if it had little chance of happening.

"Who do we talk to?"

"I'm not that famous," Nicole said. "I just play the parts
and I'm lucky to get them. I don't tell people what to do."

"Why not?" Eve snapped. "Didn't I teach you anything?"

"Yes, Mom," Nicole said dryly. "You taught me a lot
about being demanding and pushy. A lot."

This time Eve couldn't understand why Nicole hung up.

After that Eve started on her campaign for a mother-daughter movie for the two of them. She called up every writer she had ever met and asked if he or she had such a script at home already, or the idea in mind, or perhaps could be persuaded to write one for them. She would have written it herself, she told them, but she didn't have time to write, what with pursuing her acting career. Sometimes, as an afterthought, she mentioned that actually she couldn't write. "But I will some day," she said. "I have a novel in me. I know that. Maybe my life."

After Nicole's new movie came out she began to be even more well known. The reviewers called her "charming," and "appealing." None of these were adjectives that had ever been applied to Eve in her life—she had always been only the bitch on the soap—and she thought how unfair it was that she had always been typecast.

Nicole got an even bigger part in another movie and began to commute to Hollywood, and eventually she broke up with Eddie and started seeing an actor she had met on her new film, a very good-looking young man named Brian, who looked particularly good with his shirt off. Eve hadn't much liked Eddie, for no particular reason she could think of except that he was her daughter's lover and probably a mother wasn't going to approve of any of her daughter's lovers until she was forced to get used to a husband, and she didn't much like Brian either.

"I'm sorry it didn't work out with Eddie," Nicole told her. "We both tried. I guess I was too young and still had a lot of growing up to do."

"Of course," Eve said. "And you're not an adult now, either."

"Well, you'll never think I am."

"Not until you prove you are."

"What does that mean?"

"Whatever you think."

Eve had a new lover of her own now, the first time she had ever had a relationship with a man who wasn't in show business. He was, in fact, in the shoe business, and he was impressed that she was an actress. He was a burly and hairy

Jewish man her age named Ben. She called him Ben the Bear.
He had been divorced for several years, he loved to go out to
restaurants, he had a good sense of humor, and he gave her
all the shoes she wanted. She had almost a hundred pairs, in
all styles and colors. Ben had money and his own apartment,
so there was no question of his living with her.

Eve was getting quite fond of him. He was a conventional
man in many ways. He still had both his parents and he
brought her to his large family for Passover and Yom Kip-
pur. In the summer he took her to his house on Fire Island,
where they socialized with married couples who were not in
show business either. His children were in college, and when
they were home they lived with their mother, so they were
not a problem. Although he was a lusty man he wouldn't let
her tie him up in bed, no matter how often she tried, and
when they had sex whatever they started out doing always
ended up with him on top...well, nobody was perfect.

She was forty now, and the birthday made her wonder if
she should look for more stability in her life, and if perhaps
that stability would come from marrying Ben. She would
never again have to worry about money or dating. She
would make him buy a co-op for them to live in, and she
would make him put it in her name, just in case he decided to
leave. She was sure she could get him to propose, and if he
didn't, then she would tell him marriage was what she
wanted. She knew he would be flattered. He was quite in
awe of her.

From time to time when she was in the neighborhood Eve
dropped by Tiffany's to look at engagement rings, just for
the styling. When Ben got her one she would have him buy it
wholesale so it could be bigger. She wanted a rock. When she
pictured herself committed to this conventional man she saw
him as a kind of anchor around which her energy would
flow, his admiration and normalcy giving her the security to
spend even more effort on her career.

She was browsing at the wedding ring counter, looking for
something that would go with her fantasy rock, when she
looked up directly into the round brown eyes of Ben the
Bear.

He looked startled. She smiled. *"Breakfast at Tiffany's?"* Eve said.

Then she noticed that there was a short, dark-haired woman with him, who had her left hand out and who was inspecting a circle of sapphires and diamonds on her third finger.

"Who is this?" Eve asked. She supposed the woman was a relative or a friend.

"Rhoda, this is Eve," he said, looking and sounding very uncomfortable. "Eve is a...uh...friend."

"Friend?" Eve said. "Who is Rhoda?"

"I'm his once and future wife," Rhoda said, and smiled with little white teeth.

"Future?" Eve said.

"We have to go," he said to Rhoda, looking frightened. "Eve, I'll call you when I get back to the office."

"Are you still seeing her?" Rhoda asked him, indicating Eve.

"Have you been going out with your ex-wife behind my back?" Eve demanded.

"I was going to tell you," he said to Eve.

"Then tell her now," Rhoda said.

He looked like he wanted to disappear into the floor. "I..."

"It was his womanizing that broke up our marriage in the first place," Rhoda said, confiding in Eve, this stranger, as if she were not his girlfriend but simply another woman who would understand these things. "Ben has a roving eye."

"I'm speechless," Eve said. Numb was more like it. She realized he'd had plenty of time on his own to do whatever he wanted, but it had never occurred to her that a fat, hairy, conventional man who was only a civilian would want to cheat on her, or even could. Well, of course he could.

"My wife and I have a history together," Ben murmured. He looked at Rhoda as if for strength and apparently got it. "I'm sorry, Eve, I never thought you took our dating all that seriously."

"Why do you think I'm looking at wedding rings?" Eve snapped.

"I never mentioned marriage," he said.

"Did you lead her on?" Rhoda asked.

"No!"

"He did," Eve said, improvising. "In fact, that sapphire band is the exact same ring he was showing to me."

"You pig," Rhoda said, and pulled the ring off her finger. She did not, however, lay it back on the counter, but stood there with it between her thumb and index finger, undecided, looking from him to Eve and back again.

"That's a complete lie!" Ben said. His face got very red. "What are you trying to do, Eve, ruin my life?"

"Like you ruined mine?" Eve said. "You're a fool if you marry him again, Rhoda. And you know what else? Ben has turned into a complete freak since you divorced him. He..." She lowered her voice conspiratorially, to a stage whisper that everyone in the store could hear. "He likes me to tie him up in bed."

"You what?" Rhoda asked Ben, wrinkling her small nose in distaste.

"She's crazy," he said. "Put the ring down." He wrestled it out of Rhoda's hand. "We're leaving. Eve, I'll have words with you later."

Eve noticed people staring, trying not to laugh. A blond woman had her mouth hanging open as if she had been incapacitated with shock. Ben pulled Rhoda out of Tiffany's, and Eve saw them getting into a cab in front. Bastard, she thought. Liar. Sleazeball. Fatso would be one lucky man if he got his ex-wife to take him back after this. And she herself was fortunate she had found out what he was like before it was too late. She turned to the salesman.

"How much is that sapphire ring?" she asked. She might as well know what he was trying to spend. "I think I'd like to try it on."

Ben called her later. "I've always been in love with my ex-wife," he said in a tired voice that sounded beaten. "I'm sorry."

"You'll be more than sorry when I get through with you," Eve said.

"I realize you're hurt," he said, "but you almost made Rhoda leave me again."

"Excuse me?" Eve said. "Am I supposed to care about that?"

"I thought you cared about me. A little."

"I do," she said, although she no longer did. "I wasted a year on you. That ought to count for something."

"It was important to me, too," he said.

"I want that sapphire ring," Eve said. "It costs forty-five hundred dollars and that's what I want. The ring or the cash, either one. Call it palimony."

"I never proposed," he said.

"You led me to believe you would."

He sighed. "If you wanted a nice piece of jewelry I would have given you one."

"Well, you didn't, and now you can."

He sighed again. "I'll send you a check."

"Damn right you will," Eve said. "Have a nice life with your midget." She hung up.

That night she had a nightmare. There was a row of men in front of her and she was cutting off their dicks and stuffing them into a meat grinder. While she did it she was horrified at what she was doing and wanted to stop, but she was helpless before the power of the dream. She woke up in tears, frightened at the depth of her anger. She lay in bed for a long time, trying to get calm, and then she got up and washed her face and meditated. I have the power, she said, but somehow it didn't seem like the right mantra. Love and forgiveness, she said, but somehow that didn't feel right either. She had no idea what to do, so finally she just said Om, and waited to find the center of her soul.

THIRTY

Billie and Little Billie were extraordinarily close from the time he was born. Unlike other working mothers who could afford it, she didn't want to hire a full-time housekeeper, especially since the woman would need to share Little Billie's room. She was content with her twice-weekly cleaning woman, a tiny, ancient Peruvian named Mamacita, who was not as old as she looked. Mamacita did the food shopping and apartment cleaning and laundry. For the first two months Billie hired a nurse. Then, from the time he was two months old, Billie took Little Billie to work with her every night at Yellowbird, in a sturdy canvas pouch that kept him next to her heart.

He was an extremely easy baby. He thought his life was normal. His mama was always available to feed him from her body, she changed his diapers in the office, and noise and people didn't bother him. Because she was nursing him Billie still didn't smoke or drink, although she never stopped missing it. Her customers, however, drank and smoked up a storm. There was nothing she could do about that, but she thought how she had grown up in a world where everyone smoked cigarettes and she was none the worse for it. Better for him to feel her closeness, her love, than to be left alone with a stranger every night.

And how people admired him! She thought a child had never had so much attention. When Little Billie became too large and active to stay in his pouch, Billie let him sit on her lap. He could sleep clinging to her, like a little Koala bear. Sometimes, when he was deeply asleep, she would put him in the crib she kept in the office. The office was also where she nursed him, since she felt nursing one's child was too intimate, too private, too important to be done in public, and particularly not in a restaurant where she was the owner. For Yellowbird she needed to be strong. A breast-feeding mother looked too sweet, too maternal, and besides, some customers found it distasteful to watch.

Little Billie was two years old now, walking, running, talking, into things, not yet toilet trained, and she was still breast-feeding him. She had no real plans to stop in the immediate future. He also ate toddler food, he was strong and healthy, and mother's milk, she knew, built up immunities and was very nourishing. His nursing time was their time to bond.

Billie had been flat chested all her life, and now she had voluptuous breasts. They were full of milk. On her tall, lean frame, they were particularly noticeable, like silicone implants on a model. She had always regretted not having what her mother called "a figure," and she loved the way she looked now and wanted to stay that way as long as she could. But it was really only an unexpected bonus. The real reward for her was the pull of her baby's strong, tiny mouth on her nipples, the electricity that passed through her body—a sexual energy that seemed united to the life force—and the look of almost bovine contentment that came over his face as he nursed, his eyelids fluttering closed, his little fist holding her finger. It was a miracle, Billie thought, that she could supply so much of what he needed, that for this brief time she could be his world, and that this world was safe.

Even when he had teeth Little Billie never bit her. "Titty milk," he would demand when he wanted it. At three he was pulling at the buttons on her blouse, and at four he could open them. He was a beautiful child with Cal's golden curls, her eyes, and the face of an angel, the best of both of them...no, better than they were. She had promised him that in her fantasy before he was born and her promise had come true: *You will be better than both of us.*

When Billie took Little Billie home to see his grandparents for Christmas, her mother demurred. "Well, Billie, don't you think it's time he should be weaned?"

"Soon," Billie said reassuringly, but she had no idea when

"soon" would be. They both liked their bonding time too much.

He was in kindergarten now, in private school. He had the vocabulary of a child two years older, his teacher reported, and Billie knew that was not only because Little Billie was bright but because all his young life adults had spoken to him as if he were one of them. She allowed conversation, never baby talk. And because Little Billie was a good listener he picked up on what the adults around him were saying. When he was restless she sometimes let him run around Yellowbird, stopping at tables when he knew the people, but she never let him get out of hand. She wanted him to be admirably intelligent but not annoyingly precocious, polite and comfortable with other people but not a pest. He had his own corner now, in the back of Yellowbird, with the things that amused him: his TV, his computer, his crayons and toys. He was already teaching himself to read.

Ever since he had been about three Billie had realized that she found being with her son much more interesting than being with anyone else. Men found her even more attractive than they ever did because of her newly big breasts, but she wasn't really interested. She knew she would be again, and that was a decision she was letting ride in the same way as her decision to wean her child. She was a responsible mother now, and sexually transmitted disease was everywhere. Right now she was content. It had been a long time since she had had a real passion, not since Harry Lawless, and she had thought nobody else could ever open her heart. This sturdy and delicate little boy, with his vulnerability and defiance and curiosity and wonder, had. His love for her was as boundless as was hers for him.

Little Billie's school day ended at two o'clock. Billie always picked him up. By then she had been to Yellowbird already to make sure things were all right, and then she came back home to rest for the evening; she would go back to Yellowbird at four to go over the reservation book. From two to four she and Little Billie would lie in her bed, watching TV, napping, talking, and most important, he would be having his snack and measure of love from her breast. They both knew that when they went to Yellowbird she would have very little time for him. Mama had to make a living.

Then, one day when she picked him up from school, Little Billie looked very distressed, avoiding the other children's eyes, and as soon as Billie got him safely at home in their apartment he started to cry.

"What is it?" she asked, concerned, holding him, stroking his hair.

"They laughed at me," he sobbed.

"Well, why?"

He pulled away. She watched him, waiting, not overstepping her bounds, and wondered what had made the other children so cruel. Finally he stopped crying and just sniffled. She gave him tissues to blow his nose and wipe his eyes.

"We did our afternoon conversation," Little Billie said. "It's like Show and Tell, but without stuff. Miss Gribetz asked us each what we have for our after-school snack when we go home. All the other kids said they have Oreos and milk, or a sandwich, or a banana. I said I had titty milk."

Oh my God, Billie thought.

"Everybody laughed," he said. His face screwed up again to cry. "Miss Gribetz didn't know what I meant and she made me say it again. I told her 'Mama's titty milk.' The kids all called me a baby."

"Oh, Little Billie, that was so mean. You're not a baby, you're just as old as they are, and you're a lot more grown up."

"Miss Gribetz is going to talk to you," he said darkly.

Billie shrugged, although she could feel his pain and her heart was breaking. She had never thought she was hurting him. "Let her," she said. She patted the bed and he sat down beside her, looking confused. "I guess it's time for you to stop eating from Mama," she said. "Everybody has to stop sometime."

"I liked it," Little Billie said in a tiny voice.

"So did I. It was a nice time for us to be together, and my milk was very nourishing for you. But you're a big boy now, and you want to be like everybody else." She made her voice cheerful, its confident tone promising him conformity, pas-

sage, friendship with his peers. "So what would you like today instead: Oreos and milk, or a sandwich, or a banana?"

"Oreos," he said, making a face.

She went to the kitchen and got them, and poured him a
glass of milk from the carton in the refrigerator, the milk she
used for her coffee. She didn't know whether to take his
grownup snack back to her bed or serve it to him at the
kitchen table, so she just stood there with the plate and glass
in her hands.

"I'm not a baby," he said, frowning, figuring out his life.

"I know. You're my big boy."

"We could still watch TV in bed," he said.

She smiled and brought his snack into the bedroom. Little
Billie jumped up on her bed as he always did and began fid-
dling with the remote control for the TV until he found
something he liked. Billie put his snack on the quilt and lay
down beside him. She felt guilty and sad, and her breasts
were beginning to hurt because they were so full and there
was no one to empty them. She knew there was a medicine to
dry up the milk quickly because her doctor had already mentioned it to her, several times, and had given her a prescription, which of course she had never filled. She would fill it
tonight.

"Will you still hold me?" Little Billie asked.

"Till you tell me, 'Go away.'"

He smiled and lay back in the curve of her arm, watching
the television set, watching her, licking the sugar from his
opened cookie, his other hand twitching just a little as if it
wanted to go for her blouse buttons of its own accord. She
yearned for him, too.

"Do you want to go to the Museum of Natural History on
Saturday?" she asked. "Or do you want a play date?"

"I bet nobody will play with me," he mused. "Not if they
think I'm a baby."

"I'll take that bet. How much money do you want to put
on it?"

He smiled.

The next day she was on the phone, lining up a play date
where he would go with his friend to the museum, thus ac-
complishing both goals. The next day, also, Ms. Gribetz

called. She had a sweet, precise voice, that of the kind of do-gooder Billie wanted to smack.

"It's about Billie," she said. "I understand you're still breast-feeding him. That can be very destructive behavior, you know, for a child who is trying to socialize with more mature children his age. Wouldn't you like me to set up an appointment for the two of you with the school psychologist?"

"I wouldn't," Billie said. "He's weaned."

"But he said—"

"It only takes one conversation to wean an intelligent four-year-old," Billie said. "After yesterday he's on the cow."

"Oh, I'm glad."

"How are the other kids treating him?" Billie asked.

"Just a little teasing, but he's really a very popular boy."

"If they try to pick on him I want you to make them stop," Billie said. "They listen to you."

"Well..." She gave a little flattered laugh. "Sometimes."

"They will. Thank you, Ms. Gribetz, for being concerned."

"Thank you for responding."

Bitch, Billie thought when she hung up. School psychologist indeed, like they needed mental help.

She reached for the still unopened pack of cigarettes she had bought the night before, when she got her prescription filled, and looked at it. Then she opened it. Although the first inhalation made her feel faint, she smoked the whole cigarette, and afterward she felt better for it. Almost five years had been a long time. She had known this major separation from her son would come one day, but she had just not let herself think about it. She also knew that all of his life, from now on, even though she was there to raise him and he depended on her, he would be growing away. That was the point, of course, but she still felt melancholy.

That night at Yellowbird she had a vodka on the rocks. It made her a little high because she was so unused to it, but she liked it as much as she had liked the cigarette. Welcome back to reality, she told herself. We all need to socialize with people our age. So for the first time since Little Billie had been born, tonight when she looked at the men at the bar she was sizing them up differently.

She looked at Little Billie in his corner, busily drawing, his head bent over his notebook, a look of intense concentration on his angelic face. Everything in her life was so completely different now that he was in it that it was as if she were living on an alternate planet. Not for one instant anymore did she ever feel alone, but she had various needs, and so did he, and so would he, and so would she. Soon, she knew, she would have to have the feel of a man again. Her son would understand. He knew he would always come first in her life, but everybody needed a play date, even a woman of forty-three.

THIRTY-ONE

Gara was fifty now, she was going through menopause, and she was newly divorced after twenty-two years. Set free into a world that valued youth and beauty in a woman and devalued age and experience, a world where casual sex might mean AIDS, illness, and death, where she didn't even know how to flirt with and charm a stranger after all these years—not that she wanted to—she thought how unfair and cruel Carl's timing had been. He should have left her when she was younger and could start again, or he should not have left her at all.

She and Carl had been separated for almost two years when their divorce became final. For one reason or another he had delayed, and each time she had hoped he might change his mind and come back to her, until finally she wished he would just get it over with and let her try to put her life together, whatever sort of life it was going to be.

She had heard he was still living with Lucie, and that everyone they had known in Paris knew it. She also felt very sure that he never intended to marry Lucie, and that his procrastination about their divorce was his way of keeping Lucie from insisting. Married to Gara, Carl could be "single."

Gara, on the other hand, had felt very married, even though they saw each other only four times. She didn't know why he still bothered to come to New York on his so-called business trips, or called her to go out with him for dinner. She supposed he still had some separation anxiety, that he even missed her. They had been friends for so long. When they did meet they made small talk, skirting the important issue, the only issue: *Do you really love her? Why do you love her more than you do me?* They talked about his business, and he told her his Paris gallery was doing well now. She pretended she was glad. His depression over getting older, over not making enough money, had driven him to find ego satisfaction with a woman young enough to be his daughter, and now that woman would be the beneficiary of his new financial success. Gara suspected Lucie had never known Carl was having business troubles, or else she would not have been attracted to him.

"Lucie's pregnant," one of his friends told her finally.

Carl's child...her husband's child. "How does he feel about that?" Gara asked, needing to know.

"He's actually very pleased."

Although she and Carl had never wanted children, this was another blow. How easy it was for him—at sixty this was the final affirmation of his continuing youth and virility, his hedge against mortality. In a world that had not gone insane, Gara thought, the child should have been his grandchild; and when the family went out people would probably think it was. His own sons were not married yet and were still childless.

Carl signed the divorce papers. During their two-year separation, while she was depressed and frightened, hoping he would get tired of Lucie and come back, the idea of having a date, an affair, had been as remote to Gara as cheating. And now she was free. She knew Lucie's hormones were surging, that she had swollen breasts and morning sickness, that she was cozily sleepy. She herself was on hormone replacement for hot flashes and vaginal dryness, her breasts reminded her of dwarf bananas, she knew she needed a face lift; she was another disposable wife. All the years of her marriage she had thought Carl would die and leave her a grieving widow, a woman of dignity; but he was alive, he had lied. She wondered if another man would ever sleep in her bed, if she would ever feel his arms holding her all night so she would not feel so unloved and unlovable.

She needed closure, a time to grieve, finality. Since Carl had not had the decency to die, she needed to make him dead in her heart.

On the weekends Gara went to her beach house in Amagansett, by herself, by choice. She cherished the absence of speech, the sound of the ocean, the foggy air, the sunrises and sunsets when the beach was empty. She walked alone for miles along the hard sand at the water's edge and tried not to think about the past. She wondered how long it would take to become a normal person again. The loneliness there was healing, unlike the way she felt in the city when she felt only alone.

She redid the apartment so it would be fresh and new, so it wouldn't be a shrine. She knew Carl would never see it again, and that was strange. She could hardly look at the things that were left because they had too many memories, but she wasn't ready yet to throw those memories away either, and she knew it was important to keep good memories, even when they hurt.

She already knew the names of the best plastic surgeons in New York because Jane had made it an active life's study, and in August, when she had the month off, Gara had a face lift. She looked youthful and refreshed, and wondered if she should have done it before, if it might have kept her husband with her for a few more years, and then she realized it was fruitless to second-guess the past. It was *her* face; she had done it for herself. She thought it was strange that Carl would never see this, either. And she would not see his child.

She had read it took a year of grieving for every five years of a good relationship. She waited. All these years she had told her patients that you finally recover and they couldn't imagine it, but she knew it was possible, even though now she herself found it hard to imagine. And finally there were whole days when she was happy, when she didn't think of him, of his domestic life there so far away, of her lost future. Now she would simply have a different future. She was determined to be stronger now than she had been when she depended on Carl for her protection against her mother, for assurance of her identity as a lovable woman. From now on she wanted to be able to take care of herself.

None of her friends knew any men to introduce her to. "We only know married people," they protested, sounding surprised to have discovered it. It seemed that when a man left his wife he usually already had a replacement ready, or if not, he was taken in the blink of an eye, even if temporarily. Someone introduced her to a recent widower at a cocktail party; he looked happy talking and laughing with the men, and ignored her, and afterward Gara discovered he had been having an affair with a younger woman while his wife was dying, and now he was going to marry her. Jane knew younger men who were involved in the movie business with her husband, but they liked Jane better than they liked Gara. Jane was safe, she was their buddy, and when they wanted a relationship they found women their own age. Everyone knew gay men; without them how would a single woman have a male pal to go to dinner with, to escort her to a party when she felt both conspicuous and invisible going alone? Gara went to cocktail parties and to art openings, remembering she had met Carl at an art opening, and to the occasional dinner party, wishing she could be seated next to the interesting man of her dreams, but it never happened.

She knew there were women who went from husband to husband, and she wondered how they managed it. She read about them in the newspapers and magazines: the super-wives who handled every aspect of their men's social lives, or the great beauties...until they faded. She had even heard of women who met their next husbands at their own husbands' funerals, but they had been of a previous generation and they needed to be a wife more than she did. She had needed to be Carl's wife. Now she doubted that she wanted to be anybody's. If she was going to have a romance, she thought self-protectively, they would find each other, it would have to happen naturally. But everywhere she went, no matter what else was going on, she couldn't help looking.

"Stop looking," people told her. "When you're looking you never find anybody."

"You have to keep looking," others said. "You have to put yourself out there, even though it's difficult and we all dread it; you have to be emotionally available. When you feel sexy inside you look sexy outside."

She was a therapist who dealt with these questions all the time with her lonely patients, and while she had all the textbook answers for them, she had none for herself. She was used to responding to a particular person, not to someone in the abstract.

Then one spring night when she was undressing after coming home from a dinner party where she had had a very good time, where she had not thought about a man or the lack of one, where she had enjoyed the friends and the evening, she felt a strange, sharp pricking under her left arm, between her armpit and her breast. She put her fingers there to see what it could be and they touched a small, hard lump the size and shape of a shelled almond, which hadn't been there before. It was a lymph node.

She knew.

You know, she thought with a mixture of panic and calm resignation. Women always say afterward that they knew. So many times they're wrong, and it isn't anything, but you always think the worst, and so you knew. But despite her attempt at logic something told her it had happened at last: breast cancer, the thing every woman feared. In all her regular self-examinations she had never found a suspicious lump in her breast that had turned out to be anything but a part of the bumpy cystic terrain that was her own particular nature, and that she had gotten used to, and her mammograms had shown breast tissue so dense that there was nothing else to be seen—so it had sneaked up on her. Now it's moved there, Gara thought, into the lymph node, while a part of her denied it, wanted it not to be true.

I'm going to have to have a mastectomy, she thought, if it's gone this far.

She spent a sleepless night, and the next morning she made an emergency appointment with her general practitioner, Dr. Lombardi, an older woman she and Jane had been going to for years, one of the last of the breed of doctors who did everything, and who telephoned you personally to nag you when you were late for your regular checkup.

Dr. Lombardi palpated her breasts and found nothing. "You must have cut your finger," she said. "Do you remember doing that?"

"Well, actually, I did," Gara said. "But that was several weeks ago."

She looked at the small scar. "You must have had an infection that went into the lymph node. That's where it always goes. The lymph nodes are the immune system. The cut is

healed so there's no point in giving you an antibiotic now.
We'll just watch it."

Ecstasy: It's just an infection! Anxiety: Why isn't it going
away? Gara continued to live her life as a normal person on
the outside, but inside she thought of nothing else, it consumed her days, while she was "watching it." There was
nothing to see, but she kept feeling it, her right hand tucked
into her jacket like Napoleon, fondling the pain, measuring
the lump with her fingertips, feeling it grow, for two months.
One day she thought it felt smaller and she was filled with
joy and relief. The next day she knew she had been mistaken
and the fear came back. Finally Dr. Lombardi sent her to a
breast specialist, an older man who had been a colleague of
Dr. Lombardi's for decades. He sent her for another incon-
clusive mammogram and gave her an antibiotic.

An antibiotic, Gara knew, should start to make a significant improvement in twenty-four hours. But nothing happened for the entire week she took it, although she had already given up hope it would; the lump was still there, and
it still hurt all the time from the tension of the pulled skin.

"I think you should have a biopsy," the breast specialist
said. "It's too big. I don't do surgery anymore, but you
should have Dr. Lombardi send you to someone."

Dr. Lombardi sent her to a highly recommended woman
surgeon, Dr. Fink, who looked to Gara, for some reason, as if
she might have gone on peace marches in the late sixties. She
was the right age, early forties, and she had a kind of
straight-talking idealistic toughness about her. When Gara
asked her if she had been an activist she laughed and said it
was true. They arranged to do the biopsy at the New York
Collective Center for Surgery, on an outpatient basis and under a local anesthetic. Dr. Fink intended to take the whole
thing out, whatever it was. It's about time, Gara thought,
afraid but relieved that the waiting would be over.

Jane offered to come to the hospital with her, but Gara said
it was unnecessary, although she would need someone to
pick her up because they wouldn't let her go home by herself. "Then I'll come get you afterward and take you to my
apartment," Jane said. "You can't be alone after surgery."
Jane didn't mention the subtext—You can't be alone if the

news is bad—and with one of the odd tricks the mind plays, this time Gara didn't even think about it.

She lay on the operating table, full of Valium, calm. "Do you want to see the creature?" Dr. Fink asked, holding up what she had removed. It looked like a small, skinned mouse, bloody and raw.

After the surgery Gara went out and sat at a metal table in a brightly lit, undecorated anteroom while a man in a white coat worked in the next room on her dead mouse. She could see his head through the glass window. Dr. Fink came in and sat across from her at the metal table.

"It's very malignant," she said.

Very malignant? Gara was surprised and completely numb. She didn't know if it was self-preservation or the tranquilizer. I guess I'm going to die quickly, she thought. Very malignant? Not me.

The doctor on the other side of the glass said something. Dr. Fink went to talk to him and came back looking happier. "He thinks he found lymphoma and breast cancer," she said. "If that's true, then it's the best thing you can have."

As opposed to what? Gara wondered.

Some time went by; she didn't know how much. "Yes, it appears to be what he thought," Dr. Fink said. "But we'll have a full report in a few days." Then she told her to call Jane to come get her.

"It's cancer," Gara told Jane. It was the first time she had said the word. She was holding on now, trying not to let her voice quaver too much, trying not to get hysterical. What was she going to do?

"I know," Jane said. "Dr. Lombardi called me already. She has an oncologist for you to call. A woman who specializes in breast cancer and lymphoma. Dr. Beddowes. Dr. Lombardi says she's the best." She handed her a piece of paper with the number.

How quickly they act when they finally know, Gara thought, relieved that she didn't have to make decisions. She knew of other women who had spent weeks researching every doctor and hospital they could before they chose someone, but she had no more time to waste, if not because of her physical condition then because of her mental state, and she felt comfortable just having been led to this specialist by a doctor she trusted. She liked that she was surrounded by women physicians. They were in the club, they lived with the same fear of breast cancer as she did; they would understand.

Dr. Beddowes sounded kind and pleasant on the phone. She gave Gara an appointment for two days later, when the full report would be in.

"Are you tired?" Jane asked. "Do you want to take a nap? Does it hurt?"

"No, I'm okay," Gara said. "I took some painkiller, and I'll take it again tonight before I go to bed."

"Let's go out tonight," Jane said. "It's your night, we'll do anything you want to. Where do you want to go?"

"I don't know," Gara said.

"It's so nice tonight we can go outdoors. We can have dinner at an outdoor café. Eliot will take us."

So later the three of them sat in a sidewalk restaurant near Gramercy Park in the mild evening, watching the throngs of people walking by. Somewhere there was music playing. I have cancer, Gara kept thinking. She felt wrapped in a cocoon of her own, set apart, vulnerable, temporary. She looked around. Everywhere there was brightness. She had never seen colors so vivid, or details so alive and intense; the buildings, the people, the trees. She didn't know if her mind at this time of fear was distorting what she saw, or if things had always looked that way and she had never noticed before.

I don't want to leave a world that looks like this, she thought. I never knew it was so beautiful. If I have to die soon, then I'm going to try to see everything this clearly for the short time I have left. As she sat there looking and listening, mingled with the sorrow that all of this might end so suddenly, she felt an odd kind of peaceful happiness, as if a vision of what the universe was really like was finally hers.

Dr. Beddowes was in her forties, with short gray-streaked hair and a round, unlined, pretty face. "This is probably going to happen to me, too," she said with a smile, "so I'm always nice to my patients so someday someone will be nice to me."

Gara smiled back, liking her immediately.

"When Dr. Fink took out the lymph node," Dr. Beddowes went on, "another one was stuck to it and came out, too, and they both had cancer and lymphoma in them. It's a very mild form of lymphoma, one of the few that's almost benign. It's called well-differentiated lymphocytic lymphoma because you can feel the lymph nodes without surgery and it's easy to watch. You don't have to worry about the lymphoma. I wouldn't even treat it. When you get an infection of any kind, the lymph nodes near the site will jump up. That's what happened here."

"So the lymph nodes were a kind of watchdog," Gara said.

"Yes. We can't find the primary source, although we know it's breast cancer, so it's in the breast. Breast cancer can go elsewhere, but it always starts in the breast. In your case we don't know where in the breast. We have to discuss what you want to do."

"A mastectomy," Gara said calmly.

"That's what I would recommend. A mastectomy probably followed by chemotherapy. And then reconstruction."

"So the whole process will take a year," Gara said. A year lost in a life that was already indefinite, but it could not be helped.

"Yes," Dr. Beddowes said sympathetically. "About a year. I'll send you for some tests at the hospital tomorrow to see if it has spread anywhere else in your body. You'll have to stop taking your estrogen replacements because breast cancer likes estrogen. Here's a book for you to read, and a list of some others you might want to buy." She gave Gara a copy of *Dr. Susan Love's Breast Book*, a thick paperback. Gara had heard of it.

She stayed up all night reading it, looking for the chances of a postmenopausal woman on chemotherapy surviving cancer. I have cancer, she told herself over and over, not really comprehending it yet. Overnight her life had completely changed. I have cancer, she thought the first thing when she woke up. It was always everybody else. Now it's me. I have cancer. She still couldn't relate to it, even though she was going through all the right motions. She was aware that she had not shed a tear. It had not even occurred to her to cry. I just want to survive, Gara thought.

And then she was at the hospital again, in an area ominously called Nuclear Medicine, drinking radioactive liquid in the waiting room, then standing in front of a clicking machine, looking at a tiny television screen and seeing there her body segmented and photographed in a series of twinkling dots of molecules on a dark background, a starry sky of her mortality, of her disease.

After the bone scan she lay on a narrow slab under a thick plastic tunnel, unmoving, holding her breath while other pictures segmented her body even more, into tiny slices, a biopsy without a knife, each a photograph of the fiber of her being.

"It hasn't shown up anywhere else," Dr. Beddowes told her happily. "When Dr. Fink does the mastectomy we'll do a lymph node sampling to see if it's spread to any other nodes. I want you to have a plastic surgeon there at the operation so you can have an expander put in at the same time to start the reconstruction."

"Why do you want to do a reconstruction?" Gara asked, only out of curiosity, since she would never have opted otherwise.

"You're so thin that if you don't do it you won't be just flat, you'll have a hole."

She obviously thinks I'm going to live for a while, Gara thought, if she wants me to look good. She felt rather encouraged.

Dr. Beddowes handed Gara a piece of paper. "Here are the names of two very good doctors. One is kind of Hollywood and the other is very down to earth. See which one you like, and of course, see which one is free for the date of surgery. I'd like to have the surgery done as soon as possible because we waited so long. Next week?"

"Give me two weeks," Gara said. "I need to tell my patients I'm going away." She would tell them she had to attend to personal matters and give them a referral doctor. It would be hard enough to deal with her own fears without having to deal with theirs. "How long will I be too sick to work?"

"You'll be in the hospital two days, and then you'll be recovering for about five, and after that it's up to you. You'll have a drain in for two weeks."

Of the two recommended reconstructive surgeons Gara picked the Hollywood type, Dr. Lister, who wasn't her idea of Hollywood at all except that she looked like a warmer Grace Kelly and was just as young as Gara's other doctors. She had no idea what the down-to-earth doctor would have been like, but she didn't have to make a choice because Dr. Lister was the only one available. She was happy with her decision. She felt as if she was in a sisterhood of bright young women. She didn't want to be parented, she wanted to be a partner in her fight to live.

"You'll stay with us after you get out of the hospital," Jane told her. "We'll take care of you. You can stay as long as you want. You have the guest room."

"Thank you."

The surgery was set for a Monday, and she was to go to the hospital early that morning. She told Jane there was no point in coming with her; she would take a cab. She was nervous, and the few friends she had told were all calling her to wish her luck or to cry. Gara was glad they were concerned and cared about her, but she could hardly bear to speak to them. She just wanted to find her inner strength and be left alone. They were outside somewhere, and she had left their world. She would need them later.

The night before her surgery, in her own apartment, in bed, Gara said goodbye to her breast. She looked for the last time at the sagging little thing she was so fond of and spoke to it silently. "You've served me well," she said to it affectionately. "Remember all those nights in parked cars with college boys who just wanted to get their hands on you? We've been through a lot together, you and I, all these years." She touched it gently. "Goodbye, and thank you."

Early the next morning at the hospital Gara found herself lying on a gurney outside her operating room, in a section where a man was lying on the gurney next to her, surrounded by his family—wife, son, daughter—waiting for his own surgery. The family kept kissing and comforting him and telling him they loved him. She wondered if they thought he would die. For the first time it occurred to Gara how alone she was. Carl was not there. They had no children. Her parents were no longer alive and she had no sisters or brothers to hold her hand. It felt odd, and she knew she had to put it out of her mind or she would feel sorry for herself, and afraid. After all, she had told Jane not to come. She could even have asked someone else. She had chosen to be this way. Was it bravado or not wanting to bother other people with her problems, bravery or her feeling of lack of entitlement?

The wife looked at her. She seemed to feel Gara's loneliness. "Are you here by yourself?" she asked.

"Yes," Gara said.

"Well, I'm sure it will be all right. I wish you luck with your operation."

"Thank you." They smiled at each other. Then Gara was wheeled into surgery.

She woke up in a dim, pleasant hospital room with an I.V. attached to her right arm and the button for a morphine pump in her fingers. A searing pain on her left side near her ribs made her touch the button, and almost immediately she felt a little nauseated and completely out of pain. What a great invention, she thought. I don't have to wait and beg. She slept. The next morning the nurse helped her wheel the I.V. to the bathroom, where she brushed her teeth and combed her hair. She was back in bed when Dr. Beddowes came to see her, her round face glowing with happiness.

"They took out eighteen more lymph nodes," Dr. Beddowes said. "There was nothing in any of them. You and I are going to grow old together."

Gara smiled back at her. How nice, she thought, we're going to grow old together and she's younger than I am. Then she realized that what her doctor was also saying to her was that she would be under care for cancer, even if it meant just checkups, for the rest of her life.

"Can I have the I.V. taken off?" Gara asked Dr. Beddowes the next day when she came by. "It's too hard for me to drag it around by myself. I could go on oral painkillers and antibiotics now."

"If you want. Your arm is going to be stiff, you know.

You're left-handed, so you won't be able to brush your teeth
or comb your hair for a while."

"I already did."

The next day she was walking up and down the hall with
the nurse, counting laps. "If you keep doing this we're going
to throw you out," the nurse said cheerfully.

The day after that Jane took her home with her. "I thought
you were going to be in a wheelchair," Jane said, surprised,
when she caught Gara emptying the dishwasher with her
good arm. "Why are you doing things? We're supposed to
take care of you. Why are you on Tylenol? Why aren't you on
codeine? I never heard of anybody like you."

Gara knew why: she needed the independence, she
needed the focus. Being mobilized and directed toward recovery would keep her from feeling too helpless and frightened.

It hurt too much to sit up in bed from a prone position, so
she used her bent leg to hold on to as if it were another person and hauled herself up. They had put a Johnson catheter
inside her wound so it could drain, a plastic bag that somehow reminded her of a turkey baster attached to a long plastic tube, and she had to empty it several times a day and
measure the fluid and write it down. Gara thought the worst
part of the surgery was the drain. It hurt almost all the time.
She pinned the tube to the top of her jeans and put the bag
into her pocket, with a loose shirt over it. When she saw her
patients she would pin it to her skirt. They would never
know.

The *Breast Book* became her Bible. After the first few nights,
lying on her back, she tried reaching the headboard of her
bed with her fingers, to keep her arm from stiffening. She
couldn't get anywhere near it, but she tried every day, and
she could see the progress. She saw drawings of lymphedema, where the arm on the side where they had removed the
breast and lymph nodes was swollen as a tree trunk, perhaps
forever. That could happen at any time. Lymphedema itself
could lead to cancer. You had to guard against infections,
cuts, pricks; you couldn't lift anything heavy or trim your cu-
ticles. One more thing to be afraid of.

What Gara was not afraid of was looking at the scar. She

had already seen drawings of what it would look like, and she had never been squeamish about her own body, only her mother's. When the bandages came off to be changed she was surprised to see a small breast-shaped hill on the side where she'd had the surgery. It was the expander under the muscle, to stretch the muscle and skin, and saline would be pumped periodically into a tiny invisible port in it to make it bigger. Her own breast was fifty-one years old, but the fake one looked only thirteen. Dr. Lister had already told her that eventually she would take care of that. If Gara wanted them to they could both look twenty.

"When you're healed we'll start you on chemotherapy," Dr. Beddowes said. "That will get rid of whatever tiny cancer cells might be floating around which we couldn't see, if there are any. Because your case is rather unusual we took it to the cancer board. Two doctors wanted you on adriamycin, but I said that was overkill. I'm going to give you CMF, which is the standard in cases like yours. That's Cytoxan, methotrexate, and 5 fluorouracil. You'll get two injections a week apart, and then two weeks off, for six months."

She gave Gara three sheets of paper, listing the side effects of each chemical. The side effects all seemed awful and they all seemed much the same: hair loss, nausea, cracked fingertips, dark nails, mouth sores, fatigue, diarrhea or constipation, weight loss or weight gain, anemia. "You're lucky that they've recently come up with an antinausea drug called Zofran," Dr. Beddowes said. "It's about a year old. The nurses will give you that in the I.V. before you get the chemo. Afterwards you might need a little Compazine, but I'll give you a prescription. This new drug is a miracle."

They're giving me poison, Gara thought, looking at the list. That's what everybody says chemotherapy is. The poison will kill all the fast-growing cells like cancer and my hair follicles, but it's also going to hurt the normal cells and make me sick. *I don't want to think of it as poison.* I want to think of it as a good thing that's making me well, and I want to help.

"I want a hypnotist," she said. "Can you recommend one?"

Jane tried to persuade her to stay longer, but after ten days Gara needed to be home. Being healthy in someone else's apartment she would have felt like a house guest, but fragile and recovering she was beginning to feel like a dependent child. She had a lot of work to do.

When she was back home a woman came to visit her from the American Cancer Society. She, too, had once had a mastectomy. She sat on Gara's couch, her face and voice so filled with empathy that she seemed to be making a condolence call. She made Gara nervous and Gara wished she would leave. The woman had brought an enormous pink cotton prosthesis that Gara couldn't relate to at all, and a handful of polyester she could put into her bra. Gara took the polyester.

"Did you have chemotherapy?" Gara asked.

"No, I didn't."

"Well, I already had a mastectomy so I know what that's like," Gara said, annoyed. "Why didn't they send me someone who had chemotherapy so she could tell me what it's like?"

"I don't know. They just send us wherever they send us." She tried to be helpful. "When I had my operation they didn't give chemo, but I'm sure if they did I would have had it."

"Oh," Gara said, liking her better for trying.

"Do you want to see my reconstruction?"

"Sure."

The woman lifted her blouse and bra. There were two large, perfect breasts with perfect nipples on them. "My husband kept saying to the doctor, 'Make them bigger, make them bigger,'" she said, suddenly cheerful.

"They're beautiful."

"Thank you. Do you like your oncologist? What do you think of your treatment?"

"I love my oncologist," Gara said. She felt angry and defensive at these questions which she knew were solicitous and well meaning but in her mental state seemed controlling and intrusive. She realized for the first time how emotionally fragile she was. "I have a very good doctor and I'm very satisfied with my treatment," Gara went on. "She knows what she's doing."

She knew she was gibbering and that she sounded odd. We have to like our doctors, she thought. We have to have faith in them. It would be too terrifying otherwise. "Thank you for coming," she said, rising. "I have to do some work now," and hurried the woman to the door.

Now it seemed that everywhere she went she met women who had recovered from breast cancer. Friends introduced her to strangers. "Stay away from all fat, oil, sugar, artificial sweetener, meat, cheese, white flour, and coffee," one woman told her. She gave Gara a strict, healthy diet to stay on for the rest of her life, and at the end of a week Gara had lost seven pounds and looked bad. This, she knew, was no way to go into chemotherapy. She called Dr. Beddowes.

"Give me a good nutritionist," Gara said, "one who will let me eat anything I want."

The nutritionist, Rachel Smith, wearing a long flowered dress, sat in a small office surrounded by bottles of vitamins and plastic models of food. She had a bubbly personality, and she, too, looked forty. "Before you start on chemo eat the spiciest food you can find to toughen up your mouth," she said. "Indian food. Curry. That will prevent mouth sores. Rub the inside of your mouth with lemon. My grandmother taught me that. Buy an electric toothbrush. Toughen up your gums. I want you to drink three quarts of liquid every day the whole time you're on chemo; two of water and one of cranberry juice. The water will flush out the chemo fast and the cranberry juice will keep you from getting cystitis, which is a side effect of Cytoxan. Buy an iron skillet, the old-fashioned kind like your mother used. Cook steaks in it. You have to eat red meat three times a week. The iron gets into the food you cook and makes it better for your blood. They didn't have anemia in the Wild West. Buy only free-range chickens, the kind that don't have estrogen and antibiotics in them. I want you to eat six to ten ounces of protein every day, minimum."

"Coffee?"

"Of course you can have coffee. I would die without it. I would prefer you didn't drink diet sodas, but once in a while it's okay."

"Chocolate cake?"

"A little piece, not a big piece. There are only four things you can't have. Tap water, margarine, which is full of poison and worse than a nice, natural piece of butter—they're going to find out someday how bad it is—chemically decaffeinated coffee, which is treated with cleaning fluid; and raw fish. If you get sick from raw fish when your immune system is low you'll never forget it."

Gara wrote it all down. She had found that her concentration was hazy lately. Rachel gave her a heavy bag of bottles of vitamins, which she sold to her at cost. There were some Gara had never heard of.

"I want you to keep a journal of everything you eat and do every day and how you feel. That way we can see if any food disagrees with you, or if it's just what's happening in your life."

"That's interesting," Gara said.

She looked surprised. "You didn't know that?"

Gara went to see the hypnotist, another young woman, who looked almost too young. She was, however, also a psychologist dealing specifically with cancer. Gara told her how she wanted to think of the chemotherapy and the hypnotist put her into a trance, which was surprisingly easy, and made a tape for her to play at home twice a day, and told her to take it to the chemo sessions if she wanted to. It told her to relax, and said that the medicine was helping her body to get stronger and healthier, and that her body was helping the medicine to work. Nowhere did it use the word "sick." At the end it said that she would awaken refreshed.

She lay on her bed and played the tape, and before it was finished she fell asleep. When she woke up it was over. She did feel very refreshed, and also relaxed, but she had missed the message. She called the hypnotist, concerned.

"It's okay if you sleep. The mind and body hear it anyway. And don't listen lying on the bed."

They arranged for her to have a hypnosis session before each of her chemotherapy treatments, until she got used to them, and each time she would get the tape. She was feeling much more confident now, with her team of supportive female doctors making her a full partner in the task of saving her own life.

She was back with her own patients now, the drain was out, and Jane had taken her to buy a wig just in case she needed it. As well as knowing the best plastic surgeons, Jane also knew the best place to get great hair. Gara had decided not to tell any of her patients she had cancer. Most of them were afraid of intimacy and afraid of being deserted, and she knew they would worry that she would die and leave them. Some of them might even react by becoming angry at her, and would stop their therapy. It would be too stressful for them to be dragged into her personal life unless she actually were dying; in that event she would have to prepare them for it.

And another factor was the income. She needed it now, more than ever, even though she had savings. Her quite inadequate private insurance had paid for the hospital immediately, but she didn't know about the rest. The coverage didn't include office visits and paid very little for surgery. This would be a long drawn out and expensive experience.

Another acquaintance sent her to an acupuncturist who was supposed to tune up her system and make her balanced, therefore stronger. He was a tall dark-haired man in his forties with a small black beard. Sitting on a chair beside the raised cot Gara was lying on, he wanted to have a therapeutic conversation with her before he put the needles in.

"Do you know why you got cancer?" he asked.

"No."

"Stress."

"Then Carl gave me cancer," Gara said, half in humor, half in bitterness.

"Carl?"

"My ex-husband."

"Wrong!" he said sternly. "You gave yourself cancer. You were stressed, you gave in to it. Don't blame anybody but yourself."

Blame myself? Gara thought. I am the enemy within? That's the last thing I need to think, that I'm walking around with a suicidal force inside me, that I can't even trust myself.

She got up. "Don't bother with the needles," she said quietly. "I'm leaving."

"I know I'm hard to take," he said, "but you won't face the truth."

She left. On the way home in the cab she realized she was

shaking with anger, but she was also relieved that she had done something about her fury—taken action, walked away. There were so few times that she had done this. Usually she wanted to be conciliatory and polite.

My cancer is not my fault, Gara told herself calmly and firmly. It's nobody's fault. It is what it is.

It is what it is...

That became her mantra. It soothed her. She knew a side effect of cancer was rage: at an interrupted life, at disease and pain and fear and loss and deformity and stolen time, at death itself. Rage and grief were natural. She would not let anyone add guilt. It's not my fault. It is what it is.

She took the jitney out to Amagansett and spent the weekend in her little gray house on the beach. At sunset, when the sky was golden, she stood on her deck and looked out over the ocean. She had never been a religious person in a formal sense. She believed in God, but she didn't know if God was the spirit that made the universe work or a person. As a child, looking at pictures of the stern, robed, bearded old men in her schoolbooks, she had mistaken the prophets for God himself, and had been intimidated, and had withdrawn. Now, looking at the line of the water that blended into the sky, Gara felt a spiritual presence. She knew God was there, and that he was on her side, and that he was ready to listen. Her doctors had told her that a five-year survival was the benchmark, that after five years of being cancer-free you were considered cured. Five years suddenly seemed a long time, but a short time for all the things she wanted to appreciate, especially life itself.

"God," she said to him silently, "I want to live. Give me five years, and then we'll renegotiate."

THIRTY-TWO

Felicity felt like a caged cat, bristling, tail twitching, wanting to get out, wanting to hide, snarling, unable to stay still. She kept up the pretense of a precise, efficient lawyer all week but never parted from her cellular phone, returning obsessively to her computer, waiting for Jason to summon her to fill up her emptiness; and on weekends she was still a secret bulimic, filling her emptiness herself, vomiting to hide the evidence. Day after day, year after year, her unhappy life just seemed to go on without changing. Time stretched and shrank with its own logic, the hours were endless. She felt wrapped in a fog of grief and confusion and self-hatred, struggling just to survive.

Russell still refused to go to a marriage counselor, and she was afraid to divorce him and be all alone. She was getting closer to forty now, and even though she looked much younger, she was aware every day that her life was passing her by. She deserved more than to be so miserable with an angry husband who thought he was her father, to be surviving on the too-brief hours of her dangerous love affair with a man who would never marry her, but she didn't know how to change anything; she felt doomed somehow, cursed and beaten.

That was when she finally decided to see a therapist. She knew, at last, that she just couldn't fix things by herself.

Her therapist was a feisty little white woman of fifty who let Felicity call her by her first name: Florette. Once a week Felicity sat on the couch across from Florette's chair in her dimly lit office, surrounded by faded chintz that was so frumpy and unpretentious it reassured her somehow, and wept. She talked about her childhood and it seemed that the childhood pain she had pushed to the back of her mind so she could continue to exist had only been waiting for her to let it leap in, full center stage, strong and alive. When she re-lived it, breaking into tears, Felicity waited for the catharsis she had thought would come afterward, but she was just as upset afterward if not more so.

"When will I ever get over those terrible memories?" she asked Florette. "It makes it worse to talk about them."

"Really?"

"No. I don't know. When can I clean up my act? I hate my life."

"You're very insightful, but it takes time for the things you discover here to actually sink in."

"I really want to leave Russell."

"Then why don't you?"

"I'll never live in a house like that again," Felicity mur-mured sadly, thinking how she loved it.

"The princess locked in the castle?"

"More like Cinderella."

"You have a good job, you make enough money to take care of yourself. You can move into your own apartment. This is New York; he would have to give you a settlement be-cause he's much richer than you are. You aren't Cinderella."

"I could marry someone else and get a better house," Fe-licity said.

"You probably could, but why do you always want to be rescued?"

"Maybe because nobody ever rescued me when I was a child."

They sat there for a while in silence.

"I never enjoyed being in my house," Felicity said, "be-cause Russell was in it."

"Then this is not about a house."

"Then what's it about?"

"Pretend you are a house," Florette said.

"Me?"

"Yes. Say 'I am a house,' and describe yourself."

Felicity pictured a room. "The floor boards are rotting," she said. "It's not safe...I have to watch my step or I'll fall right through. The walls are tilted, not right...I feel..."

"You feel...?"

"Scared."

"When you can describe yourself as a safe, well-constructed house where you aren't scared, then you won't need Russell or Jason," Florette said. "You have to learn to believe in yourself."

It was Christmas now, and Felicity bought presents for both her husband and her lover. Her firm had done very well this year and the partners had decided to have a cocktail party in their offices. These days at office Christmas parties spouses were encouraged to come, for the sake of propriety and to keep anyone from getting drunk and doing something that might be embarrassing. Nobody had a good time and they always left as early as they could. Still, you had to show up.

Russell refused to go with her. He said he had a meeting, but she knew that wasn't the reason. He didn't like being Mr. Felicity Johnson in her world; he wanted to be the rich, successful Russell Naylor in his. Felicity ordinarily would have been delighted that Russell wasn't going to come and stand in the corner looking sulky and judgmental the way he always did at parties given by her friends, not his, but she knew the firm's big clients had been invited, and Jason might be there with his wife, so she didn't want to go alone and unprotected. If Jason was going to bring his wife and pretend to be happy, then she wanted to be able to hang on to her own husband's arm and pretend to be happy, too.

"After the meeting I'll just be home watching the game," Russell said. "Take your time."

Christmas decorations were up, and there was a large fir tree in the reception area, decorated with doves of peace so it wouldn't be too religious and offend anyone of another faith. There was a bartender, and a bar. The attorneys who weren't married had brought dates. Felicity sipped a glass of white wine, looking around, and realized she was the only person who was there alone. Then she saw Jason walk in with a woman she knew was his wife, and her stomach churned with anxiety.

"Hello, Felicity," he said, cordially but very formally, to make it clear that theirs was purely a professional relationship. If he's any more formal, Felicity thought, she'll know for sure.

"Hello, Jason. Merry Christmas," Felicity said.

"Merry Christmas. Felicity Johnson, this is my wife, Thelma."

She's a dumpy middle-aged woman, Felicity thought, encouraged, but still she felt sad and left out. "Hello, Thelma," she said, holding out her hand, smiling. While the two women shook hands Felicity could see Jason from the corner of her eye, and she wondered if he still wanted her. He was looking so noncommittal. She wanted to run away.

Jason took Thelma's arm and walked her to the bar. Felicity didn't know what to do so she turned away and busied herself with being charming to everyone she knew, and then she glanced back at Jason and caught him looking longingly at her. She felt happy immediately. He did still want her! His wife was apparently oblivious. Felicity wondered if she should leave right now to make him jealous, but she couldn't bring herself to leave before he did. She went over to talk to Jack Allsop, a brilliant trial lawyer trapped in a nerd's face and body, who always looked damp. Behind his back the secretaries called him "Allslop." He was with a very attractive, intense-looking woman with a lot of long red hair.

"Hey, Jack!" Felicity said jovially. "Are we having fun yet?"

"No, we're not," the woman said.

"This is Eve Bader," Jack said, introducing his companion. "And this is Felicity Johnson."

They shook hands. Felicity noticed that Eve Bader's hand was almost preternaturally hot, as if she was running a fever. "You're a lawyer here?" Eve said.

"Yes."

"I'm an actress."

"Really? How interesting."

"I just closed in a show off-Broadway, *Trashed Cars*. Did you see it?"

"No," Felicity said. "I'm sorry."

"That's okay," she said brightly. "It only played two performances." She smiled and Felicity laughed. "But I got a lot of movie interest from it."

"Well, that's wonderful."

"Eve was in a soap opera for five years," Jack said proudly. "People stop her on the street."

"I'd like to get away from all that," Eve said. "I'm a serious actress."

How up and alive she seemed, such a life force, such an optimist, Felicity thought. Such a contrast to me. I wish I had so much energy.

"Why don't you get us drinks?" Eve said to Jack.

"Be back in a minute," he said. "Felicity?"

"Sure."

"So what kind of law do you do?" Eve asked.

"Publishing, mostly. How long do you know Jack?"

"He's just a friend. I'm not going out with any more civilians. They're even sicker than actors, and actors are sick enough."

Felicity laughed. For the first few moments she had been so taken by Eve's presence and energy that she hadn't even noticed what she was wearing, which was unusual because she was very conscious of clothes. She looked now, and was surprised to see that Eve was wearing a formal black tail coat, the kind a man would wear, with a bit of flirty white lace showing under it, and a very short black leather skirt.

"Nice outfit," Felicity said, although she wasn't sure whether she meant it.

"Thank you. One of my thrift shop specials. I don't believe clothes make the woman; the woman makes the clothes."

Felicity smiled. She glanced at Jason, and saw that he was still looking at her. She was actually beginning to have a good time. Before she met this outrageous woman she had felt too vulnerable, but she didn't anymore.

"Which one here is your husband?" Eve asked, having seen Felicity's wedding ring.

"Oh, he's not here. He doesn't like parties."

"Never?"

"Not often."

"Are there any playwrights or screenwriters here?" Eve asked, swiveling her head.

"Some. But we handle mostly novelists and nonfiction writers."

"Mmm," Eve said. "Well, they're good to know too because they might have projects. Can you introduce me?"

"Sure."

"Come on."

When Jack came back looking for them, with glasses of white wine for them in his hands, they were already across the room. He looked over at Eve, crestfallen. Felicity felt sorry for him, but she had never seen anyone operate like Eve Bader and she was also fascinated. Eve had an abrupt way of talking and she almost crackled. She cut a swath through the party with Felicity in tow as the liaison, getting writers' business cards and giving out her own, which had her name and number and her agent's name and number on them. On the bottom of her card below the two phone numbers there was a tiny drawing of two birds, and the line: *Kill two birds with one stone.*

"I designed it myself," Eve said. "Business and personal, get it?"

"It's great," Felicity said. Eve handed her one.

"We ought to go out and have a drink some time," Eve said. "Does your husband let you out when there isn't a party?"

"He doesn't like to," Felicity said. "But I would like to."

"We'll find some new places, have some fun. You know, get a group of interesting women together, compare ideas."

"That would be nice."

"Give me your card and put your home number on it," Eve said, holding out her hand.

Felicity gave her the card. When she looked around for Jason again she realized he and his wife had gone. She felt a sinking in the pit of her stomach, as if an elevator had gone down too fast. He has a right to go home with his wife, she reminded herself, trying to be sane, I have to go home to my husband—but it hurt just the same. She felt abandoned and unloved. She always dreaded going home to Russell, but she wondered if Jason really minded going home with his long-suffering mommy-wife after all. When would she ever get over this obsession?

Jack made his way to Eve's side through the thinning

crowd. He had one glass of wine in his hand and he gave it to Felicity. "Where's *my* wine?" Eve demanded.

"I couldn't find you so I gave it to someone else," he said.

"That's how you treat me?" she said. "I'll get my own."

"Get one for me, then," Jack said.

"You don't drink."

Felicity laughed. Something about Eve somehow cheered her up. "You guys fighting," she said. "You're going to fall in love."

"No love for me," Eve said. "Sex and my career. That's it. Love makes you interested in the wrong things."

"Like commitment," Jack said. "And intimacy."

"I have a commitment to my career and I'm intimate with my life," Eve said. "No more broken hearts. They're a waste of time."

"I'm going to call you," Felicity said.

So that was how she became friendly with Eve Bader, a kind of woman she had never known in all her life. After a while Felicity began to think no one had ever known anyone like Eve. This was neither a compliment nor a criticism but simply an observation. They met for drinks, and told each other their life stories. Each, of course, left some things out—whatever was too humiliating or too private—but they confided enough to feel they were friends. They met again, a few weeks later, and then more frequently, and then regularly, and eventually Felicity told Eve she was having an affair. Eve already knew she was miserable in her marriage. Felicity never told her the name of her lover; she always referred to him as "my friend." Even though she enjoyed Eve's humor and energy, there was something in Eve, even after all this time, that she didn't quite trust enough to confide such a thing, something about Eve that was at the same time recklessly volatile and curiously cold.

It was only after a year that she stopped liking Eve, that the things she had found amusing and eccentric about her finally became annoying; but by then there was nothing she could do to separate from her without using a blowtorch, and Felicity was too sensitive to hurt anyone's feelings. She didn't know what flaw it was that made her such a bad judge of people. She had adored Russell and she had been delighted by Eve, and now she saw them both so differently. The only person she knew wouldn't change was Jason, but what she was afraid of was that he would leave her.

She still fed off Eve's optimism and energy, particularly when she was depressed and lonely, but she also didn't know why she put up with Eve's egotism and insensitivity and just plain embarrassing bad manners. Sometimes she almost liked being with Eve, but most of the time she wished Eve would stop calling her.

It made her feel even more vulnerable than ever to think she knew so little about human nature, to be suckered in that way and then disappointed, as she was with her friend; even betrayed, as she had been with her husband. Sometimes she talked about the problem with her therapist, but there were no answers. It was not a question of having changed and matured through time, or through therapy, but an actual blind spot. She had absolutely no shrewdness, no guile, no instinct to protect her from the wrong people until it was much too late.

THIRTY-THREE

Gara wondered if she should tell Carl that she had cancer. For what purpose, she wondered. To get his sympathy? To bond? Because we once loved each other so much and he will care? To make him feel guilty that he deserted me to deal with this terrifying tragedy alone? He never called her anymore, and she knew she would have to call him because she didn't want to write a letter. If she called him, Lucie was likely to answer. Gara pictured him alarmed, flying to New York to see her, offering checks for her huge medical expenses. Then she pictured him saying he was sorry about what had befallen her, and never calling again. She didn't want to deal with either of these possibilities, since solicitousness would make her weaken and love him again and cold-heartedness would make her angry, which was not good for her, so she kept putting it off.

Dr. Beddowes confirmed their original decision that a mastectomy had been the only choice, since the biopsy afterward had revealed three kinds of cancer in Gara's breast, which she said was very common. One was in the milk ducts, one under the nipple, and the other was a marker for possible eventual cancer in either breast.

"But let's assume that it was a marker for the cancer you already had," Dr. Beddowes told her optimistically.

"But what if it's not?"

"Later on, when you've finished your chemotherapy, I'll probably give you tamoxifen to keep you from getting it in the other breast, just as a precaution, and only because it's good for your bones and will keep you from getting osteoporosis when you're older. Tamoxifen suppresses the estrogen in your body, but it has a side effect of acting just like estrogen on the bones and cholesterol."

Chemotherapy, tamoxifen...estrogen suppression...would she ever have sex again?

One of the friends Gara had told introduced her to two other women who had had mastectomies. The three of them had dinner together. Both of the other women were married. They were both three-year survivors. One had been between two health insurance policies and found herself not covered: she'd had her mastectomy and a reconstruction from a flap of muscle in her abdomen done in a public hospital by a resident. She said he was very kind.

"I look like the Bride of Frankenstein," she said happily. "But I don't care. My husband keeps saying he's just so glad I'm alive. We had planned to grow old together and that's all we want."

That was all I wanted, too, Gara thought, saddened.

The other woman was in her late thirties, and she and her husband wanted to have a baby, so she had opted to have a mastectomy and chemotherapy instead of a lumpectomy and radiation. She hadn't bothered to be reconstructed, and her husband didn't mind. She had a prosthesis, an expensive artificial breast and nipple that she had sent for separately from a catalogue, to match her own. She glued them on. Her breasts looked very perky. She and her husband were still trying to start their family.

"The worst part was the chemotherapy," she told Gara. "They didn't have the antinausea drug then and I had to smoke grass to keep from throwing up. We got a drug dealer. My husband and I would sit around the apartment getting stoned. I don't know what I would have done without it."

"I guess each of us is happy with her choice of what kind of reconstruction to have," Gara said.

"Oh, yes," they agreed enthusiastically.

She tried not to let herself think that she was the only one of them who was going through all this alone, who had no one to say he was just glad she would still be there. I am glad for myself, she told herself. I want to live.

She went to physical therapy, where she worked on apparatuses to regain the mobility of her left arm and shoulder. At home she practiced all the time.

"When am I going to be through with this?" she asked.

"When you can do this," the therapist said, swinging her arm in a big circle, showing her.

"You mean this?"

"You did it!"

"You never asked me," Gara said.

"I've never had a patient who sprang back as fast as you did," the physical therapist said. "I'm embarrassed to discharge you until the end of the week, so can you keep coming back anyway till then?"

"Yes, if you'll massage the scar."

Afterward her nutritionist sent her to a personal trainer who was experienced with postsurgical patients, and would go with her to the gym and train her three times a week throughout the chemotherapy so she would be strong. He was big, young, and muscular, and while she pedaled the stationary bike he told her about his problems with his girlfriend and Gara gave him professional advice. She also, of course, had to pay him, although he did not pay her.

She was impatient to start chemo, to save her life, to be clear and clean. The chemotherapy was given in a windowless room in her doctor's office, painted a drab beige, with fluorescent lighting overhead, and a raised desk in front for the nurse. There was a row of beige leather lounge chairs for the patients, with I.V. stands next to them. No music, no plants, no daylight, nothing. It was claustrophobic and depressing. She willed herself not to be afraid.

The first time she went to chemo Gara made Jane come with her because she didn't know what physical reaction to expect, but after that, when she knew nothing debilitating would happen, she was, as always, the only patient who arrived alone. The other women came with solicitous husbands or daughters, who whispered to them in the waiting room and then waited patiently outside for them to be finished, to take them home. Gara played her hypnosis tapes on a Walkman, read *People* magazine, drank cranberry juice the nurse brought her. She willed the slender veins on the back of her right hand to come up, full and ready for the tiny needle, told them not to hurt. They hurt anyway.

Sometimes she was the only one in the chemo room, and sometimes there were other women, cheerfully taking off their uncomfortable hats to reveal pale bald heads, offering home-baked chocolate chip cookies, chattering to other women they knew; or silently hunched into themselves, frightened and miserable, wondering about their lives. There were the ones with the I.V.'s in their hands and the ones with the shunts in their chests, whose veins were used up. There were the ones, like Gara, who still had hair. After a while, even those who had been friendly fell silent, because the process took a long time, and because, no matter how brave they were, they all knew why they were there.

She knew her schedule. Right after chemo she went directly to the gym and worked out, full of energy. She looked very white. The next morning she woke up flushed and healthy-looking. The third day she was too tired to get out of bed. It was not a sick and exhausted tiredness, it was a kind of calm lethargy. The least thing seemed too much effort. She arranged her patients' appointments accordingly.

After she had been on chemo for a month her hair started falling out in an unstoppable cascade every time she combed it, fluffy piles in the bathroom sink. "It's falling out," she told Jane in despair.

"You know what?" Jane said. "I have a friend in Los Angeles who had chemotherapy for breast cancer, and I just remembered she bought some kind of scalp treatment she could put on at home and it helped a lot. I'll call her and find out for you. California has everything new, organic and mystical. If they don't have it, who will?"

So now Gara got up an hour earlier every morning to apply her scalp treatment, which stained all her towels beyond repair and made her hair fall out a great deal less. The hair that was left looked stringy and burned, and people who didn't know why told her she should stop going to her dreadful hairdresser, whoever he was, and find another one, but at least she didn't have to wear the wig. Somehow that was a kind of triumph to her.

Between the exhaustion and the things she had to eat and

drink and the exercise and meditation and tapes to listen to and chemo sessions and doctor's appointments and blood tests and the hours she spent on her regular work, there was no time to think of anything else. Concentrating on herself was not selfish, it was good sense. These days, during that fall and winter, Gara almost always spent Saturdays and Saturday night with Jane and her husband, stayed up late talking, and sometimes slept over so they could have breakfast together, as if they were her family. During the week she saw a few friends for dinner sometimes, and still went to parties when she felt up to it, although the sight and smell of wine made her sick; and when she was at those parties people told her how happy she looked. They did not tell her she looked drawn and gray-faced, although she knew she did.

"You're the bravest person I've ever known," Jane told her. "Eliot thinks so, too. He said, 'I don't know when Gara cries. She must, sometimes.'"

"I don't," Gara said. "I don't know why."

"And you're cheerful! I know I wouldn't be if it happened to me. I would be hysterical and sobbing."

"Nobody knows how they're going to react to an emergency until it happens," Gara said.

She and Jane made jokes about her disease, which in their opinion had opened the door to entitlement. Life was too short to put up with bullshit anymore. Never would Gara have to spend time with another bore, go where she didn't want to, suffer fools gladly, be hypocritically polite. "I don't have to do that," she and Jane would say, and add in a whiny voice, "I have cancer." Then they would laugh.

People told her she seemed happy, and the odd thing was that she was happy. She tried to figure out why.

Well, she had been given a reprieve, for one thing. Her doctor told her she had a seventy-five-percent chance of living a normal life span; that was what statistics said. This was the first time in her life when everybody and everything was focused on her well being and survival; her doctors—all those good-mother figures, young enough to be optimistic, old enough to be wise—praising her fortitude and stamina, explaining away her fears, even hugging her. It was not a return to infancy, since her own mother had been too protective and she had been helpless; rather it was both protection and collaboration.

Yet now, sometimes, for long moments until she made herself stop, Gara missed May. She missed her more than she missed Carl. May would have been at her side every moment, bringing her things she needed. May had liked it when Gara had been sick, had made her stay home from school at the slightest cough, put her to bed, fed her.

But Gara also remembered that she had hated missing school and not being with her friends, and that unless she was really sick she had felt trapped. If May were here she would have worried about Gara too much, made her be too brave in the wrong way, would have tried to take away all her painkillers after the mastectomy because May was afraid of painkillers and refused to take them herself. May would have bitten back sobs of grief and fear and made Gara turn into the one who comforted the other, pained by her mother's pain, frightened of her mother's "weakness," because May prided herself on the fact that she never cried.

Gara wondered if she was like her mother after all. May felt it was too personal, too cowardly, too embarrassing to shed tears in front of other people, even her family. May ate not only to avoid sex but also to sedate herself. Is that why I never cried when I heard I had cancer, Gara asked herself, and not ever, not once, through this whole ordeal? But I never needed to, she remembered; I never even thought of tears. No, she thought, I am not like my mother. I am independent. May never was independent because she had me.

Cancer had changed her, made her see life in a new, better way. It was a cliché but true: when you wanted to live more than anything else in the world, you realized how trivial everything else was.

But that was until the bills started coming in. *We do not pay for injections*, the computer printout from Blue Shield announced when her large chemotherapy bills came back to her unpaid.

Gara called to protest. "You're not covered for office visits," the woman on the phone said, sounding bored and irritated. "Look at your policy. We don't pay for injections."

"This is chemotherapy!" Gara said. "Not just injections. I need it to save my life."

"We don't pay for injections." Now the woman sounded angry, as if she spent all day talking to protesting, unreasonable idiots who thought having paid enormous premiums gave them the right to anything.

Gara knew she should write a letter to someone with more authority, or even get a lawyer to explain it for her, but exhausted and drained from the chemo Blue Shield refused to cover, she put it off. She was too immobilized to fight or even to let herself get angry. I'll do it when I'm well, she thought, thankful she could afford to pay it on her own.

The expander under her chest muscle deflated. There was a leak. Luckily it was only saline, which had been absorbed harmlessly. When Dr. Lister tried to fill it up, it deflated again by the next morning. She told Gara it had never happened to anyone before. The company that manufactured the defective expander wanted it back for tests when it would eventually be removed for her reconstruction, when she was well enough. But now, when Gara looked in the mirror, on one side she saw a flat chest with a washboard of wrinkled skin where it had been stretched, like the chest of some ancient man, and on the other side the remainder of what she used to be. I guess I won't go out on a blind date again for at least a year, she told herself, resigned. Even I can't stand to look at it, and it's mine. She bought a latex breast to put in her bra. It looked and felt real, but it fell out every time she bent over.

She finished her six months of chemo in time to celebrate the New Year. It was just in time, because the pads of her fingers had begun to split and bleed from the methotrexate. Her last session it took an hour and a half to find a usable vein in her hand; the others had collapsed. Her bravery had collapsed, too: she couldn't make the veins stand up, she couldn't push away the pain in her hand, her fingertips stung; seeing the blessed end in sight, she just wanted it to be over. Her nails were bluish black, her hair was thin and pathetic, her eyebrows almost nonexistent, her three or four eyelashes not worth putting mascara on, but she had never had mouth sores, never been nauseated except at the gym, never had cystitis, had maintained her weight, and she was going to be ready soon for reconstruction. Her drawn and grayish face looked fifteen years older, but nobody ever mentioned it. Why would they?

Gara scheduled her first reconstruction to take place over the Easter holiday, so it would seem normal to her patients (and everyone else) for her to "go away." She was starting to look better. She'd had her destroyed hair cut off in the very short little-boy bob she now noticed on so many middle-aged women who were not waif models, and which suddenly seemed to hint of secrets she had never before suspected. It's the chemo cut, she thought to herself; does she or doesn't she?

The surgery was done under general anesthesia because Gara's plastic surgeon had to make a pocket for the implant underneath the chest muscles, and she felt it would be too painful under a local. "It's not like breast augmentation," Dr. Lister had said. "It's much more precise, because you don't have a breast to go over it and cover up any imperfections of placement." Dr. Lister had chosen silicone for her despite the furor that was currently surrounding it. "If a patient has a breast to go on top of it, I use saline," she said, "but it's too wrinkly and bouncy for you. If you had saline your breast would look like a pool toy."

"A pool toy!" Gara said, and she had to laugh. "But is silicone safe?"

"I've taken silicone implants out of women who've had them for thirty years," Dr. Lister said. "They're very strong, and they don't leak. The ones that used to kill women were when doctors put shots of silicone directly into their breasts, in little clumps, and it would wander to their lungs and organs. There really is no proof that the new ones cause autoimmune disease. Since the lawsuits, only one company has been chosen to manufacture silicone implants now, and to get one for you I have to put you on a protocol. All that means is you come in for checkups, which you would do anyway."

"But what about the women who did have problems and won their lawsuits?" Gara asked.

"I still think you'll be safe."

"Okay," Gara said, because she really wasn't afraid.

The company who made her implant was the same one that had manufactured her expander. They examined it carefully and had no idea why it had been defective.

After her surgery Gara went to Jane's, enjoyed being pampered for a few days, and then went home, impatient to be independent. She had a drain again, but this time she didn't mind, because it was temporary, and she also had a round young breast, which was permanent. A nipple would have to be made later, sculpted from her chest skin, and the nipple and aureole would be tattooed to duplicate her real one in color. This was a new technique and Gara was glad they had discovered it; formerly the nipple had been made from a little piece cut from the patient's vulva, and the very idea made her cringe. Why hurt in two places when you could hurt in only one? She would also have to have her real breast lifted so they would match.

The artificial breast sat on her chest like half an orange, because that was its nature, while the real one looked deflated. Now Gara was putting the polyester she had saved into her bra on the right side. In the summer, when she had her month off, Gara had her remaining breast lifted and rounded to match it to the new one, and a small saline implant put in to complete the transformation. Before all this happened it would never have occurred to her to have her breasts lifted; it seemed too vain, something for a movie star to do, but now that she'd had it done she wondered why she hadn't done it years ago. They still didn't really match, and they weren't quite the same height, but those changes would be made later in yet another operation.

"They never match the first time," Dr. Lister said. "If you'd had a double mastectomy they would be perfect, but there are just too many variables when one is real."

It takes one operation to lop it off, Gara thought, and six to put it back on.

Blue Shield refused to pay for either of her hospital stays for reconstruction, with various excuses ranging from not paying for plastic surgery to incomplete information about the dates she had been in the hospital and how many pieces of equipment had been used. She was covered as an inpatient, and they kept insisting she had been an outpatient. She immediately started to worry, even though she kept telling herself it was bad for her health not to stay calm, and the worry increased. There were delays, letters sent back and forth, repeated phone calls made by Gara to people whose names she wrote down and couldn't reach again, who kept asking for hospital and surgery records the hospital insisted had been supplied and which they said they never received. She went higher up and finally found a woman who she was able to talk to every time, but it did no good anyway, except that this one acted nicer. The hospital accused the insurance company of lying and delaying, and the insurance company accused the hospital of the same thing. Now Gara had copies of her records, of files, of correspondence, but she still owed thousands of dollars and she wasn't even finished with all her surgery.

Every month the hospital sent her bills with increasingly stern computer printouts on them. "Hospital bills are *your* responsibility," they kept reminding her. "We will have to take legal measures." She knew she had the coverage; it said so in her contract. Why didn't her insurance provider provide it?

Finally, after a year, when the hospital thought she was a deadbeat and she was too stubborn to prove to them otherwise, they wrote to her and threatened to send a collection agency to get their money from her, to take away her home, her car, to ruin her credit rating. Sometimes now she found herself trembling with rage at the injustice of all this bureaucracy, because it was being used against people who had been ill and still feared for their lives, and because many of them really had no money and were probably terrified.

A man from the collection agency wrote to her telling her to call him to straighten this out before she got into trouble. Gara called him. "Why are you persecuting me?" she said. "I'm a sick woman, I have cancer, I don't need stress. Stress will give me cancer again."

He seemed sympathetic, a little nervous. "Well, I wouldn't want to make you sick again," he said. He kept her on the phone for forty-five minutes telling her how he disliked the system, telling her horror stories of other patients who had

not paid their bills, and how the insurance companies had
made their lives a living hell. Then he offered to give her another month if she would get after the hospital. A month
later they went through the same thing. She thought that
having to listen to him telling her the same stories for forty-
five minutes was part of the living hell.

When it was time for her next surgical improvement Dr.
Lister put her into another hospital, where they didn't know
a bill collector was after her, and which Dr. Lister thought
Blue Shield might be more inclined to pay. Blue Shield
wouldn't pay them, either. Then the new hospital said they
would send a collection agency unless she started paying a
little bit every month, so she did. She wondered how women
who had been mutilated the way she had been ever could afford to be made normal-looking again, and thought how unfair it was to add this financial worry to everything they
were going through. When they told you that you had cancer
they told you that you might die, but they didn't mention
that you would also go broke.

She hired a lawyer, finally, who wrote a stern letter to the
CEO at Blue Shield, pointing out how they were harassing a
sick and vulnerable person, causing her stress, which in her
condition was to be avoided. They paid her first disputed
hospital bill immediately, and the second one eventually.

She had recovered from the effects of her chemotherapy,
and her youthful and healthy-looking face had reappeared
as if it had never been away. Everyone asked her if she'd had
a face lift. That was when Gara really understood how debil-
itated she had looked under chemo; no one had told her she
looked sick, but now they told her, surprised, that she looked
wonderful, and asked what she had done. As a bonus her
hair had grown back thicker than ever. She wanted time to
go faster so she could reach her five-year survival mark and
feel safe, but at the same time she wanted it to go slowly so
she could savor the good things about each day. She wanted
all her reconstructive surgery to be finished so she could forget about it, but she knew she would never forget about it.
She looked different than she had before, and she always
would.

Her insurance company wrote to tell her the rules had

been changed: she could buy a Major Medical policy now without being turned down for a pre-existing condition, with no questions asked; this was the policy she had been turned down for years before because she had ripped her knee ligaments in aerobics class and had been in physical therapy for a while. A little late, Gara thought, but she bought the policy. This time, if she had cancer, they would pay for almost everything. I hope I never need it, she thought.

She didn't think about cancer all the time the way she had in the beginning. There were many hours when she forgot about it entirely. Looking at herself after her shower, she had to remember. Getting dressed, she remembered. Hearing about women she had known who did not survive it—and there *were* those, who always seemed to have their recurrence unexpectedly—she was filled with fear. When she went for her checkups and blood tests, first every three months, then every four, then finally every six, she was only frightened for the week before she went to the doctor's office, wondering if this time her reprieve would be denied.

A married friend she had known years ago in Paris, when she and Carl had been married, passed through New York on business, alone, and invited her out for a drink. Carl had married Lucie, he told her. They had a little girl, named Adrienne, after the painter friend who was her godmother.

I wish I could see a picture, Gara thought, and then, no, I don't. I don't know these people. They are no longer in my life.

"Carl speaks French fluently now," the friend said. "But remember how awful his accent was? It's still awful." She knew he was trying to make her smile, but he only made her sad. "The baby is bilingual," he went on, "as most French children are."

"She's American," Gara said. "Her father is American."

"Of course. You're looking great. Better than ever. You know, we all liked you much more than we like Lucie. She's a child, really, very shallow. Some women always remain children, no matter how old they are."

And some don't, Gara thought.

"I'll be in New York for a week," he said. "Why don't you call me and we'll have dinner?"

"All right," she said, but she never did. Dinner took too long. They would talk about the old days, or the new ones, about things she didn't want to think about or know about. She wanted closure. Carl's marriage should provide it, but she still had to be careful not to ask for information, not to live vicariously, only to remember that they both had secrets from one another, which was as it should be because they were no longer even friends.

Gara was not looking for a man anymore. She wasn't ready yet, and wondered when she would be, if ever. She felt too vulnerable, too afraid of being rejected. She knew of women who had been left by their husbands and lovers when they got cancer, because the men said they were afraid to watch them die. What if she met a man like that—fearful, insisting on promises kept? What if she met one who thought her body was ugly, and wouldn't wait around long enough to care about her in the first place? She still needed time to heal in many ways, and she knew she was atypical in hiding what had happened to her, that most women with breast cancer went public as soon as they knew they had a chance to survive, became activists, told friends and strangers in an effort to help others and themselves.

An unhappy childhood is the wound that never heals, Gara told herself. All these years she had told her patients it took time to uncover the past, and then to understand it, and finally to get safely beyond the harm that had been done—to develop a kind of scar tissue, but she couldn't seem to do it herself. May had brought her up to be perfect, or at least to pretend to be and fool people. The mother who had forced her to sit at lunch with a bottle of smelling salts under her napkin so the boy she didn't like wouldn't tell his mother she had fainted and was therefore imperfect and undateable and unmarriageable and unlovable had taught her too well.

Spring came. Gara was a three-year survivor. Her odds were getting better all the time. "You *had* cancer," Dr. Beddowes told her cheerfully. "You don't *have* it, you *had* it. Think of it that way. See you in six months."

"Of course."

"I have news," Jane told her on the phone. She did not sound at all happy. "We're moving to Singapore."

"Moving?" Gara's heart turned over. "To that place where they *cane* people?"

"They don't cane women."

"Oh, great. How long will you be there?"

"I don't know. Eliot has a TV series that's going to be made there. An hour once a week. If it's a hit we may be there for years. I have to go with him, or I won't have a marriage, but I hate everything about the idea. I'll miss my family and friends, I'll miss you terribly. It's too hot there, I mean really, really hot, and you go to prison if you drink anything alcoholic, and I won't know anybody."

"Sure you can drink," Gara said. "It's the home of the Singapore Sling."

She was used to Jane's absences on location, but they had always been known to be temporary, finite, an adventure. This sounded ominous. What would she do without her best friend, now that she was all alone? Maybe the series wouldn't be a hit. She didn't want to wish them bad luck, but she knew Jane was hoping the same thing. "Why would he want to live there anyway?" Gara asked.

"I don't know. He says it's an opportunity. He's excited." Jane sighed. "He says he's tired of Hollywood and wants to do something different."

"The mid-life crisis. At least he wants you to come with him. He's not just running off like my ex-husband. When are you leaving?"

"Next month."

"So soon!"

"He's been talking about it, but I never really believed it would happen. And now it will. We're subletting the apartment. I'm glad at least I was able to be there for you when you were sick."

"Me, too," Gara said. She still felt numb with surprise, but a big lump of loneliness was beginning to gather in her chest.

"You have to visit," Jane said. "We'll have a big house and lots of servants. My kids are going to visit. I want everyone to come."

"I will," Gara said, but she didn't know when.

"August in Singapore, what a treat," Jane said sympathetically, knowing, as always, what Gara was thinking. "When the only thing you like to do in August is go to your house on the beach. But we'll have fun."

"Yes."

"I'll visit you back here when I can."

"Of course." But she doubted it. She knew Jane; Jane complained and hated a place and then she settled in.

"We'll write to each other."

"Absolutely." Neither of them was a good or faithful letter writer; Gara had never gotten so much as a postcard from location, even when they were in Africa.

"And we'll call each other. You'll call me, won't you?"

"You know I will." But Gara knew that the three-hour time difference from New York to Los Angeles had always seemed insurmountable—whenever each of them thought of the other it was the wrong time to call—and she wondered how often they would speak when Jane was in Singapore.

"I hate this," Jane said.

"Me too."

And then she was gone.

It was strange to be here in New York knowing her long-time friend wasn't, odd to pass Jane's apartment building, look up at the lights, and know strangers were moving around in those lighted rooms, living lives that seemed an intrusion. So many losses... Gara felt adrift. She had always had friends in New York, but everyone was busy with their work—working too hard, traveling for business—and their private lives and their families—college-bound children, aging parents—so to see anyone you had to make plans far in advance, and those plans were likely to be canceled for emergencies of one sort or another. It was not that she had seen Jane so often or spoken to her every day, but they had always been there for each other and had known it.

They called each other a few times, and then the calls tapered off, as Gara had known they would. They knew they would see each other again, but not for now. Gara continued to go to dinner parties, to cocktail parties, to art openings, dealing with the shyness, trying to have a good time, and now she realized she was going there looking for new women friends.

She met Felicity Johnson at a fund-raiser for women politicians, where both had gone alone. They started talking and liked each other immediately. Felicity was very pretty and bright and bubbly; she had an honesty and vulnerability about her that touched Gara, and she had a good heart. She told Gara about her unhappy marriage and Gara told her about how Carl had left her. They commiserated and made each other laugh. By the time they knew each other better and Gara saw the other side of Felicity—the deep depression, the confusion, the painful self-doubt—she already liked her enough to feel protective toward her and want to try to help.

She met Eve Bader through Felicity. At the time Gara thought Felicity liked Eve more than she actually did. Gara thought Eve was flamboyant and funny, a character, and Eve made her laugh, too. She had never met anyone like Eve. The three of them began to go out to dinner together once in a while.

Then at a huge dinner party where Gara had, as usual, gone alone, and, as was not usual, had arrived early, she met Kathryn O'Mara Henry, who had also gone alone, and who, she soon discovered, always arrived everywhere early so she could meet people. Kathryn was a beautiful, sophisticated-looking woman, and Gara had no idea how old she might be. The phrase "of indeterminate age" came to mind. Kathryn's face and bearing were those of a young woman, but her knowing eyes and expensive jewelry belonged on someone very mature. She sailed right up to Gara and introduced herself, and Gara thought she was brave to be so friendly in a room full of strangers.

The morning after the dinner party Kathryn called her and made a dinner date. They went to the Sign of the Dove and met at the bar, and in ten minutes Kathryn had picked up three men. Gara didn't know how she did it.

She admired Kathryn's spirit. Kathryn was a woman who loved New York and made the most of it. She had seen every Broadway show, some several times, she went to every new exhibit at every museum, she saw every good new movie, she had tried every well known restaurant, and she walked everywhere, even across the park. She did not work, although she said she had worked for most of her life and that now she deserved to have fun.

"Give us the best bottle of wine you have," she would demand of the waitress. "We deserve it." Then she would pick up the check, because she was also generous.

There was a recklessness to her generosity, a kind of *I'll show them* attitude. Gara did not know whom she was showing, or why, for a long time. "If I run out of money, I'll make more," Kathryn would say. It was known that her former husband was extremely rich.

Gara introduced her to Felicity and Eve, and soon the four of them had become, without knowing how it had happened, a faithful little group. They began to have a weekly dinner together in various neighborhood restaurants, and one night Felicity suggested they go to Yellowbird. Kathryn wasn't crazy about it and disliked the food, but the other three liked the music and the ambiance, and even Kathryn had to admit she liked the quantity and quality of men. They all liked Billie, and thought she was a character and a half. Eventually Yellowbird became their club, an eccentric and comfortable gathering place where they felt at home.

THIRTY-FOUR

"Isn't this our anniversary?" Kathryn asked. They were all in Yellowbird, and it was spring. The sky had still been light when they arrived, a pearly grayish color behind the dark buildings, and all of them had walked to get there, except Felicity, who never walked anywhere if she could help it because she was always in a hurry, even when she was on time. "It was about this time last spring when we had our first dinner together here."

"A year already?" Eve marveled. "Where does it go?"

"To my friends," Felicity said, holding up her glass. "To friendship."

"To health, life, and love," Gara added.

They all nodded and clicked their wine glasses, and smiled, while Janis belted out her blues on the sound system, turned down softly, because it was still dinnertime and people needed to be able to hear themselves talk.

At her customary seat at the bar Billie watched them and overheard. She had never had close women friends, the way they seemed to be, but she had so many casual friends of both sexes in Yellowbird that she never felt it as a loss. She had a rich, full life, she thought, everything she wanted. Having Little Billie had changed everything for her. Still, it was nice for them to hang around together the way they did, to meet so regularly, and to think of acknowledging their friendship with an anniversary. She would send them a free drink to help them celebrate.

"I really must love you guys to have eaten all these bad meals here with you," Kathryn said, laughing.

Well, no free drinks for you, Billie thought, changing her mind. Then she decided to send them a good bottle of wine anyway, for being faithful spenders, and to show them who was boss. She knew the expensive one Kathryn liked.

"To Billie!" the women cried happily, toasting her with their free wine. "Our Billie!"

"Yours?" Billie thought. She smiled and nodded graciously in recognition of their appreciation.

It was a good night in Yellowbird tonight, crowded with most of her regulars and the usual strangers who had heard about her place or had simply wandered in. There was a good-looking man alone at the bar whom she might talk to later if he didn't have a date coming to join him. Little Billie was in his booth in the back, doing his homework with the Larchmont Ladies, behaving himself, not pestering her to let him go home to make trouble with his friends. Billie couldn't understand why those other parents didn't take more interest in their children. She always kept an eye on him. Perhaps that was because she had to be both parents to him, make up to him for having deprived him of a father on purpose.

It was late, after ten o'clock, when a new couple came in and were seated at table four. The woman looked vaguely familiar: the pale freckled face, the frizzy blond hair. While they were eating Billie walked around the room to see if everything was all right, and passed their table.

"Ms. Redmond!" the woman called out to her.

"Yes?" Billie stopped.

"I'm Lola Gribetz, Billie's kindergarten teacher. Do you remember me?"

Aha. That one. How could I forget you, Billie thought. You wanted to send us to a loony doctor. "Of course," she said graciously.

"This is my date, Walter Norris. We went to the movies and then we came here totally by accident, spur of the moment, just to try a new restaurant, and there you were."

"Yes, I am always here," Billie said.

"And that must be Billie, back there in the booth! I don't remember all my children, but of course I'll never forget Billie."

"People don't," Billie said. She wasn't sure Ms. Gribetz meant it as a compliment.

"I'm going to go over to say hello to him," Lola Gribetz said. "Is this a special occasion?"

"Is what?"

"That he's here so late."

"No," Billie said.

"Is he often here?"

"Whenever I am."

"Oh. Well." Her smile seemed a little forced.

"Enjoy your dinner," Billie said, and moved on.

Later, when they had finished eating, she saw Lola Gribetz making her way over to Little Billie's booth, and she felt a twitching of something that was very like alarm. This had never been anyone's idea of a family restaurant, although she thought of it that way. It was just a different kind of family. Stodgy as they liked to appear, the Larchmont Ladies looked like what they were—men in drag—and she was sure Little Billie's former kindergarten teacher would notice. She would probably be shocked.

When Lola Gribetz came back to her table she looked more bewildered than shocked, which Billie took as a good sign. "Excuse me," she said, lowering her voice to a whisper, "Ms. Redmond...aren't those *transvestites?*"

"Well, yes they are. One of them is a whiz at math. Billie has been getting A's since he started getting tutored."

"Well, surely..."

"Surely what?"

"Well, you, I'm sure you...well, you..."

"I what?" Billie said.

"Nothing."

"Little Billie has grown into quite a little person since you saw him last," Billie said. "He's started writing stories. They're very good. I think he's going to be a writer someday."

"I'm sure he finds plenty of material here," the Norris man said, with a laugh that wasn't entirely pleasant.

"If he does," Billie said, "it will give him a good start."

She moved on, and when she caught the waiter's eye she motioned to him to give them their check. She didn't like their attitude, she didn't like their vibes, and she didn't like being criticized. She didn't want them hanging around drinking coffee half the night; she would rather have the table empty. She felt disquieted, and she wanted them out of her sight. She was relieved when they left.

"Miss Gribetz acted weird," Little Billie said when she was putting him to bed.

"How so?"

He shrugged. "She asked me questions."

"What kind of questions?"

"Like she was still my teacher."

"School questions?"

"No. About my life."

"Did she do that when she was your teacher?" Billie asked.

"You remember, when we had our afternoon conversations back in kindergarten? She would ask us what we ate, what we did for fun, when we went to bed. That kind of stuff."

"Well, it's probably just her way of making conversation now," Billie said. "It's polite to answer people, but you have a right not to tell them anything you don't want to. You could ask them a question instead."

"I should have asked her if she liked her dinner," Little Billie said with a grin.

Billie kissed him goodnight. "Sleep well, my love."

What an unpleasant coincidence, she thought, having that woman walk into my restaurant. I hope she never comes back.

The next evening, when Yellowbird was full and noisy, and Little Billie had eaten his dinner and done his homework and was playing a computer game, a middle-aged gray-haired cop walked in, wearing a blue uniform with a big gun in a holster at his belt, and a mean look on his face. He meandered around the room, looking at everything, and then he strode purposefully to Little Billie's booth and started to talk to him. Billie naturally went right over there as fast as she could.

"What's the problem, officer?" she asked. She didn't like the idea of a cop scaring her son.

"Are you Mrs. Redmond?" he asked.

"Yes," Billie said.

"Officer Peoples," he said, showing her his badge. "We've had a complaint about the minor child Billie Redmond, and the conditions he's living in, and I'm here to see if we should take the child."

"Take him where?" Billie rasped. If she could have shrieked, she would have. Little Billie looked terrified, as if he was going to be arrested, and she wasn't entirely sure he wasn't.

"Away from the home, ma'am."

Immediately every nerve in her body was at attention. "What's wrong with his home?"

"That's what we're going to find out. The complaint was about here."

"What's wrong with here?"

"It's a bar. It's late at night. People are drinking."

"People drink in their homes, too," Billie said, keeping her tone respectful. Except for the all-too visible gun, bulging there in its holster like an iron phallus, she would have told him to get the hell out. "This is where I work. I own this place. I have my child with me in my workplace." Where had she heard that line? Eve! "So I can keep an eye on him and be sure he's okay."

"A child his age needs his sleep," the cop said. He was writing in a little pad and Billie didn't know if she was going to cry or throw up.

"Look here," she said, showing him her office with Little Billie's cot in it. "When he's tired he sleeps here, and then I take him home."

Officer Peoples wrote some more. Little Billie hadn't said a word, and the look on his frightened face wrung her heart. Then the cop looked up from his note pad and glanced at her. "What happened to your voice?" he asked. "And that scar on your neck—your husband cut you?"

"There is no husband," Billie said. "I was mugged. That's why I want to be sure my son is safe. You never know, these days, with violence everywhere."

"That's true. But you could get a baby-sitter."

"Oh, right, some lunatic or some irresponsible thirteen-year-old."

The cop looked around. "I was told this was a gay bar."

"Are you out of your mind?" Billie said. She was glad the Larchmont Ladies didn't come every night, and weren't there now. "Does this look like a gay bar in any way, shape, or form? This is a neighborhood family restaurant."

"What time are you going to take him home?"

"Soon. He gets very good marks in school. Obviously he isn't tired."

For the first time Billie realized the room had gone quiet, and everybody was looking at them. That bitch Gribetz had done this, turned her in as an unfit mother, threatening her child, and as a nice little bonus ruining her business. The customers didn't know what was going on, but they knew it wasn't good.

"I'm fine," Little Billie suddenly said, finding his voice. He peered up at the cop. "Do you want me to show you how I surf the Internet? Ask me a question, anything you want to know, and I'll look it up for you."

"You're a bright kid," the cop said, looking pleasant for the first time. Billie knew it wasn't the child he was angry at but her, although he could have fooled them both. "You're nine?"

"Yes, sir. Almost ten."

He closed his note pad and put it into his pocket. "I'm not taking the child tonight," he said, "but I have to file a report and then you'll be hearing from Child Services."

"About *what*?"

"They'll need to see the apartment and see the mother."

"Oh my God," Billie said, appalled. What was this anyway, a police state? People turning her in, coming into her home, invading her privacy, investigating her life? She wished, for one surprised, angry, unsettled moment, that her parents were there to defend her character, and that she were not so alone. "We live in a wonderful apartment," she said.

"I hope so."

He left, and she saw that Little Billie had tears in his eyes. He had been trying not to cry. Billie put her arms around him and took him into the office, and then she held him and tried not to cry herself. If she had, they would have been tears of frustration and rage...and also fear.

"Are they going to take me away?" he said.

"No," she said, because that was what you told a child, you protected him from everything that was unreasonable and insane, as best you could, but how did she know?

Twenty-four hours later someone from Child Services called. Billie was stunned at the alacrity with which they had pounced on her, since she had always thought that they were overloaded investigating real cases. Since the cop had seen with his own eyes that the child's life and health were not in immediate danger Billie managed to put off their appointment to see her apartment for a week by saying she was going to be on jury duty. That sounded respectable.

"You may need to get me a lawyer," Billie said to Felicity Johnson the next time she came in, since she knew Felicity was a lawyer herself. Then she had to tell Felicity what she needed the lawyer for, since they were specialists, and naturally the four women were appalled at what had happened.

"You have a right to take your child to work," Eve said. "I took Nicole to work with me when I was on *Brilliant Days*, when she was little."

"That wasn't a bar," Felicity said.

"Neither is this," Billie said, but they all knew Yellowbird wasn't a tea room either.

"This is disgusting," Eve said. "It's a feminist issue: The child in the workplace. I'm going to do something about it."

"Don't do anything," Felicity said. "Let Billie handle it. She's doing fine."

"Yellowbird is the same as day care, you know," Eve went on. "Except it's night care." She laughed. "Night care, get it?"

"Leave her alone," Gara said.

"You know, she's kind of right," Billie said. "Everybody here loves him."

"They'll see that," Felicity said. "And if they don't agree you'll call the lawyer."

Billie talked to the Larchmont Ladies about her dilemma, of course. Although several people suspected it, few people actually knew that Gladys, aka Ralph, was a cop in his other life. He didn't know Officer Peoples, though, because this was a matter for Billie's local precinct, and Gladys, who did not want to be recognized, strayed far away from his own workplace to come here.

"Maybe we shouldn't come back," he said, and there was such concern and regret in his voice that Billie felt a rush of kindness toward him.

"No," she said. "This is a free country. You didn't do anything wrong. Just don't come in next Wednesday, because the social worker will be here."

She got a little paranoid about telling them that. She hoped they wouldn't tell their friends they had been requested not to come, and have someone decide to turn this into a gay issue in which she was the villain. She had enough troubles with issues already, and she had never been a political animal of any kind.

The social worker, Ms. Lambert, arrived at their apartment at ten o'clock in the morning. Little Billie was at school, and Mamacita had cleaned the apartment so carefully it looked like a model for a home magazine. Billie had already changed her clothes three times and finally decided she would wear jeans like she and everyone else always did; this wasn't supposed to be the Brady Bunch. When the doorbell rang she stood still for a moment to quiet the pounding of her heart, and then she opened the door.

The woman had smooth dark hair and a scrubbed face with no makeup on it, she was wearing a suit, and she looked about nineteen. Billie's heart sank. Was she supposed to be judged on the most important event of her life by a teenager?

"Come in," she said.

Ms. Lambert got right to work. She, like the cop, had a note pad, and she also had a tape measure. "Is this Billie's room?"

"Yes."

She measured it, and wrote in her pad. Billie held her tongue. What did those people think, that she would make her son sleep in a closet? His bedroom was almost as big as hers, and he was a lot smaller.

"How many other people live here?"

"Just me and my son."

"This is his bathroom?"

"Yes. It's a two-bedroom, two-bathroom apartment, as you see. We also have a doorman, I'm sure you noticed."

Ms. Lambert nodded. She was looking at Little Billie's neat bathroom as if it were the natural right of every child to have something as nice as this for his very own, instead of thinking he was lucky to have a successful mother. The Brady Bunch used to share, as Billie remembered. Suddenly Billie was enraged at the whole thing.

"Why do you people waste your time with me?" she said angrily. "Think of all the mothers punching their kids, burning them with cigarettes, scalding them, shoving their heads down the toilet! Women living with crazy drug-addicted lovers who hate their kids, who torture them! Child molesters, sadists, lunatics! Kids who have no food because their mother is too stoned to get it or spends all her money on crack cocaine! You should be somewhere else, preventing some child from getting killed."

"We know there are many tragedies in this city," the woman said. "My caseload is much too heavy as it is. But I don't know what kind of mother you are until I find out, and you don't have to yell at me."

"I have to yell at somebody," Billie said. "This upsets me."

"We have to be as sure as we can that no child falls through the cracks in the system. Billie was reported, Billie must be investigated."

"What cracks in what system?" Billie said. "He goes to private school. He's there every day."

Ms. Lambert proceeded to the kitchen and looked in the larder and the refrigerator. She wrote in her pad again. What was she writing? Too much sugar?

"He gets a well-balanced dinner in the restaurant every night," Billie said.

"I'll see that this evening. And I'll also get the chance to interview your son."

That hurt. It was as if Little Billie had terrible secrets of neglect to tell them, that they still didn't trust her. They were trying to turn him into a stranger.

"This is a very pleasant home," Ms. Lambert said. "I don't know why you would want to keep him out of it and make him stay in a bar all night."

"Yellowbird is a restaurant that happens to have a bar in

it, like all restaurants unless they don't have a liquor license yet."

"The more reason it's inappropriate for a nine-year-old."

"My father owned a roadhouse in Plano, Texas," Billie said. "My Mama and my brother and I hardly ever saw him unless we went there. He worked very hard all the time, the way I do. Sometimes I really missed him. It was a thrill for us to have dinner at his place. When I was Little Billie's age I was entering my Daddy's contest nights for kids, singing. Later I sang there on a regular basis. It didn't hurt me any growing up around a bar and restaurant; what hurt was wishing we could be together more."

As soon as the words had come out of her mouth Billie was surprised. This was the first time she had realized how lonely she had been for Les Redmond as a child, for his laugh and his strength and his proud and tolerant smile. She remembered her mother having dinner there once a week, at her special table down front, just so she could see him for what should have been a regular family meal, and she also remembered that she and her brother had been there, too, and for the same reason.

"He did the best he could for his children," Billie said. "So do I. I come to this from experience. You may think it's bad, but I think it's better than any alternative you could think up."

"We'll see," Miss Lambert said. "I'll be at Yellowbird tonight."

Billie went to work with Little Billie and gave him his supper, waiting for the social worker. The restaurant started to fill. Then she heard a growing noise outside, a kind of chanting, and saw that the customers were coming in with curious looks on their faces. She went to the door and looked out.

There was a line of women, marching in front of Yellowbird, and they were all holding up placards. *The child should be in the workplace with his mother* some of the signs read. *Rights for working mothers* read other signs. And one, in homage to the old Simon and Garfunkel song, read *Mother and Child Reunion.* Eve Bader was carrying it.

Just then Ms. Lambert arrived, trying to make her way through the protesters to get into the restaurant, and behind her came a camera crew from Fox TV News, and Penny Crone with her little crewcut and a mike in her hand.

"Billie," Penny Crone said gruffly, shoving the mike in front of her face, "is it true you keep your nine-year-old child in your bar?"

"Who are these people?" Billie said to Eve, wildly.

"Why do you have your kid in a bar where drag queens go?" Penny Crone persisted.

"Who called the television?" Billie said in despair.

"I did," Eve said. "I told you there was a way." She pushed herself in front of Billie and held up her placard so the cameraman could get a shot of it, and also so it would not obscure her face. "I'm Eve Bader," Eve said into Penny Crone's mike. "I recently appeared in a CBS television movie about this same issue, and I have a statement to make on behalf of Billie Redmond. She is a caring, single, working mother who..."

"Oh, God," Billie said. She ran into Yellowbird and slammed the door before she had to hear another word. Ms. Lambert followed her.

"My goodness," Ms. Lambert said. She was scribbling.

"You don't have to write it down," Billie said. "We'll all see it on television tonight and I'll be a lot more famous than I want to be."

"Where is Billie?"

"Come on." She took the social worker to Little Billie's booth to meet him. Billie had prepared him for this interview and told him just to be himself, but still she was nervous and angry that a little kid had to convince a bureaucrat that he belonged with the good mother he loved.

"Will you leave us alone, please?" Ms. Lambert said.

Like then he'll feel free to tell you what a sadist I am, Billie thought. Somewhere a kid is probably dying this moment from being banged against the wall, and you're here looking for drag queens. She went back to the bar to attend to her customers and the reservation book, but her eyes kept scanning the back of the room.

Ms. Lambert finished with him, finally. She looked at her watch, and wrote the time down in her little note pad. There was no clock in Yellowbird. It was not even supposed to be the nineties. "I'll call my supervisor in the morning when she comes in, and you'll hear from us," she said, in a tone that was carefully neutral. There was no sign of reassurance, nor any warning of coming disaster.

As soon as she left Billie had a big glass of vodka on the rocks.

"Mama," Little Billie said, coming over and taking her hand. "Don't worry. I was stupendous."

"You were? What did you say?"

He shrugged. He looked tired. She thought it was from the emotions of the evening, but she wondered whether he should have been home in bed. Then she realized that if he were home he wouldn't go to bed anyway. He would be playing with one of the neighbor kids or watching television or banging away on his computer. At least he doesn't have television here, she thought.

He doesn't have kids his age either. Maybe she thinks I'm wrong. Maybe I *am* wrong... Do these people just punish you? Don't they even give you a chance to do different?

She took Little Billie home after the TV news was over, so neither of them would have to watch it. She was too afraid someone would say she was bad. And then all she had to do was wait.

Ms. Lambert called her in the morning. Billie had sent Mamacita to take him to school so she could wait for the call. "We're going to let the child stay with you for now," Ms. Lambert said, "on the condition that you make certain changes."

"What changes?" Billie asked, feeling nervous.

"You have to get a baby-sitter or some member of your family or an adult friend to stay with him in your apartment at night when you go to work, so he doesn't have to go to Yellowbird. It's an inappropriate place for a child. Billie has to be home, under proper supervision, and he has to go to bed at a normal hour."

"I could manage that," Billie said.

"This has to be done immediately."

"Okay."

"I will be back to check."

"Fine."

"He's obviously well-nourished, well-dressed, clean, and cared for," Ms. Lambert said. "It's his mind we're worried about."

"You won't have to worry about it anymore," Billie said.

In the afternoon when she picked up Little Billie from school Billie had a talk with him. "How would you feel about Mamacita staying here to baby-sit for you when I'm working at night?"

"Which night?"

"All of them."

He hunched up his shoulders and squinted his face at her like a little troll. "Is that what Miss Lambert said?"

"She'll let you continue to live with me if you stay out of Yellowbird. She says it's for adults."

"If a family brought their kid and they had dinner there, would she make them leave?"

"I don't know. People don't bring their kids."

"If I stay here, could I see my friends?"

"If their parents say it's okay."

"I'd sort of like it," Little Billie said. She realized then that he would probably like it a lot, but was too polite to say so because he knew it offended her. Every time he had wanted to be with his friends at night instead of with her she had been unhappy about it.

"Mamacita is afraid to go home so late at night," Billie went on, "so she would have to sleep in your room with you. Is that all right?"

"I'm too big for that. Couldn't she sleep in the living room?"

"If she doesn't mind."

"We could get a folding bed," he said. "We would have had to get her one for my room anyway."

"Okay."

"Well, that's settled," he said. "You need to bring back all my stuff."

"I'll do it tonight." He looked so pleased it hurt.

She wondered if she had kept him at Yellowbird too long, and if she had been selfish. She had thought she was protecting him, and he had always seemed so adaptable she had thought he enjoyed being there, but now when she scruti-

nized her motivations she realized she had bribed him with
creature comforts and protestations of love. Little Billie got
along with adults, which was good, but he was still a child,
with a child's innocence. Her approval meant more to him
than anything because she was his mother. He would do
anything she wanted, but he was growing up and he had
needs of his own that she couldn't ignore anymore. She remembered their mild arguments. Little Billie really did want
to be home in his own apartment, but he was willing to
please her in the end, even when he put up a fuss.

This was one more rite of passage. In a few more years she
wouldn't have to pick him up at school, he would be zipping
all around the city by himself on the bus. He would lock his
room and do secret things in there. He would like girls. His
Mama, soon if not already, would be the woman who had
brought him up, not the woman he most wanted to be with.
We all do the best we can, Billie thought, like our parents
did; but when she hugged Little Billie goodbye to go to work
she missed him already, not just for tonight but for the rest of
his life.

THIRTY-FIVE

"I'm so happy to be here with my friends," Felicity said, sipping her wine, "and so miserable at home." The four of them were in Yellowbird, and Aretha was singing "Chain of Fools" on the sound system, a song Felicity thought was singularly apt for herself. It was a song Billie liked, too, and had it played often, but Billie said it was really about men. Felicity knew she was complaining again, that she always complained about Russell, like a howling, trapped animal, but she couldn't help it. Her frustration ruled her life. "Russell has been away on a business trip for the past two days, and I wish he would never come back," she went on. "It's so nice to be in my own house without worrying that he's going to yell at me. It's so peaceful. He's coming back tomorrow afternoon and I'm dreading it."

"I'm tired about hearing about your husband," Kathryn said. "If you're so miserable, get rid of him. I got rid of mine, except for the one who died."

"Well, Kathryn, you're very courageous in every aspect of your life," Gara said.

"I never thought about it," Kathryn said. "I just did what I had to, to survive."

"I know."

They all knew Kathryn's story, briefly at least: that her mother had killed her father, that he had been brutal and her mother was set free, and Felicity sensed that all of them had somewhat the same kind of dysfunctional childhood, even though it had appeared in different ways. Why else had they bonded? They were four women who were totally different, and yet in some ways they had each passed through the same tricky terrain. Every one of them had been an outsider.

She sensed that each of them had felt abandoned and afraid. Felicity wondered how much longer they would all have to carry around the destructive baggage of the past without moving on, and thought that of the four she was the one who was in the worst place in her life. Kathryn was the only one of them who was always happy, or so it seemed. Eve hid whatever she was feeling under bravado. Gara was afraid to live. And so am I, Felicity thought.

"Let me tell you how I got my apartment and my money," Kathryn said. "Does anyone mind if I smoke?"

"Yes," Gara said, "but we want to hear the story too."

Kathryn lit up. "My last husband, Mr. Henry, came from family money. His father had made his fortune in fertilizer. There wasn't a farm in the East that didn't use something from Henry Chemical."

"So he was the Shit King," Eve said brightly, with a grin.

"No, no, that's organic," Kathryn said. "His was made in a factory. But my husband didn't work for his father, although he was a major stockholder in the company; he had been a professional tennis player, and when I married him, he was selling medical supplies. He was rich, rich, rich, but he was also cheap, cheap, cheap. I didn't know that when I married him, but I found it out soon enough. But I put up with him because I wanted my kids to have a decent father and a happy home. Which they did, until my oldest son, Jim Daniel, when he was fourteen years old, was in a terrible auto accident and lost his arm."

"Oh, no!" the other women gasped.

"My son was never the same after that. He dropped out of school, took drugs, and seemed so angry. He was particularly angry with his stepfather, when there seemed to be no reason for it. They had always been devoted to each other. Well, some years later, Jim Daniel explained it all to me. Jim Daniel had let us all think he had been out in the car alone, experimenting the way kids will do. But the truth was my husband, Mr. Henry, had been the one driving the car. He was drunk. He ran away from the wrecked car leaving my injured son in it, so no one would know he had been there, and he made my son take the blame."

"My God!" Felicity said.

"As you can imagine, I was horrified," Kathryn said. "I had never been happy with Mr. Henry, but there was no way I could continue to live with him after that. So I hired the best divorce lawyer in town to go after him. The bomber and I hatched up a plan: We threatened to make the circumstances of the accident public if the divorce went to trial, and we made him give me ten million dollars to keep it quiet. I figured that was what I deserved in punitive damages, but I never would have gotten anything near that in a mere divorce. Mr. Henry had a fit, of course, but there was nothing he could do. The publicity would have ruined his life."

Extortion and blackmail, Felicity thought, surprised. Kathryn could have done it another way; most people would have.

"I set up a nice little trust fund for my son," Kathryn went on cheerfully, "and then I went to New York, which was a city I'd wanted to live in many years ago when I was eighteen and couldn't; I bought the apartment I'm living in now for a million and a half, and put the rest of the money with a conservative private banking firm. I'm set for life."

"Amazing," Eve said admiringly.

Felicity and Gara exchanged glances. Felicity knew that Gara, too, thought Kathryn's financial triumph was rather startlingly cold hearted, or perhaps it was the way she was telling the story, as if it was just a lighthearted escapade in her long life. What kind of a sleazy lawyer would give her that kind of advice? Felicity wondered.

"Why do you always call him Mr. Henry?" Gara asked.

"Because I never really knew him, did I?"

Eve laughed. "Frontier justice."

"I had a rough time in all my marriages—no, not really in the first one," Kathryn said lightly. "The only decent thing I got out of them was my wonderful children. This time I finally got something else."

I guess I can understand that, Felicity thought. People who have enough money don't understand what some other people have to do to get it.

Then Kathryn turned suddenly serious. "I should have stayed married to my first husband," she said. "He was the only good one. Now when I look back, I see how wonderful and kind he was. But what did I know? I was a kid, and I didn't want to be married to anyone."

"Maybe you'll marry him again," Felicity said.

"It's too late," Kathryn said. "It never could have worked. It still wouldn't. I didn't love him."

"Well, look who's here," Eve said, looking up and starting to sparkle. It was Eben Mars, the potato farmer/poet, her erstwhile lover, wandering in. Felicity knew Eve had not been with him for a while now, and while the other women thought it was over Eve didn't think so. "I think I'd like to see Eben this week,' she'd say, and would call him. Sometimes she got lucky.

He came up to their table. "Sit down, Eben," Eve said, shoving her chair over to make room and pulling out an empty chair from the next table without apologizing to the people who were eating there.

"I'm not intruding?" he asked. Felicity remembered then what a gentle voice he had.

"Of course not," Kathryn said.

He sat between Eve and Felicity, and Eve introduced everyone again. "Has everyone eaten?" he asked.

"We just ordered," Eve said. "Eben, do you want to share a chicken-fried steak?"

He shook his head and looked at the menu. "I just want a salad."

"He's a vegetarian but I'm trying to cure him," Eve said. "A man needs meat."

"Meat makes you die," he said mildly. "Especially here."

They all laughed. He looked different tonight, Felicity thought, and then realized he was wearing a suit. He looked quite nice in it. "Where's your husband tonight, Felicity?" he asked.

"Not here and I'm glad of it," Felicity said.

He ordered his salad, and another bottle of wine for the table, and then he turned toward her again. "If I had known you were here I would have brought you my book," he said. "I'd be interested in your opinion of it."

"She's not an editor, she's a lawyer," Eve said, sounding annoyed. "Eben gave me a signed copy, I'll lend it to you."

"Thank you," Felicity said. His eyes met hers and she noticed that they were green, flecked with gold. She could feel something tonight that was different from the first time they had met and she realized she was attracted to him, and that he was to her. Perhaps they always had been, but she had been so obsessed with Jason and Eve had been so quick to zero in on Eben that she had put the disquieting feeling out of her mind. Now it came back. They smiled at each other. Gara and Kathryn were talking to each other and didn't seem to notice the undercurrents, but on the other side of him and left out of their moment Eve was watching them carefully, and she looked displeased.

If only another man besides Jason liked me, Felicity thought, an intelligent man, like Jason but available, then I wouldn't feel so worthless, and maybe I could have the courage to leave my situation. Just somebody to show me I have a chance at a life again after this. I need that, I need it so much. This man is single, he's free, and a man whose poetry is good enough to be published must know something about the human heart.

"It's odd, but I feel as if I've known you a long time," Felicity said to him.

"I feel the same way," Eben Mars said.

"Even though we're strangers."

"But maybe we're not."

"I'm so miserable in my marriage," she sighed.

"You shouldn't stay in an unhappy marriage," he said to her. "No one should. Life is too short to be so sad."

She felt like putting her head on his shoulder. He exuded protectiveness like musk, or perhaps that, too. Felicity began to feel the familiar sexual pulsing. She crossed her legs, but that only made it worse. "I don't know what to do about my life," she said. "I feel so trapped."

"But you must leave him if you feel that way," he said.

She sighed again. "I guess I'm just used to being unhappy. I had a crazy childhood; my mother beat me. My husband bullies me and it must feel normal to me."

"My mother beat me, too," Eben Mars said quietly.

"She did?"

"She took out all the frustrations of her life on me. I think that's why I chose the wrong woman to marry, and why I'm so afraid to connect. I'm afraid the woman is going to hurt me if I give her any power. A little boy's mother is very, very powerful."

"So is a little girl's," Felicity said. "My mother was unhappy in her marriage, too, and she would drink and chase me around the house with a belt."

"Mine used a bread knife," he said.

"No!" Felicity said, horrified. They looked at each other. We are truly the walking wounded, she thought; this man is my soulmate. "Did she ever cut you?" she asked.

"When she could catch me."

"Mine, too, with the buckle," Felicity breathed.

"You can't let yourself stay in a bad situation now," Eben said. He put his arm around her and Felicity didn't know whether to cry or to smile. "You have too much going for you. You deserve to be happy. Don't keep thinking you're the little girl who somehow deserves to be punished, or the victim of the bully who ruled over you when you were little. You're a grown woman now, as old as she was when she hurt you, and you can take your own destiny in your hands."

"Thank you for saying that," Felicity said. "I wish I had the courage."

"Your friends will help you," he said.

You help me, Felicity thought, so strongly she almost spoke the thought aloud. *You* be my friend.

"Why are you talking about the past?" Eve snapped at them. "The past is long ago. Latch on to your power like I do and you can do anything. People who sit around and complain are weak and self-indulgent."

"You think that because you don't see the gray areas," Eben said to Eve.

"What do you mean?" Now she was really angry. "I do so."

"You see everything in black and white," he said. "It's good or it's bad, you like or you hate, you're right and they're wrong."

"How would you know that?" Eve shot at him.

"We've had many conversations, you and I."

"You do see things that way, Eve," Felicity said thoughtfully. "He's right."

Eve's eyes bulged and her lips compressed into a little red line. She's going to have a stroke right here at the table, Felicity thought in amazement. Why is she so angry? And even while she was thinking it there was a perverse pleasure in telling Eve what she really thought of her, with this gentle man who knew Eve, too, protecting her, the way her father should have protected her against her mother. Felicity felt a little shiver of pleasure in the face of Eve's enormous and harmless rage.

"Do you think you know me?" Eve demanded, glaring at Eben. "You haven't the faintest idea what I'm about."

"I think I do," he said.

The waiter had brought their food, but only Gara and Kathryn ate. Eve, who was usually ravenous, was too angry, and Felicity and Eben had been too busy talking to each other.

"Well, you don't," Eve said.

"I'm going up the street and have a drink at a new piano bar that just opened," Kathryn said. She put down her credit card and gestured to the waiter. "Does anyone want to come or do I go by myself?"

"I have to get up early tomorrow morning to work," Gara said.

"Oh, you never want to go anywhere," Kathryn said to her.

"That's almost true," Gara said, and smiled.

"Then I'll go by myself," Kathryn said cheerfully. "Maybe I'll meet my next husband."

Gara and Kathryn paid their checks and left. Felicity and Eve and Eben kept sitting there, finishing the wine, then finishing the mineral water, then ordering after-dinner drinks, which none of the four women had ever done there before. Felicity realized that Eve didn't want to leave her alone with Eben because he had once been Eve's lover, and perhaps might be again; and that Eben didn't want to go anywhere with Eve but that he didn't want to leave either. As for herself, she didn't have to run home to Russell tonight, and sitting here next to this attractive and sensual man who understood her she was having such a good time she didn't want the evening to end. In spite of Eve's bad mood....

"Well, I'm leaving," Eve said, finally. She got up. All of them were a little drunk.

"I should go, too," Eben said. "May I put you both into cabs?"

The three of them left together. They stood on the sidewalk in the pleasant night, watching as two rattletrap cabs jockeyed for position to get them as passengers. Eben held open the door of the first one for Eve. It clanged rustily off into the night as he opened the door of the second one for Felicity.

"Come and have a drink with me," he said. She nodded, and he got in with her and gave the driver the address of an apartment house Felicity knew must be his. *What am I doing?* she thought. But she didn't care; she felt dangerously alive.

He lived in one of those clean and nondescript high rises that had been put up in the 1960s, on a side street on the East Side. There was a doorman, and an elevator that was self-service at this late hour. When he opened the door to his apartment it was unexpectedly large, with picture windows, the blinds pulled up to the frame, facing a little village of other people's apartments, their blinds pulled up, too, except in the bedrooms where they were asleep. In a city so crowded and with such lack of privacy people began to think themselves invisible. Felicity saw the blue glow of television sets, everybody watching the same nightly news.

Eben put on music. He offered her some wine. Felicity turned off her cell phone. He showed her around the apartment: his bedroom, the guest room for his daughter when she came to visit, his office where he wrote.

"I feel guilty about Eve," Felicity ventured. "I mean..."

He took her hand and the shock went right down her body. "There was nothing between Eve and me," Eben said. "She would call me to get together once in a while, so I'd say okay. It was nothing. She knew that."

"I knew that, too," Felicity said. "I just wanted to hear you say it."

"I just did."

He led her back to the living room and they sat next to each other on the living room couch and told each other everything that had happened to them since they were born. She was aware that this shared grief was a kind of seduction, but she was still so new at it that she found it touching and beautiful. It was finally past one o'clock in the morning, but she wasn't tired and she wasn't worried that Russell had probably called her several times. Russell was dangerous and frightening, but she would tell him that she had been exhausted and had gone to bed early, right after dinner at Yellowbird, and he would believe her. She felt charmed tonight. She was not worried about work tomorrow either, because she felt as if she might never need sleep again. The music played on, intoxicating and new, evocative of no other moment but this.

Then finally, as if on some joyous impulse, Eben swept her into his arms to dance, and at that moment Felicity felt he had swept her away to a wilder place from which she might never return. A moment later they were kissing, his mouth soft and generous, and then they were undressing each other. They didn't even bother to go into the bedroom the first time they had sex; he simply pulled down the blind and they did it on the living room rug. He did everything Russell had not wanted to do to her, and she did everything that she had not wanted to do to Russell, and they both screamed with pleasure when they came.

"Oh God, help me, Eben, help me," she begged at that moment when she didn't know what she was saying, "Please help me leave my husband."

The next time they did it in his bed, and slept, and then again. She had never known a man who was so lusty. When, in the early morning, she finally had to leave, to bathe and change for the office, Eben stopped her at the door and entered her a fourth time, standing.

"Leave your husband," he whispered into her hair. "Live with me."

In the sanity of morning sunlight she laughed because it sounded like love play, but she was also flattered, and a part of her believed him. She had found a man who was her sexual equivalent, and who was romantic and kind, and when she left Eben Mars, Felicity was stunned and already in love.

When she turned on her cell phone again there were four

voice mail messages. Two were from her husband, and two were from Jason, who knew Russell was out of town and had wanted to see her. It was as if she had forgotten Jason. She didn't even want to see him right now. As for Russell, she wished he would disappear. There were also four messages at home; two from Russell, the last one wishing her a good night, and two from Eve.

"Where are you?" Eve's voice demanded. After Eben had reassured her she had forgotten Eve, too. Eve probably wanted to dish. She would have to be careful about Eve, and for the first time Felicity was a little nervous.

Eben called her at the office as soon as she got there. "You are the sexiest woman I have ever known," he said softly. "I wish I were with you right now."

"And you are the sexiest man and I wish the same," Felicity answered back.

"Come by on the way from work," he said. "Please. Please."

"I don't know if I can..."

"When will he be back?"

"This evening," Felicity said.

"Then come to me before. I need you. Just for an hour and I'll let you go. Please..."

She was getting wet thinking about it, hearing his voice. "All right," she said.

"I want to take you to dinner," Eben said. "I want to show you off. I want you to walk in my potato fields with me and afterward I'll write a whole book of poems for you and make love to you forty-five times. A hundred and forty-five times. I want you to leave him. I'm going to make you leave him."

"I wish you would," Felicity said.

"I think I'm falling in love with you," Eben said. "I want to take care of you. I want to make you happy."

"You already are," Felicity said.

THIRTY-SIX

Eve undressed for bed, throwing her clothes on the floor. She had noticed Eben's attraction to Felicity all evening, and what was more insulting, Felicity was encouraging it. Felicity was such a basket case with that husband and lover that she had to cry on everybody's shoulder. She should know that Eben was not what she thought, not a man to rely on to change her life, that he was just a smart man who was a good fuck and furthermore, he belonged to Eve.

Felicity should be home by now. Eve called her, but all she got was the voice mail. Probably Felicity was in the bathroom, so after a while Eve called again. Again no answer. Now what? Was she asleep already? Eve looked at the clock on her bedside table, and a half hour later she called again and hung up before the voice mail clicked through. Then she called a fourth time and hung up again. She thought of calling Eben, but if he didn't answer she would have to hang up on him, too, and if he did answer and said he was alone it could easily be a lie. Also, calling to check up on him would make her look as if she were chasing him, and it was important that he knew she was just as strong as he was.

She was so suspicious and restless that there was no question of even trying to go to sleep. Eve got up and dressed again, in jeans and a sweatshirt, and then she went downstairs and hailed a cab. She got out on Eben's corner and walked. There was nobody on the streets tonight; it was a weeknight, and people were at home, asleep, preparing their brains and bodies for the next day at work. She knew exactly which windows were Eben's apartment because she had been there several times, and when she looked up she saw that they were all still lighted and the blinds were up. From across the street she could see everything. She just wanted to know if he was home and what he was doing.

What he was doing was dancing with Felicity. Eve couldn't believe it. He whirled her in his arms like Fred Astaire, and then they kissed. But instead of an old movie fade-out, what Eve saw standing there was Eben kissing Felicity with every appearance of the beginning of foreplay, and then rushing to the window and pulling down the blinds in one forceful snap.

Eve knew the bastard was fucking her friend. And her friend, her *married* friend, with a lover of her own, was fucking Eve's property. No matter what any of them said, it wasn't over until Eve decided it was over. She stood there for a while longer, but it was creepy on the deserted street, and Eve knew from past experience that Eben liked to have sex several times in a night, so they could be at it for hours. She walked, fists clenched, face grimacing in fury, until she found a cruising cab, and then she went home.

She didn't fall asleep until it was nearly light, and then she overslept. She had wanted to see what time Felicity came in to work. But by the time she woke up and called Felicity's office she was in a meeting. Eve left a message, and then called twice more before she got her.

"Don't you believe in calling back?" Eve said instead of hello.

"I'm sorry," Felicity said. She sounded even sweeter than usual. "It's been crazy here today. I just got your messages."

"So you spent the night with Eben," she said harshly.

There was the briefest pause. "What are you talking about?"

"I called you and you weren't home, and then I went by his apartment and I saw you both in there, kissing. Don't deny it, I know it was you."

"I wasn't there," Felicity said. She sounded scared. "It was probably someone else. You told me you think he has lots of women."

"None who look like you."

"How do you know?"

"Don't bullshit me," Eve said. "I want you to meet me for lunch."

"I can't."

"Yes you can. You'd better meet me. I can make a lot of trouble for you. Meet me in the coffee shop near your office, the one on Madison Avenue with the turkey sandwiches. One o'clock."

"I have a meeting at two," Felicity said.

"What I have to say to you won't take a whole hour," Eve said.

They met in the Viand coffee shop, a crowded, narrow little room, and sat in a red vinyl booth facing each other. Eve ordered the warm sliced turkey sandwich she liked and Felicity ordered a Greek salad which she actually seemed calm enough to pretend to eat. The eating was a kind of social fencing. Eve was too angry to be hungry, and she knew Felicity was much too nervous.

"What's the matter, Felicity, aren't two men enough for you?" Eve began.

"You know I'm afraid of my husband," Felicity said. "I would never, never go to any man's apartment when he's out of town. My husband calls me all the time to check on me, and he's violent. He'd be capable of coming home unexpectedly just to see if I was there. He would kill me if he thought I had another man. He would."

"And you know I've been seeing Eben," Eve said. "I have rules. The most insulting thing in the world, the thing I consider unforgivable and totally out of line, is to have one of my woman friends go out with a man I've been intimate with."

"Intimate?"

"Yes."

"I wouldn't call what you and Eben had intimacy. You fucked him. From time to time."

"And he's one of my toys in my playpen," Eve said. "As long as I want him there for that reason he's mine, and no other woman has a right to go near him. Ever. Even when I'm finished with him, he's still off limits."

"Even then?"

"Yes."

"I'd better tell every man who plans to go out with you

then," Felicity said lightly. "If he has sex with you his dating life is forever over."

"I'm telling you to stay away from him. You're my friend. You're not allowed."

"I'm not seeing him," Felicity said. "This was a total misunderstanding on your part. You're my friend, too. I care about you. I wouldn't do such a hurtful thing. I completely understand."

"I hope so," Eve said. "I can tell your husband, you know. I can also tell him about your lover. *Jason*...I don't know his last name, but the first name's enough." She watched Felicity pouring artificial sweetener into her iced tea and noticed that her hand was steady. Could it be possible that wasn't Felicity in Eben's apartment in the first place? The lights had been pretty dim and she was far away. "I'll be watching you," Eve said.

"Watch as much as you like." Felicity sipped her tea. "We've signed a few new producers and playwrights at the firm recently," she said with a friendly smile. "I always have my eye out for someone to introduce you to who could help you with your career."

"You do?" Eve said, surprised and pleased. "When can you do that?"

"Soon. I'm looking."

"Oh," Eve said. "Well, I'd appreciate that. I always need contacts."

"And which of your girlfriends has the most?" Felicity asked. "I do!" She was beginning to sound so enthusiastic that Eve was swept away, too. They smiled at each other.

"I can help you," Felicity said.

"That's great," Eve said. She would pretend to drop the Eben Mars issue for the moment. Felicity would think she had won and Eve would get what she wanted more than anything in life: a boost for her career. She never wanted to have to choose between sex and success, one shouldn't have to, they were separate things, but once in a while one had to back down a little bit and keep the emotions in the wings. This didn't mean she wouldn't keep her eye out to see what Felicity and Eben were up to. Eben was still her toy, and she didn't want anyone to make a fool of her. She didn't get a hard young prick like that very often, especially these days, when all the men she met seemed to be scared to death.

That evening Eve walked past Eben's apartment building and looked up to see that he had pulled down all his blinds. It would have looked as if he had gone away, except that she could see light behind them. So Felicity had told him, and now he was being careful to protect his privacy. Eve wondered what kind of discussion they had had. She took a cab to Felicity's street and walked past the townhouse she shared with her husband. Lights were on there, too, and on the second floor she could see a middle-aged black man watching baseball on an enormous television screen. She had never seen Russell Naylor, but Eve was sure it was him. She waited a while until she saw Felicity crossing a different room, dressed in a robe and carrying a box that looked as if it had a manuscript in it. So they were in for the evening. If she didn't know better, Eve would have thought it was a nice domestic scene.

She went back to Eben's building, which was on her way home. There was a pay phone on the corner, and Eve called him. "I'm bored," she said when he answered. "Why don't I come over and you give me a drink?"

"I'm getting ready to drive back to the old farm," he said. "Rain check?"

"Sure." She thought for a moment. "Are you taking someone, or would you like to take me?"

"You?"

"Why not? I'll come back tomorrow on the jitney."

"I have to be alone," Eben said. "I'm working on a new poem."

"To Felicity?" she asked mockingly.

"She's a lovely woman, but no."

"Well," she said. The operator's voice came on asking for more money. Eve hoped he had no idea where she was.

"Goodbye," Eben said, and hung up.

Eve stood there for a while, annoyed at being rejected, even though it wasn't the first time he had turned her down. She saw his lights go out, finally, and she waited to see his car nose out of the garage in his building, but it never did. Nor did he come walking out of his front door. He was in for the evening, too, and he had lied to her. She was sure he was with another woman. Eben liked to be alone, but he also had one woman or another around all the time. Wait till she told Felicity. She hoped Felicity wasn't stupid enough to have fallen in love with him.

On the other hand, she hoped Felicity had. It would serve her right. From what Eve knew of Eben Mars, the only person he was in love with was himself. Eve started to walk home, and on the way she had another thought which was quite disturbing. What if Eben was staying in town because he wanted to see Felicity tomorrow? What if they had started on a real affair?

If he had been with a woman tonight he would have told me, Eve thought; Eben doesn't care about my feelings. He knows I don't love him. In fact he likes to tell me about his other women, just to be sure I keep my distance, he's so neurotic. It can't be that he's *saving* himself for Felicity? Eve felt a twinge of pain, and the anger started up again, making it hard for her to breathe.

It would never work for them, of course, Eve thought. Eben Mars would never marry a black woman. For all his antics and pretenses of being an artist, deep down he was much too conventional. Of course I'll tell her, Eve thought. I'll call her tomorrow morning at the office. That's the least I can do.

She was joined to them now, to Eben and Felicity, to whatever they were doing and about to do, until it played itself out. Felicity thought the triangle she was in was with Eben and her husband, but she was wrong. The triangle was with Eben and Eve.

THIRTY-SEVEN

Suddenly Felicity realized that Eve had become her unwelcome and unexpected appendage. Ever since that night with Eben, Eve had started calling her at the office every morning as soon as she got in, and Felicity dreaded it. There was always the interrogation about whether she had seen him or heard from him, and Felicity's denials, and Eve's unasked-for comments about Eben's risky character, a man who would not settle down, especially not with her, a woman he could not take home to his mother. (Felicity knew more about Eben's mother than Eve did: a woman who came after her son with a knife. Why would he care what she thought now that he was away from her?) Then came the repeated questions about the state of Felicity's marriage, and whether she had seen her lover. Felicity didn't ask how Eve had found out Jason's name; Eve could find out a great deal when she put her mind to it, and she obviously had. Felicity got off the phone as fast as she could, and then she told her secretary that if there were any more calls from Eve, she could not be disturbed.

She had been sneaking off to see Eben every day, and he called her constantly on her cell phone, talking about their grotesque childhoods, trying to search out the roots of their subsequent problems, sometimes reading his poems to her, always telling her he loved her. Felicity had never had such passionate sex in her life. The man was insatiable, and so was she now, addicted to him and her multiple orgasms, a woman who had been starving for affection and finally was more than filled. She was not bulimic anymore, food didn't matter, she was floating. But also Eben was romantic, he was kind, he was loving. He had held her all night, even in his sleep, that night they were together, and she wondered if it was this tenderness she needed more than the spectacular sex, if the protection and reassurance of his arms around her, her head on his shoulder, was what drew her to him the most. He was the closest thing she had ever had to a best friend, and compared to Eben, Russell seemed more domineering and harshly critical than ever and Jason seemed selfish and stingy with both his time and his feelings.

Jason had reappeared, of course, not knowing that everything had changed, and Felicity was avoiding him, which of course made him want her more. The attraction she'd felt for him, the obsession, had vanished like a puff of smoke. All those years when she had believed he was saving her marriage were over. Now she did not want her marriage to be saved.

Eben kept begging her to come to stay with him for a while in his house in the Hamptons, to take her vacation early, to be his. She called Gara, who she knew had a house there.

"I need to get away for two weeks. I'm going to take my vacation early. I want to stay with Eben, but of course Russell mustn't know, so could I say I'm staying at your house at the beach?"

There was a brief pause. "Do you think that's wise?" Gara asked.

"If you don't want me to, I'll understand..."

"No, it's not that. What if he finds out?"

"He won't," Felicity said. "I'm going to leave him anyway. This is the first time in my life I've been really happy."

"You should leave some things at my house in case Russell decides to surprise you."

"I will, but he won't," Felicity said. "He doesn't know how to find your house. He won't even ask. I know him. Russell is too macho to make a fool of himself."

"I hope you're right," Gara said.

Felicity arranged her vacation time with her office, explaining it was an emergency of a personal nature, and then she told Russell. "I'm going away for two weeks," she said. "By myself. I want some time alone to think about our marriage. I've been miserable for a long time."

He looked astonished—no, horrified—and unexpectedly

vulnerable and in pain. "I didn't know you were that miserable," he said.

"I'm going to Gara's house in Amagansett," Felicity went on. "I need to be peaceful and away."

"And what exactly are you going to think about while you're there thinking about our marriage?"

"Whether I can go on like this anymore," Felicity said.

"You act like I was a monster," Russell said. His voice was boyish and wounded, the sort of tone that would engender guilt, but she was beyond that now. He had hurt her too long and too often.

"You were."

"What did I do?"

She sighed. "I can't discuss it now. I'm burned out and tired." She knew he could see her resolve and he wouldn't try to hold her back.

"You'll give me your phone number, I hope," he said.

"Yes."

"And you're taking your cell phone?"

"Yes. But don't call me on it all day long the way you do. Otherwise it will be as if I never went away at all."

"I won't bother you," Russell said. "I called you only because I wanted to know you were safe. I still have to do that. I worry about you. It's dangerous out there in the world. I worry that you'll get mugged, that you'll be in an accident.... Baby, I hope you can solve this problem, whatever it is. I didn't even know there was a problem. You should have told me, but I know you, you keep things to yourself. I love you and I don't want to lose you."

How sad his eyes were, how bewildered. Why had he never been this human before? She supposed she had to leave him to make him into a good husband, but she didn't want him anymore, good or bad, she only wanted to be free so she could start her new life.

"I know," Felicity said. When she hugged him goodbye they both had tears in their eyes.

She knew now that sadness would be part of it, too, the tearing apart of two people who had become family, but as soon as she was in her rented car driving east on the Montauk Highway, she was happy again. Eben was in his own car, next to her, he on his car phone and she on her cell phone, and they looked at each other at high speeds and smiled and talked all the way. Outside their windows was the blue, blue spring sky, and the brown fields, the hidden seeds waiting to sprout into summer abundance. Soon there would be tomatoes and corn and sunflowers, and later his potatoes. The trees had green leaves now, again, and their future together seemed as fresh as nature.

"I love you," Eben said on his phone.

"I love you more," Felicity answered.

In his large brown farmhouse, they had sex the moment they walked in the door, and afterward he made lunch for her and they talked, and then they had sex again. They slept, and drove to the beach, where they made each other come wildly in the deserted dunes. The water was still too cold to swim, so they went back to his house where they took a shower together and had sex, and then she made dinner for him, and they talked more, about everything, and then they went to bed. She thought there must be something wrong with him, a man who had an almost constant erection—that he was a love addict, or a satyr—but she wasn't complaining. All night he would wake up, put it in, go to sleep, wake up, put it in, as a kind of reflex, as if he were doing it in his sleep, or in his dreams...or in hers.

Every day and every night were the same.

Sometimes they went to the movies, arriving separately and sitting in separate seats in case anyone knew him. Russell called once every day, at Gara's, where Felicity called in to retrieve the messages, and then she called him back with one excuse or another for her absence. Whenever they spoke he sounded beaten, tentative, melancholy. He never called her on her cell phone; she understood that had been their connection to each other when he had thought they were happy, and now it had too many memories. Felicity didn't know how she felt about him, and she didn't want to think about it. She knew now that very soon she would leave him.

"This will be our bedroom," Eben said. "And this room I'll make into a private gym so you can work out. Would you like that?"

"Oh, yes," Felicity said.

"This is my office, and this will be your office. We'll come here every weekend. During the week we'll live in my apartment."

I'd like to redecorate that apartment, she thought, but she didn't say so. It needed more life and color. She knew that by this time next year she would be married to him.

She went to Gara's house once, just in case Russell wanted her to describe it to him. It was a sweet little house, and Felicity knew why Gara found it and the ocean it overlooked so restorative. While she was there, her cell phone rang. It was Jason. She winced.

"Why haven't you returned any of my E-mail messages?" he said.

"I'm away. On vacation."

"With Russell?" He sounded panicked, thinking he had done something stupid by calling. "I didn't know."

"With a girlfriend," Felicity said. She didn't want Jason to know about Eben until she had left Russell and it was all acceptable. Maybe she would never tell him. She had not thought about Jason or wondered what he thought for several weeks. "But you shouldn't call anyway. I'll leave you a message when I get back."

He understood it was risky and he was glad to back off. She knew he would never leave his wife, and she also knew that if he did she wouldn't want him.

"Oh, I don't want this vacation to be over," Felicity sighed to Eben.

"Neither do I, but it won't be. We'll have more. I'll take you to the Caribbean in the winter. We'll lie on the beach."

Just before they left to go back to the city Eben cut an armful of flowers for her from his garden, and then he got his camera. He took a photograph of Felicity standing on the lawn with the flowers in her arms, and called her "my faun."

"My satyr," she said, laughing, and then he let her take a picture of him.

Felicity wrapped the flowers in wet newspaper, but by the time she got back to the city they were dead. She felt sad, and missed him already. She pulled off one to press in her wallet as a remembrance, and left the rest in the car. Russell was waiting for her in their living room. She wondered why she had never noticed before how really old he looked. She knew she couldn't spend the night in his bed, that their marriage was over, and that she had to tell him tonight.

He offered her champagne, as if her homecoming were a celebration. She took some for courage. "How was your trip?" he asked.

"I thought about a lot of things. I made some decisions."

"And?"

"Russell, I want a divorce."

He looked as if she had hit him. She had tried to leave him before, but he had known she would come back. Now he knew she wouldn't, because she knew it.

"Don't," he said. "Oh, don't. I'll make it better. Let's try to work it out." He was actually in tears, this tough man, this old street fighter, the husband she had always feared; he was crumbling and she looked away so she would not have to watch him being in such pain, because it pained her, too.

"We'll have to go to a marriage counselor in any event, a few times," Felicity said evenly, "in order to get the divorce more easily. I want a separation right now, so tomorrow we both need to get lawyers. Unless you want us to go to a mediator, which will expedite things. A divorce will take a separation of a year, but if we get a mediator they can run it through the courts in a few months. I'm going to sleep in the den tonight, and tomorrow I'll pack my clothes and get a hotel room. Then I'm getting my own apartment."

"A marriage counselor?" he said hopefully. He had always adamantly refused to go, but now he sounded as if a marriage counselor would somehow save them. No one can save us, Felicity thought, but it will mollify him and I need someone on my side. She wondered if Russell had heard anything else she had said.

"Yes," she said. "I'll try to get an appointment as soon as possible."

There was nothing else to say. She couldn't look at his yearning eyes and told herself he was only being manipulative. He was a businessman, he worked with unions, with tough negotiators. He knew how to intimidate and back down and threaten and promise and close a deal. She knew what he did, and now she was going to try to emulate it. You can make the deal you want, Russell had told her once, only if you're willing to walk away.

She didn't even discuss money. That was how much she wanted to leave him. Besides, the lawyers or the mediator would do that. This was not the time to push Russell into a fight.

She slept in the den, the next morning she got a hotel room, and now she and Eben were free to see each other as much as they liked. Felicity was virtually living in his apartment, and on weekends she went to his house in the potato fields, where they continued their interrupted vacation. One weekend he had his blonde, green-eyed, eight-year-old daughter, Ondine, there, and the three of them watched Disney videos and ate takeout pizza. Felicity loved his daughter with all the frustrated motherly instincts she had been forced to hold back because of Russell's intransigence, and when Ondine asked her to tuck her in she knew the little girl liked her, too. She couldn't wait to have the child share their life more often, and she wanted more....

"How would you like to have a little mulatto baby?" Felicity asked Eben one night, when they were having sex.

"I'd love it," he said.

How happy she was. After all these years, she deserved it.

"So you left your husband," Eve said on the phone.

"Yes. Finally."

"I guess you think it's going to last with Eben," she said in a nasty tone that meant *You are an idiot if you do*.

"Eben and I are friends," Felicity said. "He's been very helpful to me during this difficult period. He went through a divorce himself."

"He'll never marry you. The word is out that you were cheating on Russell with him. There's gossip. I bet Russell won't give you any money. By the way, what have you done about Jason?"

"If there's gossip I'm sure you're the one who spread it," Felicity said.

"*Me?*"

"I have to go now," Felicity said.

"I *hate* that woman," she said to Gara on the phone. "I hate her, I hate her."

"You don't have to take her calls if they upset you," Gara said.

"Yes I do. She could make trouble."

Now she had to deal with Jason, finally. There was no question of letting him touch her now that she was in love with Eben. She almost recoiled at the thought. Felicity agreed to meet Jason at their lunchtime apartment. She had already told him she had left Russell, and when she got there he knew right away that another bad thing was going to happen.

"Jason, we have to stop seeing each other," she said.

"Why?"

"Because we're not on the same turf anymore. I've left my husband and you're still with your wife."

"You know I can't leave my wife."

"I don't want you to. I'm leaving you. I hope we can always be friends, and of course we'll continue to work together whenever you need me, unless you don't want to."

"How did my little love slave get so cold?"

"I want another life without either of you. I felt guilty and bad and dirty. Now I feel good about myself."

"I knew you would leave me if you ever left him," Jason said sadly.

Felicity let him kiss her goodbye and hug her, and she felt sad, too, but not really. Then she left the apartment and went back to the office.

The next day Jason sent her flowers and a note at work. He had never sent her flowers or written to her in all the years they had been seeing each other. *I'll always care,* the note said. *Love, Mr. Master.*

Master, Felicity thought. Ugh. Who was I then, what kind of fool? But she did like the flowers, and she knew she loved Jason in a way, and always would, as an old friend who had been so important in her life during the time she had needed him. After so long of course she was fond of him, but if she never saw him again she wouldn't mind at all.

The marriage counselor had done no good, and now the divorce mediation was proceeding. Felicity felt uneasy continuing to waste so much money on a hotel, so she went out with a broker to look for an apartment to rent. She had been living with Russell for so long in their townhouse, which they owned, that she hadn't realized how expensive rent in New York City had become, and everything she could afford on her salary seemed small and claustrophobic. Finally she found a cozy little one-bedroom apartment on the East Side, near Eben's, for more than she felt she should really spend, but it was on a one-year lease, which she knew was all she would need. She was able to rationalize the unexpected expense by reminding herself that she had left a millionaire and his luxurious lifestyle, and their beautiful townhouse that she had decorated and that she sometimes missed very much, and she deserved to live in a decent apartment, in a decent neighborhood, to make up for what she had lost.

Russell, of course, would not give her a penny at this point, until the court made him do it, and he had not let her take any of the furniture, not even things she had paid for herself. She sneaked away half the dishes and half the silver when she was taking her clothes.

"You abandoned me," he told her. "Don't think you have any chance of getting the house."

"I don't want the house. I want money for my share of it."

"You want what?"

"After all these years of marriage..."

"I paid for the house. Your share is zilch. You should have waited for me to die, Baby, till death do us part, and then you would have had it all."

Only the good die young, she thought, but she didn't say anything because she couldn't afford to antagonize him at this stage in their negotiations.

Eben called her four times a day, advising, consoling, encouraging, monitoring her progress, offering friendship and love. It made her feel safe to have him so close to her and on her side.

"My husband has turned into the angry businessman now," Felicity told him. "He's talking tough, and no one does it better than Russell does."

"Husbands on the verge of a divorce always try to starve their soon-to-be-ex-wives out," Eben said. "He'll have to give you something eventually. Don't give up and don't let him cheat you of what you deserve."

"I just want to be free of him," Felicity said. "I've wasted so many years of my life."

"I want you to be free, too, but I want you to stand up to him. I care about you."

"I know."

She did not tell him that she didn't care about her house anymore because he had offered her his.

Eben came to see her new apartment when her bed arrived, and brought food and wine, and they had sex for the first time in her own place, and while she was glad he was there it also seemed strange. She had thought she would like to be independent to do what she wanted, but it was oddly like a date, and when he left in the morning she felt hollow. When he invited her to come to his apartment the next night, the way she always did, Felicity was somehow relieved. She had made her little apartment look very sweet, with her own imprimatur, but she didn't feel comfortable there yet, and she wondered if she ever would, because it was only an interim refuge. She felt comfortable at Eben's, in his apartment in the city and his house in the country. She felt comfortable with him, not with herself.

THIRTY-EIGHT

When Gara was being seated at their table at Yellowbird she saw Kathryn walking over from the bar to join her, with her glass in her hand. Kathryn had recently switched from wine to vodka on the rocks, because she had heard that vodka was less fattening, something about the sugar content, and because after quite a few she had less of a hangover. Tonight Gara could see that she had already had quite a few. It was interesting about Kathryn; she drank more than any of the other women in their group but insisted she hardly drank at all and said she got drunk on one drink, when of course the others could count and sometimes did. She said she worried about drinking because her father had been an alcoholic, and that was why she claimed to be very careful.

Gara certainly couldn't blame her if she wanted to anesthetize herself. The strenuous daily workout with her trainer followed by the daily aerobics class, the hours of tennis, the energetic walking, vigorous sports all day brought up her endorphins, and the alcohol did whatever it did afterward. She knew Kathryn was carrying grief from her past—Kathryn had told her bits and pieces in a totally matter-of-fact way—but Kathryn always insisted the past didn't matter and you couldn't dwell on it or ever feel sorry for yourself. But it was Gara's nature, and her profession, to wonder about Kathryn, how she had so much strength to deal with what had been a brutal childhood, and to enjoy life so much. Sometimes she wondered if Kathryn was really so happy, or if she had locked herself off emotionally since earliest childhood just to survive. She wondered about Kathryn's doomed marriages to the wrong men. Kathryn said they had just happened. But Gara knew nothing "just happened." There was something tough about Kathryn, but whether it was the nature of a survivor or the bravado of a woman in deep pain was a question Gara often asked herself. One day soon she was going to try to find out more.

"Well, we're the first, as usual," Kathryn said cheerfully. Her skin and hair were glowing, and she was wearing her new thin white wool Chanel suit, which was the suit of the year that spring, and hers was the original.

"How beautiful and elegant you look," Gara said.

"Thank you. You should buy one. It would look good on you."

Gara smiled. "I forgot to buy anything new this spring and now I probably won't bother."

"If you're not nice to yourself, who will be?" Kathryn said.

"That's true," Gara said. "Maybe I will. The copy."

"Not the copy! You're not a copy. So where is the rest of our group?"

"Well, Eve left a message she has a business dinner and won't be coming, and you know Felicity, we're lucky to get a glimpse of her these days, but she promised to come and she'll probably bring Eben." Since her separation from Russell Felicity was able to do whatever she wanted, but she was still careful when she and Eben were in public together, never went out with him alone, and usually stayed home with him, because she didn't want to exacerbate the situation while she was negotiating her divorce.

"What do you think is going to happen with those two?" Kathryn asked.

"I don't know," Gara said. "I've always had my reservations about this relationship because it happened so quickly and conveniently, but I want it to succeed so much that I also sort of believe in it. It would be so good to see Felicity settled and happy. She would be one of the fortunate ones who was able to change her life after she thought she never could. Eve is still upset, by the way."

"Eve?" Kathryn sipped her drink. "He never liked Eve. She should give up and find someone else. It wouldn't be hard for her, she's so pretty."

"You think Eve is pretty?" Gara said. That was a strange

and mild description of Eve that would better suit anyone else.

"Don't you?"

"Well, dramatic-looking, interesting, attractive, but hardly pretty. She's much too angry for that."

"I don't look at people's inner lives the way you do," Kathryn said. She held up her empty glass to the waiter. "Give me another vodka. The good kind, from Russia, made from potatoes. I always forget the name."

That's not the only thing she's forgotten, Gara thought. She ordered a glass of white wine.

Billie Holiday was singing scratchily on the sound system, her voice full of such pathos it made Gara nostalgic for things she didn't even know about. Billie Redmond came over to their table, eagle eyed, to make sure she wasn't wasting a table for four on only two. She was looking sexy in tight jeans and cowboy boots and a lace shirt, and a belt with a huge silver serpent on the buckle.

"Are the others coming?" she asked, by way of hello.

"Absolutely," Kathryn said.

"I was just wondering, Billie, were you named after Billie Holiday?" Gara asked.

"I don't know. Nobody ever mentioned it."

"How is Little Billie doing?" Kathryn asked. "It still feels strange here in Yellowbird without him."

"For me, too. But he's annoyingly happy in his new life as an ordinary kid. Not that he'll ever be ordinary. He's much too smart."

"Little Billie is a very special little boy," Gara said. "I miss him." But she was glad he was out of there.

"He doesn't miss us at all," Billie said. "Kids break your heart, but they don't know it, and we can't tell them, because they're supposed to break your heart. He's also my greatest joy. Try the okra. It's new." She moved on.

"Tell me more about your life growing up," Gara said to Kathryn.

Kathryn shrugged. "I don't remember much. It's like I wasn't there, but I know it was happening to me. There are big gaps. I don't want to remember, to tell you the truth. The murder, well, there were so many accounts in the papers that weren't the way it was, and then I just blocked things out of my mind, I guess, so sometimes I wondered which was right, my memory or the newspapers. My mother wouldn't talk about it for years. And you know, I was married, I was very young, I had two babies, I was overworked, so I feel as if I missed most of it."

"What about your childhood, before that?"

"Well, I was away most of the time. I was in boarding school. I remember the teachers. I respected them and liked them. I really don't remember my childhood, except I know it was full of fear because my father was so violent and abusive."

"You mean, before you went away...?"

"Yes. Before. And during and after. I know I came home for vacations from boarding school to spend time with my family in that madhouse we lived in, but I just don't recall. I had fun with my friends, I remember that."

"Do you know why your mother sent you away? Was it to rescue you?"

Kathryn shrugged and took another swallow of her drink. "I suppose so. My father finally slugged me. I guess he was changing the way he thought about me."

"And...?"

"Then it would have been dangerous."

"So do you think that was why your mother killed him?"

"No," Kathryn said. "It was something to do with the other woman. I don't remember. My mother said shooting him was an accident, so I believe her."

"Do you think he deserved it?" Gara asked mildly.

"Oh sure. I don't like to say anybody deserves to die, but none of us were sorry about it."

"It's interesting."

"It would be for me, too, and I'd like to remember, but I can't."

"Did you ever go for therapy?" Gara asked.

"No, I have no use for shrinks. You're the only shrink I know and put up with, but that's because we're friends and I'm not your patient."

Her tone was light, but there was anger beneath it, and Gara knew it was time to back off, for now. She wondered if

Kathryn was really blocking all these memories as she claimed, or just didn't want to relive them by talking about them. Either was possible, and either would make sense. When Gara was first in practice it had been widely believed that traumas should be unearthed and dealt with, that the pain should be ferreted out and felt again, like a kind of root canal without anesthetic, and then the patient would be free. Now there were theories that said it was unnecessary, that you could simply go on and live your life. Gara believed this was valid, and faster, and less debilitating. It was obviously what Kathryn believed.

"The one thing I regret in my whole life is what happened to my son," Kathryn said. "My last husband betraying him in that way. I'll never get over that, and neither will my son, I'm afraid. The money I got him didn't help him inside. Poor Jim Daniel. Sometimes I know he's lost to me." Surprisingly for Kathryn, who never showed emotion because she considered it weak and boring and embarrassing, her eyes filled with tears.

Gara knew the story. Kathryn had told them all one night. They sometimes reminisced about their lives, even when it hurt. In their friendship, between the laughter they shared, and the banter, always came the revelations.

"I have a picture in my mind of Jim Daniel as a little boy," Kathryn said. She was in control again, the tears forced back. Now she only sounded nostalgic. "With his little cowboy boots about three inches long, and his toy gun, and his cowboy hat sliding down over his eyes, and that bewildered look on his face as if things kept happening to him and he couldn't figure out any of them. And then for that awful thing to happen to him...I feel so responsible, I can't help it, I just do."

"Of course you do," Gara said. "But it wasn't your fault. Just keep remembering that."

Felicity came in then, looking exhausted but happy, her hair loose. In her short, tight black dress Gara couldn't help noticing Felicity had lost a lot of weight, and she had been slim to begin with. She remembered when she had been in love and never needed to eat. "Hi!" Felicity said, grinning, and sat down next to Gara.

"Where's your boyfriend?" Kathryn asked.

"Shh. He's not my boyfriend. He'll be here any minute. Should I order wine by the glass or do we want a bottle?"

"A bottle," Gara said. She told the waiter with a gesture. He knew what kind of wine they liked at the moment and brought it right away.

"Have I got news for you," Felicity said. "My husband has a girlfriend already. In my house, in my bed, her clothes in my closet."

"How do you know?" Kathryn asked.

"He wanted me to come over there to discuss getting back together again. Russell is always trying to get me back because he doesn't want to pay any alimony, but I went over to the house because I missed it and I thought maybe if I tried to be friends with him he'd be less intransigent. Well, I went upstairs to the bedroom and there were some of her clothes where mine used to be. And there was a *blonde hair* in the bed."

"You looked in the bed?" Gara said.

"The bedspread wasn't on. You bet I did. My husband, who is so critical of my friendships with white people, so sanctimonious, has a white girlfriend."

"Maybe it was a blonde weave," Gara said.

"Girl, I know the difference between a hair and a weave." They all laughed. "I was really annoyed and jealous that he's replaced me already," Felicity said.

"But you have a boyfriend."

"That's true."

"And Russell is still trying to get you back."

"That's true, too. I feel sorry for her."

Eben Mars came in, in a T-shirt and jacket and chinos, and pretended surprise to see them. "Well, look who's here," he said.

"Eben!" Felicity said, pretending the same surprise.

"May I sit down?"

"Of course." He sat next to Felicity.

"You promise Eve isn't coming," he said to all of them.

"That's what she said. Unless she drops by later, looking for us," Gara said.

"Oh, no!" Felicity said.

"Did I ever tell you I love your friend Felicity?" Eben stage-whispered to Gara. "That she's a wonderful person and she's changed my life?"

Felicity beamed. "And he's changed mine," she said.

"That's what I'm here for," Eben said. "That's what friends are for, isn't it? Aren't you helping her, too?" He looked from Gara to Kathryn and back to Felicity.

They nodded, because they weren't sure what it was that they were supposed to be doing. Complicity, secrecy, a listening ear, a beach house; yes, that was all part of it. But Eben's use of the word "friend" in reference to himself rang a little warning bell in Gara's mind. People in love were also supposed to be friends, she knew, but somehow it made him seem detached, even altruistic, a man with a mission. Gara didn't know why she felt that way, but she did, and she didn't like it.

THIRTY-NINE

That summer Felicity and Eben were idyllically inseparable, and the greatest pleasure of all for her was when his
daughter had two weeks with him after she came home from
camp, and Felicity could pretend the three of them were a
family. She never tired of playing with the little girl, and
when Ondine cuddled up against her or hugged her, Felicity's heart was full. She didn't know what kind of mother
Ondine had grown up with, but she felt it must have been
difficult for the child to see her father with different women,
some of whom were kind, some not, and to have the kind
ones go away never to return just when she had gotten to
care about them.

She and Eben drove by to say hello to Gara in Amagansett
a few times. Kathryn stayed with Gara for several weekends,
and in between Gara's gay friend Brad was an almost constant fixture. In August Kathryn went to Italy to stay in a big
house she had rented with another well-divorced woman
friend. Eve had two lines in a movie that was being shot in
New York, but the way she talked about it you would think
she was in the whole thing. Actually, it was her daughter,
Nicole, who was in the whole thing; she was one of the two
leads. Billie sent Little Billie to sleep-away camp at his insis-
tence, his first time; and she closed Yellowbird for two weeks
in August and went away somewhere with a man she had
met.

Felicity wished she knew someone to introduce Gara to.
Although Gara had a busy enough social life, and did not
mind being alone when she had to be, it seemed a shame that
she couldn't find love, much less a date, and that she had decided she never would. Gara was such a good person and

had so much to give, and she was so attractive. In her new happiness Felicity wanted everyone else to find a lover, too.

In September Russell gave up and let Felicity have her divorce. Or perhaps she was the one who had given up, because he kept their house, and the money settlement he gave her was unfairly small. But she was a woman with a well-paying career and no children, and she wanted to be free of him, she wanted to marry Eben Mars, so nothing in her marriage to Russell seemed worth fighting for. She wondered if Russell was still with the blonde woman, and if he wanted to marry her. She had always known that if she left him he wouldn't stay single for long; he needed someone to bring his dinner to the television set and worship him like the little woman.

A few days after her divorce had become final the four friends celebrated the significant occasion at Yellowbird. Billie sent over a free bottle of wine. Eben had said it would be better if he didn't come along, since Eve would be there, and that he would meet Felicity later at his apartment.

"To freedom!" they all said, raising their glasses.

"To my new life and to happiness," Felicity said.

"I hope you don't think you'll find it with Eben," Eve said. She tried to look like a concerned friend, but actually she looked bitter and mean.

"Eben who?" Felicity said, and laughed. She could hardly wait for their dinner to be over so she could go to his apartment and feel his arms around her.

"Those of us who didn't find boyfriends this summer are going to find them this fall," Kathryn said cheerfully.

"You said we'd find them last spring," Gara said.

"So I lied. But this is a new season. You'll see."

"I don't even want one," Gara said.

"You will when you meet him."

How lucky I am, Felicity thought, to have my life settled, to be peaceful at last. She excused herself, pleading work from the office, as soon as they finished their main course, because she didn't want Eve to try to share a cab with her. Ever since she had moved to the East Side last year Eve always wanted to share a cab, she never paid, and this time she would certainly be looking to see if Felicity was going to Eben's.

She didn't have a key yet to Eben's apartment, and when

he opened the door, wearing the dark blue bathrobe she had given him, Felicity felt relieved and safe. He looked so handsome in the robe that she could hardly wait for an excuse to buy him more clothes. "How was your dinner?" he asked.

"Fine." She waited for him to say what he usually did: "I haven't hugged you for twenty-four hours," or, "for an hour," whatever it happened to be, keeping track, melting her heart, but he just led the way to his bedroom without a word and they undressed. He seemed a little distant and she didn't understand, but then when they had passionate sex three times the way they always did she felt reassured.

"I was thinking," Felicity said, lying with her arms around him and her head on his shoulder, "We should make our reservations now for Christmas in the Caribbean because all the good places will be full. Russell and I used to make them a year in advance when we went."

"A year!" Eben said. "How could anyone know what he wanted to do a whole year away?"

"A little compulsive," she said, but she didn't mean it, really.

"I don't know if I want to go to the Caribbean," Eben said.

"You talked about it so often I thought you did."

"Well, I changed my mind," he said vaguely, looking off into space as if he was avoiding her eyes.

"Okay. Then where would you rather go?" He didn't answer. She felt an odd jolt of anxiety, and thought perhaps she shouldn't pursue it.

What she wanted to say was, You're acting different and I want to know why; but she had an idea. She knew Eben might be a little nervous now that she was actually single, and that she would have to lead him through these first difficult moments by not putting pressure on him, by being as sweet and winning as she had always been, and let him see she was not going to demand anything he was not ready to offer freely. Before she left in the morning he made breakfast for her, as he often did, and then he made her late for work by insisting on having sex again. She felt better, as if he was his old self again.

When she got to the office Eve called. "So did you meet Eben?"

"Why would you think that?"

"You're single now, you're free, you can do what you want."

"That's exactly right," Felicity said, "and stop bothering me."

That didn't stop Eve; you could hit her with a mallet and she wouldn't notice. "I just want the best for you," Eve said, "because you're my friend."

"Thank you. I need to go to work now." She hung up.

Eben had called six times a day when they were forced to hide and be apart, but today he did not call at all until almost five o'clock. Felicity worried at first that something had happened to him, and then she wondered what had kept him so busy that he could not find time to call her, but he didn't mention it, and she thought she shouldn't ask. "I'm going to drive to the Hamptons in an hour," he said. "I have a meeting. I might as well stay there Friday, too, and then you can come out for the weekend."

"All right," Felicity said.

She would give him space, if that was what he needed. She saw her therapist, who agreed. After all, Eben had not done anything definitive yet to show that he was a man who wanted only what he couldn't have, or that he was afraid of intimacy, or any of the other dreadful possibilities. But the next two days Felicity worried and obsessed, as she had done with Jason, and although her therapist had reminded her that it was her nature to be sure she had been abandoned, and that soon she would have the weekend with him, still she couldn't stop.

She got to his house in the potatoes Friday evening, and she made dinner for them, which they ate on his terrace by candlelight because it was dark early now, and things seemed the same as they had been before her divorce. The sex was as wild as always, and when they slept he held her close. There was a part of him, she knew, that needed her. The body did not tell lies when it was asleep. But then the next day when they were walking on the beach together, the deserted part of the beach where only a few months ago they had joined recklessly in the dunes, he said, "I think I'm going to go to a health spa for two weeks by myself."

She was stunned, paralyzed. "Oh?" she said, while she thought what she should or should not say. By himself! For *two weeks*? The two of them had not been apart since they be-

gan their affair. She looked out over the gray sea and wondered if that was what her life would be like soon, just that
empty, and she knew she would not be able to bear it.

"Mmm," he said.

Maybe it would be good for him to be alone to think, then
he might miss her. Or maybe he wasn't going at all, and was
just saying it, testing her. "That might be nice," she said
mildly, as her fingernails cut into her palms, her hands in the
pockets of her jacket, so he could not see.

Another three weeks went by and Eben's new pattern of
calling her only once a day turned into missing a day altogether. However, he said no more about going away alone,
so Felicity bided her time. But something else was new; by
not communicating he had an excuse not to see her every
night, and then it was not for two nights, and then when she
was at his apartment his phone rang on several different occasions when she could tell that he was talking to women
who were returning his calls.

"Who was that?" she asked finally, when she couldn't dis-
semble anymore.

"We should definitely be going out with other people," he
said.

"Why?" she asked, although she knew why; he was tired
of her, she had failed in some way, or in many ways. Her
whole world was falling apart. Imagining the worst still
hadn't meant it was going to happen, but now it was. Her
heart felt as if his hands had tied it into a deformed knot of
pain, and the pain shot through her whole body and covered
her skin with a sheet of fire. It was the adrenaline, the blood
rush of an animal facing death.

"We've been too intense," Eben said.

"Intense? I thought you loved me," Felicity said.

"I never said I loved you."

"You did! All the time!"

"I never said I loved you, I never brought you flowers.
You must have misunderstood."

She stared at him. Yes, this was Eben, the same Eben who
had made promises and planned their future life together,
who had loved her, and who she still loved just as much as
she had a few moments ago; but now, for him, everything
was different. "What did I misunderstand?"

"Look, you have no claims on me."

"But you said..."

"I offered you friendship," Eben said. "I wanted to help you."

"Help me?"

"Isn't that what you asked me to do, the first time we went to bed together? You asked me to help you leave your husband."

"Oh, God," Felicity whispered.

"So I did."

"Is that what it was?" Her mouth was so dry from panic that she could hardly speak.

"That's it."

"But you loved me. You did..."

"I have always had feelings for you, you're a wonderful person, but I never loved you. I was just caught up in the excitement of your leaving."

I gave up everything for this man, she thought.

"I have to go now," she said. She left his apartment as quickly as she could because she didn't want him to see her cry.

When she got home to her still strange new apartment she called Gara, sobbing, and told her everything that had happened. " 'The excitement of my leaving' meant the thrill of taking me away from my husband," Felicity said. "Why didn't Eben want me? Is it because I'm black?"

"It was a perfect Oedipal situation for him," Gara said. "He was taking his mother away from his father."

"But he hated his mother. She was in a miserable marriage and she took it out on him, just the way my mother did on us."

"And you were in a miserable marriage, too."

"What will I do?" Felicity wept. "I'm so frightened. I'm all alone."

"I know, I know," Gara kept saying soothingly until Felicity got herself under control again. "Think of this," Gara said. "Eben is neurotic, and totally narcissistic, but you should thank him for helping you do what you wanted. You would never have left Russell without him. Eben was your interim person."

"I thought he would be my husband," Felicity said.

"Be thankful he never was. You *will* get over it eventually.

I know it feels like you never will, but I got over Carl and I spent all my adult life with him."

She could not conceive of being happy again. "What did I do wrong?" Felicity said. "What's wrong with me? Why didn't he want me?"

"It's not your fault. It's his nature. If you have a pet snake and you take care of it, and then one day when you're reaching into the cage to feed it, it bites you, it's not your fault. It's because it's a snake. Snakes bite."

"Snakes bite," Felicity repeated dully, hanging on to it. "Eben is a snake. Snakes bite."

"Call your therapist and get some extra sessions," Gara said gently. "You're in extremis, she'll find the time. Work the situation out with her. And above all, don't blame yourself."

But of course she blamed herself; she always did. In the morning, with her eyes red, and dark circles under them from crying and sleeplessness, Felicity went to the office. As usual Eve called first thing.

"Well, did you see Eben last night?" Eve demanded instead of saying hello.

"I have something to tell you," Felicity said. She might as well tell Eve now, let her get her satisfaction, and get rid of her. "I dated Eben for a brief period of time after I officially left my husband, but it's over now. We broke up."

"Ah," Eve said. "Are you very upset?" She was trying to sound concerned, but she could hardly hide her elation. She assumed, correctly, that Eben had done the leaving.

"I'm reasonably upset," Felicity said.

"He'll be back, you know," Eve said. "But he'll never stay long."

"I don't want him." But she did, she wanted him more than anything in the world.

He never called.

She had thought this confession would get Eve off her back, but she was wrong about that, too. Now Eve called every day with a report of what Eben was up to, who he had been seen with, where he had been seen alone, or simply to talk about him, as if the fact that they had both been wounded by him now made them sisters...or perhaps she was really calling just to gloat.

Felicity herself could not bear to be alone. She cajoled

friends to have dinner with her, even ones she didn't much like, so she could be out every night; she went to every function she heard about, even though she was too unhappy to enjoy them; and she went on blind dates where she often had to flee to the ladies' room so they would not see her break into tears. She missed the sex with Eben so much it was like a fever, and she missed the love and the holding, and the promise of happiness she had believed in. Everything he had done had been manipulative, offering her from his life what she was about to give up in her own. He even knew how much she wanted a child and had served up his daughter on a plate. She couldn't get him out of her mind. She called Gara several times a day for comfort, crying, leaving messages on her machine, she broke down at the office behind her closed door, she wept in restaurants, she had turned into a fountain.

"Stop that, will you," Kathryn said impatiently to her one night at Yellowbird. "Get off it. It's over. Go on with your life."

Kathryn could, Felicity thought. I'm not Kathryn.

"No man is worth it," Billie advised her. "Trust me. I know."

"Eben took a woman to the Caribbean," Eve reported at Christmas, and that hurt Felicity more than anything else he had ever done. She should have been with him, that had been her trip. "This one seems serious," Eve added. "I bet he marries her."

"Eve, could you be a little more helpful?" Gara said.

"I am being helpful," Eve said.

"I mean, shut up."

How long did it take to get over such heartbreak? Felicity couldn't eat and she was getting so thin it frightened her. She remembered her mother when her lover had left her: pining, grieving, starving, scary. Again, she had turned into this woman she never wanted to be. When would she ever find her own way?

FORTY

Gara wondered what was happening to their little group of friends. Things seemed different; there were new tensions, new agendas. For a while they still went to Yellowbird every week, but Felicity cried all the time and sometimes simply vanished into herself as if she had become invisible. "The space traveler," Kathryn called her. She might as well not have been there at all.

Kathryn was ever more restless, and said she felt she was wasting her life by always going to the same restaurant, so sometimes now they met elsewhere, trying new places Kathryn had liked or wanted to find out about, and on these occasions they evaded Eve by telling her they weren't going out together because each of them had made other plans. Felicity could not bear to be with Eve, Gara was angry at Eve because she was tormenting Felicity, whom she felt protective of, and Kathryn really didn't care either way.

"I haven't seen you for a while," Billie would say with some accusation in her voice whenever they came back to Yellowbird, which they always did eventually because Gara missed it. "Been away?"

Yellowbird, Gara knew, would go on as long as Billie wanted to work, and she wasn't ever sure whether Billie missed them or the money they spent there. Billie intended to send Little Billie to college in eight years, and by then college would be even more expensive than it was now. "Really busy," they would answer.

"Eve was here," Billie would say. "With some guy." She never sounded particularly pleased that Eve was so faithful to her.

Christmas had gone and Gara was relieved, but now New

Year's Eve loomed ahead. Brad the Consoler had gone to the country for the holidays, to stay in a beautiful house with several other gay men, old friends, none of whom were lovers, none of whom even had lovers to spend their vacation with or families they liked enough to see. He had called and said it was turning out to be one of the best vacations he'd had in years. Since neither she nor Kathryn nor Felicity had a date, nor any prospect of one, Kathryn decided the three of them should spend New Year's Eve at the Sign of the Dove because it would be so festively decorated and because they had a special with hors d'oeuvres and all the champagne you could drink, followed by dinner.

Kathryn and Gara were used to being alone by now, but Felicity was not. They stood in the crowded upstairs room that had been made into a bar for this night, all dressed up, and Felicity looked grief stricken. Couples and small groups were chattering at little tables, while waiters passed around caviar and smoked salmon and pâté. There were platters heaped with oysters at the bar beside the bottles of champagne in military rows, like an army ready to advance and make them happy. Gara was determined to have a good time, but it hadn't happened yet. The banal glamour of the luxurious food only depressed her, and she didn't feel like getting drunk. Kathryn, in a glimmering silver dress, had fastened on to a young couple from Norway who had come to New York for the first time, for the holiday, because they were on their honeymoon.

"I'm in love," Kathryn announced, with the open-faced blonde couple in tow. "Aren't they sweet?" They looked pleased and shy, and also as if they would like to get away from her. As soon as she went back to the bar for more champagne they melted into the crowd.

I should be grateful I have something to do and friends to do it with and the money to afford it, Gara thought, but the only time in her life she had not dreaded New Year's Eve had been when she was married, and then she and Carl had both virtually ignored the bittersweet holiday on purpose; a bit of caviar and champagne at home and asleep before the ball dropped from the tower in Times Square.

"What are we going to do for the millennium?" Kathryn asked. "We have to do something spectacular."

"I'll be dead," Felicity murmured.

"You'll be married," Kathryn said. "Have a drink."

They sipped their champagne. "I want to take a house somewhere warm for February," Kathryn said. "It's a shame you guys have to work or you'd come with me." She waved and smiled at the young honeymoon couple across the room and they waved back. "Why don't you take a winter vacation?"

"Can't," Gara said.

"I blew my vacation, remember?" Felicity said.

"Well," Kathryn said cheerfully, "maybe I'll just go by myself. I always meet people."

Felicity looked around with a desperate look, and Gara knew she wanted to bolt. "Tonight is just another night," Gara said to her. "Get through it. It's okay."

"I'm tired of you sulking," Kathryn said to Felicity. "Look how nice this all is."

"Have pity," Felicity said. "I'm trying." Her eyes filled with tears.

"I'm going to talk to those people, I know them from my trip to Italy," Kathryn said, and disappeared, surfacing at a corner table where everyone was laughing.

"I need to go home," Felicity said.

Gara felt abandoned by Kathryn and depressed by Felicity. Felicity's mood was too catching. "Stay for a while," Gara said. "Don't just leave me."

"All right," she said, distantly, already vanishing into herself and the sad place where she kept reliving parts of her life. "At least when I was married to Russell I wasn't alone," she said.

"You claimed you were."

"You're right." Felicity flashed her a hint of a smile. "Just keep reminding me, please, how unhappy I was."

"You were miserable. You were bulimic. You kept saying you hated him."

"Thank you."

Gara was relieved when the waiters announced dinner was to be served. They went downstairs to the main rooms, which were bright and colorful and festive and glittering, with cozy tables and a gourmet dinner with wines. Gara remembered the times she and her parents had gone out somewhere to celebrate when she was a child, and how she had sat there with the grownups, vaguely bored, vaguely lonely,

and thinking: When I grow up I'll have my own life and it
will be different. Well, she was grown up now, and this was
her own life, and somehow it wasn't that different at all.
Even Kathryn, who was normally chatty, had fallen silent,
defeated for a moment by the palpable gloom.

There was a band afterward in the downstairs bar, and the
flashing lights were almost black. Kathryn was her old self
again, and was dancing with a man. "Dance!" she cried to
them. "Dance!"

"I'm leaving," Felicity said, and did.

Gara stood there for a few moments, watching the danc-
ers, feeling invisible. There were balloons and pointed hats,
and streamers, and people were counting the minutes to
midnight.

I'm alive, she thought to herself. I'm alive and I'm not sick
and there's tomorrow. There was no one for her to speak to
so she spoke to God, as she sometimes did these past few
years because it made her feel so much better. Thank you,
God, she said silently, for giving me my five years, and for
loving me, and for helping me to help myself. I told you I
would renegotiate, and now I'm doing it. I want more.
Many, many more.

She did not ask that she might meet a man in the New Year
because it seemed impossible, and also because love and sex
seemed to bring with them so much grief. She only asked to
continue to be well and to appreciate her days. She asked to
be able to help her patients and send them on to happier and
more productive lives. She asked for Felicity to recover soon.

At midnight the revelers gave a cheer. And at two minutes
after twelve she felt free. It was over, and she was not
obliged to go through the Happy New Year bullshit for another whole year.

"I'm going," she said to Kathryn. "Happy New Year." She
took a cab home alone, surprised and grateful to find one.

Kathryn called her the next morning. "I left right after you
did," Kathryn said. "I wasn't having much fun."

"I thought you were."

"No. I was bored."

"We'll have better times this year," Gara said.

"Of course we will."

FORTY-ONE

Kathryn was moving on. It was time, the New Year was calling, and she had places to see, people to meet, things to do. She had known, when she had been bored during that New Year's Eve dinner, that it was time. Life was short, and she had many years to make up for in the years she had left, however many they might be, until she was too old to care. She could not imagine ever being too old to care.

Despite the constant heavy blizzards that made New York unappealing, she sublet her beautiful Fifth Avenue penthouse apartment for an outrageously large sum of money to a couple who wanted to stay there for a year, and planned her itinerary. First she would go to California to see her mother. Her mother was in her eighties now. Her mother's husband, Arlo, had died, leaving her the beauty salon and enough money to live comfortably, and by now of course the salon was sold, so she had more. She was living in a little apartment in Marina Del Rey, with a terrace that overlooked the Marina with all the sailboats and yachts, and enjoying her retirement.

Kathryn had talked to her mother on the phone, planning her visit. She wanted to take Sheila on a nice trip, and offered to take her wherever she wanted to go. It had occurred to Kathryn, after Gara had tried to make her remember things that night at Yellowbird, that her mother had saved her life. Now that so many years had gone by she and her mother got along very well, although they didn't see each other very often.

"Arlo and I used to go to Hawaii," Sheila said. "I'd like to go back."

"Done deal."

She would also visit her children, Kathryn thought, scattered as they were around the country, but she wouldn't stay long. A few days always did it with grown children, no matter how much you loved them and how much fun you had. Then, for the months of February and March, she had the rented house in Palm Beach, where some of the women she played tennis with were going to be, and after that she would go to Canyon Ranch. Spring would be the time for Paris. In early summer she was planning a safari in Africa, which she had never done. In August, back to a house in a different part of Italy, or maybe the south of France, with a different recently divorced woman friend, Pamela, since Susan, the one she'd spent last summer with, had remarried.

After that, who knew? She would see where the breezes blew her. Whenever she missed New York she could always come back for a while and stay at a hotel. But there were so many places she hadn't been to yet, so many things she hadn't done, that Kathryn doubted she would miss it for a long time, although of course she would always keep her apartment. The apartment was one of her trophies. It was also a good source of income.

She called Gara to say goodbye. Gara seemed sad at the thought of her deserting them again. "Let's have a going-away dinner," Kathryn said.

"At Yellowbird."

"Oh, no, do we have to?"

"Please? Felicity will want to come, and I guess we should have Eve. It will be like old times."

"I have never been attracted to old times," Kathryn said, laughing, "but we did have fun together, and we will again."

When they met for dinner and sat at their usual table there was a small wrapped present at her place. "What's this?" Kathryn asked.

"From me," Felicity said. "It's nothing, really, just the thought that counts."

Kathryn was touched. She opened the package and there was a Janis Joplin CD with all her most famous songs, the songs they had heard so often at Yellowbird. *Freedom's just another word for nothing left to lose*, the card said, in Felicity's precise handwriting. *I love you, Kathryn, and I will miss your great spirit. Felicity.*

"Oh," Kathryn said, "thank you." She was beaming, but

there was a lump in her throat. What a sweet woman Felicity was. "I want to find out you're happy when I come back," Kathryn said sternly.

"I'll try."

"I'll give her some of my power," Eve said. "Then she can move the world. Or one prick." She laughed. "Get it? Move one prick?"

"We get it," Gara said dryly.

"Gara doesn't believe in mysticism," Eve said. "She is wrong. Sex is mysticism. The yin and the yang of the two opposing spirits, always conflicted, always needing one another."

"Whatever works," Kathryn said.

They ordered their usual broiled chicken, and Eve her chicken-fried steak, and they had a bottle of very expensive wine, which Kathryn insisted on paying for even though she was sticking to her vodka and wouldn't have any of it. "I hate that you're leaving," Gara said, "and I'm going to miss you. Who's going to buy us Montrachet?"

"Visit me. I'll be in so many wonderful places."

"What a life you have."

"You wouldn't want it," Kathryn said. "You live for your work."

"Well, I do love my work, that's true."

"Maybe I'll get bored and want to work again some day," Kathryn said. "You never know."

Billie came over, wearing red satin jeans and a tiny black sweater, with a red silk scarf around her neck, hiding her scar. Kathryn thought that even if she went to aerobics class every morning of her life she would never look that good in tight pants. Billie was a knockout.

"So Gara says you're leaving New York," Billie said. "I can't imagine wanting to live anywhere else."

"I'll be traveling, not settling down," Kathryn said. "And just for a year."

Or maybe forever, she thought. She didn't say it. It occurred to her then, apropos of nothing in particular, that New York was such a strange city that if you came back and didn't call anybody you could be here for years and they would never know it. Or you could walk down the street and run into six people you knew, from all different areas of your life. She had been in this town for eleven years, and she knew how mysterious it was. She had made more friends than any of the other women she knew, even Gara, who had been born here.

"Well, that's nice," Billie said. "I guess."

No, not more friends than Billie. Billie knew the whole world. But Billie's friends were mostly men, and Kathryn's friends were mostly women. Being horny and actively hunting made all the difference. Kathryn knew that in the unlikely event she met a suitable man and fell in love she might change her mind, but right now she didn't care if she never had sex again. She didn't even care if she never fell in love again.

Alastair Uland, she thought. Wow, that was a name from the past. He was the only one of her husbands she had ever loved, and she certainly had no idea why. He and their life together was so far away now it was less than a memory, more like a dream, or a story that had happened to someone else. Everything, Kathryn thought, that had happened to her had happened to a person she no longer was, who she would never be again. Every cell in her body had been replaced many times, and so had most of the people. Pare down, move on, live for the moment. The moment was all you had. That was her philosophy now, and it was what she intended to live by. It unquestionably made life simpler.

FORTY-TWO

Sci-fi was in the pipeline for fall '96 on TV. Alien invaders, alien abductions, scary things coming down from the sky. Strange life forms in business suits working alongside human beings. Scientists who believed, and those who scoffed, constantly being tested by bizarre events. Eve was called to Hollywood to read for a pilot.

The one-hour prime-time show was to be called *They Are Here*, and it was rather lighthearted and fey as those shows went, although there was plenty of action, too. Her character was named Cornelia, and she was a space alien who was also a scientist (weren't they all?) and it wasn't a lead or even one of the large supporting parts, but Cornelia was going to appear in every segment even when she had no lines. Eve knew it was her chance. Although she had put down television as being beneath her, when push came to shove she was ready to take a small recurring role because she knew that when the producers and the public got to see her work she would get a bigger part and then, finally, she would be a star. She was absolutely convinced of it. Apparently everyone had forgotten about her troubles on *Brilliant Days*, or perhaps people who did nighttime didn't keep up with soaps. At any rate, when she arrived for her audition everyone was cordial, and a few days later her agent told her she had won the part.

It was odd to be back in Hollywood again, and it would be odder still if the pilot was bought and she had to stay. The soft, warm air brought back memories, even though the traffic was worse, the sky was discolored with smog, and she was a good deal older and wiser. She would rent a little house, Eve decided, in Studio City near where the show was to be shot, with a palm tree in the backyard, or maybe even an orange tree, and possibly even a pool. This time she wouldn't have to support Nicole. She would be able to spend all her time and money on herself. Orange Fiestaware, she thought. And I've always wanted to put a ceramic flamingo in my yard.

Eve was euphoric. She couldn't stop bragging to Gara and Felicity and Billie in Yellowbird. She was sorry Kathryn had left town and wouldn't be able to know the news, but when Kathryn turned on her TV she would see. "I don't want to lose my apartment because it's cheap," Eve told them, "so I'll sublet it. If you know anyone who wants to sublet, let me know."

"If the pilot gets bought and the show is a hit, you could be in California for five years," Felicity said hopefully.

"True. I could give up my apartment then. I could go from one series to another and buy a mansion in Bel Air."

"I certainly hope this works out for you," Felicity said. "My fingers are crossed."

"Mine, too," Gara said.

In the spring, when Eve went out to shoot the pilot, Nicole insisted she stay with her, since she had broken up with Brian and was in between boyfriends and said she would enjoy the company. Nicole was quite a faithful little thing, Eve thought; she'd had those two long-term relationships and even though she met attractive men all the time at work she was careful who she dated. Nicole had a two-bedroom garden apartment in Beverly Hills now, in a white building that looked like a large private house, on a tree-lined street. She was driving a BMW convertible, like all the rich high school kids, but she had paid for hers herself and she only looked like a kid. It always amazed Eve how young Nicole looked, even though she was twenty-nine. It gave her a very wide range of roles.

Eve didn't have to worry about memorizing her part because she had only two lines: "Here's the laser, sir," and "No, he's not here." Waiting to be made up she flipped through *Vogue* and wondered if she should color her hair with more red in it so it would photograph better.

She was in the swivel chair under the hot lights. What were they—they were putting latex on her head! What was that thing? It looked and felt like a too-tight shower cap, and it had brown spots on it like Homer Simpson's boss's head, and they were gluing lumpy plastic on her face! "What are you doing?" Eve shrieked.

"Don't wiggle," the makeup woman said sternly. Her name was Trellis, and she had made herself up to look like a member of a rock group, and was wearing black nail polish, which Eve had given up a year ago as being too common.

"They won't be able to see my face," Eve protested. She was horrified. How would anyone know who she was? All she could think of was that humiliating day long ago when she had played Yahoo the Clown for a bunch of little birthday brats in Beverly Hills. "I'm allergic to this shit!" she shrieked.

"Nobody is allergic to it. Hold still."

At least she could move her mouth, at least she could talk. The mask was surprisingly mobile. If you looked closely and you knew her you could tell it was Eve Bader, otherwise nothing looked familiar except the eyes. At least they had left her eyes. The eyes that were the mirror to the soul.

"Nobody told me I would be doing this part in full drag," Eve snarled.

Trellis laughed. "What did you think? You're a space alien."

"So are the people on *Third Rock from the Sun.*"

"But they're in disguise as humans, remember?"

Eve crossed her arms and set her lips. There had never been any description of the space aliens in the script she had read, and she had really not given their appearance much thought.

"You might want to cut your hair short," Trellis said. "This cap really messes it up, and it's very hot, too. Unfortunately they haven't found a way for it to breathe."

"I will *never* cut my hair," Eve said.

"Suit yourself."

On the set Eve drank bottled water through a straw and cursed her agent. Even though she had only those two lines, she was in some other scenes in the background and they wouldn't let her leave. She had been appalled at the way she looked in the mirror and when she looked around at the other space aliens toiling away in their laboratory, she felt like one of the Munchkins in *The Wizard of Oz.* Who was going to discover her now?

The director, Nelson Gruen, was a tall, thin young man

who looked as if he should be dating Nicole. "Good work," he said, patting Eve on the shoulder as he went by.

Good work? Suddenly Eve felt her depression lifting. He had noticed her, he had singled her out. People *would* know who she was. Maybe not that she was Eve, but that she was Cornelia, and then they would read *TV Guide*, which would surely write about the show, and there would be a group picture, at the very least, and she would be identified. Her part would be bigger by then. Maybe she would have a love interest. She glanced at the other space aliens and then at the humans and thought that she could easily be matched up with either species. After all, she had the power. This show was going to do it for her, at last. She was sure of that.

"They made me wear a mask," she told Nicole that night at dinner. Nicole had taken her to Spago to celebrate. "My skin still hurts. I have very delicate skin, you know."

"People will love you," Nicole said. "Just behave yourself."

"What does that mean?" Eve asked, insulted.

"Do your job, be nice, don't ask them to change anything. Do what I do. You'll be working forever."

"And since when did you become the mother and I the child?" Eve said.

Nicole actually thought for a moment. "I don't know exactly," she said. "But I like it better this way."

"I have something to say about that, you know," Eve said. Nicole only smiled.

As she had hoped, the pilot was picked up, and they were going to start to shoot the series in mid-July, to go on in the fall. Eve sublet her apartment for six months, without telling her landlord, who frowned on subletting because he would rather she leave so he could raise the rent, and told him the bearded artist who would be staying there was her cousin, house-sitting while she was in Hollywood becoming a star. She was going to go out to L.A. in early June so she would have plenty of time to find her little dream house and fix it up before the hard work began. Of course she had to have a going away dinner at Yellowbird.

"Why do we have this table?" Eve asked Billie when she got there and saw Gara and Felicity sitting where the sight lines were not good. "I don't like this table."

"We're busy tonight," Billie said.

"Well, I'm going to Hollywood tomorrow to become a star, and this is my swan song here, so I want my table changed. I want that one."

Billie shrugged and picked up their menus. "Come on, star," she said.

Eve smiled, and sat down where she could see everything. "I heard that Eben has a woman living with him this summer in the Hamptons," she said to Felicity. "She's twenty-four."

"Good luck to her," Felicity said.

"I don't care anymore," Eve said.

"Neither do I."

The truth was Eve didn't care; Eben's sex life had become nothing more than interesting gossip. She was sure to find a good replacement for him in Hollywood, maybe even a live-in lover again, like the old days. But this time of course both she and her man would have money. Eve felt that she was on the threshold of the best of all possible worlds.

Felicity left early, looking tired. Eve, however, was wide awake. "Let's go somewhere to have a drink," she said to Gara.

"No, I don't think so. I'm tired, too."

"Well, I want to do something."

"I want a cab," Gara said.

They paid their bills and started to leave. "Aren't you going to say goodbye to Billie?" Gara asked.

Eve shrugged. "She was never very nice to me. She's moody."

"Moody?"

"Don't you think so?"

"No."

Eve waved and smiled at Billie, who waved and smiled back. They headed for the door. There at the front booth was Nelson Gruen, her young director, sitting with a good-looking older man, in his fifties, Eve thought; not exactly her type, a little too elegant and snobby-looking, but she was leaving New York anyway. "Well, hello, Nelson," Eve said, stopping, pleased to see him on a social basis so she could bond.

He looked at her for a moment. "Oh, Eve," he said.

"What are you doing in New York? And in Yellowbird of all places?"

"My roots are still in New York, and Yellowbird—this is

Michael Hinthorn, Eve Bader—Yellowbird is Michael's hangout."

"I've never seen you here before," Eve said to the older man. "We must come here on different nights."

"Or maybe on the same night sometimes," he said. He held out his hand to Gara. "I'm Michael Hinthorn."

"I'm Gara Whiteman."

"I've seen *you*," he said.

"You have?"

Eve couldn't imagine why he had noticed Gara and not her. Nobody ever noticed Gara; despite her sometimes bright clothing, she always seemed to be wearing the protective coloring of an animal at risk.

"Why don't you two sit down for a minute?" Michael said.

That was all Eve had to hear. She sat down next to Nelson, and Gara sat across from her next to his friend. "I hope we're not interrupting your discussion," Gara said.

"The discussion was finished, and now we're just relaxing."

"Michael is my lawyer," Nelson said. "He makes my deals. Eve is in the show."

"Ah. And you, Gara?"

"I'm a therapist," Gara said.

"We all need one of those," Nelson said.

"Would anyone like a drink?" Michael asked. "Eve? Gara?"

"White wine," Eve said.

"Thank you," Gara said. She was looking more comfortable now, but she had her arms wrapped around her breasts again in that mannerism of hers, which she apparently wasn't even aware of. What did she think, that they were going to fall off? I must do that some time in a scene, Eve thought, if I ever do a breast cancer movie. There would be plenty of them to do, she was sure.

Michael ordered a bottle of white wine. "I come here for the music," he said. "Sometimes late at night. As far as I'm concerned the best music was written between the midsixties and the mid-seventies."

"That's what Billie always says," Gara said. "Except for her few favorites from the past."

"Did you ever hear her night tape?"

"Oh, yes."

"That was Billie."

"I know."

"I'm looking forward to starting work," Eve said. "I'm leaving tomorrow to settle in."

Nelson was looking at her with a squinty-eyed look. "So you're Nicole Bader's mother," he said.

"Yes, and I taught her everything she knows."

"You taught her well."

"I also taught myself," Eve said, a little defensively. After all, *They Are Here* was her show, not her daughter's.

"You must be very proud of her," Nelson said. "She's so talented, and so beautiful."

"Oh, I am."

"It's nice to see your children follow in your footsteps," Michael said. "You always think they won't want to. My daughter and son are both lawyers, too."

"And your wife?" Gara asked.

"Ex-wife."

"Oh." It was obviously not his wife's occupation she was interested in but his marital status, and of course he knew it, too, because he was smiling. But then she looked away and busied herself with her glass.

Poor Gara, Eve thought, she'll never know how to flirt with a man. I wonder how she ever got her husband.

They stayed there until midnight. After they had finished the bottle of wine Gara got a little more friendly with Nelson's lawyer, and Eve was relieved because that gave her the chance to have Nelson to herself. She wanted him to remember her, so he would make her part bigger and give her more lines. Eventually she offered to fix him up with Nicole, since he was apparently such an admirer of hers, and they were both available. He said he couldn't think of anything nicer.

"She doesn't run around," Eve said. "She's a very serious girl."

"I'm serious, too."

"You'll be my son-in-law," Eve said, elbowing him, and laughed.

"Then I guess I'll have to hire you all the time, won't I?" he said, laughing, too.

You think you're kidding, Eve thought. Just you wait. She

thought she would never be able to stop laughing, and although they didn't know what she thought was so funny, or why she was so manic, eventually they were all laughing just as hard as she was, for no reason at all.

FORTY-THREE

The morning after they had met at Yellowbird Michael Hinthorn called Gara and invited her to go to a screening with him of the new Bertolucci movie. *This is a date*, she thought, feeling younger than she had in years, and unexpectedly excited, the way she had been when she was much younger and dating, looking forward to fun. It was safe but intriguing: an event, out with other people to protect her, doing something interesting, maybe even flirting, knowing a man was curious enough about her to want to spend a few hours in her company. She could not imagine falling in love. She was not unaware of what she had done all these years in her ambivalence; she had protected herself, and avoided men even when she was asking people to introduce her to one. She had never even noticed Michael Hinthorn in Yellowbird, although he had noticed her. She had been content, she had made her compromise. She didn't know if the compromise had come from fear or realism, but she had made her world safe and comfortable, and that had been enough.

But one night a month ago, alone as always in her apartment, just as an exercise Gara had made a theoretical list of the kind of man she would want to meet. Number one: I should feel comfortable with him. That was essential. Two: Intelligent and interesting to talk to, hopefully even funny. Three: Likes to go out and do things with me. Four: Presentable enough to fit in with my friends. She did not ask for gorgeous, just acceptable. She did not think she was asking for anything too unreasonable.

She had not asked for Emotionally Available, although she knew that should have been at the top of her list. She was not emotionally available, so why should he be? She just did not want him to be involved with another woman, because then he would not fit number three: Likes to go out and do things with me. What she was looking for, she realized, was a companion. Of course, eventually, she would have to deal with the sex part of it, because if she only wanted a companion she could go out with Brad. She knew she wanted sex, too, and she didn't know if she would have the courage ever to go to bed with a man again. You couldn't have sex in the dark forever, although people said you could, and what if he recoiled? He would have to love her first. If he really loved her enough it wouldn't matter. But she could not imagine that kind of love happening to her anymore.

They met at the screening room in an office building on the West Side. In the crowd outside the little screening room she saw him before he saw her, and she thought again that he was attractive. She had thought that when she first saw him at Yellowbird, but then she had withdrawn into her shell and not let herself think about it at all. Watching the movie they sat in huge comfortable upholstered seats, and did not touch, although they glanced at each other from time to time. She didn't know what that meant.

The movie was called *Stealing Beauty*, and it was apparently about a very pretty young woman with enormous, mobile red lips, who was looking to lose her virginity, and all the men who were eager to help, or just to know her, or to watch her. The scenery was spectacular. Gara thought of Carl, and the trips they had taken, and then she glanced at Michael and wondered if they would ever know each other well enough to want to go to Europe together. Now that she was sure she had her life back there were many things she wanted to do.

"I liked that," he said afterward.

"So did I."

"Where do you want to have dinner?"

"I don't know."

He took her to a small French bistro on the East Side. Gara had a few glasses of wine for courage, and over the salad and grilled fish they talked about the movie and others they had seen, about books, about art, about his clients and hers (the little she could reveal), and about ideas. Neither of them said a word about their pasts. Not about former marriages, not about affairs since then, not about dysfunctional childhoods.

The closest they came to any discussion of the past was to tell each other what schools they had gone to, and that they had both grown up in New York.

There was something about living in the present that Gara found surprisingly reassuring. It was as if they were both too tired to reopen old wounds or to grieve over old losses. If they liked each other it would have to be through instinct, through enjoyment of the moment, through little things they did that were considerate or made the other smile. Eventually, she knew, they would have to pry, or at least hint, but right now everything was fresh and new, and...she felt comfortable with him.

"I'm glad we met," he said to her when he walked her to her door.

"Yes," Gara said. "Thank you for the wonderful evening."

She was not surprised when he kissed her goodnight. She had felt he would when she saw the instants of hesitation and resolve cross his face, and when he did, she liked it. Then he was gone.

I'm glad we met, she thought, remembering his voice when he said it, liking his husky voice, his charming smile, his thick, gray-flecked dark hair, the way he dressed, the sense she had that he was in very good shape, younger than Carl, still eager but not looking for youth and beauty like that girl in the movie if he was content to be here with her. The one thing she had not noticed was his eyes. She didn't even know what color they were. She had been too afraid to look into his eyes, because then he might see her.

It will all take time, Gara thought. Maybe we can be friends. I would love that, having a man to go out with. I expect nothing more, and I am still amazed to have this.

When Michael called her two days later she was surprised it was so soon, and unexpectedly happy that she would see him. He took her to an art gallery opening downtown, where he bought a drawing for the new apartment he had moved into and was still fixing up after his divorce, and then he took her to dinner in SoHo. When they talked about their usual nonthreatening intellectual subjects, enthusiastically, appreciating each other's opinions, rising to gratifyingly unexpected heights of insight like two well-matched tennis players, Gara realized how hungry she had been for just this kind of intelligent conversation. In her world of single women it had all been jokes, laughter, repartee, commiseration, complaints, and always, always the subject of men. Would they find one, did they want one, how they had lost one, or gotten away from one, how could they get one; the existence of these unconquered men hovering on the horizons of their lives like some kind of rainbow.

When they were drinking their espresso she felt as if she had been doubly filled, mind and body. "Thank you for another wonderful evening," Gara said.

"You know what I like?" he said. "That we never talk about ourselves."

She looked at him. Did he mean it, or was he being ironic? Perhaps both. "There's plenty of time for that," she said.

"But I think I know you already," he said. "You're a good person."

"That's very perceptive."

"Aren't you?"

"Yes. And are you?"

"I try to be."

"That's a step."

She had never flattered him, feeling uncomfortable verbalizing anything positive for fear he would run away, or that her discomfort with emotion would make him think she was being insincere. But now as they smiled at each other she thought that he must know that she liked him. She looked at his eyes. They were blue.

We must be the two most terrified people in the world, Gara thought. That night when he kissed her goodnight at her door they both opened their mouths and fed on each other. We're not too scared for that, she thought. But she didn't ask him up, and he ran away as soon as she turned to go in. "I'll call you," he said, his voice trailing away from his flight.

She knew he would.

"So you've found another frightened bunny," Felicity said at dinner in Yellowbird. There were only the two of them now. Felicity was delighted Gara was dating and wanted to hear all about it. "He sounds just like you."

"It's good," Gara said. "We can learn to trust together. Or not. Somebody must have done an excellent job of destroying him."

"Like you were damaged. Like we all were. That's why we find each other."

"Maybe you're right," Gara said.

"Think of it this way," Felicity said. "If it doesn't work out with you two, at least he will have been practice. Then you can find another man. But maybe it will work. Just have fun."

"How did you get so mature, finally?" Gara said.

Felicity smiled. "I've been working really hard with my therapist, and also it's been almost a year since Eben dumped me. Sometimes I still get very upset when I remember all the lies he told me, but I'm okay now. I would have been happier if it had worked for us, of course, but I see him as he is. He will never make any woman happy for long. He isn't happy either. But he was my bridge person."

"Bridge person?"

"Bridging my two lives: Slugger's Baby, and a free, independent woman. I know I still have a long way to go, and I want to learn."

"That sounds good," Gara said.

"I spoke to my parents a few times on the phone," Felicity said. "My mother has reconciled with my father, but only because she's sixty-five years old and her last boyfriend left her and she doesn't think she'll ever get another one. My father is glad she's being nice to him. I think in a funny way my mother has fallen in love with my father, finally, because she needs someone to take care of her and he's willing to do it. Of course she keeps yelling at me for divorcing Russell. She says I'll never get such a good husband again, and that more likely I'll never get one at all."

"That's supportive," Gara said sarcastically.

"I realized that I'm still trying to get her love and approval, even though I don't approve of what she does. But it's becoming clearer to me that it doesn't matter that I'm not the daughter she wanted me to be. I want to become the woman I want myself to be."

"And you will," Gara said.

They were getting ready to leave when Michael came in, looking around. Gara knew the person he was looking for was her. He had said he was going to be out with a client and she had said she was going to have dinner with Felicity at

Yellowbird. She was surprised at how happy she was to see him.

"That's Michael," Gara said, waving.

"He's cute."

"Do you think so?" But she thought he was.

He came over to their table, obviously glad to see her. Gara introduced him to Felicity and he sat down. Walking by, Billie gave them a knowing glance. Billie, who always knew which man at the bar would like her, also knew which of her customers would discover each other. Often they were mismatched, but nothing surprised her, neither when they met nor when they broke up. On the sound system LaBelle was singing "Lady Marmalade," and the energy in the room was high. Michael ordered more wine for them, and as soon as she had finished hers Felicity insisted on leaving them alone together, making a great show of looking at her watch.

"What were you two in such deep conversation about?" he asked.

"Parents and childhood."

"Oh." He nodded noncommittally.

The wine had made Gara bold. She leaned over and looked into Michael's face. "What kind of parents did you have?" she asked.

So then he finally told her, and about his childhood, and as he did Gara realized that his was as bad as hers had been in a way that was both unique and similar. A father who had abandoned him while physically remaining at home; a helpless, demanding mother who had spousified him, leaning on him too much and too often to make him be her little man; and finally, a wife who had left him, the way Carl had left her. He sketched in his life with short, sharp strokes, and as she listened Gara thought how lucky she was that he had not ended up as another confused caretaker of the nonthreatening wounded, those wary and conflicted men entangled with women young enough to be their daughters.

And then she thought: But I am the nonthreatening wounded. For all my bravery and independence during the time I was trying to save my life, the other part of me remains, too. He can probably sense it, even if he doesn't really know. And I thought I was so good at fooling everybody.

It was late; they both had to leave. He walked her to her door, their cab waiting, and they kissed in that same brief,

frantic way that was almost experimental. She thought for
the first time that some night she would actually invite him
up.

After that when she thought about him she was often
physically aroused, a feeling she had thought was lost to her
forever. She looked at her breasts in the mirror, and touched
them, wondering what he would think, pretending he was
with her and didn't notice. In the years that had passed she
had begun to think of the artificial one as real, as much a part
of her as the other. It was part of her; she was who she was.
"He'll like the whole gestalt," she would tell her women patients, trying to convince them that the unreal standards of
beauty they tried to live up to were so mingled with who
they were as lovable people that all would be well. "If you're
his fantasy you can vomit and he won't care," she would say.
Was she his fantasy? And did his fantasy also include the
specter of the recurrence of disease and a possible early
death? Gara did not believe she would get sick again, she
was sure she would live a normal life the way all her doctors
felt she would, but what would he believe? Would he think
caring about her was worth the risk?

I won't have to find out if I don't let him near me, she
thought. It felt comfortable to have more time, to be guarded
again.

She allowed herself to think about him only when she had
nothing else to do. When her work day was finished, when
she had been to the gym, when she had done her professional reading, then she could relax and let him enter her
mind and take over. She knew it was not obsession if she
doled out these little periods of emotional passion in this
way. She and Michael had been out together twelve times
now, and sometimes when she thought about him she was so
nervous that she never wanted to see him again. She wondered if he noticed. At other times she thought she was in
love. She hoped he did not notice that.

They always went somewhere or did something: movies,
theater, art galleries, parties, happier with each other than
doing it alone; they never sat across from each other at a little
table and talked about their emotions and the relationship,
but they glowed when they were together, she saw it. And at
the parties they sat together and talked to each other as if

they had just met and had forgotten there was anyone else in the room.

Now when she looked in the *New York Times* every weekend to see what there was to do in New York Gara always thought about doing it with him, elated at the thought of discovering something new in a photography exhibit, or an art exhibition, or a play. She had never been like Kathryn, a self-starter. She and Michael recommended books to each other, albums. His taste was eclectic, far ranging, and her mind ranged along with him, opening, alert. He told her often that he liked her, that she was growing on him—and, ambivalent, she made sure it meant nothing to her when he said it, told herself he was conceited to think she cared—and then when she was alone she pulled out the memory and relived it in the safety of her isolation.

I'll give him six months to become dependent on me, Gara thought. Then I'll invite him up.

Of course, it happened much more quickly than that. One night he simply rode up in the elevator with her. Then, when he was at her door, she said, "Come in." He did.

Suddenly Gara remembered the first time Carl had come to her apartment, so many years ago, that masculine presence filling the room, making her apartment seem girlish and small. Now her adult apartment seemed too precise, too lonely, too self-centered; and as if it had a life of its own, adapting warily to Michael's step, his energy, the space he took up by existing at all. He looked at her books, her records, her art, her photographs, trying to know her.

"Is this your ex-husband?" he asked, picking up a framed photograph.

"No," Gara said, smiling at his mistake. "It's my father." Her father in that picture had been the age of a man she could be dating now.

"Then is this Carl?" He indicated another, which was. She had kept out one photo of Carl, finally, because he had been her family, and because their time together had been mainly good and that was something to remember.

"Yes," she said. He put it down and didn't comment. His curiosity was assuaged now and he didn't care.

She looked frantically through her collection of CDs for something with no memories. In despair, finally, she put on the radio; late-night jazz playing softly, hoping it would be a long time between commercials. It would be difficult to try to have sex during something so unromantic and intrusive as a commercial, but silence seemed frightening, like something watching her.

Then he kissed her, and she remembered how much she liked it. They kissed for a while, and along with the growing passion she sensed his fear as if it were her own. She told herself that everyone was nervous the first time with someone new, but she knew for her it was worse, because it was the first time in years. Then what was he nervous about? Performance? Rejection? Or crossing the boundary between friendship and something more complicated and threatening: emotional intimacy, the most demanding and alarming thing of all?

They went into the bedroom. She put on a dim light so he would not be able to see what he was not supposed to see, and in that dimness she saw that he had a good body, in shape, but gone to some softness around the middle, which made her like him more because it made him vulnerable, not perfect, thus perhaps less likely to judge her. Then when they were naked and partly hidden under the sheet she had pulled up, he had his fingers on the artificial breast, trying to stimulate the nipple he thought was real, and she put his hand gently on the real one, as if she had a preference and a preference was reasonable.

She began to relax under his hands, his lips, her hands and lips roaming over him, too, remembering the joy of making love to a man, feeling happy that he wanted her and that he was giving back to her the pleasure she had not had for so long. But when he finally entered her it hurt sharply at first, and she wondered if she had closed right up from disuse. What must he think, that she didn't like him? He knew how difficult this was for her and was gentle, and didn't seem to mind what he somehow instinctively sensed was the result of long abstinence, and after a while she began to enjoy it, and felt as if she had found her own self again. He didn't seem nervous anymore, nor was she.

What a wonderful thing, Gara thought, to have a friend and sex together in the same person. Neither of them said anything about love; in fact, neither of them spoke at all.

Michael slept with his arms around her, as Carl had years ago. She thought she could get used to that again, and thought the women he had gone to bed with before her were lucky. She felt more affectionate toward him than she had ever before, and more tolerant of herself. She felt feminine again, and blooming. No matter what happened tomorrow, tonight had been the resurgence of possibility for her as a desirable woman and a sexual being.

In the morning she made coffee for them, and they drank it together at the kitchen table. "How long ago did you have breast cancer?" Michael asked casually. So he had noticed after all.

"Five years," Gara said. "I'm okay now."

"I'm glad."

They didn't mention it again. They read the newspaper, and then they went off to their separate work lives. He kissed her goodbye. "I'll call you later," he said.

We'll see about that, Gara thought.

But he called her that night, with plans for things they would do later in the week. They picked a play and a movie, and a restaurant they wanted to try. He said he wanted her to meet two of his good friends. So life would go on, and they would continue their discovery of each other. She knew she could not ask for more, and that was really all she wanted.

FORTY-FOUR

It was a crisp fall evening, and Gara was meeting Michael at Yellowbird, a place they still went to from time to time because they liked the music and the atmosphere, they liked Billie, and because it had a sentimental relevance to them because it was where they had met. She got there a little early and sat in the booth they had begun to call their own, and looked around. On the sound system Janis was singing "Try." "*Try, just a little bit harder...*" Don't we all, Gara thought; sometimes it works, sometimes it doesn't.

She looked at the unfamiliar faces in the room and thought again, as she had almost two years ago, that New York was a city always in flux, where people were constantly remaking their lives. It was like the filing system on a computer: folder within folder within folder, neatly hidden away but accessible. You could navigate skillfully from place to place, from old friend to new friend, or hide and see no one. Sometimes people wondered what had happened to you; more often they just thought you were busy. Often you were. Sometimes they thought you didn't like them anymore. Sometimes you didn't. As you remake your life, Gara thought, you also remake yourself.

Eve's show was doing well, and she was still in Hollywood. Gara and Felicity had watched it once, to see her, and had gotten a good laugh at the way she was disguised. Although she had a small part, Eve had hired a press agent, who occasionally put things in the newspapers as if she was important. The most important thing about Eve—still and probably always—was that she was Nicole Bader's mother, a role she had never wanted in life but which had helped her get what she did want, a career.

Occasionally Gara got a phone call from Kathryn, from Palm Beach or Italy or Hawaii or Paris or Canyon Ranch, and Kathryn was always busy and cheerful, regaling Gara with her adventures. "I deserve this," Kathryn kept reminding her, and Gara agreed. She told Kathryn she was seeing a man now, and Kathryn was surprised. "Well," Gara told her, "I'm surprised, too." It had occurred to her many times in the past few months that she, the unlikeliest one of them all, was the only one with a relationship.

Felicity and Gara were still close friends, but Felicity didn't come to Yellowbird anymore. Felicity said the food was dreadful and the atmosphere reminded her of a middle-aged singles bar. When they had dinner together they went to elegant restaurants, the sort Felicity had gone to with Russell, where she could now go with the people she chose. She was still looking for a man, either black or white, still with a toe in each world and not quite figuring out where she needed to belong, still hoping she could have a baby before she was too old, but she was not frantic about her social life. Sometimes she said she was lonely. Sometimes she said she was happy. The one thing she never seemed to be was afraid.

Billie, of course, was still Billie. Some things never changed.

But some did, of course. Gara looked over at what had been their favorite table, and there were four women sitting there, with one man, and they did not look like tourists; they reminded her of herself and Kathryn and Eve and Felicity and Brad. She almost resented that these strangers were sitting at "her" table, totally unaware of all the things that happened there during the past two years. The strangers were laughing and talking and drinking, looking around to see who was coming in, and Gara felt a kind of nostalgia for whatever those Yellowbird evenings had been in her own friends' lives, in that time that somehow now seemed so long ago.

They could be us, she thought. They all have their secrets. They're all survivors of something. As were we. As we are now.

Everybody in Parish, Mississippi, knows that come sundown things change....

Ben Rader was back in town, and, as chief of police, he intended to use his power to investigate his friend's mysterious death. He soon realized, though, that he was up against blackmail, drugs, even murder. And his only key to the truth was Eve Maitland, a woman he wasn't sure he could trust.

HELEN R.
Come Sundown
MYERS

MIRA BOOKS

Available in May 1998
at your favorite retail outlet.

MHM436

A wonderful novel that continues what
Jane Austen's *Sense and Sensibility* began!

JULIA BARRETT

THE THIRD SISTER

In *The Third Sister,* Julia Barrett faithfully
evokes Jane Austen's style, characters and ambience
to tell just what happens when the youngest
Miss Dashwood meets two eligible suitors.
Which man will she choose? Which man will she love?
The gentleman or the scoundrel?

MIRA
BOOKS

Available in May 1998
at your favorite retail outlet.

MJB446

ALL THAT GLITTERS

by *New York Times* bestselling author

LINDA HOWARD

Greek billionaire Nikolas Constantinos was used to getting what he wanted—in business and in his personal life. Until he met Jessica Stanton. Love hadn't been part of his plan. But love was the one thing he couldn't control.

From *New York Times* bestselling author Linda Howard comes a sensual tale of business and pleasure—of a man who wants both and a woman who wants more.